A WALK IN ALIEN CORN

Lar Redmond grew up in Emerald Square on the edge of the Liberties in Dublin. He was educated at Rialto School and at James's Street Christian Brothers. At the outbreak of war he joined the Irish Army, and in 1941 he went to England to work as a carpenter. He later returned to Ireland with his wife and child, and worked as a foreman for his father's building company.

Lar emigrated to Australia in the 1950s after the collapse of his own building firm. He worked for many years as a foreman and a builder. He won two bursaries to the University of Adelaide for writing, and had his first short story published in Australia in 1963.

In 1967, Lar returned to Ireland. Since then he has appeared many times on television and radio, and has had dozens of short stories and articles published. *Emerald Square*, his first bestselling novel, was originally published in 1987. A collection of short stories, *Show us the Moon*, was published in 1988, followed by this, his second novel, *A Walk in Alien Corn* (1990).

A WALK IN ALIEN CORN

LAR REDMOND

Glendale

First published in Ireland 1990
by The Glendale Press Ltd.
1 Summerhill Parade
Sandycove
Co. Dublin

British Library Cataloguing in Publication Data
Redmond, Lar
    A walk in alien corn
    I. Title
    823'.914[F]

    ISBN 0-907606-80-6

Origination by Phototype-Set Ltd., Dublin
Printed in Great Britain by Southampton Book Co, Southampton.

1   Santry Court

At the gates of Santry Court I presented my 'Indefinite Leave' pass to Arse Face Brennan, the sergeant on duty, who grunted, opened the gate, and with a sigh of relief I walked out into Civvy Street and freedom. The big bastard who reluctantly opened the gate had hated me from the first day he laid eyes on me, though he had never succeeded in 'nailing' me on any charge.

Luckily, he was not in charge of 'Dirty C', my company. The machine gunners had to suffer him, a big, ugly, country 'get' with an ill streak in him. Deliberately, I put my hands in my pockets and sauntered away. As expected, a bull-like roar broke the silence of a lovely summer afternoon.

'Taike yer hands out a' yer pockets, Redmond!'

I turned casually, surveyed him critically, with the slightly puzzled air of one who cannot quite identify what he is looking at. I watched him grow red, then purple, as he shook the gates, like a frustrated gorilla, mad with rage. By the time I reached the footpath, he was on the verge of a stroke. I thought I would help it along a bit.

'You can piss off, Arse Face,' I called back softly, putting a brazen face on the incident, even though inside I was trembling with fear. I was safe, thank God, I was back in Civvy Street, my heart pounding with fear I would not show. I took one last look at the sergeant, grinned infuriatingly, but it was a 'put on' grin, for I was terrified of this man, and now he gave me additional reason to fear him even more.

'By Jaysus,' he roared, 'if ever I get yeh back, y'ill rue the day yer mother spawned yeh, yeh Jackeen bastard.'

What he was roaring at was a slightly-built young man, with a saintly face, small, only five feet four in height, with the long eyelashes of a movie star, a slightly feminine face, that belied what lay behind. That was why Arse Face hated me. I did not look like his idea of a soldier, or a man, though I was both. I was twenty-one years of age, I looked about seventeen, but I was a fully fledged carpenter, with a well developed body from hard work, and I packed a punch. The first soldier who got the bright idea of calling me 'girlie' had ended up in the Medical Hut, though it had taken a week of taunting before I had found the courage to take him on. At heart I was really a coward, and abhorred violence.

I had hated the Army, every stupid moment of it, and this sergeant, in particular had made my life a misery, his ever watchful eye just waiting for a chance to get at me. He represented everything I detested, but somewhere at the back of my revenge was the feeling that I might pay dearly for my contemptuous defiance. I had grinned into his spittle froth, I had addressed him as 'Arse Face', a nickname he hated, I had returned his hatred with interest, but even I had no conception of how dearly I would pay for a small show of bravado, how this angry encounter would alter the course of my life.

I turned on my heel and started to walk towards Dublin. I was finished dying for Ireland at thirteen and tuppence a week, fed up with the boredom of a neutral army. There was no way we were going to take the North now that it was stuffed with British, Canadians and Yanks, and that had been my sole aim in joining the army in the first place. The foolish thinking of the time was that if we got the Brits with their pants down, we could finish the partition of Ireland once and for all.

Here in the South, a civil war had been fought over this issue, and in Southern minds it was only half time, but

6

events had proved us all wrong. There was going to be no fight, Ireland was not going to be invaded, the Yanks would see to that. England was not going to be invaded until Herr Hitler had conquered Russia, and, as the world knows, that was going to be never.

Clear across the city my beloved mountains straddled the skyline, and somewhere at their feet, in Walkinstown, my family lived in a brand new ten-roomed house. Here my well-heeled father was prepared to sit out the war. It was a better house than most officers could claim as home, and well I knew it. I had the background that goes with being an officer, all the trappings, plus, except for one thing: I did not have enough formal education. My younger brothers and sisters attended Terenure College and Loreto Convent respectively, but there had been no money to keep me on at school, much less college. Dad had left it too late to make his pile, too late for me anyway.

I had met several University students in the Army Depot, where the initial training had to be done, where, at the end of three months, the officers were chosen, and it was then I discovered that I could outmatch any of them when it came to a discussion on literature or poetry, and could bowl most of them over. That did not help me. Without the Leaving Cert, I was sunk, slotted for life. I could become, like my father, a wealthy builder, but, if I could not start my own business, I was debarred from any job above the level of foreman carpenter.

I was a blue collar worker, branded forever, as surely as an Indian Untouchable. Above the well of my life hung the jaw bone of an Ass, invisible, and all the more potent for that. I swung through the tiny village of Santry, making light of the few miles, and soon the hedges and fields gave way to the suburbs. Before five o'clock I was in O'Connell Street, under the magnificent column of Nelson's Pillar. Dublin was quiet as it had not been for a century, its life muted by a shortage of petrol. The trams for Howth and Dalkey rested in Nelson's shadow, the last of the Mohicans, for with a world war looming, staring them in the face, the city fathers in their wisdom had committed the city to bus transport, and these empty streets were the result.

I had half an hour to wait for the 77 bus to Walkinstown and Tallaght, for there were only two per day. This was neutral Ireland, a quiet place, removed from the mainstream of life. I sat on the granite Liffey wall, watching the river race past. It was in full spate from a night of rain, the sea that held the river back had receded, and the gulls screamed and fought for food on its garbage-strewn surface.

Home! I was home. This was my city, I had been born not far from here. Over Westmoreland Street the Ballast Office clock kept time for Ireland, the very bricks and cobblestones were old friends of mine, I could never be lonely here. Crossing to the bus stop as time drew near, the city suddenly sprang to life. The offices and shops had closed, and suddenly O'Connell Street, wide and all as it was, was filled with cyclists. Thousands of them poured into the street, girls with lovely legs and pretty dresses, and sombre-suited men who all wore bicycle clips on the ends of their trousers. It was one of the unique sights of the city, this twice daily parade of people on two wheels.

I whistled up the pretty girls, getting many a smile, but had to quit as a small crowd gathered for the bus, for they were all neighbours of mine. Travelling on the Tallaght bus at that time was like belonging to an exclusive club, far removed from the pushing and shoving of mere city dwellers. The neighbours knew me as the son of 'the Builder', white collar workers all, Electricity Supply Board office workers, Civil Servants, State Transport office Wallahs, all sheltering under the umbrella of State, all of them with at least the School Leaving Certificate. They had been where I had never been, to secondary school or College. I was accepted because I came from the biggest house on the road, my family had the most money, but above all because my father was a gentleman.

And so we left the city behind, with me in my smart Civvy Street suit, savouring every moment of it. Up Dame Street, past Christchurch, and into the seething Liberties with its falling down Huguenot tenements, past Patrick's Cathedral, weaving our way up the Coombe and Cork Street through the darting bikes, and then past Emerald Square, the place that had moulded me for life. The Square is on the perimeter of The Liberties of St Patrick's: we roared past it, and Dolphins Barn chapel, where I had made my First Communion and Confirmation. Everything around here was part of me. We tore over Dolphins Barn Bridge and the Grand Canal, where I had learned to swim, and then the last of the houses were left behind and we were in the green fields of Crumlin, broken only here and there by a few cottages.

I got off at the Halfway House, for I needed a little respite before facing home. A single farm cart, with a horse feeding quietly from its nose bag, stood outside. The pub divided two roads, a minor one that went to Tallaght and a main road that went all the way to Cork. A hundred yards away a thatched cottage, with a well beside it, gleamed white and gold in the sunset, and from the fields all around came the calls of corncrakes, and the lovely musical notes of the cuckoo. It was a quiet pastoral scene, and this was where I belonged.

The hated army was behind me. At whatever cost, I was never going back there, unless the Irish Free State came under attack. I went into the pub. It was dark and cool, and the surly owner even cooler. He knew who I was, but gave no sign of recognition. He did not like the few new arrivals within his small community, and served them grudgingly. He was a bachelor, a member of a religious organization called 'The Sacred Thirst', and had spent a lifetime serving drink to farm labourers who could not afford it. He had a bitter, lined face, he wore a bowler hat and drainpipe trousers, was about fifty years old, and had never had a woman or a drink in his life. He scorned motor cars, and the war had proved him right, and his smart pony and trap were known far and wide. I drank my bottle of stout, ordered another, and idly speculated on the mind of a man who hated drink and yet could earn a comfortable living dishing it out. He would serve drink to a labourer until he was falling drunk and leave him to stagger home to a wife who need expect no money that week. He was a bloody hyprocrite, but no worse than the clergy, Catholic and Protestant alike, who ran posh boarding schools for the sons and daughters of the rich, and belted the bejaysus out of the poor.

It was the Catholic Church, my Church, who had collected money in every parish in Ireland, to buy bullets for Franco, that misbegotten son of a bitch who had crucified Spain. I'd have to pretend to go to Mass this coming Sunday to please Mam, but my trout rod would be tied to the cross of the bike, and I'd be gone early, with a Tommy can and sandwiches, and the makings of tea, to spend another glorious day fishing the Dodder. I did not want to hurt my mother's feelings, but if it came to the crunch, I would!

Mass parade in the Army was supposed to mean just that. One paraded for Mass, and marched to the chapel, Protestants excluded. We had only two in Dirty C. But when you reached the chapel, you were allowed, at least in theory, to exercise discretion as to whether you entered the building or not. I had refused, only to be brought to attention by a sergeant who liked me, and marched into the building. My refusal was over a bigoted sky pilot who excluded the Army from the main body of the church, and made them get Mass in the Sacristy, because, he declared from the pulpit, we were seducing the young women of the town. In this particular town, the women did not take much seducing, but anyway, willy nilly, I was marched into the crammed Sacristy to endure a three quarter hour sweatbox, with only the distant murmur of the congregation and the tinkle of bells as the Eucharist was blessed, to tell you that you were in God's House. There was going to be no more marching under orders for me from now on. I was twenty-one, and I would go my own way, even if I had to confront my own mother.

I finished my second bottle of stout, ignored the surly

landlord, and walked out. It was a glorious evening, after a perfect day, in a lousy summer. Our house was only up the road, and as, I rounded the bend, it stood proudly alone in its large garden, with the blue Dublin mountains as a backdrop. All around me the countryside was alive as it never would be again. Passing Norton's farm I spotted half a dozen rabbits in the fields, a covery of partridge sailed over my head, and the sky was full of clamour as thousands of crows flew home to roost. The corncrakes and cuckoos were still at it, blackbirds and thrushes were on every hawthorn bush singing goodbye to the day. Yes, it had been a perfect day. Even if it had pissed rain all day it would still have been perfect. Any day a natural born civilian gets out of the army, any army, that is a perfect day.

When I reached home Mam and Dad were in the vegetable garden. My father was still a young man of forty-seven, so, with no building to do, he had taken up gardening, and the family were self-sufficient in the matter of vegetables all year round. The large greenhouse grew a summer crop of tomatoes, and, in winter, lettuce, and lovely chrysanthemums for Christmas. Here was a little sheltered corner of the garden where the bronze small-flowered hardy variety chrysanthemum grew. Mam had taken them from the back yard in Emerald Square, via a three-bedroomed house in Crumlin, and here they had reached their last resting place, as she had herself. She loved them, and I myself have never had a garden without them.

There was a small greenhouse that was occupied solely by a vine, which gave a crop of reluctant grapes, grapes that longed for a sunnier clime, and were homesick. In the orchard, apples, plums and pears flourished, young trees getting better by the year, and the blackberry was everywhere in August, just there for the picking. The family did the picking, and Mam was busy bottling fruit and making jam until winter came knocking at the door. Our family had come up the hard way, Mam had not forgotten. Herself and the girls looked after the hens, about fifty of them, and chicken for dinner was no great event in our house, with eggs plentiful too. There was little we lacked. We even had three bee hives, tended by my brother, that kept the trees fruitful and provided honey in the comb, delicious on breakfast toast. There was little about this house of ours that was not productive, everything was put to use, except the gleaming new motor car that was chocked up on concrete blocks, and would remain so until the war ended.

This was the home to which, by herculean effort, we had aspired, and I had been part of that effort. The hall stand told its own story, with its college blazers to remind me of all that I had missed. I looked, with my long-lashed eyes and delicate face, very much a part of it, but I was not, quite. I had been through the crucible of The Liberties and the building sites, and the Irish Army and Dirty C Company had completed the job.

I looked like a soft target, a mere boy, but I was a grown man, fit, as Dickens remarked, for anything from pitch and toss to manslaughter. I hated boxing, but when driven into a corner by a bully, I could fight with unparalleled fury, simply because I was always so frightened. I had the courage of a cornered rat.

'You're looking a bit peaky,' said Mam, kissing me, 'I'll have to build you up. I'm glad you're out of the army, it didn't suit you at all.'

I gave her a big hug, shook hands with my father, and thanked him for getting me out.

'It was a mistake, Lar, you were never cut out to be a soldier,' he said. 'Though I'm proud that you were there when you were needed.'

'Mam?'

'Yes.'

'Is the point twenty-two and the trout rod still in my bedroom?'

'Yes, Lar. Nobody was allowed near them.'

'Right then. There'll be rabbit and trout on the menu again soon.'

'Trout,' said Mam sighing happily. 'I'm longing for one. It'll be like old times, Lar.'

It was great. I was home at last. Together we went into the house, Mam made me a late tea, and I wolfed down bacon and eggs, and white pudding, for I was starving. Mam was already beginning the process of building me up.

'I'm thinking of going to England,' I said suddenly.

She turned on me like a fury.

'You're going to no England, me bucko, until you spend some time with your family. You need a month's rest by the look of you. And there's no need for you to go. Your father will give you some pocket money, and you can help with the garden.'

'All right, Mam,' I agreed quietly. There was no use in upsetting her, and anyway it would take at least a month to get a travel permit, if ever I got one. I was only on 'indefinite leave', and that did not entitle me to leave the country. I would be lucky if I could slip through the net. But go I would. That bastard of a sergeant would never get the chance to work me over. Already my bravado at Santry Court was changing my life.

2 Westland Row

In the month that followed I occupied myself by helping in the garden, shooting rabbits, and coming home from mountain valleys with trout and mushrooms. It was a time of peace, walking in the mountains, listening to what the wind had to say. It was the calm before the storm. The newspapers were full of advertisements for tradesmen, and one day I stole quietly in to Dublin, and signed on with an English Agent, then went to Dublin Castle and applied for a travel permit, and held my breath. Nobody at home knew. Mam, especially, did not seem to realise that I was merely on 'indefinite leave', and could be called up again on the whim of some officer; that the bullying sergeant had not forgotten me, that I stood in imminent danger of being hauled back. I bitterly regretted that I had taunted him, but it was too late for regrets. All I could do was hope that, in the confusion of the under staffed Permit office, I would slip through. Boarding the ship would be another hazard, for there were military police looking out for people like me.

At the end of five weeks, I saw the Agent again, permit in hand, and was given the date of my departure. At home I slyly packed, and had my clothes and tools in the luggage room at Westland Row railway station long before the day. In the dawn, one morning, I left a note for Mam, walked to Crumlin crossroads, and boarded the first bus that came along. I was nearly broke. Mam would have given me money, I knew, but I was close to her heart, and could not bear to face her tears. Nor could I tell her that I was going for the duration of the war, however long it lasted. I could never face the risk involved in coming home again. Like Cortez, I had burnt my boats, but, at the back of it all, I was elated at the thought of travel and war.

I had read enough books for the present. If ever I hoped to become a writer, this was the time for living, for living in danger if it came my way, and then also, there was the rising excitement of English girls ahead. All my information told me that they were a lot more givish than their Irish counterparts, who were terrified of losing their virginity. Contraceptives were illegal in Ireland.

Also, they had been too well brainwashed by the Church. The awful example of one among their number who had been unfortunate enough to be put in the family way was enough to deter them. For that scarlet woman there was no alternative except to flee to England, and never come back. Most of them became prostitutes on the streets of English cities like London, and some, not many, prospered on the wages of sin.

The eleventh commandment operated superbly in Ireland: 'Thou shalt not dip thy wick without a jockey's licence'. And I, who had known no woman for too long, was slowly going mad for need of one. I kidded myself that I was too fastidious to avail of a whore, but the truth was that I had no money, and was also afraid of getting a dose of 'the Johnny Rocks', the Pox. There were notices in all the public toilets warning incipient breakers of the eleventh commandment of the dangers of promiscuity. Gonorrhoea, syphilis, and the crabs on the rocks, were enough to deter only the most foolhardy spirits, and, for those who transgressed, Steven's Hospital, on the banks of the Liffey, was highly recommended. I never wanted to qualify for that . . . .

Dublin that Monday morning, 10 September 1941, was its usual noiseless self. I entered the railway station from a silent street. It was like going into a mad house, for here the

15

business of exporting the native Irish was going ahead like wildfire. I collected my luggage and joined a small crowd of men who all stood beside carpenters' tool boxes. One of them I knew slightly, he having been a foreman on a site alongside one of my father's. He grinned when he saw me, and shook hands.

'Howayeh, Lar,' he said.

He was a rugged-faced good-looking man of average height, whose name was Paddy O'Toole. He preferred to be called 'Tooler', the man with the dirty name, he would say, grinning.

'Hello, Tooler,' I said, smiling. 'What are you doing here? Don't tell me there's no work for even the likes of you?'

He was a noted joiner and carpenter of great skill.

'Nope,' he said, 'It's the bloody boat again for me. This is the third time since '39 . . . Jaysus! I hate the thought of what I'm facing.'

'Is it that bad, Tooler?'

'No, it's just that I'm gettin' too old for this lark. It's okay for young fellas like you.'

He looked me over critically. I weighed ten stone exactly, and I looked well. 'It won't take you long to get yourself a Mot. The English ones 'ill go for you.'

Please God, I thought, but said nothing about my wish.

'How old are you, Paddy?'

'Too old, thirty-eight.'

'Jesus, that's not old.'

'It is when you're not married, an' haven't the money to get married. That's when thirty-eight is really old. I take it you're for Taylor-Woodrow, Lar.'

'All the rest are too. There's fourteen of us.'

He glanced around at the mayhem that was the station. The engine of the train, fuelled on peat and timber, hissed impatiently alongside the platform, throwing sparks into the morning air like a small fireworks display. Shouting men and Labour Agents were all about, mustering their respective gangs. Ireland was on the hoof, sold as surely as any black slave to a southern plantation. Here all the big building firms of England were represented, Taylor-Woodrow, a mickey mouse firm up until '39, now coming alongside Langs and Sir Robert McAlpine whose McAlpine's Fusiliers, all Irish, were to make him a multi-millionaire.

The English Agents had come up with a novel idea for finding their respective gangs. They provided them with different coloured rosettes, and the labourers due for England wore them like bulls at the Horse Show in Ballsbridge. God help them, they wore them with pride. It meant that they had a job, that they belonged to somebody, that they had status at last, lowly though it was.

There were crowds of them from Connemara and the still over-populated areas of the Gaeltacht, men who shouted at each other in Irish, who had no suitcases, but carried only brown paper bags with a shirt and a change of socks. Wild looking men, for the most part, who looked strangely out of place against the station background. They belonged on stony ground, with the rocks rising behind them to some bare mountain. They belonged to the wild bog and the cry of the curlew. There they would look at home.

What I was observing was the blood letting of a place that had never ceased to bleed since the famine, where emigration had become the norm, where women reared sons and daughters for export and 'God blessed them' when there was a few dollars in the post. That tide had turned, and it was to England that they went now. Dublin to them was the hated Pale, where the Jackeen lived, a place in Ireland, yet not of it, a city, peopled by men and women who were not English, but would never be acknowledged by them to be Irish. I knew that, I had met a few of these Culchies before and had not been backward in telling them where the revolution took place. 'In O'Connell Street, me oul' flower, that's where the British were licked. They were never beaten in Ballyslap!'

At the end of the platform a colourful knot of girls, mostly from Dublin, had gathered together in mutual protection against the swarming mass of rosette bearing bulls, all of them in their bright new cheap 'Pinnys', all carrying a Woolworths suitcase, with handbags from the same five and ten cent store. I saw none with an overcoat. Winter would soon be upon them, but what did that matter? Where they would be going they would soon be able to afford a good overcoat, they were going to earn great money in England's factories. There was one, a lovely blonde, that I kept looking at until she gave me a fleeting smile, glancing with one eye from behind her Veronica Lake hair-do. All the blondes were imitating the Hollywood star, whose blonde tresses swept over one eye. As time went by so many of them were dragged into machines and scalped that the managements insisted on hair nets worn at work.

Among the men from the West there was one who stood out, not because of height or good looks, plenty of the others were finer figures of men, but because he wore, with conscious pride, an English wartime 'Utility Suit'. He was the boyo who had returned, the one who had told the others how good the crack was in Cricklewood, or Camden Town, or wherever, for no matter where they landed it would always be Cricklewood where they were. They would live in workers' camps, and build England's airfields and factories. Always they would cling together and live apart from normal English society. They would be known as 'Long Distance Men' by the Brits, and they would grow old before their time from hard work and harder drinking. When the war ended they would rebuild the shattered cities of Great Britain. If England was conquered they would work for the Germans and, just as willingly, rebuild their broken cities too. It was all one to them as long as the money was good, and the crack was there.

These men I was observing came from a hard background, grindingly hard. They had been cutting bogs and piling rocks since they were children. Christ only knew what made them so big and strong, for it was not the diet of spuds and tea that did it alone. There must be something

18

else in the soil of the West to produce such strength.

They were men who knew how to snare a rabbit and poach a salmon, how to tickle a trout and silently bring down a deer on his local Lordship's estate. For me it was a very different proposition. I wanted travel and adventure, above all I wanted to see an air-raid, I wanted to experience life in the raw. When the war was over I would return to my father's firm, and Dublin. My plans did not include leaving my beloved city, at least not for keeps.

'That wan,' said the Utility-suited man in a loud voice to his friends, ''d make a fine ride on a Saturday night afther a few pints.' He pointed to my beautiful Veronica Lake. He had a Mayo accent heavily overlaid with Cockney. Some of them around laughed with him. He was obviously the experienced hard chaw amongst them. I flushed with rage. Tooler gave him a glance of unconcealed contempt.

'That's one Culchie who has been over beyond teh see the time,' he said to me. He grinned knowingly at my reddening face.

'Yeh better get used to it, Lar,' he said. 'Y'ill meet plenty more from the same dirty stable where you're goin'. Anyway, what the hell brings a nice young fella like you here? Sure there's no need for it. Your father is a snug man.'

'Maybe,' I said swiftly, 'but I'm not going to louse on him for the rest of the war. I want to earn my own way . . . and see a bit of the world.'

'Half your luck, Lar,' said Tooler. 'I wish I could change places with you.'

The train gave a piercing whistle, and, lugging our accursed tool boxes and cases, we struggled aboard. The train was packed, there must have been a thousand Irish on it that morning, as there was every morning. Not two per cent of them would ever see Ireland again. And the man at the head of the Irish Free State, who dwelt in a Celtic Twilight was not four miles away, snug as a bug in a rug. From his house in Blackrock he could, every day of his life, watch the boat going out and never fret about its cargo.

The Irish Free State stood proudly alone. In his mind the flag of freedom had been hoisted and Ireland had told the world that it would make up its own mind. He had one hundred thousand soldiers armed to the teeth with ancient rifles from World War One. With most of them you wouldn't hit a haystack at over a hundred yards. This was our finest hour. He never came to Westland Row to see Ireland on the hoof, wearing badges of shame, or he might have been projected into the real world and have left the Celtic Twilight forever.

The Mail boat, the Leinster, turned out to be a dirty old ship, well past her best but still able to denude the glens and hills of Ireland of the living. We fourteen carpenters from Dublin kept together beside our luggage and tools, which we had stacked on mid-deck beside a canvas-covered hold. Most of these would remain cardboard figures in my mind for life, I only came to know two of them well. Tooler was the first. It was a lovely sunny morning with a freshening breeze as we came out of the Bay into the open sea, and Wicklow and the old Sugar Loaf mountain soared blue above the magical green. Soon Ireland was gone, but the wind was now blowing with increasing force, and we faced into a storm I would never forget. What made it worse was that the sun shone all the time. Within an hour the old tub was wallowing like a sick pig, burying her snout deep in the oncoming hill of water, then righting herself laboriously, a tired ship, before skidding down the other side of the hill to bury her snout once more.

The Irish girls, in their pretty frocks, were looking sick, and my own stomach was starting to turn over. Since we had been at Westland Row I had noticed one carpenter who stood alone and apart from the rest of us.

'Ay, Tooler,' I shouted above the wind, 'who's your man over there?' I pointed to a fine six foot figure of a man, bearded, handsome, very like the dead leader, Parnell.

'Trevor Baird,' shouted Tooler. 'A bit of a bolix.'

'But what . . . ?'

Tooler put his fingers to his ears and beckoned me to

follow him. We found a place out of the gale, under some stairs. Tooler lit a Woodbine, I lit a Goldflake and resumed where I had left off.

'Well, Paddy,' I shouted, for there was still noise all around us, 'I was going to ask you why he keeps apart from us.'

'He's too good for us, or so he thinks. He's a Dublin Protestant, his oul fella was a wealthy man . . . a builder. But yeh see in his time he had the choice of all the Protestant Church work, yeh know, time and material, no price involved . . . Protestant gentlemen diggin' wit' the same foot. It wasn't so easy for yer man over there. Times had changed.'

'Why? Was he a builder too?'

'Yeah, an' he lost all the money his oul' fella left behind him.'

'But if his oul' fella was a builder, your man must have known his job?'

'He did all right, I'll say that for him. But his oul' fella had trained him too well. He tried to take up where the oul' fella left off, talkin' down his nose at the men, giving them the surname treatment, "Morning, Jordan. . . . Morning . . . ." expecting teh be called "Sir" . . . . That didn't go down wit' the men. Times had changed.'

'How?' I asked, pretending I did not know.

'We were sick of his kind talkin' down to us. Their time was gone, but Baird still tried teh keep things goin' as they had always been. That was his mistake.'

'What happened, Paddy?'

'The fellas lay down on the job, they wouldn't do a decent day's work for him.'

'When he sacked a couple they brought in the Union. He deserved what he got!'

'He must have been a right bolix,' I said, laughing.

Tooler did not laugh. 'Yeh know Lar,' he said quietly. 'He wasn't the worst of the fuckers, an' that's not sayin' all that much for him. But he was fair, fairer than most. It was just that the time for his kind lookin' down on mine was over.

The British were gone, bet out a' the South, his side lost, mine won. Baird is a pukka sahib, left stranded among the Fuzzi-Wuzzies . . . .'

He burst out laughing, and I grinned along with him.

'What's so funny, Paddy?' I asked.

Paddy gave another roar of laughter, but somehow managed to answer me.

'He thinks he's goin' home,' he gurgled, 'he thinks th' English 'ill know that he is really British . . . a Protestant like them . . . that's what he thinks . . . Jaysus,' he roared, 'they'll lump him in wit' the rest of us, an' call him Paddy. That's what I'm waitin' teh see.'

He had not all that long to wait either. Holyhead was half an hour away, and the Mail Boat stank as we entered the shelter of the harbour. We went back to our mates and tool boxes, and I tried not to look at my lovely Veronica and her gay friends. They were huddled together in a sickly knot, green of face, some of them really ill. My blonde lay sprawled face down on the deck, her new dress all soiled, and her face wore a deadly pallor. All along the rail men were still vomiting and dry retching, and the dirty old tub would have to be well hosed down before she went back for another load of . . . .

'Dirty Irish pigs,' remarked one of the crew, who of course had been in no way upset by the storm. 'Fucking pigs'. I was too ill myself to do anything about this remark, but my stomach was slowly settling. I had been on the point of vomiting for some time. How I held it down I will never know.

And then we were ashore, lining up for the long wait while every man's travel permit was checked and double checked, and, all around, singing Welsh voices, just like the Cork ones we had at home. None of the Welsh appeared to be in a position of any importance, they were checkers of tickets, porters, handlers and so on. The job of screening the neutral Paddys was solely in English hands. When my turn came at length I found them to be condescending, rude and aggressive, we were treated as 'smoked whites', little better than the wogs and blacks of their colonies. That

22

the Brits were the greatest fighters in the whole world I freely conceded, for hadn't they nearly beaten us?

Trevor Baird, the Dublin Sassenach, was just in front of me. There was an insignificant looking little bastard with a mean face on him, who constantly patrolled our queue as if looking for something that was there but hard to locate. I kept my eyes well away from him, I did not want trouble. In the end it was Baird he singled out. I think it was the beard that did it, a quite unusual thing for a young man to wear in those times.

'You there, Paddy,' he barked pointing to Baird, 'step off the queue.'

There was a stunned silence from Baird.

'Are you fucking deaf, Paddy?' snarled the little man.

'Are you talking to me?' said Baird incredulously.

'Too fucking right I'm talking to you. Now move your arse off the queue, and follow me.'

With a scarlet face the big 'Prod', who thought himself British, stumbled after the small little ferret of a man towards an office at the end of the platform. This was quite apart from the normal procedure and was evidently the point of interrogation for suspects. I turned to Tooler, grinning. 'I wonder what he thinks about the Brits now?'

Tooler laughed quietly. 'The Paddy bit 'ill sit on his chest like a poultice of wet slack,' he replied.

'A bloody pity about him,' said I, 'the bloody Quisling'. Quisling was a new word that had come courtsy of Herr Hitler. We moved forward without incident and, after an hour, boarded the train. There was no sign of Trevor Baird rejoining the rest of us, unlucky bloody thirteen, I thought. I was still quite ill, my stomach had not settled, in short I thought it a sorry way to enter England. And I was still smarting over my treatment by the English, though it had not been any worse than the rest. We dumped our tool boxes along the corridor, and seven of us filled one carriage, for there was already one man there, another 'Dub' as it turned out, a glazier by trade, headed for London. He had thick glasses perched on a long skinny nose, which was merely the extension of a long skinny face and head, which in their turn perched on a long skinny body. There was not a bloody pick on him, I thought, but could not help noticing his merry blue eyes and the wide mouth made for laughter.

'Let me have men around me that are fat,' said the immortal Bard, 'yon Cassius has a lean and hungry look.' . . . Well, he was entitled to his opinion, but I would have trusted the man before me against a dozen fatsos.

It was too warm in the motionless train. I left the carriage and went to a window in the corridor, and stuck my head out for some fresh air. There appeared to be some sort of a row going on somewhere, for I could hear shouts of rage, and then from a room directly opposite me the glass flew out, and the little ferret-faced bastard who had gone on patrol came flying through. He was covered in blood. Then from the door came the big Dublin Prod, a policeman staggering behind him, nose bleeding. Baird had 'tapped the Claret . . . .'

Behind again, there followed three more coppers, batons swinging at Baird who was intent on boarding the train. They closed on him, raining blows as he tried to open a carriage door, and, with a snarl, he turned and fought. A terrific right stretched a huge policeman unconscious on the platform, and, bleeding from a dozen blows, Baird fought to the last. Two more policemen joined in before they pulled him down, with Baird roaring like a bull, no affected accent now,

'Yiz fuckin' English pigs,' I heard, 'yiz whore's melts . . . . Here's another one,' he screamed, staggering to his feet, leaving policemen all over the ground. Of course the result was never in question. He was floored by sheer weight of numbers, and the train whistled and blew steam as we slowly chugged away from the station. It left a small knot of men kicking something on the platform. And then I was sick. Everything that I should have vomited on the boat came up now, and it was ten minutes later before, pale and shaken, I rejoined my companions.

24

'Are you all right?' said a big blonde-haired man who I found out later was from Waterford.

'Yes, thanks, Blondie,' I said. 'Did you see what they did to Baird?'

'We all saw it,' said Tooler.

'What'll happen to him now, Paddy?'

'Well, afther they've done kickin' 'im, he'll be charged, then it's accordin' teh the Beak he comes before as to where he's sent, an' how long he gets . . . . Jaysus help him, the poor bastard, but he'll know what nationality he is before they've finished wit' 'im!'

'A bad business,' said the glazier with the thick glasses, 'I don't see me likin' this kip very much. Any more a' that an it's back teh Alice for me. By the way, boys,' he added, 'my name is Mick O'Hagan.'

'So Alice is the Mot, is she?' said Tooler.

'Yis,' said Mick. 'I'm married this ten years. Best day's work I ever did, gettin' married teh Alice.'

He looked at Tooler. 'Are yew married, Tooler?' he said.

'No, Mick.'

'Yew'er leaving it a bit late, aren't yeh?'

'Yes,' said Tooler, 'I should a' done the job years ago, but I kept puttin' it on the long finger. Had it too cushy in Dublin before the war. Didn't want teh be strapped down wit' a couple a' kids maybe . . . .'

'Yew were a bloody fool,' said O'Hagan. 'Where's the Mot now?'

'Cryin' back home I suppose,' said Paddy sombrely, 'By Jaysus, this is the last time I'm leavin' Ireland without bein' married. I'm goin' teh live like a bloody miser an' get a few quid together this time.'

'Yew shouldn't have waited this long. Yew should 'a got married last week. Yew should, yew know. I would.'

'What, get married on nothin'?'

'All yew need is a job, whether it's in England or Ireland. The rest comes later. A man thinks an' acts different when he's married.'

O'Hagan reached overhead, took down his case, and

produced a large brown paper bag and a flask. He looked compassionately in my direction.

'Yew're lookin' a bit sick, Lar,' he told me, 'here, this'll buck yew up in no time.' He handed me a delicious ham and lettuce sandwich and a cup of strong tea. It was sweet and brown, and I wolfed the sandwich. Mick gave me another, which I did not refuse, and handed the rest around among the boys. 'A decent ould Dublin skin,' I thought, and handed him back the cup. O'Hagan grinned.

'Yew're lookin' like yer mother's son again,' he said, 'yiv got a bit a' colour back.'

Tooler and the others were enjoying the sandwiches made by the heavenly Alice.

'Thanks, Mick, God bless your Missus,' I said, and meant it.

'I see what yeh mean by bein' married,' said Tooler. 'What was the Missis doin'? Tryin' teh fatten yeh up?'

'Yis, she been tryin' that since we met. Good job I met yew lads, I'd enough food teh take me to Tibet, don't mind London.'

Outside, the alien country flashed past. We had long since left Wales, with its bare mountains, stripped of trees for pit props. On a slate-grey mountain I had seen a line of men, like ants, disappearing into a hole in its side. I wondered what they were mining, and shivered at the thought. I would never go down a mine, to be no better than a mole, burrowing for money in blackness. I would sooner be dead.

These English fields flying past I soon discovered were much larger than the ones I was used to in Ireland, three or four times as large, and the farm houses I saw in the distance were many times bigger than their Irish counterparts too. There was little to indicate that I was in a country at war, that England had its back to the wall, and was fighting for its very life. Far away, once or twice, I saw barrage balloons straining at their cables, indicating the presence of an airfield. Outside the towns that would have been cities in Ireland, the neat, cultivated plots, or allotments, as the English called them, were everywhere. 'Growing for Britain'. I noticed one or two old men working at them, but, for the main part, they were empty. The factory workers who slaved all day came here at night to try and lighten the burden of the British Merchant Fleet, who lost thousands of tons of shipping in the Atlantic to the marauding U Boats. Lost too were the brave men who sank with them.

'How did you an' Alice meet?' said Tooler, to pass the time.

'Well,' said Mick, 'that's a gas story tew . . . . I was out Ballsbridge way, glazin' this old toff's house . . . lousy work, hackin' out old putty and replacin' . . . . Well, anyway, about ten o'clock, this fine buxom blonde cem' upstairs teh where I had one a' the window sashes out an' was puttin' back the glass, an', decent enough, she had a tray with a small pot a' tea and some scones. We got talkin' and she was very nice me. I fell for her straight away, right there an' then.'

'How old were you, Mick?'

'Gettin' on a bit . . . . Thirty-tew. Time I was married.'

'What kept you single so long, then?' said Tooler.

Mick grinned. 'Well Paddy, I didn't have a mot, like yew, and then, although me job wit' Dockrells seemed safe enough, I'm not Clark Gable an' the mots weren't exactly queued up, if yeh folly me.' And suddenly I took a love for this man and his decent honest ways, and told myself I would try to be like him always. I would face the truth if it killed me, for sometimes I was inclined to bury my head in the sand and hide myself from myself.

'Go on, Mick,' I said.

'Well, I found out her name was Alice McVittie, that she was supposed to be a lady's companion to th' oul wan that owned the place, but what that really meant was that Alice worked at everything . . . shopping . . . makin' up beds . . . a "skivvy" more or less, for a lot of the houses in Ballsbridge are on their last legs as regards money. So no money, no servants. This oul' wan, Alice told me, had lost most of her

27

money in the Wall Street crash. Well, the lovely big blonde cem' again in th' afternoon wit' more tea and cakes, an' goin' home, I passed through the kitchen. It was an excuse to see her, teh thank her, for the job was finished. An' so was I if she didn't go along wit' what I had in mind . . . .'

'Fell for her hard, eh, Mick,' said Blondie, in his soft Waterford brogue. 'Didn't you?'

I took stock of Blondie enviously. He was everything I would have been myself if God had willed it so, six feet tall, broad-shouldered, as good-looking as a Hollywood movie star, a big young man, and well-dressed with it. His 'Crombie' overcoat was above my head, on the rack.

'She was,' said O'Hagan, 'what they used teh call in the twenties, "my big moment". Anyway, sis I teh her, "it was nice meetin' yeh, Alice," for she told me I could call her that, "an' the job bein' finished I won't be seein' yeh again . . . ."

'"An'," ses she, "Michael, why not?"

'"Well," ses I, and me heart was dancin' wit' delight, "no betther man if that's the way yeh feel about it."'

'So yeh started goin' out together,' said Tooler.

'Not half. Tew days later I met her and took her to the Royal, an' after the show we went teh the Bar. I had a small one an' a pint, an' Alice didn't drink, so she had lemonade, but she never blinked an eyelid when I ordered the second pint. I was tryin' teh get me courage up . . . . Yeh see I couldn't believe me good fortune that a lovely big woman like her 'id fancy a fella like me, but she did. Believe it or not, Ripley, she did!'

'Can yeh prove that?' said Tooler, to raise a laugh.

'I can,' the Dublin glazier replied, 'we've tew kids, a boy aged nine and a girrill a' seven. But teh get back teh the Royal, it was now or never for me. I'd never get up the pluck again, so straight away I asked her would she consider marryin' me. And do yeh know what she said? She said "Yes", that's what she said, "but y'ill have teh know more about me, Michael."'

It seemed that the ample Alice was a North of Ireland

Presbyterian, and would understand if Mick called it off.

'"No way," sez I, "There's tew things we'll never fight about, one is religion an' the other is politics. So if that's all right wit' yew, Alice, it's us for the long haul together." I'd had enough politics after the Rizin' in '16 . . . I was in that.'

'Don't mind me saying so, Mick,' said Blondie, 'but you look a bit on the young side to have been there.'

O'Hagan laughed heartily. 'Well, Blondie, yeh won't believe this, but I was only sixteen, an' I stood for three whole days behind some sandbags in Church Street, armed wit' a Pike, if yew don't mind.' I stared hard at him. Surely he must be joking . . . .

'A Pike,' I echoed. 'Jesus, now I've heard everything. You're joking, of course!'

'I'm not jokin',' said O'Hagan, 'that's the truth. The oul' dealers around kept us in tea and grub, an' kept beggin us teh go home tew our mothers, but we wouldn't. When the Volunteer force surrendered, we marched to the Rotunda Gardens and formally did likewise. And the Brits gave us a kick in the arse, and sent us home.'

'Only kids,' I said.

'Yis . . . . But this one grew up in a hurry, an' I was well versed when Lloyd George unleashed the Black an' Tan scum on the country. I saw a few a' them across the Jordan.'

'So you were a Shinner, like my father?' I said.

'Yis . . . . I knew your oul' fella. A sound man.' In an instant the past was upon me, and, with the ears of a little child, I listened to the terrifying roar of men locked in battle on the streets of Dublin, and saw again a shattered O'Connell Street, pavements covered with masonry, bricks and glass, and over it all the shadow of Nelson on his magnificent column, his blind side turned on the city below, and bronze Daniel O'Connell, still on his granite pedestal, with his four angels, their wings protecting 'The Emancipator', one of them scarred forever, shot through the 'diddy'.

I was a child of that revolution, now in the mists of my past, but here before me was the indisputable evidence that it was a very recent past, for O'Hagan was only about forty-one. And we were both taking a walk in alien corn.

A squadron of Spitfires roared low over the train from a nearby airfield, bringing me back to the present with a jerk. The Battle of Britain was over, the young eagles of the air had faced those of the Luftwaffe, and, over the green fields of Kent and Surrey, they had fallen out of the sky in numbers, but the fat homosexual, Goering, had lost his nerve, appalled at German losses, not knowing that the RAF was down to its last few planes, that another day's onslaught by him would have left England at the total mercy of the German bombers. Such are the fortunes of war.

'Anyway,' said Blondie, 'I'm sorry for interruptin' you.'

'Well,' said O'Hagan, 'we went together for three months, for we set the date that first night, but, a' course, I was mad teh go teh bed wit' Alice. But I kept that to meself.'

'Did you have any trouble getting a priest to marry you?'

'Yis . . . the Catholic Church doesn't believe in mixed marriages, but the priest changed his mind in a hurry when I told him the Presbyterian minister was willin' do the job. He wasn't . . . but the lie worked. So, just before our marriage date, we crossed the Border teh meet her father.'

'Yeh must be a brave man,' said Tooler, 'to be game to meet one a' them fellas?'

'I was, at that time anyway. Yeh see, Tooler, I never had a bit in me life, an' Alice was a virgin too. She was twenty-eight, an' needed a man, an' me, I'd nearly lose me mind everytime I thought of sleepin' wit' a woman . . . especially a woman like Alice.'

'How did things with the oul fella go?'

'Polite, very cool, we stayed overnight at Alice's farm house, a tidy spread, an' told them our intentions. The mother never opened her mouth at all. The oul fella had a mouth like a bulldog chewin' a wart, an' how in the name o' Jaysus the pair of them ever produced Alice I'll never know.'

'And you left the next morning,' I said.

'Yis, but before we left the oul fella called me into the sittin' room to have a talk wit' me. Siz he, "I'll not go behind the bush an' pretend I'm glad to meet yeh. I'm not, and I'm sorry me daughter didn't marry one of her own. However I'm bound to say that you appear to be a decent sort of a man, but I fear for your marriage".

'"I have the same problem wit' my people, Misther McVittie," I told him, "but we'll be happy, Alice an' me . . . ." And I felt like tellin' him "Fuck the begrudgers" . . . but I didn't."

'"An' what about my daughter's religion? Is she goin' teh change that too?"

'"No," ses I, "Nor will I change mine. We're free people, the pair of us."

'"An' what about the children? I suppose they'll be brought up as Taigs?"

'"The boys will, the girrils 'ill go with their mother's religion. That's the way it was hundreds a' years ago, before the Border came . . . before Cromwell came . . . in a mixed marriage. I take it yew won't be comin' tew the weddin'?"

'"No," ses he, "we'll not meet again."

'"I'm sorry about that," ses I, "for yev only wan daughter, an' y'ill never see yer grandchildren . . . . Anyway, goodbye." We shook hands an' that was that. We never did meet again.'

'There's terrible bigotry in Ireland on both sides,' said a middle-aged man who up to this had spoken little.

'Well,' said O'Hagan, his very blue eyes twinkling behind his heavy glasses, 'me an' Alice weren't much concerned about anything except gettin' married. Jaysus, I thought the day 'id never come 'till I'd sleep wit' her. An' the word got out on the job, someone found out the date, we were married on the twenty-fifth of July . . . a Saturday, an' then the rousin' up started . . . y'know, the way fellas 'ill rib yew up, shoutin' "Aye, Mick, y'ill be all right next Saturday night . . . y'ill be introducin' Fagan . . . heh heh . . . ." An' me passin' it off, shoutin' back that it wouldn't be the first time,

31

actin' the hard chaw, an' me a virgin boy at thirty-two years of age . . . . What I knew about women yeh could write on a stamp . . . .'

With the others laughing, and the time flying, I had grave thoughts about a country that could produce a virgin boy at thirty-two and a virgin at twenty-eight. Surely there was no other country could match this, and there were thousands of them in the Irish Free State. The Church held the cities, Dublin included, in the same vice-like grip as they did the people of Ballyslapadashamuckery, and yet this train was packed with our fellow countrymen who thought of Dubliners as 'smart aleck Jackeens'.

'Well,' said Tooler, 'tell us the rest, Mick.'

'Well,' said Mick, 'we got married, very quiet, an' then we were on the boat for a week's holiday in the Isle of Man. I'll never forget it. It was all like an excitin' dream, I mean, this was the day, tonight was the night, an' O'Hagan, the Phantom Rider, would strike again!'

I joined in the roar of laughter that followed this. This man was outrageous by any standards, even Dublin ones. Eventually he continued the saga of the deflowering of the willing Alice. Their hotel room had overlooked the sea front at Douglas, Mick had gone the limit and booked the best suite in the place. Between Alice and himself they had found the deposit for a small house on the South Circular Road, and had worked side by side for three months redecorating it. The bedroom and kitchen were furnished by the time they were married, though they had never sampled the forbidden fruit. They had come to each other as Adam and Eve had done, driven by want and love, as innocent as the couple in the Garden of Eden. And here it was, Paradise on earth.

'Alice was all flushed an' shy, yeh know the way women get, an' she went inteh the bedroom teh change for dinner . . . . A' course I was tew shy tew folly her, but I was like a fly on th' edge of a sugar bowl, rubbin' the hands together wit' delight. "This is it," I said tew meself . . . "this is it." An' then, bejaysus, Alice came out a' the bedroom an' she was cryin'. "Jaysus, Alice," I told her, "don't tell me you're sorry yew married me." . . . "Oh no, Michael," she ses, "It's just that me . . . well, you know what happens to a woman every month . . . . It's all the excitement, Michael, that has brought me on before me time. Oh, Michael, I married you for love, and I can't be a wife to you tonight. I'm sorry . . . ." an' she was burstin' her heart cryin' . . . .'

'So I put me arms around her, an' said it was all right Alice, love, an' I told her I loved her so much I could wait forever if necessary . . . I was always a good liar . . . an' that I didn't marry her just for that, an' she dried up her tears and smiled . . . an' I was fuckin' ragin'.'

We were all in stitches now but O'Hagan had not finished. When our laughter had subsided a little he added, 'Her period kept up the whole week of our honeymoon, an' she still had it when I went back to work, an' all the fellas tellin' how much weight I had lost, an' asking me did I go up wit' the blind now when yeh rise it, an' me givin' back smart answers, an' all the time I was still a fuckin' virgin boy.' We were still laughing as the train pulled into Crewe.

O'Hagan looked across at me. 'I suppose, young Redmond, yew think I'm a dirty old man, don't yew?'

'No, Mick, I don't, I know well you're only telling the truth.'

He gave me a penetrating stare before replying. 'Yew'er no virgin boy,' he said at length.

'No, thank God,' I said, 'but I haven't had all that much experience. I'd like to get some more.'

'Yew're in the right country for it,' he replied.

'I hope so.'

'That's what brought yeh t'England, isn't it?' said Tooler.

'Among other things . . . .'

This was where we parted from the Dublin glazier who had lightened our long journey, the unlucky thirteen headed for Coventry, he for London. He shook hands with me last, his train was on the far platform almost ready to go.

'Goodbye, Lar, an' good luck,' he said.

'The same to you, Mick.'

I looked up at him and saw that his eyes were blinded with tears. 'I'll need it,' he whispered, 'Jaysus help me, I'm lost without Alice . . . Goodbye . . . .' I felt my own eyes mist over as I watched him go.

3   Coventry

There was no doubt now, in Crewe Railway Station, that we were in a country at war. The platforms seethed with British and Commonwealth forces, army, navy, and airforce, with a generous sprinkling of women wearing the uniforms of all three. We stuck together closely in this military tide, and Tooler went to find out when we could get a connection to Coventry. He returned with doleful news, we would have to wait three hours.

We took turns in guarding the luggage while the rest queued outside the tea rooms for stale buns and weak tea. It was the best we could do, and, at seven o'clock, in the late September twilight, we boarded the train at last. Night came soon and we pounded through the dark in a blacked-out juggernaut. Once, we pulled into a siding for over an hour while the distant roar of guns and explosions came to us across the quiet fields, and bright flashes lit up the horizon. This was it, this was the excitement I had been seeking, with the world in an uproar I wanted to be where it was at. The pity was that it was not all going the way my Walter Mitty dreams had predicted.

I was tired, I was hungry, I was depressed and missing home. Sorrowfully I wondered how many tears Mam had shed because of me, her favourite son. All the others were blondes, I alone had inherited her small stature and dark brown hair. It was eleven o'clock when we reached Coventry, or what was left of it. We were all asleep, and stumbled out into the blacked-out station, where we waited for half an hour for the firm's truck, which never came. So this was the way of it for itinerant workers, no one to meet us, no one to guide us. Eventually, we set off down a narrow street, hefting our accursed tool boxes that grew heavier with every step.

It could have been worse, at least we could partially see where we were going, for a half moon lay on its back in a clear night sky. 'If only,' Blondie snarled, 'we knew where we were fucking well going, everything would be all right.' Eventually somebody spotted a small light shining dimly through a door, on it the magical word 'Police'. Tooler knocked softly, and a big policeman stepped out. It was a 'watch point', hardly bigger than a telephone box. He stared in some dismay at our weary platoon.

'Oi, Oi,' he said, 'an' wot 'ave we 'ere?'

Tooler told him in a few brief words.

'Well,' said the Law, who was in no way friendly, 'caw'nt 'ave thirteen Irishmen wandering around Coventry at night. Oi'll get you fixed up until morning.' It was only a couple of years since the IRA had set bombs off in this city, and the Irish were not popular.

'Any chance of something to eat?' said Blondie.

'Not an 'ope,' said the copper. 'This way.' We trailed disconsolately down the narrow street, with its cobblestones flanked on both sides by piles of bricks that had once been shops and houses. Before a towering mound of rubble the policeman produced a key, and led the way into an underground air-raid shelter. He flicked on the light, revealing a double row of bunk beds, with no mattresses, their steel springs shining coldly in the light. There was a heavy smell of damp and must, mingled with the sickening odour I had smelled in the street outside. It was sweetly revolting, like no other I had ever known.

'This 'ill 'ave to do for tonight,' said the copper, 'We'll get you lot sorted out in the morning.'

He turned, went out into the darkness, and locked the door behind him.

'This,' said Tom Hogan, a quiet man of around thirty, 'is a right fuck up.'

His remark summed up all our feelings, but we were too tired to discuss it. We all lay down on the bare springs, covered ourselves with our overcoats, and tried to sleep. I awoke to a cold dawn, shivering, and walking stiffly towards the open door. Outside, some of our gang were already assembled, gazing open-mouthed at the handiwork of Der Führer, who had ripped the guts out of this city, cored it as one would an apple.

Overhead, only a couple of hundred yards, the spire of Coventry's ruined cathedral soared aloft, pointing the way to Heaven, and the Germans who had destroyed it. The big copper of the previous night was there, and in the daylight I could see that he was a sergeant.

'All out,' he shouted into the air-raid shelter. 'Your truck 'ill be along about now. Cum' on, move it.'

When the last had stumbled out he locked the door, and walked away.

'Nice friendly sort of a fella,' said someone. We were all showing the strain of our long drawn out ordeal of the first day and night in England. Presently, along came the truck, and we sullenly loaded our gear aboard, and shivered in the cold wind as the open truck headed out of Coventry. We were headed for Stoneleigh Abbey, and the galvanised iron bubble huts that would shelter us. They had concrete floors, they were unlined, much less insulated, and one could either freeze or fry in them, according to the season. One pot-bellied stove to keep them above freezing point in severe weather, three coarse blankets, two sheets and one pillow, no locker or wardrobe of any kind, you lived out of your suitcase.

'Smashin',' said Tooler, 'reminds me of the fuckin' Gresham Hotel.'

The large camp was silent, the rest of the workers long since departed, 'going to it for Britain', and we made our way over to the dining hall where they had a late breakfast for us. They gave us a book of tickets which would entitle us to be fed for a week. Breakfast over, and back in our hut, a truck squealed to a halt outside.

'Cum' on, lads,' roared a north of England voice, 'doan't you know there's a waar on?'

We were all getting into bed when this happened, we were worn out. Presently, after a couple of more arrogant roars, the driver shut off the engine and came into the hut.

'Doan't thee intend to go to work today?' he snapped.

'No,' said Blondie.

'What!'

'No . . . fuck off.'

'Wait till Bateman 'ears of this! 'e'll fix thee.'

'Fuck you and Bateman,' said Tooler. 'An' if he has any friends or relations in America, fuck them as well.'

'We've had a rough time,' said Tom Hogan quietly. 'We need the sleep.' And that was that. We slept all day, turned up early for dinner, ate all we could get, and were ready to go to work the following morning. It would be the first real day's pay any of us had earned for a long time, and we were eager to start. The arrogant driver of the previous day grinned when we loaded our tool boxes, but made no comment. This truck had a canvas cover under which we sat on wooden benches screwed to the floor. I found myself beside the biggest Irishman I had ever seen. His name, predictably, was Paddy Murphy, and I think he came from Mullingar. His hands were like shovels, his bone structure awesome, an old trilby hat, stretched to its limit, perched precariously on the young giant's head, for he was only nineteen. He had the guileless face of a child, his blue eyes calmly looked on a world gone mad, he had not a bad turn in his body.

'Are yiz comin' on our job?' he asked softly.

'I think so,' said Tom Hogan.

'There's no work on it for carpenters, anyway,' said Murphy, and started to sing to himself. He had a fine voice for ballads, and I enjoyed him singing for the fifteen minutes it took to get on site. Then the truck skidded to a halt beside a hut, the men bailed out and headed for a

38

deep cutting beside the road. Their picks and shovels were at the bottom of it, and we, the unlucky thirteen, started to unload our tool boxes. The Ganger approached us from the hut

'Righto, you lot,' he barked, 'fall in. Oi 'ave picks and shovels 'ere for you.' Every man jack of us wore carpenters' overalls, had a rule projecting from the side pocket, and a pencil behind the ear. So this was it. This was what the feared and faceless Bateman had lined up for us. Blondie winked, stepped forward, and grabbed a pickaxe, then whipped out his rule and measured the handle.

'This pick,' he told us, 'is two inches longer than the Union allows.'

'What length is it?' said Tooler.

'Three feet, if yeh don't mind.'

'Take two an' a half inches off it.'

Blondie opened his tool box and took out a saw, grinning. Tom Hogan now spoke up.

'The Union rule allows two an' three quarter inches.'

'Well,' said Tooler judicially, 'we'll settle for two and five eights.'

'An' a sixteenth,' said Blondie.

'Leave the line on when yer cuttin' it,' Hogan added. Blondie placed the pick down flat on his tool box and swiftly cut the handle across.

The Ganger, being jeered by a crowd of Paddies, was slowly turning purple with rage. Two more truck loads of men now pulled up behind our one, and stood around, enjoying the fun. They were all from west of the Shannon, some of them shared our hut, for I recognised them from the night before when they had practically ignored us. Now, in the face of the common enemy, they cheered us on.

'Good on yeh, Dubs,' came a shout, 'show the bastards what Irishmen are made of.' So it was acknowledged by them now that we were Irish, and suddenly, in a moment of truth, I realised that I was, after my own fashion, as parochial as they, that most of their stand-offish ways were due to shyness and fear of the unknown. In future I would go forward to meet my fellow countrymen, and find many gentlemen among them. I would come to hate Dubliners' jeering description of country people as 'Culchies', and never again think it, much less use it. I would come to know well the people whom Cromwell had given the choice of "Hell or Connacht", whose ancestors had taken over a lunar landscape of rocks and bogs, with the few good acres of that province occupied by the victorious Sassenach. Even the salmon and seatrout that swam in from the Atlantic and raced up their rivers were denied them, yet somehow they had survived, piled rocks around the fields, some no bigger than a tennis court, built their tiny cottages with the same accursed rocks, and made their little plots fertile with seaweed, sometimes drawn from more than a score of miles away.

'We'll show them,' Blondie roared. 'Back on the truck, men.'

In the hut the Ganger was frantically phoning Bateman in the Coventry office, while the men from beyond the Shannon cheered us, and filtered away to work. Dublin Jackeens had been accepted at last, and from now on we could do no wrong. The man called Bateman was responsible for their joy in our defiance, for he hated and despised Irishmen, considered them no better than pigs, that their proper station in life was at the bottom of a ten-foot trench. We had shown him something different.

The truck driver was leaning against the hut, gleefully listening to the Ganger's report, but Tooler soon took the grin off his face.

'Aye . . . Yew . . .' he called, 'home James and don't spare the horses.' Tooler, as a foreman, had been used to giving orders, and could match any Englishman for arrogance if it came to it.

'Move,' he roared into his gaping face.

'Oi'm not movin', 'oo do you think you are?'

'Me, Pat O'Toole. How would yeh like four flat tires?'

'An' a nose teh match?' said Blondie, who was backing Tooler to the hilt. It seemed that these two had emerged as the natural leaders of our gang. He walked over to the truck, and started to unscrew the valve cap on the back tire. The driver, outguessed, and suddenly afraid, made for the driver's seat, and Blondie screwed back the valve, and joined us on the truck. So it was back to Stoneleigh camp, and another endless day without earning a penny.

At three o'clock Bateman sent for us. The old Irishman who led us to his office whispered a little information about the man we were about to meet. Bateman had been one of the Black and Tans who had ravaged Ireland, and got the mother and father of all hidings in the process. His natural contempt for Paddies was reinforced by a very real hatred of the people who had beaten him. We filed into his office, which was occupied by a scared looking typist, and the Bucko himself. For me it was instant hatred. It was his ilk that had filled my childhood with nightmares, it seemed to me we had met before, and perhaps we had! Our eyes came together at once in a glare of mutual hatred.

'Why aren't you people at work?' he snarled.

'We were employed as carpenters by your agent in Dublin,' said Tom Hogan quietly. 'We're all Union men and we don't do labouring work.'

'You'll do it here.'

I studied the old bastard intently. A big one, with no spare fat like the sergeant I had baited in the Army, but over fifty, I guessed. Well, if it came to it . . . .

'No way,' said Hogan. 'If you've no work at our trade you might as well send us home.'

'You'll starve before I do. You'll report to the same place tomorrow morning if any of you want to eat!' His plan was to withdraw our meal tickets, but that did not work at all. The entire staff in the kitchen was Irish.

We filed back to the hut. It was Friday, and we faced a miserable weekend without money. Blondie, who seemed to have plenty of cash, gave me and Tooler a loan of a couple of quid, until pay day, whenever that would be. Saturday, with its time and a half, and double time for the afternoon shift, came and went without a shilling earned. Around us, on Saturday night the boisterous life of the camp went on apace, with plenty of drink and fags flying, over in the canteen, where insipid English beer was served with black market whiskey under the counter. It was somewhere about nine o'clock when someone told me that the young giant from Mullingar had been badly beaten up while drinking. I said I was sorry to hear it, and went despondently to bed. This was not the England I had expected. I should have been in Coventry by now, in a pub, looking for a girl, and finding one.

It was so long since I had had a woman that the want lay on me like an inescapable pestilence. Aggravated by the fact that I was lobbing around all day, the longing rarely went away now, a good day's work would have lessened it. I was dozing off when I felt someone gently drawing back the bed clothes from my face. I looked up startled, into the battered face of Paddy Murphy.

'Jesus, Paddy, what happened to you at all?'

''Tis all right, Dub,' he said softly. 'I'm just lookin' for someone. Go asleep now.'

'I heard three of them did you over. Is that right?'

''Tis . . . . Sorry for disturbin' yeh. Go asleep, Dub.' He left as gently as he had come. I was nearly asleep when I heard the screams.

I jumped up and ran to the door. Outside, a bright moon filled the night with silver magic, it was almost as light as day. Murphy had found what he was looking for and had two unfortunates with their heads tucked under each mighty arm, screaming as he dragged them behind him.

In the middle of the wide, cinder strewn square he flung them face down on the ground, placed a Brobdingnagian boot on the shoulders of each man, and began to lash them with the weapon he had picked up. It was a quarter inch steel bar used to reinforce concrete. He lashed them alternately about twenty strokes each before honour was satisfied, and walked away, leaving them whimpering into the cinders. Well, I had come over to England to see life, real life, in the raw, and the brutal scene I had witnessed was just that. The carnage in Coventry, its heart ripped out in a single night, was just another facet of man's inhumanity to man, but I would not have gone back to our cushioned existence in Walkinstown for anything. I was young, in my own quiet way I was wild, and, above all, I wanted to be free.

There were only three of us in the hut to witness Murphy's vengeance, the rest having headed for the flesh pots of town, and now the door was flung open, and they erupted into the hut in tearing spirits. They were boisterously gay, but not drunk.

The Dubs, it seemed, had suddenly become very popular with the men of the West.

'Begod,' said a fine red-headed six-footer from Mayo, 'but ye're a great crowd a' Jackeens the way yiz handled the Ganger. Yiv taken on Bateman too, I'm told.'

'Yes, we won't go down the cutting.'

'But what'll you do?'

'Blondie and me have plans for that get on Monday.' The big Mayo man sat down on my bed and took a small bottle, filled with clear liquid, out of his pocket.

'A dhrop a' the "Crathur",' he whispered, "All the way from Connemara. Have a swig." I did, and I nearly exploded. It was dynamite, lunatic soup, depth charger that nearly blew the roof off my head.

'Jesus,' I gasped when I could speak again, 'what kind of paint stripper is that?' The men from the West stood around in fits of laughter.

'That'll put lead in yer pencil for Bateman,' said the red head. 'Did yeh know he was a Black an' Tan?'

'Yes.'

'Did anyone tell you he has a special hatred of Dubs?'

'Why?'

'He got his game leg in Dublin. The Shinners shot him up.'

'Pity they didn't finish the job,' I said with venom. My hatred of this man was such that I, normally a coward, was prepared to take him on, but I had no fear at all with Blondie to help me.

43

'Did any of you hear about Murphy tonight?' Yes, they all knew, he had been looking for the third man who had assaulted him, but had been stopped by a Scot from entering the hut. There had been words between them, the Scot had flung down the gauntlet and challenged Murphy to fight him the following morning.

'Murphy 'ill kill him,' I predicted. The others were not so sure. This man had been a professional fighter, weighed fifteen stone, and feared no one. Murphy, at seventeen stone, had youth and weight in his favour. Too bloody much youth, said the men around me. The Scot, at thirty-two, would half kill him. And besides, he had taken a terrible beating today.

When the lights went out a couple of men who had been whispering, came over to me.

'Will yeh write a couple of letters home for us tomorra', Larry? We heard you were good with the pen.'

'Sure I will, lads.' I went to sleep, slightly shocked.

Sunday morning I was up early, and one of the few at breakfast. The 'hung over' camp slept soundly, but eleven o'clock saw every man jack headed for the hut where Mass was celebrated. Not to be the odd one, I went. The fight was due to take place at twelve noon. Murphy presented a dreadful spectacle. Overnight the bruises, that could only have come from boots, had turned greenish purple. Big and all as he was he was only a man, and I feared for him. I even said a couple of 'Hail Marys' for him, for, like most Irish agnostics, I went back to my religion when the tough times came.

The Mass finished, we headed for the cyclone fence that shut the camp in and prevented us from walking the broad acres of Stoneleigh Abbey. It was a lovely morning, the sun blazed down on the green and ancient oak trees that had seen the yeomen of England use their devastating long bows in battle. The Scottish and English contingents were already there, the challenger stripped to the waist, and a finer figure of a man a woman never clapped eyes on. My heart sank. Beside him Murphy looked as awkward an an

44

elephant, but an elephant, when aroused, is the most dangerous of all the animals, and this gave me hope.

Murphy lumbered out to face his opponent, who was already dancing around, limbering up. Suddenly Murphy charged, but it was not at the Scot. It was at the crowd. He had spotted the last of the trio who had beaten him up, and now he felled him with one mighty blow on top of the head. His pals carried him off, and now an ugly mood was abroad as Murphy faced the Scot. The men from the West had been right. Murphy was no match for this man. Time and time again a straight left, followed by a crashing right, found poor Paddy's battered face. The English and the Scots went wild, urging their man on. Murphy was reeling all over the place, and then went down to a barrage of heavy punches.

He lay on his back, bleeding from a dozen cuts, looking vacantly at the tranquil Autumn sky. And then something snapped in me, and I, who knew myself to be a coward at heart, went mad, and, shaking, stood over him.

'Get up and kill him,' I screamed. 'Never say your mother reared a jibber.' The code of Dublin's Liberties that I still lived by, notwithstanding our mini-mansion in Walkinstown. Murphy blinked and focussed on me with difficulty.

'Kill the bastard,' I roared. Paddy staggered to his feet, to be met with an open-handed slap across the face. The boxer was going to play with him now, the slap was meant to wake him up. It did!

With a roar and a scream like a bull-elephant, Murphy charged, head down, arms flailing, forcing the Scot back against the cyclone wire fence. It was four feet high. One of Murphy's terrible punches got through the other's guard, and he was lifted off his feet, over the fence, unconscious before he landed, jaw broken in three places. The Irish outnumbered the others by two to one, so any thoughts they may have had about tackling us were swiftly put to one side. And me? After Murphy, I was the hero of the day. The men who had so lately resented Dubliners took me to their hearts and to the pub, and had me half twisted before dinner. I had to sober up before I could write the letters.

Tomorrow morning, we had decided, we would march into Coventry, and present our case to the police. It was 'simply honour our contract or send us home'. The truck came for us again after breakfast, this time with a very subdued driver. Blondie told him half-heartedly to fuck off, for the rest he was ignored.

It was another late autumn day of glorious sunshine when we set off through the fair fields of Warwickshire, and I could see, at close range, what I had only glimpsed from the train, but the conclusion was the same. There was simply no comparison between Irish farms and English ones. Their fields were bigger, their houses four times the size, everything about them was on a larger scale, indeed some of the houses were mansions. Our fine house in Walkinstown would never have made the splash here that it did at home. As we drew near the city, houses bigger than ours were a dime a dozen, the homes of company executives.

I tailed off behind the others to take a good look. Below me, in a hollow, the sunny town stood around a black hole, through which the graceful spire of the cathedral soared. Around the perimeter of the black hole a thin line of old slate-roofed houses squatted, like crows, all that remained of the Coventry that was gone. They, in turn, were surrounded by the gay red and yellow roofs of the new city that the car industry had built, an English Detroit. Eventually we were marching glumly through the prosperous suburbs. An odd house here and there had 'copped' it but the main damage was confined to the old city. More by luck than anything else we came to the narrow cobbled lane where we had slept that first night.

'Are yeh sure,' said Tom Hogan to Blondie, 'that this is the place?'

Blondie nodded. 'I think so anyway, Tom.' I did not think so, I knew, for that terrible cloying sweet smell was again in my nostrils.

Tom Hogan, as the least hot-tempered of our gang, had

been elected spokesman. We trooped into the police station, and the big sergeant opened his eyes when he saw us.

'Oi, Oi. Wot 'ave we 'ere?'

Tom quietly explained the situation, ending up by saying that if there was no work for us at our trade, then we should be sent home.

'So,' said the sergeant, picking up the phone, 'your firm 'ave broken their contract?'

'I don't think so,' said Tom reasonably. 'It's one of their manager's fault. He hates Irishmen and thinks the only fit place for us is at the bottom of a trench.'

'He's a Black and Tan bastard,' I blurted out. 'He's . . . .'

'Shut up,' said Tooler. 'You've too much to say for your age. Just bloody shut up.'

'Wot did that young fella say?'

'Nuttin' really, Sarge. He's just a hot-headed young fool.' The sergeant gave me a hard stare, he would know me again, then spoke into the phone. From the other end we could hear Bateman shouting defiance, but the sergeant soon settled his hash.

'Listen 'ere, you,' he snarled, 'Oi'm not 'avin' thirteen Irishmen walking around Coventry, broke. Got that?'

We heard Bateman's voice shouting again, but the sergeant roared him into silence.

'You'll 'ear more of this,' he roared. 'I'm getting on to your firm in London, now. An' my report on you will do you no good, believe me, no bloody good at all.' He slammed down the phone and turned a red face to us.

'Now listen 'ere, lads,' he said, breathing hard. 'Oi'm not surprised that you're angry, but take my advice, don't be provoked by this man into doing anything that would get you in trouble. Just go back to the camp an' leave it to me. Will you do that?' Hogan nodded, thanked him, and said, yes we would.

'Good lads,' said the sergeant who seemed at last to have taken a liking to us. Rooting in a drawer he produced a twenty pack of cigarettes and told us to ''ave a smoke on the road back', and then gruffly told Hogan to bugger off, when he tried to thank him.

Outside the station we had a smoke and I asked if anybody wanted to see the cathedral, but there were no takers. They slouched off moodily back to camp, and I went back into the police station. I wanted to ask the sergeant some questions.

'Fiery young bugger, aren't you?' he said with a smile. 'Wot can I do for you?' I grinned back, delighted. So the whole bloody country wasn't composed of Batemans, or vicious little Ferrets such as had greeted us at Holyhead.

'I just wanted to ask you what that terrible smell in the street is. Every time I get it I nearly vomit.'

For answer the big man came from behind his desk and led me outside. A few yards down the narrow street he stopped before a huge mound of rubble, broken bricks with great slabs of reinforced concrete topping the pile, their rusting reinforcement protruding from them like twisted guts. Great iron girders that had been through the firestorm lay around, curled like liquorice sticks, and a crane was busy lifting them onto a truck. They would be re-forged to make tanks, to be used against the German General, Rommel, who was giving the Brits a lesson in tank warfare in the Western Desert.

'That,' said the sergeant sombrely, 'used to be Woolworths. There were seven 'undred people sheltering in the basement when it got 'it by a blockbuster.'

'Jesus!'

'There's plenty of bodies under that lot, I'd say. That's where the stink is coming from . . . I wasn't in the Great War for nothing. I'd know the smell of death anywhere, blindfolded.'

'Really, sergeant? Seven hundred people. Christ, no wonder it stinks.'

'That's what I was told anyway, son. I wasn't 'ere the night of the Blitz. The sergeant 'oo was died the same night as Woolworths. Oi'm 'is replacement.'

So that was that little mystery cleared up. I thanked him

and walked the couple of hundred yards to the cathedral.

Nothing had been done since the Germans had destroyed it. On that terrible night, when the citizens had had to face a Blitzkrieg from the sky, the incendiary bombs had rained down, setting the city ablaze, the second wave of bombers had had no difficulty locating their target, and had kept things livened up by dropping 'Blockbusters'.

I found an entrance, into the ruined cathedral that lay open to the autumn sky, and looked in awe at the piled up debris. The charred and broken remains of the huge trusses that had supported the roof lay piled up on the floor, some of them hung with stalactites of lead, with pools of the same mineral stuck to the floor. It was a scene of unbelievable destruction, of something that had once been beautiful, but now had the pathetic grandeur of a ruin. Incredibly, a charred cross still stood at the east end of the ruins, surely a sign, a miracle, that could only have come about by the power of God! I did not know then that this cross had been made from the same beams that littered the floor, that it was the work of the people of Coventry, that, after the crucifixion, the glory of Calvary would return. I found myself on my knees before it, praying.

The habits of the years die hard. 'Give me a child,' said a Catholic priest, 'before he reaches seven years, and he is mine for life,' and so it was with me. I had rejected a tyrannical priesthood in Ireland, but would still remain a Catholic forever.

A Catholic-Protestant, one who could see greed and privilege clearly, who could spot a 'Whited Sepulchre', but would always retain a 'hot line' to Heaven through Jesus Christ.

'How shall I enter the Kingdom of Heaven?' the rich man asked of Christ.

'Give all your wealth to the poor,' he was told.

Until my Church, which was lousy with money and land, started to strip itself of some of its wealth, and give to the poor, until that day, I would never go back. And that day would never come. Jesus had been a carpenter, like me, and knew what a hard day's work was all about. The angry young man who had kicked over the stalls of the money changers outside the Temple was for me! That he had paid with his life for this one action I had no doubt, for he had struck at the root of all evil. Indeed, I thought, he had sealed his fate when he said, 'give all your money to the poor', for he had menaced the social order of the day, just as people like me would not be forgiven by our modern Pharisees, for we menaced them.

Protestant ministers who rode to hounds, and Catholic priests who coursed hares, and went drinking, why, I reflected, they were all one. The ministers were the younger sons of Establishment families, and patronised their flock. The priests who were not exported to carry God's message to the heathen, were the sons of wealthy farmers and publicans, and guaranteed by the Church never to be sent abroad unless they requested it, and, to their credit, many of them did. But the ones who remained in Ireland, by their bigoted, parochial outlook, made it obvious that they had never been more than a mile or two from a cow-pad.

I rose from my knees and made my way nearer to the cross. The Jesus that had hung there must have been a very dirty Jesus indeed, before he crumbled away in the holocaust, feet and legs blackened by smoke, wounds concealed by soot, but surely this was the way Mary last saw her Son. Scourged unmericully, jeered by the mob, brutally beaten on his staggering way to his crucifixion, yes, the statue that was here no longer, must have looked exactly like him before it turned to dust.

I blessed myself, stumbled across the piled debris, and out into the street. Back at the camp, my companions in misfortune were sitting disconsolately on their beds. Blondie, on the other hand, was going out. He had, on his first night in Coventry, picked up a girl, and now he was going to her place for the day, and night! He would not be back until morning. We had a brief consultation and agreed that the next morning, if we had heard nothing from Bateman, we would head for his office and front him up.

Blondie, all six feet of him, strode off, my envious gaze following him all the way to the gate. Jesus . . . what would it be to be six feet tall, and as good-looking as he? And I knew what it was like. He could get all the women I wanted, and that number was legion. I ate some bread I had saved from breakfast, for mavericks like us received no lunch, and went to bed. I was sick and tired of traipsing Coventry without a butt, or a penny in my pocket. I went to sleep, longing for a cigarette, but with a vengeful mind made up that Bateman would pay dearly for this.

'A cripple', I had been informed, who needed a stick to walk. He would need more than a stick if I had my way. First and foremost he was a Black and Tan, one of those who had terrorised my young mother and me, whose rifle butts had smashed through our Georgian door, whose boots had pounded on a gracious staircase, destined to echo down the corridors of my mind forever . . . I slept the long afternoon away, and somehow the day came to an end. The Western contingent stayed home that night, the crack was good, and my new friends kept me well supplied with cigarettes. About eleven o'clock Paddy Murphy came in, looking worse than ever, but evidently in genial form, with a good few drinks on him. The bruises would soon go, but it would be a long time before his Scottish opponent drew another week's wages.

Grinning, Murphy approached, picked my ten stone off the bed as if I weighed nothing and cradling me in his huge arms paraded around the beds.

'Would yeh have a look at it,' he roared, 'with the face of an angel and the temper a' the Divil himself. The best Jackeen that ever came out a' Dublin.' Then he set me back down on my bed again, and, squatting beside me, shoved a five pound note in my hand.

'Don't offend me by refusin',' said the Mullingar man. 'Yeh haven't earned a shillin' in the last week, an' that's not charity, it's a loan, between friends,' he added.

Well no one in his senses insulted a man as big as Murphy, besides, I was dead broke, and, with what I had in mind, would probably be deported tomorrow.

'Sure, you'd do the same for me, wouldn't you?' said the big slob.

'I would, Paddy,' I said, and meant it. 'But you have Buckley's chance of ever seeing that fiver again. Blondie and me are going to have a show down with Bateman in the morning. We'll probably be arrested and sent home.'

'To hell wit' the fiver,' said Murphy, 'an' good luck to yeh. It's time that bastard was fronted up be someone.' We shook hands on that, Murphy went away, and I was left to my erotic dreams of Blondie and his . . . what? 'Doxy,' I thought, remembering Pepys's *Diary*, and wished I had a 'doxy' myself. Mortal sins did not bother me anymore.

As long as I could remember I had walked in fear of the 'Confessional', but not now. The last time I had gone was six years ago, when I was sixteen, and had to confess the terrible sin of looking at girls' legs and thighs when their skirts blew up. Girls riding bikes on a windy day were my speciality, and I had entered the confession box in a state bordering on hysteria. The dark, cloistered, muffled place, with barely enough room to kneel down, the sound of the small sliding door going back, and the voice from the darkness. 'Begin your confession, my son.'

'Bless me Father, for I have sinned', the ritualistic open-ing, and so to my sinful addiction of watching out for girls' skirts blowing up, the further the better. He was what was known as an 'easy' priest, and he had gently told me that legs were legs, just that and no more. 'Why,' he went on, 'there is really no difference between a man's and a woman's, they both support the human body,' and I should give up my sinful ways. But, I thought, if there is no difference, why am I here to confess?

'For your penance, my son, say six Our Fathers and twelve Hail Marys, and stop thinking that there is any difference.

That had been the first time I had ever left the confessional without feeling cleansed! I had done more than look since then. I had felt Kathleen's and Sheila's legs

52

in the dark one night, and they were lovely and soft. And what was the use of going to confession when I knew damn well I would feel them, any chance I got, and progress rapidly along the shameful road that led to going to bed with a woman. I could tell that priest now, if he still did not know, bloody well I could tell him the difference.

And still, before sleep took me, I remembered the joyful days of my boyhood, when my small sins had been forgiven, coming out of the chapel with a lovely feeling of purity, bounding like a deer down Dolphins Barn street, never to sin again. And wished it could have remained so, always, that the terrible driving urge for women would leave me, but I knew it never would.

Jesus of Nazareth, on the charred cross that had brought me to my knees that day, who had said, 'Let him who is without sin amongst you cast the first stone', who told the woman taken in adultery, 'Go and sin no more', whose feet had been wiped by the hair of the prostitute, Mary Magdalene, surely he would understand how it was with me? That if, right this minute, I could be fortunate enough to come upon another Mary Magdalene, I would gladly pay her price, and, in my heart, bless her in her giving . . . and taking!

I woke up the following morning in foul humour, primed for what lay before me. Blondie arrived back about nine thirty, nodded significantly, and together we made for Bateman's office. On the way I took careful stock of Blondie, and marvelled at his cheerful appearance and bounding good health. I had never seen him look better, he gave the lie to everything I had been told in my childhood about sex. He should have looked pale and wan from too much of 'the other', but he looked as fit as a fiddle while little celibate me had dark rings under the eyes and was certainly no advertisement for a sexless existence. Tooler caught up with us as we neared our quarry.

'What are you tew up teh?' he said.

'We're going to sort out Bateman,' said Blondie quietly.

'Right then, I'll give yiz a hand.'

'You won't Paddy, you have too much to lose. What about your woman in Dublin? Lar an' me have nothing to lose. It's all one to us whether we're sent home or not. It's different with you, and you know it.'

'All right, then,' Tooler conceded. 'But I'll be close by if I'm needed. I'm told he's a tough old bastard.'

We parted then, Blondie opened the office door without knocking, and in we went. Bateman glanced up sharply from behind his desk, and then went on writing. We stood before him until he was forced to look up.

'Well,' he snapped, 'what brings you two here?'

'You know well what brings us here,' said Blondie. 'We want a job at our trade, or to be sent home. We won't work as labourers, and that's that!'

The typist on the far side of the room, I noted jealously, was eating Blondie with her eyes.

'You'll work at the work I have for you,' Bateman snarled. 'I'm making special arrangements for your lot that'll make you glad to join the other Paddies in the cutting.'

A heavy walking stick lay on top of the desk. I snatched it up. I hated this man and it would only be poetic justice for a Dubliner to beat him with the stick my city had made him carry.

'A Shinner gave you this,' I said, hefting it, 'and here's the son of a Shinner who owes you one.'

'Right?' said Blondie.

'Right,' I said. We had planned it well, and now Blondie moved to the right and I to the left. We would attack him from two sides at once. I saw the typist put her hand over her mouth, about to scream as Bateman came slowly to his feet, and we closed in. There was not a sound in the room, you could cut the tension with a knife.

And then the phone rang, it exploded like a bomb, making us jump. Bateman reached out and took it. Blondie and I came to a halt, frozen in the act of committing an assault.

'Yes, sir,' said Bateman into the phone. 'They'll be on their way within the hour.' He put down the phone, and I the stick.

'You lot are going to London,' he ground out.

'When?' Blondie roared.

'Now,' snarled Bateman. 'Pack up and fall in outside your hut. You'll be at the railway station in half an hour.'

'Fall in,' I sneered. 'I'm not in the fuckin' army. Don't tell me to fall in, you old bastard.'

I was hyped up to hell, baulked of my revenge.

'C'mon, Lar,' said Blondie. 'Yiv got what yeh wanted.'

Yes, I had, but I knew only a sense of shame. If my mother or father had seen and heard their son they would have died of shame. If they ever heard that I had spoken, Liberties style, and effed and blinded in front of a woman they would have disowned me. I could almost hear my gentlemanly father's cutting censure. 'You dirty little gurrier, you've been better reared than that. Take yourself off, get out of my sight.' An hour later we hefted the tool boxes onto the train, and away we went, bound for the big smoke, and, if the dear Jesus was kind, we might at least be able to earn a week's wages.

4 London

It was only a two hour journey from Coventry to London. I wondered what the great city had in store for me. As we drew near to it the barrage balloons were all about, straining at their ropes in a rising storm, for the sky was black, and, even above the noise of the train, the thunder rumbled, and the sky was lit with flashes of fork lightning. One barrage balloon, higher in the sky than the others, received a direct hit, and burst into flames. Fascinated, I watched it slowly fall, a ball of fire that set two others alight as it came to earth.

Our unlucky thirteen, as we called ourselves, were scattered along the train, for it was packed to capacity, so full that the officers, with their drawling Oxford accents, had to mingle with the common herd in the second class carriages. I was glad to be away from the others, for sometimes I welcomed the prospect of sitting alone, studying the human race, and this was a unique opportunity to study the class distinctions that made up England. The working class, in or out of uniform, were easily identified by their accents, the establishment by theirs. The white collar workers all wore the same sort of uniform, bowler hats, rolled umbrellas, white shirts. The 'blue collar' working class seemed to run to jerseys, caps and loud scarves, stolid men who knew their place, and England's place in the world.

They looked up to the officers in more ways than one,

for the upper class were taller, and quite obviously had been better fed in the hungry thirties. Hitler had called England a 'C3' nation, but forgot that that only applied to the lower orders, and surely these Andy Capps around me were the lower orders.

The train slowed down as we moved through a mighty huddle of slate grey roofs, with here and there a terrace blasted from the face of the earth, but hardly noticeable in this mighty sprawl. Soon we were at Euston Station, a gigantic place, of steaming monsters and scurrying people. It was time to pick up the accursed tool box again, and I wished I had never been forced to become a carpenter. Why the hell had I not opted for glazing like O'Hagan who had only to carry a glass cutter, a putty knife, and one chisel for hacking out? Working for my father I had never had to carry a box of tools any distance, but now I was starting to hate the badge of my serfdom, its impossible weight dragging the life out of me. It surely hung around me like a millstone.

Somehow we managed to group around Tooler, who had done it all before, and who would now lead us across London, or rather under London, for he made for the Tube. We descended into the bowels of the earth by escalator, searching for the train that would take us to Paddington and then on again to Southall.

'Wot time is it, mate?' said a cockney to me.

'Half two,' I replied, Dublin style.

''alf two is one, Paddy,' he replied, grinning.

I heard the distant rumble of an approaching train, and then it came, the cloying breeze of London's Underground, sweet-scented, hot, the smell of women and sex.

The Cockney had heard our accents, and now he thought he would try it on with Tooler.

'Wot do yer fink of our Underground, Paddy?' he said.

Tooler scowled. He had no liking, like the rest of us, for being addressed by total strangers as 'Paddy'.

'Like shite down a sewer,' he snapped.

'In other words,' I told the Cockney, 'we are not

57

impressed, nor are we amused!'

The Cockney blinked in surprise. It was obvious he had never tangled with Dubliners before, and had become used to getting the better of soft country lads, like big Murphy. He would never beat us, who all came from a city noted for its acid, sometimes blasphemous, quickness of tongue.

And then they came, the women, the joy of my young heart, tumbling off the train while we scrambled on, red heads, brunettes, blondes, big-bosomed, slim-waisted, underweight, overweight, bright-faced or serious, young women and not so young, and all had the exact same hallmark that had got Adam into trouble with Eve.

"Jaysus,' said Blondie as we hurtled through the darkness, 'I'd love a woman this night!'

'But you had one last night.'

'I'd like wan every night, an' so would you.'

And that was the truth — me, whom women seemed to look through, who was living a life as celibate as any priest, or maybe I should say Tibetan Lama, for plenty of the priests, in Ireland anyway, were not stuck for a bit of 'nooky'.

'Paddington,' said Tooler, and the bloody tool boxes and cases going up this time to emerge in the railway station. We were all shagged by now. Bateman had given us no money for expenses. I gave Blondie back the three quid I had borrowed, and went into the tea rooms with the two quid left from Murphy's fiver, stood a few of the boys tea and cakes, and bought some fags. Which left me as broke as the rest. Money was like that with me, it took wing at my touch.

The train ride to Southall took no more than half an hour, and I cursed like a trooper when I saw the Alpine climb we had before us to reach the street, two bloody flights, I told Blondie, who was panting beside me. But that ended the hardship for that day anyway. A covered lorry awaited us outside, we clambered aboard and a few minutes later had reached the firm's headquarters, on

Lady Margaret Road. Here, a smiling personnel officer met us, told us we were a fine body of men, gave us three quid each, and said that he could not possibly have us join the firm thinking that it was not a good one. The money was hardship money and would not be stopped from our pay. We would start here the following morning, he would find interim jobs for all of us until he found out which of the firm's sites were most in need. He was urbane, charming, if slightly patronising, but he managed to smooth our ruffled feathers in jig time. A decent man on the whole, I thought, he really could not be blamed for talking down to us a little, it was just that his class-ridden society had made him so. It was five in the evening by now, and we again boarded our covered wagon, headed for Shepherds Bush and the firm's hostel. The tool boxes were left in Southall, thank Christ, for I think I would have demolished mine if I had had to carry it one foot more.

The hostel was a couple of large houses knocked hurriedly into one, and quite near the Chiswick Empire. I was, I thought, in the ''eart of the Hempire'. It was also the place where all my heroes came from, all who had made my literary world one of joy.

Bacon, a dishonest rogue, fined £40,000 for admitted corruption while Lord Chancellor, retired in disgrace, never to hold office again, lucky to have not been left a pauper, the fine, in effect, being remitted by the King. He was sixty then, and for the next five years did the work that was to make him immortal. His essays have never been bettered, nor ever will be, such a concentrated 'literary pemmican' that had stunned my mind when I had come across him, when he led me, in my otherwise unguided pursuit of literary excellence, to other essayists who, though not endowed with such weight of thought, were a delight to read. I discovered the lovably improvident genius, Oliver Goldsmith, of whom Johnson said, 'he touched nothing that he did not adorn.' His boldness of thought, which tallied well with my own about the clergy of the two Islands, flabbergasted me, for they were written over two centuries ago, directed at the clergy of England, an endeavour which must have carried danger with it.

'A priest in England,' he wrote, 'is not the same mortified creature as a Bonze in China; with us, not he that fasts best, but eats best, is reckoned the best liver.' Boswell's description of Goldsmith as an 'inspired idiot' made Boswell more of an idiot than even nature had intended him to be, and nature's intent, in his case, had been formidable. The great Johnson had loved and admired Goldsmith, for Johnson's gruffness of manner concealed a heart as big as Oliver's, all he lacked was Goldsmith's charm.

After I had eaten dinner I went for a stroll about the blacked-out city. It was not as dark as I had expected, even when full night came on. I had been born in a city, I took note of landmarks so as not to get lost, and continued my reflections on the literary giants who had lived in this place. The list was endless, and then came the staggering thought that the people I loved best, who had had more influence on my life than any others, were English! And yet, so far, most of the people I had met on this island were detestable. What was the solution? For there had to be a solution to the problem posed. The answer when it came was simple. I was a square peg in a round hole, born on the wrong side of the tracks, as the Yanks put it. I was in the same league as Jack London and Charles Dickens, Emile Zola, and many other working class writers who had had to study, spare time, to appease the yearning inside them to express themselves. I was too indisciplined to apply myself, too in love with life and living to waste my golden years in the intense application required. I was trying to step outside my class, and so I belonged nowhere. I had two faces, one for the companions I found myself among, and then the secret one, the secret me, who would have loved to have been with the likes of Charles Lamb and his companions, and 'You, my darlings, my midnight Folios!'

Ireland was now taking over from England as the centre of literary excellence. The process had begun a long time ago with Dean Swift, and was continued by James Clarence Mangan and many others, Wilde, Shaw, Seán O'Casey, and the one and only James Joyce who reigned supreme now, though banned in Holy Ireland. Like O'Casey he had fled the narrow nationalistic Catholic tyranny.

But even most of these, I grudgingly admitted, were not truly Irish, but Anglo-Irish, like the Dublin born Brit who had found out what he really was at Holyhead. Like poor Oscar he now languished in an English jail.

Returning from my ramble, as I drew near to the hostel, I spotted a tiny sign in the blacked-out window that said 'Café'. I went inside. It was only a small place, working class, with the inevitable Juke box, gaudily lit up, playing Glenn Miller's 'Kalimazoo'. A few teenagers were standing around. I went to the counter and bought a cup of tea and a doughnut, and sat down at a little table. Across the room, at another table, a buxom blonde toyed with a tea cup, and now she looked over at me and smiled. 'Jesus,' I thought, 'I'm alive again. A woman has noticed me.' She was young, not more than eighteen, and stacked. She had everything a woman should have, and all in the right places, and I felt desire rise in me, swiftly, like a volcano. I smiled back. Instantly she was over to my table.

''ello, good-looking,' she said. 'Let's 'ave a loan of yer eyelashes.'

I felt myself blushing furiously, under her smiling gaze. She told me her name was Doreen, and asked me what I was doing drinking tea? 'I thought all Irishmen drank only beer or whiskey.'

'I suppose you thought all Irishmen were six feet tall too, Doreen,' I said, playing for time, to get over my shyness.

'Aren't you going to buy me a cuppa, Pad?' she said.

'Certainly,' I told her. 'Would you like a cake with it?' After all I had three quid intact. It was going to have to see me through to payday, but that was only a few days away.

'Would you sooner take me to the pub, Paddy?' she said softly, her eyes promising all kinds of delights if I would do so.

'I'd sooner take you there, Doreen, than drink tea here, but I'm paid next Friday, and, if you still want to go with me, I'll call for you here.'

'Are you broke, Paddy?' she asked.

'No . . . just a bit light on. And my name is not Paddy. It's Larry.'

'You wouldn't 'ave five bob to spare, would you?'

She had the slightly husky voice of the cockney, which I found infinitely alluring. She was heavily made up, scarlet fingernails, blood-red lipstick, violet eye shadow, but nothing she could do to herself would disguise the fact of her ample charms. Lovely full breasts, the deep cleft above them peeping through her low-cut frock, a soft, swelling belly and wide hips above a good pair of legs. I gave her ten bob and made a date for Friday night.

I would only have three days pay due to me, but the firm was going to pay us a full week, and stop the loaned money at one pound per week. I floated on air until Friday evening, and then I woke up sharpish. The firm did not pay us a full week, it had only been a rumour, there was no way I could go to the 'caff' for Doreen who, I was sure, if not 'Brass' was very close to it. I worked away sullenly all day Saturday, even the double time for the afternoon shift did nothing to raise my spirits. I was torn apart by desire, I was young, too young to cope with the forces that my manhood had unleashed, I was ashamed of my longing, I was all mixed up. There was no one to tell me that I was a perfectly normal young man, all my information via the Church had convinced me that I was some kind of sex maniac. Sunday morning found me at Mass with Tooler and Blondie. I always sought the solace of the Church when I was in trouble, and I prayed earnestly to God, asking him to take this terrible longing away from me. I even seriously contemplated going to confession.

It was only the memory of the gobshite priest who had asked me what was the difference between a man's legs and a woman's that stopped me, for had I been asked that again, I would have told the sky pilot in no uncertain terms. We returned from Mass to lunch at the hostel, and, that being done, a weary afternoon stretched ahead. We read the Sunday papers, especially the *News of the World*, which was banned in Ireland, and I wallowed in sin and sex for a couple of hours, reading of many a rape and wondering when I would be driven to a similar outrage.

Outside, the marvellous autumn weather persisted, and truly the Americans' invasion of England had brought an Indian summer with it. There had been any amount of Americans in London and elsewhere while the 'Lease Lend' deal operated, but only a few short weeks ago, at seven on the Sunday morning of 7 September, the Japanese Air Force had devastated the Yankee Navy at Pearl Harbour, and brought America into the war. Again luck had saved the Brits, as it had once before turned against my own country in favour of the 'Devil's Children', and scattered the Spanish Armada to the four winds. Luck had deserted Napoleon on the field at Waterloo, even Wellington, another one of the Anglo-Irish breed, had admitted that it was a close-run thing. England lost every battle except the last!

'Anyone care,' said Tooler yawning, 'to take a trip to the East End of London? I knew a waterside pub down there on my last trip over, an' I was wonderin' if oul' Mrs Clarke an' her daughter still run the place . . . or if it is still there at all. Any takers?'

I jumped up, and Blondie followed. Anything was better than this bloody place, and I had wanted to see the devastated East End, but had no idea how to get there. It took us an hour or more, but in the late afternoon we stepped off a bus, and, after quite a long walk, came to where Hitler had struck, and struck hard. On this quiet Sunday afternoon the wrecked streets, warehouses and factories stretched as far as the eye could see. We wandered up one silent street only to enter another. Artisan-type dwellings that had once housed a mighty population lay open to the sky, or well piled under it. The pavements were spotless, a thing I found particularly unnerving, for there was no living soul around and it suggested that the ghosts of the dead housewives came out at night, and, in my over-active imagination, swept the pavements before their front doors. I was walking through a twentieth century Pompeii, a haunted place. Tooler's pub had been beside the water-front, but he could not even begin to identify where it had been. Old Father Thames swept past, polluted, dirty, indifferent to the affairs of men, a dead river in a dead land, a Buck Rogers aftermath of a war in space, that one might expect to encounter on Mars. I shivered.

The blitzed area could have comfortably swallowed any Irish city, maybe even Dublin! This was the blow with which Der Fürher had hoped to knock out the British Empire, and had nearly succeeded. No other city in the world, I thought, could have taken such a hammering and survived. This city had almost been knocked out once before by the Great Fire of the middle ages, when Samuel Pepys, who loved the company of a 'Doxy', had watched all his taverns swept away, as Tooler's had been, where Samuel would go no more, and feel the legs of a buxom widow, 'white as milk, though monstrous fat'. And yet, London had refused to die then as now. Within a few years it was bigger than ever and had continued to grow ever since, and had kept my own beloved city under its iron heel. I marvelled all over again at the foolhardiness of a few dreamers who had dared to raise an Irish flag over the GPO in Sackville Street, and take on the might of this enormous symbol of Empire. In every tube station now Churchill could be seen, cigar jutting out, defiant as this city, London incarnate! But I saw London differently, a battered old prize fighter, bleeding from a score of wounds, staggering up in the smoking dawn, after another terrible fight night. And, with blackened teeth in a broken mouth, raise a clenched fist to the sky, roaring, 'Bastards . . . German bastards, I'm still here . . .', and fight on!

'Let's leave this place,' I said quietly.

'Aye,' said Tooler, 'let's do that.'

So, another ride underground back to Shepherds Bush, and yet again, as the train came, the rush of warm air from the tunnel, laden with the scent of sex. What in God's name had gone wrong with me since I came to this city? Going to Mass in the morning, vowing never to slide so far down the slope of sin again, and all my holy resolutions blown to hell and Connemara by the sweet scented tepid air of the underground.

It was early October now, the nights were longer, winter was almost upon us, though the sun still shone with summer vigour. We broke our journey in central London, and spent an hour drinking insipid English beer with lacklustre thirst. The sight of all he had known formerly, gone forever, had depressed Tooler, who glumly sipped his drink as if it were poison. There was no Irish whiskey on offer, the Scotch was rationed to one or two at most, and, around nine o'clock, we mooched our way down into the bowels of the earth again for our return journey to the Bush. Again, the whoosh of scented air as the train approached, the uncanny wind that excited me so much. The women that tumbled off in droves had never looked more desirable, the few drinks had heightened my want, and Blondie put it into words on the train.

'Jaysus,' he said above the noise, 'I'd give me hearts blood for a woman this night.'

'So would I,' I said, and that was the understatement for the year of 1941. At Shepherds Bush, we went into a pub just around the corner from the hostel, and sure enough, as I had expected, there was Doreen. She was sitting with an older woman, it was a quiet, old fashioned pub, and I figured it was probably her landlady. I was correct.

65

She saw me at once, and when the older woman left for the 'Ladies' she sidled up beside me.

'You never turned up on Friday night, Paddy,' she said reproachfully. 'I waited for you.'

I was very sure she had not waited alone too long, but apologised profusely.

'The firm let me down, Doreen,' I told her, 'I just didn't have the money to give you a good night.'

'WIll you give me a good night next Friday night, Pad,' she said.'A REAL good night?'

'If you give me one,' I said, greatly daring.

'I will, Pad, I will, promise, cross my heart.' I slipped her ten bob and she was back sitting quietly when the older woman came back.

'Who the hell was that?' said Blondie, flabbergasted. He was not accustomed to being with small men, and being completely ignored, especially by blondes bursting at the seams, blondes like Doreen who exuded sex from every God-given curve on their beautiful bodies.

'Oh . . . just a friend of mine, a girl-friend,' I said, offhandedly.

'Looks a bit "Brassy" to me,' said Tooler glumly.

'That,' said I, emboldened by drink, 'is exactly what I need, and come next Saturday night, I'm going to have.'

'Jasus,' said Blondie in his soft brogue, 'you're a sly one, Lar.' The pub closed then, and, on the way out, I managed to whisper a few words to Doreen.

'Make it Saturday night, Doreen. I'll give you a real good time because I don't work on Sunday and can rest . . . .'

'Okay. What time?'

'Eight o'clock . . . outside the "Caff" . . . not inside. Okay?'

'Yes, Pad, okay.'

I worked away at mickey mouse work with a light heart the following week. Five of our unlucky thirteen left us for places north on Wednesday, a further three went after them on Thursday, two more on Friday. It was obvious the firm had been making work for us, merely a holding operation until they could put us on 'site'. . . . There was now only Blondie, Tooler and myself left, and I wondered why. I found out on Saturday morning, when Tooler, who was easily the most skilled among us, was offered a permanent job in the Joinery Works in Southall. He took it gratefully. What he had dreaded was exactly what I was looking for. Big sites, army camps, and airfields had been Tooler's undoing before, the lonely men, the wild drinking, the 'Crack'! The local town and tavern, and a woman if you could get one.

Blondie was to leave for Dover Monday morning, I was to go north to Warrington.

'There y'are,' said Tooler. 'I knew why they left us till last. I knew they had something up their sleeve, though I'm surprised about meself.'

'I'm not, Paddy,' I said. 'But what's this about me an' Blondie . . . the up the sleeve bit?'

'Kept yeh segregated from the rest . . . now they've split you tew up, an' well apart from each other. That's what your facin' up to the Black an' Tan got yeh.'

'Divil a damn I care,' said I.

'Nor I either,' said Blondie, 'but I'm sorry they broke up the gang.'

'So am I,' I lied. In fact I wanted to get far away from Tooler's paternal wing, and away from Blondie too, for I figured that if he was around I stood little chance of getting a woman. Imagine an obliging landlady opening the front door to the two of us. There was only one outcome to that one. Blondie would sleep with the landlady and I could sleep on the landing. I wanted to get out of his good-looking shadow. I still wondered at Doreen's lack of interest in him last weekend.

It never occurred to me that she might prefer small men to big ones, dark ones to blonde ones, that every eye formed its own beauty.

'Tonight's the night,' I said to Blondie on the way home, 'I think I'm on to a good thing.'

Blondie grinned. 'I don't think I am, I know I am,' he said. 'Do you remember the woman that was with your blonde?

67

Well, she chatted me up while you were in the toilet, an' when we went back to the hostel, an' all was quiet, I crept out an' slep' with her. What de ye think of that?'

'Jesus,' I exclaimed, 'how in hell do you do it?'

'Aisy,' said Blondie in his soft brogue. 'You'll get the hang of it soon. Th' English ones don't flash their eyes an' give themselves away in front of everyone. They just look at yeh straight in the eye for a second, an' and after that it's up to you. Y'ill soon learn, Lar.'

'Don't you think she's a little old for you, Blondie? After all, you're only twenty-eight.'

'What different does that make, Lar? Sure all cats are black at night. She's a fine figure of a woman, and bloody great in the sack. And she's only forty-one. I suppose you were too busy lookin' at your blonde to take any notice of her.'

'That's true all right, but a fella like you could do better than that!'

Blondie looked at me cooly. 'Could I now?' he replied. 'Well, I'm not in love with any wan woman, Lar, an' this wan has everything I want, includin' loads a' money. How does that affect you? And she's nuts about yours truly.'

'Well, Blondie, if you're happy, I'm happy for you. But you don't love her do you? I mean, you wouldn't marry her, would you?'

'No, I'd never marry any woman, that's what makes it so aisy with this one. I just love them all, I love their lovely soft bodies, I love their red-tipped breasts, their soft thighs, and most of all, the softness and delight that lies between them.'

I stared at Blondie with some surprise. His face had a far away look about it, and really he was lost, soliloquising, talking softly to himself. There was a kind of 'Synge' flavour about his speech, a touch of *The Playboy of the Western World*, a play I hated, and, with other young Dubliners, I sent it up all the time. 'Misther,' we'd say to the publican, 'wid yer long arim, an' yer sthrong arim, would yeh be afther pullin' us a pint?'

Nevertheless, my friend, who was not of Ireland's western

world, had just peeled back the centuries and spoken Gaelic to me in English.

'Besides,' said Blondie, 'I've no need to worry about puttin' her up the pole. I hate wearin' them things, an' she told me no need to worry, she had that fixed years ago.'

'Lucky you,' said I.

'I hope you're as lucky,' said my friend. 'There's the bloody hostel,' he said as the truck squealed to a halt, 'I'll see yeh Monday mornin' before we leave . . . .'

'What about your dinner? Will I not see you then?'

'What . . . with the widow waitin, an' the place drippin' with black market luxuries? Not bloody likely, an' her for afthers? Yeh must be coddin'!'

I burst out laughing. I could not help it. Blondie was so down to earth with life. He came to terms with it as it was, whereas I castigated myself endlessly, looking inwards, engaged in the perilous game of self analysis.

'De yeh know the liveliest thing on this planet?' said Blondie, as we went to the wash house.

'No, but I suppose you'll tell me!'

'Its a kitten, a kid, an' a young widda . . . . Don't forget yer Uncle Blondie told yeh that.'

The time between dinner and meeting Doreen outside the 'caff' was measured in light years. I was there, standing in the warm darkness half an hour before she came, and when she did she had to shake me to notice her, for I was far away, trying to define, apart from my coming encounter with an English girl, the vibrant excitement that seemed to be a heady undercurrent that ran beneath everything in this city. All day long the radio never stopped blaring out nostalgic love songs. Vera Lynn, bananas about the 'White Cliffs of Dovah' and prostrated for 'Never Saying Thanks For That Lovely Weekend'. If Blondie was any barometer to go by, the women, left at home when their husbands were called up, were lonely, they worked in numbers now in factories, they had their own money, and the social order that had prevailed since World War One was breaking down. Birth control had been practised in England on a wide scale in the hungry thirties, when a new arrival was a thing to be dreaded. When, in some cases, condoms could not be afforded, Durex brought out a washable French letter as durable as a bicycle tube. 'Terrible things, they was,' a cockney on the job had told me with feeling. 'Like 'avin' a bath wiff yer socks on! Honest ter Gowd, mate, they was that thick you could patch 'em!'

When I had done laughing I had told him he was having me on, and the next day he presented me with a brochure from the Durex company that had opened my eyes. It was a lavish production, a coloured 'glossy' from pre-War days. They made French Letters for all climates, from the Frozen North of the 'rigid digit' to the tropics, where the largest of the English Colonies lay, and flaccid floozies of aristocratic lineage did it out of pure boredom, 'The heat, my dear, one is inclined to . . . well, you know . . . .'

The condom the cockney had told me about was there sure enough, and was cheap at the price. It was known as 'The Workman's Friend', and cost five bob, another sign of class distinction. There were no mentions of price in the upper class section. If one had to ask the price one could not afford them anyway, but 'One had to keep them away from the servants, y'know, who might stop breeding more servants. And really, my dear, that is the function of the lower orders, I mean, where would our soldiers come from if servants didn't have them?'

'Dreaming, Pad . . . ? You 'ave the eyes of a dreamer,' and in the velvety night she linked her arm in mine, and led me like a lamb, very willingly to the slaughter.

'Where are you taking me, Doreen?'

'To see the Wizard of Oz,' she said, and the cheap perfume she wore came to me, sweeter than the scent of the roses in the garden of Omar Khayyám.

'No, Doreen, be serious,' I said, my heart was thumping like mad.

'To the White 'eart,' said Doreen. 'It's a lovely place, Pad, they 'ave singing at the Mike, an' the lights are low, 'cept at the Mike, of couwse, an' we'll be at the back.'

70

'Of "cowse",' I said, imitating her. The coming night spread before me like a carpet in the house of the old Persian poet.

The lounge in the White Hart was bigger than any I had been in before. There was a small stage against the end wall, with a pianist and a 'Mike', and, as the night wore on and the drink made them bolder, the procession of patrons to the stage was endless. The drink made me bolder, too, and Doreen, lapping up gins and tonics, was furtively compliant, the lights were low, and the Vera Lynns, Bing Crosbys and Perry Comos, who sang with all their hearts just waiting to be 'discovered', went unnoticed by me.

Doreen was very experienced, and knew just how to toy with a greenhorn like me. It was a little bit of everything, a brush with a soft breast as she leaned across to stub out a cigarette, a sly nibble on the ear, a stolen kiss on the neck, and then, just before the National Anthem played us out, she kissed me with open mouth, and I nearly went wild. I had never been 'French kissed' before, and it rocked me. By the time we got outside the pub she had me in a state bordering on imbecility.

Shepherds Bush was only a quarter of a mile away, and in this fantastic autumn, for it was well into October, it was nicer to walk, at least with Doreen. In the blackout one could do with impunity what could not be done in the light. Several times she French kissed me again, and I held her tight, so tight that she gasped. But she loved it, I could see that! Certainly, she did not love me, but she loved men and sex, and I was a man and mad for sex. We did our furious loving in the black shadows thrown down by buildings, for the moon was high.

Coming near 'the Bush' Doreen drew me up a cobble-stone lane that had the deep recessed doors of warehouses. She stood back in one, and I stepped in after her and wrapped all her charms in my ardent arms. Here, and right now, was what I had come to England for.

'Doreen . . . Doreen,' I whispered as my right arm slid down the thighs and up her light skirt and, Jesus Christ, this was it. She was all ready and had no knickers on!

Doreen, who was panting with desire, suddenly stopped me in the final act.

'You 'ave a little present for Doreen, 'aven't you, Pad?' said my passionate Juliet.

'Yes . . . for God's sake, how much?'

'Three quid, Pad.'

I found the notes, handed them to her, and knew the inexpressible relief of being inside a woman again. no torturing erotic dream this, all heaven in a London lane. As the climax of the love act came, the air-raid sirens started to wail all around, and suddenly Doreen twisted and tried to break free, but I held her in a vice like grip and would not let her go.

'My baby,' she screamed. 'Let go, you bastard!'

Well, I freed her, it was all over anyway, and I know knew why the English called love making in a standing position a 'knee trembler'. I watched Doreen's fleeing figure as the ack-ack guns opened up, silhouetted against the flashes in the sky, and then came the roar of London, the battered old bruiser, the giant who hurled bolts of lightning at the sky. From nowhere, a fiery cross drifted through the moonlight, and blew apart only a few hundred feet above the ground. All around the musical tinkling that I had wondered about suddenly filled the air, and I was hit with a tiny piece of shrapnel on the shoulder. I hastily jumped back into the shelter of the doorway.

No thunder storm I had ever been through could match the fury of this man-made one. Low down, another German plane, badly hit, roared overhead, deafening me, and disintegrated with its cargo of bombs about four hundred yards away. I threw myself down to the ground by instinct, covering my head with my hands, shaking, terrified beyond reason, and how long I lay there I do not know. Not long anyway, for I heard the sound of ambulances racing past the end of the lane, and slowly I came back to the horrible land of the living. The cobbles were a shambles of broken slates and glass. I found that the backs of my hands were bleeding, but they were only scratches. This had been a small 'sneak raid'. The days of the London blitz were gone. One by one, the planes that had devastated this city were beginning to litter the endless steppes of Russia.

Gradually the roar of the battered old giant subsided until at last, with a few savage grunts here and there, he grew silent. The 'All Clear' sounded, and all that was left was the melancholy wail of the ambulances with their cargos of dead and dying. And the armless or legless, or mindless ones that would live on and remember this night forever, like myself. I put out my hand to lift myself off the ground. It closed around a roll of notes, bank notes . . . . I stared at them for a long time for they were three in number, Doreen's wages of sin.

I stumbled back to the hostel and into bed, worn out. All around me the men were talking about narrow escapes they had had during the raid, but I was sick inside, sick of myself, of my barbarous behaviour, the naked savagery I had displayed when she had cried, 'My baby', and tried to flee. The fact that she was English and a part-time prostitute made no difference. She was a woman, the same as my mother and my sisters. What in God's name would they say if they knew of this animal of a brother? Some time, in the small hours, I fell into an exhausted sleep, to awake to a world of horror, horror at myself.

Tooler remark to me that I looked washed out, and I felt it, but I could not dare to tell him or anyone the enormity of my sin. That would be reserved for the dark and silence of the confessional, for I made up my mind to go again. But how anyone, even a loving God, could forgive a lecher like me, I could not comprehend. Tooler and I went to Mass together, and I prayed earnestly for forgiveness and for a small sign, a tiny light in the darkness, anything that would help to expiate my sin. Rape! 'Pray all you like, me bucko, but that is what you are guilty of,' said Conscience. 'You dirty little Dublin gurrier!' The Mass made no difference to my state of mind. I had myself on the rack and turned the screw harder than any priest of the Inquisition would have done.

The *News of the World*, formerly a source of sinful delight, suddenly lost its charm that afternoon when I came across a case of rape. I had been reading of other crimes besides mine, and was getting a little solace from the fact that the world was full of sinners, when the words of the judge in the rape case jumped off the page at me . . . .

'The fact that the woman was of dubious morals in no way excuses your animal-like behaviour. Even if, as you claim, she was a common prostitute, she still remained a woman, a human being who you subjected to the most appalling violence . . . I therefore sentence you to life imprisonment with hard labour and recommend that there be no remission . . . .

Jesus, my heart turned over, congealed inside me. I ran outside and walked the pavements for hours until the blackout came and I could creep back to bed. But one thing had become clear during my long walk. I would not go to Warrington the next day. I had three pounds belonging to Doreen, and the least I could do was to stay back, find out where she lived, and give her the money. Sod the firm, I would work that one out tomorrow. Feeling a little better, I went to sleep and dreamed of Doreen. I woke up sweating, but I had slept the night through and felt a lot better.

At eight o'clock the firm's truck came for Blondie and me, and we boarded it, bound for Euston Station. We both had travel chits and once inside the station we shook hands and wished each other well. 'All the best, Blondie,' I said. 'You never know when we might meet again?'

'Goodbye Lar, watch yourself,' said the handsome one and stroke off. Neither of us liked saying goodbye, so it was a brief affair. I mingled with the crowd, waited a couple of minutes and made for the luggage room. I checked in the abominable tool box and my large suitcase. As I turned around to leave, I bumped into a grinning Blondie.

'Holy Jasus,' he burst out laughing, 'you're another hidden rogue . . . like me. You're not lavin' either!'

'No,' I said, laughing too, 'I have some unfinished business to attend to.' The laugh was forced, what I wanted to do, had to do, was best done in secrecy. And then it hit me like a bombshell. Blondie was going back to the delights of the buxom widow, stealing another day of bliss while the going was good. The widow was Doreen's landlady, and all I had to do was go with Blondie. My praying had not been in vain, God had sent me, through the sinner, Blondie, the means in some small part to atone to Doreen. Blondie assumed I wanted to go back for the same reason as himself, but told me I'd have to be careful, she did not allow men in the place, ever.

'What about herself and you?'

'That's different,' said Blondie smugly. 'She owns the joint. I'll lave tomorra, but London is not far from Dover. I'll be up often enough teh see she doesn't stray from the path of virtue. Yeh have teh keep it up to them, or they get strange ideas.'

'How the hell will I get to see Doreen if she's that strict?'

'Aisy,' said Blondie producing a Yale key. 'I'll lave the front door open, an' you give me a couple of minutes with the widow, then you can come in, but take off your shoes and go quiet. And, for God's sake, don't close the front door in case she hears you.'

'I'll leave it open?'

'Don't worry, your Uncle Blondie 'ill remember that he does not remember banging the front door. If you play it safe you'll be okay, Lar.'

'What room does she live in, Doreen, I mean?'

'Right at the top of the house, the attic. But, for Jaysus sake, go quiet, especially on the second floor. There's a nosy oul' bitch there with ears like a fox.'

It all worked exactly to plan. I heard the buxom widow giggling as I crept past her door. Good old Blondie keeping her busy, a real pal, I told myself, until I realised he would have done the same anyway. I arrived at the top of the house without making a sound, and stood there listening. All was silent. With my shoes in my hand I gently tapped on Doreen's door. No answer. I tapped again softly, insistently, and in the end I heard a bed creak and the muffled sound of feet on linoleum. The door opened a few inches, held by a chain, and Doreen's sleepy face confronted me. She looked a lot younger with the make-up scrubbed off, and innocent, although I knew she was not. She also looked frightened out of her wits.

'Wot you want?' she whispered.

'Nothing . . . I just came to give you this. You dropped it on Saturday night.' I handed her the three pounds and she gave an audible gasp.

'I downt believe it,' she whispered. 'An honest man . . . at last! Come in, Pad.' She slipped the chain off the door and ran silently back to her bed, but not before I had a glimpse of an enchantingly curvy bottom, and legs as white as milk, though not like Pepys's Doxy, 'monstrous fat.' I gently closed the door. Doreen indicated a chair in the centre of the room, and I sat down. She was propped up on one elbow, her blonde hair resting against a blue pillow, a flimsy slip covering her generous breasts.

'Got a cigarette, Pad?' she said.

'Sure.' I threw her a packet of Goldflake and a box of matches. 'You can keep them,' I told her. 'And I'm sorry about the other night, Doreen, really I am. I just came to give you the money and say goodbye. I'm off to Warrington today. S'long, Love.'

I rose from the chair, trying not to see her obvious charms, opened the door, and was closing it when I heard her.

'Down't go, Pad,' she hissed. 'Come back'. I re-entered the shabby room and my heart started to thunder in my chest. Doreen, either by design or accident had exposed one breast, and now she stubbed out the cigarette and crooked a finger and smiled.

'Come on in beside me, Pad,' she whispered. Like a sleep walker I went towards her and in a second I was kneeling before her kissing her breasts. Doreen heaving great sighs of happiness, me in my seventh heaven, knowing now that any time a woman exposed her breasts and crooked a finger I would always be there, that they did not even have to do

76

that to get me. I was hooked on the fair sex, dependant upon them for my very existence, for life was not worth living without a woman.

'Get undressed, Pad,' Doreen gasped. 'Hurry.' I tore off my clothes and slid in beside her, and now at last I knew again the absolute bliss of a young woman as sexually aroused as myself. We made love for an hour, and then lay back exhausted. Doreen lit two cigarettes and gave me one. 'You're marvellous, Pad, d'you know that . . . an' lovely an' gentle? Anybody ever tell you that?'

'Not lately, Doreen. I'm terribly ashamed of the other night.'

'Why?' Doreen was genuinely shocked.

'Because when you wanted to run away to your baby I . . . I . . . held you against your will until, well, you know . . . until . . . Jesus, I'm sorry, Doreen. I never did that or anything like it before.'

Doreen smiled and snuggled happily up to me.

'You was never that far gone before, Pad, I bet. That was my fault, for I know no man can stop when he's that far gone. You're no different from all the rest, 'ceptin' you're nicer. You speak beautiful too, Pad, anyone ever tell you that either?'

'No, not that I can recall.'

'The girls in Ireland must be bloody dopey then,' said Doreen. 'Don't they ever do it over there? They bloody must, for there's Paddies all over the world.'

'They're afraid, Doreen. They want to all right, but they are scared. You see, there's no French letters in Ireland. It's a crime to be caught with one.'

'Jesus,' said Doreen, 'fancy living in a place loike that!'

'Aye,' I said running my hand over her soft thighs, 'fancy that! Fancy some more?'

'Not 'alf,' said Doreen and turned to me. A sudden thought struck me like a blow. 'Doreen . . . I'm not wearing anything, did you know?'

'A couwse,' said my passion Poppy, 'but I am. Got caught once, never again. C'mon Pad, make love to me.'

And this was the creature who had forgiven me, pardoned me, explained myself to me, and now wanted me to love her, and I did, with great tenderness, even love, kissing her neck and breasts until she moaned with pleasure, and then the coupling, the wild ride among the stars, where all was dark red passion, and the lovely spiralling down slowly from that height, with all the world becalmed, silent, at peace.

The thought came to me that this time yesterday I had been in the chapel, torn apart, pleading with God to forgive me, and promising never to sin again . . . and yet a woman only had to crook a finger twenty-four hours later and I would, like Judas, betray Him all over again. Doreen lay languid against me, and was willing to be loved again. And again I made love to her, until we had loved each other silly and were half out of our minds with happiness.

'That was lovely, Pad,' she said. And so my time in the Garden of Eden was over, and now I must go. It was already past two o'clock but I had no mind to travel this day. I went boldly back to the hostel, crept in unnoticed, and went to bed. At five, the hostel manager shook me awake.

'Cor blimey, Mate, what are you doing 'ere? I thought you was in Warrington by now.'

'I had some unfinished business to attend to,' I told him boldly. 'I'll go tomorrow.'

He grinned. 'I know the bloody business you 'ad to attend to, bloody young bugger. Don't you know there's a . . . .'

'Waar on,' I interrupted. 'But I did my bit for England this day,' and I burst out laughing when I thought of Blondie at it downstairs and me upstairs, 'going to it' for oul' divarsion, our English Roses not neglected or left to bloom alone.

All the manager could do was laugh with me. I had never felt more relaxed, life was good, and I did not give two Highlanders' you know what about, 'the Waar', the Church or Taylor-Woodrow who employed me.

'I'll ring up Warrington and make some excuse for you,'

said this good Cockney. 'But don't play me up, Pad. You'll be off in the morning?'

'Yes, word of honour.'

'Right then, we'll say no more about it.'

Doreen was surprised to see me walk into the 'caff' that night, but immediately dropped the young man she was talking to, and came over to me. She looked radiant and I told her so, smiling.

'Bloody Blarney,' said Doreen, 'I 'ope you don't think you are comin' 'ome with me tonight . . . .'

'Of course not, Love, we'll just go for a drink, have a kiss and a cuddle, and then I'll be gone.'

'Okay,' said Doreen without conviction. Her intuition was dead right, for I did spend the night with her, while downstairs an uproarious party was in full swing. It was cold and grey and sorrowful the following morning as Doreen said goodbye. As for me I almost wept to leave this girl alone, for somehow, like so many other women were destined to do, she had stolen into my heart and I would sigh for her, until I met the next one. It would be the same for Doreen, I knew, but I also knew that we two would never forget the short time we had spent together, that my natural antagonism towards the Sassenach would soften a little because of her, that I would always think of her with a kind of loving. A kind of loving, but not love! A poet named Campbell had written, 'Love's fire needs renewal, of fresh beauty for its fuel, Love's wings moult when caged and captured, only free love soars enraptured.'

That was for me! In the year of 1941 Ireland was 'rearin' them yet' and I was actually naïve enough to think that there was such a thing as free love, that you could have your cake and eat it too. I had not yet realised that all things in this world had to be paid for, especially happiness.

It was six in the morning as I walked to the hostel from Doreen's loving embrace. She had, as is the way of women, become quite sentimental at the last, and had shed tears, and upset me. After breakfast I headed for the railway station and the luggage room, and was on the nine-thirty to

Warrington, going north. I was tired and depressed as the train chugged out under a winter sky, for now at last the Indian Summer was over, and winter blew an icy blast at old London. I had become quite fond of the city, a cautious relationship though, one that a lion tamer would have with his favourite lion. London had been good to me, it had given me money and one of her 'doxies' to spend it on, money well spent I thought, but, at the same time, never again would I stand in an alley for a knee trembler. That day was gone. I had enough experience now to know that my quota of women was there for me as it is for every man, that I did not have to be blonde and six foot tall to get one.

Doreen had thought me beautiful and had envied the long eyelashes that I detested so much. I had the key to the world of women now, I need never lack one. But, despite all that, I had a sense of impending disaster. North I was going, and I hated North with its icy suggestion of an Alaskan climate. My mind had been coloured against it by *Wuthering Heights*, and the brutish dialect of the young Heathcliff. But there was nothing I could do, Civvy Street was no different in wartime England than being in the army, and anyway I was seeing a bit of the world.

Nine hours later, in the arctic cold of a lowering winter night, I stumbled off the train, half frozen, for the carriages had been icy cold. Warrington fulfilled my worst fears. A dark, slate-grey city with narrow streets, many of them cobbled, flanked by, two up, two down, shabby dwellings. There was no truck to meet me, so I booked the tool box into the luggage room, and started off through the night. As usual I was compelled to go to the police station. They advised me to go to the 'Sally Arms', maybe they could do something for me. The police were cold and hostile, made me produce my yellow identity card that all Irish people working in England had to carry, asked me who I worked with, where I had come from, and kept me sitting on a hard bench for an hour while they checked with London.

A steel-eyed Lancashire get told me to report here every month, and not to forget that I could not travel more than twenty miles without police permission. He left me wondering if the colour of the card had been deliberately chosen to mark Irish workers as cowards? Eventually I found the 'Sally Arms', and went gratefully inside. The place was full of lonely young soldiers who were drinking tea and eating home-made buns, while cheerful young ladies of the upper class were charming and smiling, and exuded chastity and sex in equal quantities.

I created something of a sensation when I arrived, for I looked far younger than my twenty-one years, was obviously lost and in need of God's help, most of them uttering muted incredulity when it was discovered that I was Irish. I was too small, too well dressed, too well spoken, to fit their concept of an Irishman. But, unaware of the insults in every breath, they were very nice to me.

I had always imagined that every Salvation Army place had accommodation for homeless men. This one had none. It catered only for lonely soldiers, but the woman in charge told me I could sleep in the armchair. I bought sandwiches, buns, and anything that was edible, for I was starving. Gradually the place became empty, the lady in charge gave me a car rug and I fell fast asleep in the chair.

5 Warrington

It was bitterly cold the next morning when I left the 'Sally Arms', and went to the firm's site at Longford, where they were building houses for the greatly expanded Royal Ordinance factory, which made presents for Herr Hitler in the shape of shells and bombs. There were huts here for the building workers, but the camp manager, a Dublin man who knew me through my father, advised me against living in them and, after one look, I saw his point. He said he would have my tool box collected at the station and he would expect me the next day. 'This is the address of the Housing Authority in Warrington. They will fix you up with Digs.'

And so some time before noon I found myself confronting a good-looking young woman who was in charge. She was expensively dressed and the rings on her fingers could have paid my wages for a year. She was upper class, condescending and contemptuous. I was sure it was my Irish accent. The type whose rich Daddy had probably got her this soft job to prevent her being pulled into the Services or hospital work. She looked through her book with a languid indifference that made it plain she 'was not used to this sort of thing'.

'Heah,' she said, 'is the address . . . . A Mrs Beeby, of 14 Acacia Crescent. It's on the edge of town, suburban house, y'know.'

She sighed wearily, indifferently. I felt my colour rising,

and, with my new found confidence with women, decided to embarrass her at least, if I could. She had on a beautiful pendant hanging from her neck on a golden chain, which rested in the cleft between her breasts. On this I fastened my eyes. She continued to speak for a couple of seconds, then faltered, stammered and came to a halt. I smiled and looked up into her furious face, with what I hoped was a kind of leer. A 'that shook yeh, yeh bitch' kind of look.

'How dare you!' she said angrily.

'How dare I what? What are you talking about?'

'How dare you look at me in that manner!'

'The cat can look at the King, Miss.'

'The food office is just round the corner,' she hissed. 'You may get your ration cards there. You will need them for your lodgings.'

'I'll need a note or a card from you to Mrs Beeby also, I believe.' Almost spitting with rage, she gave me a card. I took another dirty look at her diddies and left.

I found the food offices, and, after some three hours, emerged with my food ration books. I picked up my suitcase at the 'Sally', thanked them and headed for Acacia Crescent. The day was nearly gone and it was freezing, a north wind giving promise of an early snow fall. The sight of Acacia Crescent was far from welcoming. It was a cul-de-sac of Jerry-built brick houses, quite new. The rough grassed area in the centre of the ring of houses held some stringy saplings, now stripped of their leaves and lashed in the rising wind.

I rang the bell of number 14, and the door was opened by a fat lady in her mid forties. She was sallow-faced, with small, shrewd piggy eyes, and a ski-slope nose that made her superior air seem comical. Not to laugh in her face, I smiled.

'The Housing Authority sent me, Mrs Beeby,' I said. She heard my accent, looked startled, and then stared blankly at me. 'You have your name down for boarders,' I said helpfully.

'Ow . . . well . . . I suppowse you'd bettah come in.' She

seemed very doubtful about letting me in at all. I stood in the hall waiting for the next move. Reluctantly she led me up the carpeted stairs. It was the only carpet in the house, which was sparsely furnished with Early American Nothing. The linoleum on the bedroom floor gleamed, the room had a bed, a wardrobe and a chest of drawers, with cheap curtains on the window, which looked directly at the backs of other houses at the end of the small garden.

'You can come downstairs when you unpack your clowthes,' she told me, standing proudly in the centre of the room, expecting me to be delighted with it. I was far from impressed. And besides, the bloody place was freezing. I unpacked as quickly as possible in order to get downstairs where there must be a fire. She showed me into the dining room, which was no less cold than the bedroom. She had just lit a miniscule fire in the grate. Jesus, I thought savagely, my stay here would not be long.

I smoked moodily, trying to get some heat from the little fire. There was no coal in the coalbox, so I could do nothing about it. After about an hour she came in with a tray, mincing her way through the door with obvious distaste. She set down my dinner on the table and I stared at it, stunned. We often left more behind on our plates at home. My temper was getting the better of me.

'Your dinner,' she said. 'I'll bring in a pot of tea now. You can leave it beside the fire if you like.'

'Mrs Beeby,' I said, 'would you mind putting some coal on that fire? . . . It's freezing in this room.'

'Ow,' she said flushing. 'Do you think sew? I thought it quite wawm!' However, she came back with a small shovel full of coal, put it on the fire, and left without speaking. The blight of penurious thrift hung over this house like a bad smell, and now I bitterly regretted my decision not to stay in the firm's huts. I would leave this house at the end of the week. At least in the maligned huts there would be humanity and warmth, no crowd of men would stand for the conditions one was expected to accept here.

Or was it because I was Irish? No, I decided, not quite.

No matter what nationality crossed this threshold, although the welcome might be warmer, the sub-zero temperature would not alter, nor would the food be more plentiful.

Although I had joined the Irish Army, like many another, with the wild idea of catching the Brits with their pants down and taking back our lost six counties, yet I had never felt real hatred for them until I arrived in their country. From the beating up of the 'Dublin Brit' at Holyhead, through Bateman and his contempt for my race, it had been an ordeal by fire. And yet . . . and yet! London had been good to me, they had called me 'Pad' and meant no harm. Doreen had given herself to me completely, and made me happy. The big sergeant in Coventry had given us a twenty pack of cigarettes, the Personnel Officer in Taylor-Woodrows had given us a sub on our coming pay. The cockney in the firm's hostel had covered up for me. There was no way I could continue to hate the whole British nation.

But I could transfer my rancour to the people of Lancashire, to the chilly reception I had received, and the pretentious bitch who owned this ice box. Presently, I heard a male voice coming from the kitchen, speaking fractured English. I assumed correctly that it was his Lordship, come back to his Jerry-built palace. Her Ladyship came in eventually and removed the tray.

'My,' she said disapprovingly, 'you 'aven't drunk your tea.'

'No', I said, but gave no reason. It had been 'shamrock tea', three leaves, and so weak that it staggered out of the pot.

'By the way, Mrs Beeby,' I said coolly, 'I'm going out and I have no key. I wouldn't want you to wait up for me.'

'Ow . . . . Will you be late?'

'I don't think so, but I might.' The 'might' was thrown in to leave no doubt that as long as I was here I would come and go as I pleased.

'Well,' she said doubtfully, 'I'll 'eve to ask 'imself about that.'

'Don't bother, Mrs Beeby,' I said cheerfully, 'you'll hear

me when I get back. I'll knock loudly enough.'

And so out into the freezing blackout I went, looking for a fish and chip shop. My stomach was rumbling with hunger, for the small potatoes, tinned peas and 'Spam' wouldn't feed a sparrow, much less a manual worker. I took my bearings carefully and mooched along the main road until I got the delicious smell of fish and chips on the breeze. Like a bloodhound I followed the scent. It was an old fashioned Chipper with benches and narrow tables screwed to the floor. The middle-aged Italian smiled.

'Yes?'

'A "One and One",' I told him.

'Buth a one an' one is a two? What you want?'

'Fish and chips,' I told him. 'That's what they call it in Dublin.'

'Ah,' he said wistfully. 'I 'ave many friends in Dublin . . . . They tell me it's a very nice . . . the people like Italianos.'

'It's a lot better than this kip,' I said bitterly, 'and the people a hell of a lot nicer.'

'Is not too bad here now,' said the Italian, as he stirred the sizzling chips. 'Was a little not so good first, when a da War break out. I spent nine month in a camp, then they let me out again seex month ago. Isa not easy.'

'Why?'

'A local man . . . he start up another feech an' cheep shop when I am in the jail. Deeficult for me to get supply of good feech . . . . Still, mosta my old customers come back to me . . . . They not too bad when you geta know them. You wanna take away?'

'No, I'll have it here.' He wrapped it in the traditional white paper, and I sat in the small enclosed space and wolfed the meal. The fish was so delicious I ordered another.

'What kind of fish was that?' I asked him.

'We call it a Rocka Salmon . . . is a Dog Fish. You like it?'

'Yes, it's smashing.'

'Isa the way I cook it,' said the Italian. 'Down the road the other fellow make a mess of it.'

86

Dog fish, I thought. The smallest species of shark. I had caught dozens of them and seen hundreds receive the same treatment I gave them. Beat their brains out, for they twisted and fouled up gear when landed, and throw them back in the sea! We thriftless Irish, I thought, we did the same with pike, and eels, fish the English and French and German went mad about, and paid dearly for . . . when they could get them.

I finished the meal, feeling a lot better, and approached the Italian again.

'Where's the nearest "caff" around here?' I asked him. 'I'd like a good cup of tea.'

'Stay here,' said he, 'and 'ave a cuppa with me. I do not geta busy until after the pubs close.'

And so I had a couple of good cups of tea and a chat with the friendly Italian. I lingered as long as possible, but then had to face home. Home! That bloody freeze box? And I swore by all that was holy that I would find a new digs at the weekend.

The snow was starting to fall when I got outside, it had grown warmer, the bitter wind had gone and this would be a heavy fall, I knew. I trudged through the silent winter night, everything was becoming muffled, and my footsteps made no sound. As I drew near the house the sense of impending disaster which had dogged me since I came North hit me once again, so that I rang the Beebys' bell with some trepidation, stamping the snow off my feet while I waited. It seemed a long time before the door opened and when it did it was His Lordship, with his large commoner wife standing nervously behind. He was about the same build as the bully, Bateman, the same expression of suppressed hatred, the same granite face and glittering eye, the same contempt for the Irish.

'I want thee out of 'ere,' he said. 'Now!'

'Why . . . what have I done?'

'You're dirty, you're Arrish!' I felt my face grow pale, and the nervous trembling start up inside me, the thing I was afraid of, the Celtic fury that when aroused did not know when or where to stop. It had once put a first rate amateur boxer, a stone heavier and two years older than me, into hospital in less than a minute, when I was backed up in the Irish Army.

'Watch your tongue, Mister,' I said, and I could not stop my voice from trembling.

'For wot?' he said with supreme contempt stepping into the porch. I stepped back quickly. This was not the way to go. I was in a strange and hostile land, pigs like this had brought sorrow to my country, but in any confrontation with this man I was likely to end up on the wrong side. The attitude of the local police had convinced me of this. The British needed workers, but when they got you here they tried by every possible means to pressure you into their army. Once there, it was 'Good old Paddy, 'elpin' us again.'

'What about my clothes?' For answer he went back into the hall, lifted my suitcase, and dumped it at my feet. The snow was falling gently, and slowly concealing the rawness of this slapped-up jerry-built estate where there might be bloody murder in a second. This old bastard was well over fifty, it was my delicate appearance and long eyelashes that gave him the confidence to insult me.

'I want my food ration books.'

'You'll get them when you pay what you owe.'

'And what's that? And for what? A bloody freeze box of a house and an Oliver Twist dinner? Is that what I have to pay for?'

'Ten shillings,' said his putty-faced wife from behind. It was outrageous! The cost of a week's lodgings was not more than one pound and ten shillings anywhere.

'All right,' I said. 'I'll have to get my money. I left it under the mattress.' Before he could gather his wits I whipped around him and up the stairs. I did not have any money hidden, but I wanted to tramp snow all over the carpet. While I was in the room I threw the bed clothes onto the floor and was back down in a flash, stamping my shoes to make sure I had left the last little bit behind.

Once outside again, I fronted her up. 'The ration books,'

I snarled. I saw her husband blink in surprise at the menace and tone of my voice. I could see him starting to reappraise me. I ignored him. Madam came back with the ration cards in a hurry and handed them over.

'The money,' she said.

'Here is all your dinner was worth, and even that's too much.' I held out two half crowns, five shillings, and deliberately dropped them on the floor.

'You can pick them up yourself,' I told her husband. I was shaking with rage, and His Lordship's attitude had undergone a spectacular change. He had perceived something in my face and voice that told him not to push his luck too far, something that told him he had made a mistake, that I was not a mere kid he could push around. I picked up the suitcase and made for the garden gate. Once there I turned around and faced the house. In the darkness of the porch I could still make out the two figures. The snow had ceased, and, from behind a cloud, the moon peeped out, casting a cold dead eye on half the world.

'How would you like to step out on the road, Mister, an' see me off this joint?' There was still no answer. 'How would you like for me to beat the bejaysus out of you?' Still no answer.

'You're a lot bigger than me,' I jeered softly. 'You're a cowardly old Sassenach bastard . . . you're a shit . . . . Now will you see me off.'

He came with a rush then. I stepped through the gate into the road and cheerfully turned to meet him. All caution had left me, discretion was thrown to the four winds, my affronted Irish was up and I didn't give a Fiddlers for the whole Lancashire police force right then. He wore glasses, I'd have them off first, and beat the bejaysus out of him.

But his bluff had been called and he stopped short of coming through the gate. I stood there but could not work him enough to come out on to the road. 'Cowardly old bastard,' I complained loudly and, picking up my suitcase, went reluctantly away.

At the Salvation Army hostel they were surprised to see

me again so soon and asked me what had happened. 'The Landlord hates Irishmen and put me out when he found out I was one.'

They were duly sympathetic but not surprised, or so it seemed to me. However, the armchair was again placed at my disposal, I drank tea and chatted until the crowd dwindled, and then went to sleep.

The next morning saw me back once again with 'Rich Bitch'. She was not so cocky this time and asked me politely what she could do for me. Curtly, I told her I wanted to see the head of the office, to see the Beebys struck off the housing roster. Within a couple of minutes I was standing before a nice middle-aged lady who seemed concerned.

'Anyway, Ma'm, quite apart from their hatred of the Irish, a dog shouldn't be sent there, unless you want it to die of malnutrition. The blight of the *gorta* is over that house.'

Surprised at my turn of speech, she asked me what the *gorta* was.

'Gaelic, Ma'm, for famine!' This gave her a giggle.

'Right,' she said at length. 'That does it. You're the third complaint I've had about the Beebys.'

She produced a massive ledger and drew a line across their names. 'That's that,' she said. 'Now, where can we fix you up?' I had already made up my mind on this matter when confronted with the stupid pretensions of the Beebys.

'I'm a carpenter, a manual worker. I need a working class house, used to people like me coming home dirty. Please don't ever again give me an Acacia Crescent.'

'This is the name of a bachelor here, middle of town, Foreshaw Street, quiet working class area, a Mr Ken Norton, number 19A. How about that?'

'Fine by me,' I said, 'as long as I get settled. Can I pick up my case here later?'

'Wait a moment,' she said, 'Mr Norton is a First World War invalid, bad leg injury, you know. He has a phone . . . just hang on and I'll have a chat with him.'

After a couple of minutes she hung up and smiled. 'You can take your case,' she said. 'He is expecting you.'

'I was supposed to start work this morning, Ma'm, and they'll be wondering where I am. Would you mind phoning the office? I'd be very grateful.'

'Certainly,' she said and handed me the phone. The Dublin Camp manager came on, and I told him what had happened.

'Okay Lar,' he said, 'You'll meet an odd bastard over here like that . . . . Don't let it get you down. By the way, you'll be booked in on full pay today. See you tomorrow morning.'

So, around two o'clock, I found myself knocking on Ken Norton's door. It was an area of narrow cobblestone streets and drab 'two up, two down' houses, each with its white doorstep onto the street, inhabited for nearly a century by the same folk, generation after generation going into the same mill, or foundry or factory, for from these shabby dwellings came the muscle that drove Britain's Industrial Revolution. And it was Britain's Industrial Revolution that had slapped up these small houses, as many as could be fitted to the acre, each with its small backyard and outside toilet. A bathroom was unheard of, but coal could be delivered through the back gate, for there was a lane running along the terraces.

There was another unbelievable use for the lane, one that I would discover soon, though, had I been told at second hand, I would not have accepted it. It was 1941, things like that were long gone. Number 19A was no different from all the rest, and there were streets and streets of them, drab prisons where Britain's working class were content to live, like cage-bred birds, knowing no better. I knocked on the door gently, and after a little wait it opened, and Ken Norton stood before me. He was of average height, painfully thin, a mere cobweb of a man with a white, tortured and lined face that told of countless days and nights of suffering.

He looked sixty or more, but his black hair told a different story. His fine-boned, thin nose overshadowed a sad, downturned mouth, but right now he grimaced in what I took to be a smile.

'Come in, mate,' he said. 'I've been waiting for you. Name of Larry?'

'Yes, Larry Redmond.'

'Unusual name, that!'

'Not where I come from.'

'You're Irish!'

'Yes . . . very. Do you mind?' Might as well get things straight right from the start.

'Takes all kinds,' said Ken. 'I'm a cockney meself . . . born within the sound of . . . I don't give a bugger where a man is from, as long as he is clean an' tidy. Like a cuppa before I go for my afternoon nap?'

'Yes, I'd love one.'

'Right. Take your case upstairs, back room. You'll find all's ready. If I've forgotten anything, yell out. Kitchen's there and the stairs are there too.'

I grinned. 'I know. I was reared in a house like this, exactly like this.'

Ken seemed surprised. 'You 'ave houses like this in Ireland?'

'In Dublin and Belfast, thousands of them.'

'Well, I never,' he said as I went through the little kitchen and found my room. This was lovely, more at home. An old-fashioned washstand with a hole for the basin cut in the top stood against one wall, there was carpet on the floor, a chest of drawers and a lovely big mahogany wardrobe gleamed in the afternoon sunlight, with a bevelled mirror reflecting it. Given a chance, I could be reasonably happy here, although my dislike of Warrington and its grimy face was still as active as ever. This was a comfortable little house, and downstairs a roaring fire blazed in the carpeted room. If the job worked out I would get down to my promised course in writing, for I had long since received my application form. All I had to do was fill it in.

I put my things away, and came down. Ken was pouring the tea, a goodly strong cup, the way tea should be made. I gave him my ration books and sat down. He had made toast and we chatted for a while. Then it was time for his afternoon nap. He handed me the key to the front door, for I had told him I was going to find the post office. 'Go easy when you come back, mate, I need the sleep.'

Upstairs, I filled in the application form for the short story course, wrote to Mam, said I was sorry for not writing more often, but that things were topsy turvy with me. I told her this was likely to be my home for a while, and sent her two quid for her birthday, which was today, as it was mine. Both Scorpios, born on the same day, there was a special bond between us that even years of silence could not break. I stole downstairs and out, found the post office close by, and headed back to Ken's snug little home. I would sleep the afternoon away, I knew, for sleeping in an armchair may be better than sleeping on the floor, but it is not much better. And I was getting too many long train rides and armchairs for my own good. Not to mention the last time I was in bed . . . Doreen, where was my next Doreen?

As I approached number 19A the neighbour next door came out. She was a small buxom woman of thirty-five, with a go-ahead thrifty look about her, a look I had noticed a lot in women of her class. Battlers . . . who had reared children in the hungry thirties, and to whom the "Waar" had come as a blessing in disguise. At least now there were jobs everywhere, her kids were at school, her husband in the Forces and working. She had never been better off. There were a couple of million like her, whose only complaint was that everything was 'on ration'. Even that was bearable, for they had just emerged from a more severe period of rationing than most wars could inflict, the bottom rung, poverty, on the dole.

She smiled as I approached. ''Appen as you'll be Ken's new lodger?'

'Yes.'

'I get 'is food for 'im most times, poor lad, 'e's crippled walking.' She had a cardboard box in her hands and now she pressed it on me. 'Be a good lad, an' leave this on kitchen table. I've been shoppin' wi' your ration books. And don't make noise, 'e sleeps on sofa in front of fire. Don't

93

think 'e ever goes upstairs to bed.'

'Is he very badly injured, Mrs . . .?'

'Lucy 'ill do, Lucy Bottle. Aye, lad, 'e is. Don't take any notice of 'im when 'e is short, like 'e can be a nowty buggah when 'e is sufferin', but lad, 'e goes through it.'

'Does "Nowty" mean difficult, Lucy?'

'Aye.' She laughed. 'I'll 'ave to watch me English around you, Paddy. You speak very well. I'll 'ave to run now. I'm on afternoon shift at four . . . Ta ta.'

I opened the door quietly and entered, carrying the box of groceries, which I left on the kitchen table. Ken slept like a dead man on the sofa in front of a blazing fire. I was to find out that he was on morphia against the terrible pain that sometimes racked his emaciated body.

From my bedroom I looked out at the uninspiring view. A sea of smoking chimneys as far as the eye could see. A swift thaw had followed the snow fall, the backyards were full of slush. I got into bed and fell asleep at once.

It was dark when I awoke, and from downstairs came the smell of cooking. I was, as usual, starving, so I dressed quickly and went down. The radio was full on, and Henry Hall was playing with George Elrick doing the vocals.

'That you, Larry?' said Ken.

'Yes . . . that's a lovely fire.'

'You going to work in the morning?'

'Yes, of course.'

'Will you need a cut lunch?'

'No, there' a canteen on the job.'

'Right then, your dinner is on the table. Come away from the fire and get stuck in.'

For the times that were in it, it was a good dinner, and I said so. 'I'm not a bad cook,' said Ken, adding bitterly, 'I've 'ad plenty of bloody practise.'

After dinner I helped with the washing up, and then we went into the small front room with the blazing coal fire, so close to the pavement that every footstep that passed was marked. Some of the footsteps had a funny sort of muffled thud, quite loud, and, my curiosity getting the better of me,

I remarked on it to Ken. He laughed, shaking his head, but made no direct answer.

'Well?' I said.

''ave a look next time one of them comes along,' was all he would say.

'What! In the blackout?'

'Cor blimey, mate,' said Ken. 'I'm in the bleedin' 'ouse so much I don't know night from day. Sorry. That's the noise of clogs, Larry. Didn't you ever 'ear it before?'

'Jasus,' I said, 'I thought they had gone out with the Indians.'

'No, they still wear 'em 'ere in the tanneries and foundries. In the morning is the time you hear 'em most, mill workers and such.'

'I suppose the lavatory is out the back, Ken?'

'Yes, you can't miss it.' It was a dark cloudy night, but I soon located the lavatory without the use of my eyes. I could smell it! As often happens before an English winter, there was a kind of see-saw between the departing season and the coming one, and this evening was mild, almost warm, as distinct from the bitter cold of the night before, and an all pervading smell of urine and worse was on the night air. When my eyes had become accustomed to the light, I groped my way into the toilet, which smelled strongly of Jeyes' Fluid. I completed my call of nature and started groping for the cistern chain in order to flush it away.

'Jaysus,' I swore angrily, and, in the end, risked lighting a match for a second. To my astonishment there was none!

I decided to make no comment on the matter, in case I offended my new landlord, and tomorrow or the next day would answer my questions. As I went indoors, the heavy pounding of aeroplanes came from above, and with a roar the ack-ack guns opened up, and the earth shook.

Ken was sitting by the fire. 'Bastards 'eading for Liverpool again,' he said quietly. 'Poor sods, they're copping the lot.'

He had switched off the light and the radio, and, in the firelight, I could see his hands shaking so badly that he gave up trying to roll a smoke.

''ere, mate,' he said to me, 'roll me a smoke, will you? I always get this way when I 'ear them bastards and the guns go off. I suppose it brings 1918 back all over again.'

I made a reasonable job of the cigarette rolling, and handed it to him. I struck a match to save him more embarrassment, and lit up myself.

'That was some war, Ken,' I said. 'I hope there will never be another like it. From what I've seen on the pictures and what I've read, that was the most frightful war of all time . . . . Bogged down in a sea of mud, hundreds of thousands of men flung at each other . . . Jesus . . . and you were in that lot?'

'Not for long I wasn't . . . . Got 'it the first day . . . . Never fired a shot . . . 'alf our Company wiped out, poor young bastards . . . never even 'ad a woman, some of them. Shot to bits on the first day at the Front!'

All was silent now in Warrington. The ack-ack guns had stopped when the planes had gone over, and from Liverpool, like distant thunder, came a roll of sound. Then the Jerries were flying back again, the guns opened up, and the terrible shaking recommenced in Ken. This was the way it was with him, crippled from that old war. I wondered how many thousands like him still lived a half life, as he did. Eventually the guns ceased, and now there was complete silence.

'We've never 'ad a bomb on Warrington,' said Ken. 'We calls it 'appy Valley!' I remained silent, shocked by the appalling truth about Ken. Happy Valley! There was no valley on this earth that could be a happy valley for the man beside me, who was staring into the flames.

'I got married the week before I was sent to the Front,' he said. 'Violet . . . we 'ad always been sweet'earts ever since school days . . . an' we took the plunge. Vi was sure I would be killed, an' she wanted me kid . . . . She was a good 'un, pity it turned out like it did. Still, that's life.'

'Yes,' I said quietly.

'Only woman I ever 'ad, she was the first an' the last. That bloody German shell saw to that.'

'A shell?'

'Yes, we was 'oled up in Ypres, that's what they said it was anyway, but it was torn apart, only bits of buildings left. I was sheltering be'ind the remains of a wall on the second floor when this bloody great shell 'it our squad, an' blew the whole lot of us to kingdom come. I was the only one left alive, an' they 'ad to lift me off the spiked railings over the basement.

'Sweet Jesus,' I whispered, but Ken gave no sign of hearing. He was back in France.

'I got spiked 'ere,' he pointed to his hip, 'an 'ere,' pointing to his fly. 'An I wasn't a bloody man any more . . . I was a year in 'ospital. Vi lived 'ere with 'er mother, an' the old woman died while I was sick. So when they sent me 'ome, I came 'ere. Been 'ere ever since . . . .

'And Violet?' I ventured at last.

'She stuck it for a year more, an' then went out to work one mornin' an' never came back. Poor little sod . . . stuck with a cripple . . . 'oo could blame 'er? She was a healthy young woman who had slept with me for a week . . . she never played me up with another man, just left me 'er 'ouse, an' never came back . . . .'

I gazed steadily into the fire which was becoming a little blurred. I was not reared in the straight-jacket of the 'stiff upper lip' tradition, I was Celtic and volatile by nature . . . . 'Poor little sod,' he had said, ''oo would blame 'er?' Here was a man, an Englishman, that I had to stop and admire, a better man than I would ever be.

'Hard lines, Ken,' I said.

'Yes, 'ard lines, mate. I only 'ope she is 'appy, met some good bloke . . . she deserved it. There was a knock on the door then, 'Will I answer it, Ken?'

'Yes, that'll be Ken an' his mother.' I opened the door and stepped back to admit the visitors, and it was as my landlord had said. Mother turned out to be a buxom woman about fifty, grey-haired and smartly dressed. Her son, Ken number two, was wearing dark glasses and carrying the white stick of a blind man.

'Just came by to see if thee is all right, lad,' said Mrs Jones. 'An' meet thy new lodger.'

'Meet Larry . . . Larry Redman . . . e's Irish,' said Ken, and he told me I was meeting Mrs Jones and her son, Ken.

'I'll have to call you Ken number two,' I said, smiling. I drew up two chairs to the fire. My landlord lay quite still on the couch.

'Is 'ip troublin' you, Ken?' said Mrs Jones.

'A bit, love.'

'Bluddy war,' said Mrs Jones savagely. 'Nice bluddy mess it made of you two. Why don't bluddy politicians 'oo start them go an' fight them!'

'Now, now, Mother, don't start up again.'

'Suppose not. We're goin' for drink. You two join us an' we'll sup ale, an' forget bluddy war.'

'Not me,' said Ken briefly.

'Cum on, lad,' coaxed Mrs Jones. 'It'd do thee good to get out of 'ouse.'

'No.'

'You'll cum, Larry?'

'Yes, I'd like to.'

Outside, Ken number two took over and led us with certainty towards the pub. A heavy fog had fallen, and for the first time I tasted sooty grit and chemicals of all kinds falling to the ground with this deadly cloud. I could see nothing, not even when I held my hand up before my eyes.

'Anybody goin' pub?' Ken shouted to the silent street. I heard a few doors open, and soon we had all formed a crocodile, hands on each others' shoulders, while the blind man strode confidently along. In the pub, we all split up. If the fog persisted, Ken would lead us all home again.

It was an old-fashioned, side street pub that never knew a stranger. I was in company and did not feel isolated, but I decided that I would never come here alone. It was too clannish, they were all right with me, but only because I was with neighbours.

'Pity Ken wudden cum,' said Mrs Jones when we were seated 'suppin'' ale. It was lousy stuff, flat and insipid to an

Irishman used to frothing Guinness and fiery whiskey but, on the principle of doing what the Romans did when in Rome, I supped it up, and tried to look as if I was enjoying it.

''e never moves from bluddy sofa,' she told me, ''e's been goin' down 'ill past three months, lad. Thought as it'd buck 'im up if 'e 'ad lodger for company.'

'Could 'appen,' said her blind son. 'Give it a little time, Mother.'

'ee lad,' said Mrs Jones, 'but the two Kens was somethin' to see twenty years ago, alf ower street'd stand to look when they cum up it in uniform!'

'Twenty three years ago now, Mother,' said Ken, quietly.

'Ken got blinded . . . .' said his mother bitterly. 'First day at Front . . . . Lukin' at 'is pal sumtimes, ah think 'e came off best.'

'Now Mother, now Mother,' said Ken cheerfully, 'doan't stawt . . . doan't thee upset thyself . . . . Cums in bluddy 'andy in fog!'

Mrs Jones was a nice woman, and Ken 'number two', a cheerful man without a trace of bitterness, making the best of a bad job, playing his cards well, coping with the rotten hand life had dealt him.

'Compared with the other Ken, lad, I 'ave it good. No pain, an' 'e's never free of it. Stay with him, Larry, 'e needs somebody to talk to . . . .'

'We had a great talk tonight.'

'That's good, 'e must like you, 'e can be a nowty buggah be times, but at back of all 'e's all right.'

Ken turned out to be exactly as described, 'a nowty buggah', but after our conversation that first night when he had given me an unintended look into his soul, I would always, in his case, turn the other cheek.

When closing time came we left the Stags Head, and went out into a night almost as light as day. The fog had been swept away, clouds scudded across the face of the moon, and the mean, cobbled streets had a faint air of mystery about them.

Mrs Jones kissed me on the cheek as we parted. 'Look after 'im, Larry,' she said, ''e's one o' the best.'

Ken still lay on his bed of pain as I came in. He told me I would find a chamber pot under the bed. 'Empty it in mornin' before you go to work.'

'Where, Ken?'

'In the outside lavatory of couwse. Where else?' Curiouser and curiouser I thought, but when I looked out of my bedroom window all the mystery of the toilet and the smell was solved.

In the bright moonlight I could see everything in the small backyard, the toilet, the back gate leading to a lane, and another smaller door, set in the top of the brick lane wall, with a small platform on the inside. Every back wall had one and every house had its full 'Bucket o' Muck' standing ready to be collected. The next morning, as I was going to work, I saw the 'Muck Truck' that came to collect the filth. It was an old Leyland from which the cab doors had been removed, this to facilitate the men jumping in and out. The body of the truck was of timber, and, straight up the centre of it, a partition had been erected. This partition carried two slatted shelves, each of which held twelve buckets each side, so that the vehicle carried forty-eight containers.

Incredibly, the men carrying the buckets of muck wore clogs and had sack aprons to protect their clothes, the whole filthy scene seemed to me like something from a medieval nightmare, with its outbreaks of cholera and typhus. And then it came to me why Europeans were able to dominate the world. The white man, it seemed, could conquer anything and this ferocious nation I lived in had come out on top. And it was, I speculated, due no doubt to the Muck Bucket, for any human being that could live through and prosper in these conditions and worse, could conquer anything.

When penetrating yet another Pacific Island, another colony, they coughed in the face of a native and wiped out a tribe. The dear missionaries, shocked at the wicked nakedness, made the natives dress up in second hand clothes, and sent them to Heaven by the thousand. With their resistance to germs and the 'instant fury' possessed by the white man, all lands fell before him. The poor savage who had to dance all night to enrage himself to make war, was no match for the white man who could sleep soundly at night, and in the morning turn on his fury like a tap. I knew I was right. Was I not one of this same white race?

By the same token, I came from a city that was supposed to have the worst slums outside Warsaw and I had little doubt that we had, but even in the city centre, where perhaps ten families lived in one tenement house and had to share a single water tap and toilet, nothing like the Warrington Muck Cart had ever been seen. I had heard of a few cottages out Donnybrook way where a Muck Cart attended, but this arrangement died an early death with the coming of a native government, as did the Dry Toilets in Irish towns. Sewage replaced filth in a hurry, and the Irish Government brought in a firm of French Cleaners to show us how to clean up Britain's 'Dear old delightful dirty Dublin'. I came from a clean city, poor but clean, and I was genuinely shocked that the Muck Cart should persist in English towns as late as the year 1941!

However, I was prudent enough to keep my mouth shut on this aspect of Warrington life, particularly as most of the residents were convinced that where I came from we kept pigs in the parlour, but sweet Jesus, this place was old-fashioned to me. Dublin had long since had tarmacadamed roads and electric lighting, here the medieval sound of clogs on cobbles had awakened me this morning, trudging to work under gas lamps that, due to the War, were no longer lit. 'Potties' under the bed, clogs, gaslight! And in the dark this morning I had smelt the malodorous presence of the Muck Cart as it rumbled past, and I had the quixotic thought of doing my Correspondence Course with a goose quill.

The bus pulled up at every stop, picking up the caged factory birds, heading for work. British women, like

101

everything else in the land were 'Going to it for oul divarsion', their husbands were elsewhere, called up, but they did the right thing by His Majesty's Forces stationed in their district. Relations between the sexes had never been warmer, there was no shortage under the blanket.

And little neutral Larry slept his virginal sleep and sometimes, most times, dreamed of a woman beside him, any woman, Jesus it was hard to be young and left out! Vera Lynn, the Forces Sweetheart sang that she walked alone, 'But to tell you the truth I'm not lonely . . . .' Well I was bloody well lonely, though unlike Vera I was no begrudger of those who were not. Vera was all right so long as she knew that 'you're lonely too', which seemed a bit on the lousy side. From where I stood nobody should be lonely, starting with me!

The job was the usual muddy building site, rows and rows of slapped up houses and two-storey flats to house munition workers, all roofed, ready to be finished, carpenters galore, but no timber. Britain was muddling through, and the national wealth was being squandered on an imaginable scale. The large contingent of cockneys on the job were frankly hostile to the powers that be, after years on the dole. Only the war had saved them from continuing poverty, and they knew that they would all be called up any day now.

'We've got the bastards where we want 'em now,' they said. 'They won't bleedin' dish out the same to us after the War, like the old Dad 'ad to suffer. We've an all party Government now, but come the end of the War, Paddy, an' the bleedin' Torys go. Bastards!'

Nevertheless, I never heard one of them even remotely suggest that England might lose the War. They would have lynched anyone of their number who even thought of it. And, when the time came, they would fight as gallantly as their fathers before them, and although they had turned to Churchill to lead them from their Garden of Gethsemene, yet at War's end they would turn on this enemy of the working class and rend him and his party apart. I had plenty of time to observe and talk during the next three weeks, but after that the long-awaited timber arrived, the firm introduced a bonus scheme, and we went to it with a will.

But that first day went slowly, trying to find shelter from the icy breeze in windowless houses, so that I arrived back at Ken's half frozen. I let myself in quietly, and stood there, lapping up the heat and comfort of the little room. Ken lay fast asleep on the couch, and for the first time I really took stock of the place. The fire, as usual, roared up the chimney, and the light was on.

On a small table beside the fire lay Ken's pipes, with a glass beside them to hold his pipe cleaners. Under the window another small mahogany table with some bric-a-brac, including a photograph, a close up, which I knew was the absent Violet. She had been very beautiful. Beside it the photograph of a good-looking young man in uniform, poor Ken, who had left his looks and his manhood on the field at Flanders, and a pity, I thought, he had not left with them.

There was a triangular cupboard in the corner that backed on to the kitchen, and, on its top, Ken had constructed, in plaster, a hillside with a glen, complete with silver paper river bed, tiny ferns and pebbles that served as rocks, and, sitting on them, miniature gnomes and leprechauns. The whole thing was skillfully done, artistically painted in dull browns and yellows, the colours of gorse, and it rose splendidly against the kitchen wall.

'Admirin' me 'andiwork, Larry?' Ken was awake again. 'Yes, Ken, there's a touch of the artist about it. It's lovely.'

'Y'aven't really seen it yet, I'll show you after dinner. So 'ave a wash, lad, an' you'll find a feed over a pot of water on the gas stove.'

In the time I spent with Ken it was nearly always this way, though sometimes I came home to find him knocked out with morphia, and no dinner. But the 'Chipper' was handy, and on such occasions I availed of it. We never discussed this when it happened. I was happy in this little house, my Correspondence Course had arrived, my evenings, even if Ken was in a 'nowty' mood, were full, and I was making progress as a budding writer. Or so I imagined.

The bit of sport in my life came from the building site, for there was rarely a dull moment there. It was almost completely staffed by Dublin tradesmen, all staunchly Union men, who stood for no nonsense from the firm. Britain needed us, we needed the money, but there was no love lost between us. The bonus scheme from the start was fiddled by the office staff, who supposed wrongly that Paddies could not add up. This was the flash point of many strikes. When the money was light on, we just jacked up and did no work at all.

Usually we marched on the office and stood shouting outside until some nervous representative was sent out to reassure us that all would be made good. It took some time for the staff to get used to the idea that we were well able to calculate our coming bonus, but eventually they were forced to the conclusion that they were not dealing with the population of some remote island in the Pacific, that these natives were far from 'pacific' and could not be fobbed off with a handful of beads. When that sad realisation dawned, a lot of fun went off the job. On one hilarious occasion my mate, Mick, had put his derisive bonus, seven and six pence, back in its packet and, during the uproar outside the office, when those inside would only dare to open the tiny pay-out window, had flung the money straight through the slot and caught the manager full in the face.

Mick Gilbey was tall and thin, a pale-faced Dubliner, an out and out Socialist. He was earnest and passionate in debate, we both enjoyed the mental tussle, though some-times we enraged each other, for I was determined to be a Capitalist like my father. And Mick had made up his mind to bring the system down. I met him the first day on the job, and spent most of it differing with him, but I had made a lifelong friend that day, and we would work well together when the timber came. This, notwithstanding the coming revolution, when the builders of Dublin would choke to death, made to eat their own ill-gotten gains.

As usual, Ken had no dinner, I rarely saw him eat anything except a biscuit or a slice of toast. 'There's a letter for you from Ireland,' he said. 'I put it on the mantelpiece.'

I grabbed it eagerly. It had come via the firm's hostel in London, a mere note from Mam, but it contained another letter. This one was from my companion of Irish Army days, Gibbo and the letter came from Edinburgh. Duffy was still with him, although he was now a sergeant, and Gibbo one of his platoon. Gibbo had fallen in love with a Scots 'nymph with a custard voice'. Any day now he would be shipped off to fight Rommel. He was, he said, 'having a big swing', and looking forward to the coming excitement of war in the Western Desert. He was getting married. My heart turned over as I read this, and I looked across at another who had been only eighteen and, like Gibbo, a virgin boy. Please God, I thought, he will never come to know the suffering a German shell can bring, and, without more ado, I brought down my writing pad and wrote by return, sending my regards to John Duffy. It was only five months since we three had marched the roads of Ireland, fighting a mock war in the green fields and dripping woods, always wet and most times hungry, and Gibbo defiantly leading the company in a song when things were really rough.

I told him how it was with me, asked him to keep in contact, and added a word of caution, about his recklessness. He could have made sergeant twice over but for it. I sealed the envelope and put a stamp on it. I would post it the following morning.

'Well, Ken, that's that.'

'Finished?'

'Yes, why?'

'Watch this!'

He limped to the kitchen, turning off the light on his way, then a yellow light came on shining on the little hillside and glen. I heard the sound of running water, and down the silver river bed came a wild mountain stream with a waterfall at its end. It was lovely, amazingly effective, so much so that a wave of homesickness swept over me.

'Well,' said Ken, smiling one of his rare smiles, 'wot you think of that?'

'Terrific, Ken. Don't shut if off for a few moments.' For I had left Warrington and its grimy streets and tall factory chimneys far behind, and, trout rod in hand, I was walking under the beech trees on the bank of a wild stream that bounded down the mountain, to join the Liffey at Manor Kilbride. Yellow furze and forsythia set the banks ablaze with colour, the great rocks strewn around were covered with soft green moss, and small trout darted for cover.

All around me the mountains were purple in the late evening sun. I was sitting on a rock, smoking, waiting for the 'evening rise' to begin. It was quiet, so peaceful, only the sound of running water . . . . Suddenly the air-raid siren screamed its warning, the roar of the Luftwaffe swiftly followed, the ack ack guns opened up, great thunderous volleys that shook the house and its shaking tenant; this was a worse paroxysm than I had seen before, for Ken had fallen off the couch while watching a creation of joy, and now twitched and jerked like a man who suffered from the St Vitus's Dance syndrome. I do not think he ever forgave me for seeing him like that.

I ran to the kitchen, whipped the little hose off the tap that created the river, poured cold water in a basin and ran back to Ken. I kept putting cold cloths on his forehead and wiping his sweating face, and then, as before, the noise stopped, and the ominous rumble from Liverpool rolled across the land. Ken slowly recovered, but before he could light the cigarette I had placed between his lips, the Jerries were back, the guns roared again, and the sweat rolled off me as I tried to hold this incredibly strong shadow of a man. Such strength can only come from fear or madness, or both, and both of us lay exhausted after all was over.

I made tea, we drank it, pots of it, talking into the small hours. We were as close as brothers when I eventually went to bed, but that night was the beginning of the end of our friendship. Ken, over the next three months, gradually retired into himself more and more, sometimes we hardly exchanged a word in a day, and I knew with certainty that it would not be long before I was asked to go. Twice I went around to Ken number two and told him I was leaving, and twice his mother and he pleaded with me not to go.

''e needs someone in t' 'ouse, Larry, 'e mustn't be left alone.'

'But he's making it plain I'm not wanted. How can I stay?'

'Stay, anyway, lad, doan't leave sinkin' ship . . . .'

'Like a rat?'

'Nay, lad I wasn't goin' to say that . . . nay, lad,' Mrs Jones protested. 'Just' doant leave 'im, lad, 'e'll get over it. We've seen this 'appen before.'

And so I stayed on, working at my writing lessons, keeping a low profile, until the inevitable came.

'Look, mate,' said Ken one night, when the snow had begun to fall again, as it had on and off all winter, 'I don't want to 'urt your feelings, but I'm not able to cope with a lodger. You'll 'ave to find another 'ouse.' I felt my face go white with shock, I had had ample warning, but, at the back of it all, had persuaded myself that he was my friend, that he needed me.

'Oh . . . when?'

'As soon as you can arrange it, Larry. I'm sorry, but that's the way it is, nothin' against you, I just want the 'ouse to meself again.'

So that was that, I would have to write a couple of letters, one to home . . . don't write until I find another address . . . the same to the Correspondence School . . . tell the Police my new address . . . go to the bloody food office again . . . .

'Ken,' I said, 'Can you give me a few days?'

'Yes, but I want you out as soon as possible.' A 'nowty buggar' he had been called, and a 'nowty buggar' he was just now, but there was no way, looking at the peaky, strained face before me, that I could even begin to dislike him.

'I may 'ave to go to hospital, mate, so make new arrangements quick.' Somewhere near the job I would make a few inquiries.

I went to work the following morning in bitter mood and

bitterly cold. The buses had stopped running, and great heavy flakes were still adding to last night's deposit. I trudged through eighteen inches of soft snow towards the housing site, where I was hoping to be told that all work was off for the day. No such luck, the job had to go forward, we were already behind time, and the powers that be were putting pressure on the builders to get finished. So, on the job we stayed, most of us hiding from the snow in window-less houses as best we could.

We were frozen, hungry and savage, for this charade of 'going to it for Britain' was silly in our case. We had no bloody timber to do anything with, had had none for a week or more. The only consolation was that we were getting paid for doing nothing, but that was not true either. If we were not producing we were suffering for our pay and harder money was never earned by men.

In the afternoon of this terrible day, the softness went out of the snowfall, it had stopped at midday, and a deadly north wind, that cut through our thin clothing like a knife, took over, and, with its breath, crusted the snow hard, and then went on to make it solid. This was the big freeze-up, this was the Arctic come to England, the Arctic demeaned by smoking black chimneys, dirty snow, and too many humans. The dignity of soaring pines, the howl of wolf packs hunting through the night, the sense of purity that rightly belongs to a white landscape, had all been removed, to be replaced by dirt and soot, and the smell of fish and chips.

More dead than alive I found my way back to Ken's little house, looking forward to at least twelve hours respite in his cosy den. I found the lock on the front door iced up, and used a full box of matches to thaw it out. Eventually I managed it, and came in from the cold. The fire was low, but the room was welcoming and warm, the light was out. Over in the corner on top of the cupboard the yellow light lit up the small mountainside with its tumbling wild stream, and I stood there entranced, transported in a second back to Ireland, away from this harsh climate and people that were alien to me . . . . But where was Ken?

I stood there wondering, then went into the kitchen, and opened the little door that led to the winding stairs. The landing light was full on, and a black shadow on the stairs startled me before I looked up. Before me, Ken's body hung motionless. I was struck dumb with horror, but my mind recorded every detail of the terrible event. Ken had fetched a ladder, opened the trap door to the roof in the landing ceiling, put a piece of timber and a rope across it. He had killed himself by jumping from the top landing with the rope noose around his neck, and his blood-congested face and staring eyes were right in front of me . . . .

For all eternity I stood there, transfixed. Then came the scream, an uncontrollable scream that I almost thought had come from someone else. I stumbled down the couple of steps, fell over a chair in the kitchen, still screaming, gone mad with fear, tripped on the step leading to the front room, falling on my face, scrambling on hands and knees towards the front door, wild to get away from this nightmare. And all the time the little river plunged down the mountainside valley, and Ken had reached his own 'happy valley' at last. I broke a couple of fingernails trying to open the front door, and then fell on to the street, with the light streaming out behind me. Almost at once came a roar of anger.

'Shut bluddy door, you daft git. Doan't you know there's a waar on?'

'Yes,' I screamed, 'I know there's a fuckin' 'waar' on, come an' see what the last one left'.

'That's a bluddy Paddy,' said another voice, as I turned and got sick against the brickwork.

'Aye, an' bluddy drunk, an' all.' They were on me then, a big policeman and an air-raid warden. The copper grabbed me. All along the little street, doors were opening, and the neighbours coming out, and in seconds a crowd had gathered.

'What's to do?'

'Bluddy drunken Paddy, that's what's to do. Cum on you . . . . Maike way there, this lad's goain' to the lock up.'

'Just a bluddy minnit, you!' It was Lucy Bottle from next door. 'What's this lad supposed to 'ave dun?'

'Drunk . . . leavin' light on in blackout . . . vomitin' in public . . . you've got eyes in your 'ead 'aven't you?'

'Yes . . . . But 'ave you? This is a good lad, what's wrong, Pad?' The terrible retching had stopped by now so that I was, after a fashion, able to answer her.

'Don't go in that house, Lucy,' I said. 'Ken has hanged himself.' Lucy bustled over, shoving neighbours aside. 'Get in there and taike your 'ands off this lad.'

It was very light in the street, for the snow made it so, and by this time I could see everything quite clearly. The air-raid warden, unnoticed, had gone into the house, and now he and the copper nearly collided in the doorway, the warden roughly pushing the policeman aside, and heaving his guts up on the snowy pavement.

'Cum wi' me Larry,' said Lucy Bottle. 'Ah'll get thee a cuppa . . . tha' needs it.' We left the gathering crowd, and, weakly sipping tea, I heard the ambulance come, and, from somewhere far off, the noise that accompanied the removal of Ken's body

'Cum on now, 'ave you no bluddy 'omes to go to?' It was the policeman, dispersing the crowd. Presently there was a loud knock on the front door and Lucy flung it open like a tiger.

'Ah've cum to taike lad to station,' I heard him tell Lucy.

'Why, what's 'e bluddy done?'

'We need statement . . . 'e found body.'

'So did air-raid warden . . . y'know . . . drunken one 'as vomited.'

'Watch it, Missus!'

'Why . . . 'ave we got bluddy Gestapo in Warrington now? Lad's avin' cuppa, 'e's in shock . . . .'

''e's wanted at station!'

'Well, 'e's not goin' to bluddy station until ah say so. you can cum in an' wait, but keep a civil tongue in your 'ead. Cum on, cum in . . . .' Sheepishly, the big copper stood beside the small fury that had fronted him up.

''appen you'll have a cuppa too?'

'Ah will that!'

'Then sit down an' we'll get things sorted out.' As stated, I was required at the police station, Ken's house would be sealed up, nothing to be removed until after the autopsy . . . .

'What about my clothes?' I said.

'You'll 'ave to manage best you can,' said the copper. 'It won't taike long.'

''appens as the lad wants 'em now,' said Lucy firmly. ''Ow wud you like to be in 'is shoes in this weather?'

'Ah've nuthin' to do wi' that, Missus, that's the law.'

'Well, law 'ill 'ave to be broken, then. Cum on, Paddy, we'll get bluddy clothes . . . now.' She stood there glaring at the policeman, a small gritty female from Lancashire, who was prepared to go to war for a stranger. A lot of bigoted ideas about the Brits were leaving my mind in a hurry.

'Cum on, Pad,' she said. 'Is 'ouse door open?'

'No . . . 'e'll 'ave to manage best way 'e can as I told you, Missus.'

'I have the front door key,' I whispered to Lucy.

'Right then . . . cum on.'

We marched out of the house and I opened Ken's door. Together we went upstairs and packed my suitcase, with the big copper looking on, unable to cope with this tigerish female.

''urry up, for God's sake,' he pleaded. 'This cud cost me me job.' We came downstairs as quickly as possible. Coming through, I re-connected the rubber hose over the sink to the water tap and turned it on. I turned off the main light, having flicked the little yellow bulb on, and there I stood for the last time, looking at Ken's turbulent river, surging over tiny boulders, and the waterfall at the bottom, with its pool below, from where it drained back to the kitchen sink, its tiny gnomes and leprechauns sitting on the banks. The copper stood open-mouthed. Lucy was quietly weeping beside me, and I was blinded with tears.

'Thank God,' I managed at last. 'His torment is over.'

'Amen to that,' said Lucy.

'Soppy pair o' buggers,' said the big copper, gulping. 'Cum on.' He went into the kitchen, Ken's river dried up in a hurry, and then we were outside forever.

'I'll taike that,' he said to Lucy who was holding the suitcase, and as she glared he added hurriedly, 'into your place.' And he did.

'Now,' he said. 'Are we ready to make statement, lad?'

'Yes.'

'Well then, cum on.'

'You're bringin' 'im by car?' said Lucy.

'Aye, Missus.'

'An you'll bring 'im back 'ere same way, woant you?'

'Aye, Missus, ah'll do that. Satisfied customers, ma'am, that's ower motto.'

'See that you bring 'im back then, e's 'ad enough for wun night.' And so, after the formalities at the police station, I was taken back to Lucy Bottle's house. Her two children, one a boy of eight and the other a girl of ten, were quietly doing their school homework and Lucy, God bless her, had made me a good dinner. I was surprised at the amount of meat on the plate, and hoped aloud that I had not left her short.

'No,' she smiled, 'Ah doant work in factory canteen for nothing. We eat well in this 'ouse, better than before War . . . I bet bluddy Tories doan't go short, war or no war.'

I finished up the dinner and stood up shakily. 'Where's my case, Lucy?' I said.

'Why? You goin' somewhere?'

'Yes, the Sally Arms 'ill put me up for the night.'

The Sally Arms woan't put thee up for the night. You can sleep on sofa, down 'ere.'

'I don't know what to say . . . .'

'Then say nuthin, an' 'ave anuther cuppa.' At half past ten Lucy sent the kids to bed, and I slipped them a few bob on the sly. I was lousy with money, I, who was always broke, had managed to save quite a bit while with Ken — staying at home and the Correspondence Course had done the trick.

Lucy made up a bed on the sofa. I would find another lodging tomorrow. It was all arranged before she went to bed. I lay in the flickering light of the fire, for these Lancashire fires never went out in winter, and my thoughts were long long thoughts. Eventually I slept, a heavy drugged sleep of exhaustion, and sometime during the night I dreamed a dream of Manor Kilbride and its mountains. I was fishing the rippling stream again for trout, and everything was lovely until I sat on a rock and lit a cigarette and Ken sat down with his purpled blackened face and asked me to roll him one. And I screamed and sprang into a deep pool and swam under to get away from the frightful vision, but I could not surface again and I was gasping out my life, struggling . . . struggling . . . crying . . . .

Lucy brought me back with a stinging slap on the face. I was panting like a man after a mile run hard. Sweat streaming off me. I was incoherent, half out of my mind.

'Sorry I 'ad to do that, lad, but you were in a right ol' state.' I could not answer her, all I could do was cry and I did not seem to be able to stop. I had been crying at the end of the protracted nightmare that had awoken Lucy, and now I could not stop.

Lucy knelt down beside the sofa and ruffled my hair. 'You're a right bluddy softie, Larry,' she said, and, leaning over, wiped my eyes. I caught the scent of the perfume she wore, and in the firelight her hair gleamed and her white breasts made her night dress bulge. I could feel them on my chest.

'Ah, Jesus, Lucy,' I whispered, and I kissed her face and breasts and somehow she was in beside me and we were making love as if the world were about to end. It happened so swiftly, with such passion, so unexpectedly . . . .

'My God,' Lucy gasped, when it was over. 'But I never meant that to 'appen.'

'Nor I,' I panted, but three minutes later we were at it again. It was lovely. I think I fell asleep just before the dawn. I was asleep before Lucy left, that I do know, and it was ten o'clock with the kids long gone to school before I woke up.

Lucy was putting curlers in her hair, and smiled when she saw I was awake.

'You'll 'ave eggs for breakfast then?'

'Yes, thank you, Lucy.' I found it hard to meet her eyes after what had happened between us.

'Gone all modest, 'ave we?' said Lucy derisively. 'I didn't see much of this last night . . . thank God,' she added smiling. 'Take what the good Lord sends.'

'Don't you feel any guilt at all, Lucy?'

'Not much . . . .'

'What about your husband, though?'

'There'll be plenty left for 'im, Larry. Why, you're not goin' to tell me you're sorry you 'ad me, are you?'

'No . . . of course not. It was lovely, you've been lovely to me, Lucy, but it's just that it's wrong . . . .'

'What's wrong about it?'

'It's a sin isn't it?'

''oo bluddy ses so? Catholic Church?'

'Your Church, too, Church of England I suppose. They call it adultery, don't they?'

'Aye,' said Lucy the pagan, laughing. 'An they call it right. It's done by bluddy adults, so ah suppose it's adultery all right.' I burst out laughing, I could not help it.

'Trouble wi' you Catholics is,' said Lucy, putting my breakfast on the table, 'that you 'ave all been brainwashed . . . ashamed to enjoy sex. An' doan't tell me I'm wrong, me 'usband is a Catholic?'

'Mmm,' I said thoughtfully, 'your husband! Suppose someone in the street tells him you put me up overnight, what'll he say to that?'

'Nowt,' said Lucy succinctly. 'Ah'll tell 'im it were on'y a boy, an' anyway, 'e knows I 'ave a soft 'eart.'

She looked out the window into the street.

'Just let any of those buggers out there open their mouths, an' I'll 'ave a little talk wi' them, whole bluddy lot of 'em 'anging out wi' soldiers in Pelican every chance they get . . . . Sum boy you turned out to be,' she added. 'any idea ah might 'ave 'ad about you been a virgin . . . well . . . !

114

She laughed heartily. 'Sum bluddy virgin, ah'll say. You've 'ad plenty of practise, ah can tell.'

'Not really, Lucy,' I said candidly. 'I've only had two women in my whole life.'

'An' now it's three?'

'Yes, that's right. And I wish it had been twenty-three, I'm always longing for a woman.'

'Well, you 'ad one last night, better start lukin' for another, me 'usband is due 'ome this week.'

'This week!'

'Aye . . . should never 'ave been called up in first place, 'e can do more damage on 'itler in factory than 'e can in Army, 'e's a tool maker . . . very 'ighly skilled, I'm told.'

I finished my breakfast, with Lucy looking at me in thoughtful silence. 'You're a very good-luckin' lad,' she said at length, 'an you 'ave a luvely body . . . must be bluddy long eyelashes that makes people think you are . . . but you're not. You're a man all right, all bluddy man! Catholic Church didn't get to you like it did me 'usband. Doesn't know 'ow as to luv a woman. Cums at me like a bull at a gate . . . . It's a sin,' she jeered, 'let's get it over quick like!'

'Does he not kiss your lovely breasts, like me?'

'No . . . nor fondle me the way you did either, bring me on luvly like until I'm mad for it . . . .' She stepped away from the table, and her eyes were full of tears.

'Oh, get out a' here, Pad, before I lose me 'ead over you. And doan't cum back! Ah mean that! Me 'usband is a good un' . . . I'm nearly old enough to be your muther. Pack up now, Pad, an' go.'

I packed quickly and dumped my cases at the door. Then I went back to her. She stood before me, an ordinary working class Lancashire Lass, with curlers in her hair. I passed thousands like her every day of my life without a second glance, yet now I wondered how the dark night with firelight gleaming on a woman's hair, and a pair of snowy pink-tipped breasts could turn a small 'two up, two down', house in a mean street into the Garden of Eden. Somewhere I had read that the higher the species in nature the more the male differed from the female. Certainly nothing about a woman's body, when it came down to the important bits, vaguely resembled a man's.

A man's body was hard and unyielding, a woman's softly designed to absorb and engulf the force of the act of love, and in it a man could be lost and drowned. That was the way of it, I decided, women's voluptuous bodies were irresistible to me, and who the hell wanted to resist anyway? I put my arms around her and kissed her gently.

'I wish it was last night all over again,' I said.

'Maybe ah do too, but get on, lad. There's no future for us. Go now.' She was still in her dressing gown, and now I made my last move. Gently I parted it and kissed both her breasts again. Lucy drew in her breath sharply, and pushed me away.

'Well,' she demanded. 'Are they as good as last night?'

'Oh yes, Lucy, but there's something missing.'

'What?'

'No perfume, Lucy, no perfume. Oh Lucy, you've destroyed my ego. I thought it was I who seduced you.'

'Well as it 'appened, you didn't. I'm lonely, an' ah fancied you from first day. I didn't notice you puttin' up much resistance, bluddy 'ipocrite.'

'No fear, Lucy, never with you. It was lovely, thank you. Give us a kiss before I go.' Lucy backed swiftly off, and shook her head.

'Get out, lad, get off. We're finished.' So I left Foreshaw Street for the last time, never to return. And I had at last come to terms with what I was, that when a woman sent a signal I would be there. That, as they dominated me and made me less a man, at the same time they blessed me and conferred manhood on me. That I was only one half of a human being, the other half was a woman! I had to come to terms with that! In joyous boyhood I had run free. Now that day was done, and manhood, instead of turning me into a king, had made me a slave!

Most desperately I wanted to run free in the world of letters and words, and fishing rods and woods and streams and mountains, without the chains that these strange creatures could put upon me, but never would I run free again!

Back again at the Housing Office, and 'Rich Bitch' was still on duty. Was it my imagination that she looked at me with new eyes? Or was it that I was now more sure of myself? Or that I was growing up in a hurry, that experience was leaving its patina on my face, that I no longer looked like a boy? Or was it because I had stopped hating the Brits?

Whatever, she smiled and gave me a new address as requested, near my work. It was after twelve, I had lunch in a 'British Restaurant', after that the same old routine, go to the station, show them my new address and phone the job to account for my absence. It all took time, and it had begun to snow heavily again as I made my weary way to number 22, Uniform Terrace, at Longford. It turned out to be a council house, a shabbier edition of Acacia Crescent. It was almost dark when I knocked on the door.

It was 9 December, 1941. The next day would be a bad one for England!

6 22 Uniform Terrace

I stood there waiting, the snow swirling around me, shivering, but there was no answer. In desperation, I pounded on the door, and it was opened almost at once by a tall old lady. Coming in out of the freezing blackout, I stood there blinking, taking stock of my new lodgings. A poor shabby home, cracked linoleum on the floor, a battered sofa, and a timber kitchen table covered with newspapers doubling as a tablecloth. But the blazing coal fire made it lovely in my eyes. Over the mantelpiece hung a cheap tasteless print, and beneath it, on a chair, a kitten was contentedly washing a paw, like a little hand with a furry glove on it.

But above all it was warm and the ugly old man rising to meet me, with watery eyes, large red sponge nose, clown's smile, wholesome good nature displayed by ill-fitting dentures, was the warmest thing of all. James Barnes, 22 Uniform Terrace, Warrington, Lancashire, night watchman on our very own building site. Dogberry! The nickname was irresistible.

'Good evening,' I said, uncertainly.

'eee, lad, I'm right glad to meet thee. Been lukin' for lodger for couple of weeks now. Meet Missus,' he added with pride. The tall old lady who was tidying the table smiled.

'Married a young 'un, I did,' she said, ''e's on'y sixty-eight, I'm seventy-wun.'

'I can hardly believe it,' I said, and meant it, for he looked far older than his wife.

''e's me third,' she added.

'I were married afore too,' said Dogberry defensively.

'On'y wunce,' she retorted, ''im an Ted Earls were after me for years. Said as I'd marry first wun back from Great War. ''e cum back first!'

Shabby though this Jerry-built house was, slapped up just before Hitler struck, I knew I would be happy here, for I had landed among a couple of characters, and already I felt at home as I had never done with poor tortured Ken. Ken's house had been very comfortable and well furnished, this one was spartan, but the 'crack' would be good.

While she was making tea, I studied Mrs Barnes. Tall, stooped, withered apple cheeks, and a pair of enormous luminous hazel eyes, flecked with gold, eyes that would coax the birds out of the bushes! Never had I seen eyes like these, the eyes of a gentle tigress, and never would I see their match again. It was easy to imagine the devastation she had caused when younger. I did a bit of rapid reckoning. It was only twenty-three years since the war in Flanders had ended, and twenty-three from sixty-eight still made Dogberry forty-five when he had volunteered for service. And this was the widow who had sent two men into that hell to win her favour. I could see that poor old Dogberry was still mad about her, for he had introduced her to me like a sultan to the warmest jewel in his harem!

'You're Irish,' she said flatly.

'Dublin,' I said defensively.

'Dublin, Belfast or Cork,' she answered. 'I wuddn't know t'difference. You're all t'same.' And shamed me for sitting there in my six guinea tailor-made suit and my suede shoes, I thought it obvious I was a city man, and she said we were all the same!

'You're very small for an Irishman, though,' she said, smiling, hitting me on a sore spot.

'Maybe, Ma'm,' I said swiftly. 'But there's smaller than me where I come from. Everybody over here thinks an

Irishman is seven feet tall, with a long upper lip, and shillelagh under his arm, an' the little divils dancin' in his laughin' Irish eyes . . . .'

'My . . . my,' Mrs Barnes interrupted, 'but you're bluddy Irish alright. Smart an' fiery . . . ! You'll do. I like a man to 'ave a bit of go in 'im. 'Ad a proper meal today, lad?'

'Not bad, Ma'm.'

'Mrs Barnes 'ill do,' she said tartly. 'I'm not t'Queen.'

'ee, lass,' said Dogberry fondly, 'thou art the Queen of this 'ouse.' She shrugged his hand from her shoulder impatiently, and Dogberry, like a faithful old watch dog who had been kicked, subsided in confusion. His light went out, his smile was gone, and all that was left was an old man who had been too often rejected.

'Got food ration books, Paddy?' she asked.

'I have, Mrs Barnes, and I forgot to tell you my name is Larry.'

'Good, then, Larry. Three can manage food better nor two. I'll go down t'food office in't marnin' and fix up.'

'An',' said Dogberry, suddenly glowering, 'tha'll not be wearin' thy good 'at! An' tha'll not be talkin' to Ted Earls! I 'eard all about thee last Sataday mornin', talkin' an' makin' up t'im. Whole street were skrikin' about it!'

And there and then she did the little jig I was to see so often afterwards.

'Me!' she said derisively, 'makin' up t'im! I cud 'ave 'im anytime I lift me little finger!'

'But 'ee'l not 'ave thee,' Dogberry said ferociously.

'Ah,' she said, jugging her way to the pantry. 'Shuttup.'

We had tripe and onions for supper, and talked a lot and got to know each other a little before I went to bed, and Dogberry to work. My room was directly over the kitchen and the fire, so the room was not as cold as I had thought it would be, but still I had to put my overcoat on the top of the bedclothes, which were on the light side. It snowed all that night, and before I went to sleep I gave a thought to the old man, out in that, all night, at sixty-eight years of age. In the trenches they had been told that they would return to a land fit for heroes to live in, and my derisive mind agreed that one would have to be a hero, a Spartan, to live as old Dogberry had between the wars.

Through the bleached hell of a freezing building job I worked the following day, talking on and off with my work-mate, Mick Gilbey, about the new Digs and the pair of characters I lived with, and the unfaltering courage of the old man.

'ee, lad,' he had said. 'Old 'itler is playin' merry 'ell wi' us now, but we'll get 'im! Get bluddy Japs an' all . . . got old Kaiser Bill in't last lot, shud' ave hung the bastard. We'll 'ang this lot, any road.'

We had grown quiet then, listening to the scream of the air-raid siren, followed by the heavy drone of German bombers flying over to knock some more 'merry 'ell' out of Liverpool. The guns opned up uselessly into the thick cloud, from close by, and the Jerry-built house jigged almost as much as old Mrs Barnes had done. From the heaped up fire a small avalanche of red hot coals suddenly spewed over Dogberry's slippers and, with a roar like a lion, he stumbled up, fist clenched at the ceiling. 'Bastards,' he shouted. 'We'll get thee.'

And then the fit of coughing took him, his red face purpled with the silent paroxysm as he fought for breath, while I hastily shovelled up the smoking coals. Gassed in the Great War, old Dogberry.

'Got whiff from Kaiser Bill,' he told me after order had been restored, and we waited for the bombers to fly back. They came faster now, one more load of death lighter, the laboured hammering gone from their engines, and the guns opened up again. And I gave a fleeting thought to the late Ken, and silently thanked God that he was dead. While the racket was on I studied the trembling print over the fire for the first time. A tall horse-faced English aristocrat, in a captain's uniform, strode towards a mansion. On the steps, a wasp-waisted beauty, with a long skirt and a plastic face awaited him, beside her two little Harry Whartons with shining eyes watched their 'Pater' with his arm in a sling, fearlessly crossing the Axminster lawn. Underneath, it read 'For England Home And Beauty'.

'And Ireland,' I thought fervently, 'you're not the only one who is rearing them yet!'

Dogberry looked at me with affection as the guns grew silent. 'ee, lad,' he said warmly. 'I saw thee lukin' at picture. That's a grand picture, lad, a right good 'un! Tha'll not 'ave the like 'o that in Ahrland.'

'No,' I said civilly. 'We have not.'

'A grand lad, 'e was!'

'Who?' I said in surprise. 'HIM?'

'Nay . . . nay, lad, but 'e were like 'im, were ower captain. Got 'is lot in Battle of Somme. Shot through lungs.' He took out an old Bruno tobacco tin, opened it, took out some papers, and started to roll a smoke. The little kitten, who had been hiding in terror, crept back and started dry cleaning its other glove. Dogberry laughed wheezily. 'ee lad,' he chuckled, 'we 'ad sum times, did me an' t'Captain an' t'lads.'

He lit his fag, drew on it, and started to choke and turn purple again. Across the fire his wife jigged in time to his coughing.

'You should stop smoking, Jim,' I said kindly, when the convulsion was over.

'Aye, lad, ah suppose ah shud, on'y cumfort we 'ad in trenches though . . . Captain smoked Turkish, 'e did . . . . Aye, me an' t'Captain an' t'lads . . . merry 'ell we gave 'em that night!' He was back on track again.

'Captain 'ad rum. Bought it hisself, ower 'is pocket for lads, 'e were like that were Captain. We were all suppin' up while barrage were on, an' when guns stopped Captain took last swig from bottle . . . . "Quiet now, lads," 'e whispered. "Folly me!" An' ower top 'e went an' us after 'im, eeee,' he said, his voice tailing off, gazing down the trenches of the years.

And I had a sudden dreadful vision of Dogberry, past his best, swallowing rum among the shivering young Kens, peering into the dark and the muck, and the sheer bloody lunacy that was Flanders, for England Home And Beauty!

'Took three trenches that night, we did, wi' 'and grenades an' cold steel . . . old Jerry don't like cold steel, but 'e were too foxy for uz that night, 'ad 'ole company lined up be'ind, an' that were the end for uz.'

'How many of you got back?'

'Me . . . an' Captain.'

'I thought the captain was shot?'

'So 'e were lad, but not that bad. It were cold as killed 'im.' He looked at his swollen feet, relaxed now, out of the crippling boots, and sighed.

'Me an' Captain got out, lay in shell 'ole all night, an' next mornin' 'e were dead an' these . . .' He raised a foot . . . 'were frost bit. Been playin' me up ever since.'

I had gone to bed then, and Dogberry to work, and now, chilled to the bone, the whistle blew.

'Seems to be an interestin' place, your Digs,' commented Mick, as we left the site together. 'Any chance of me movin' in? These huts are terrible . . . some of the fuckers'd make you feel ashamed to be Irish . . . . Will you ask the oul' wan for me?'

'I will, Mick,' I said delighted. 'You'd be great company for me.' Overhead, the sullen clouds, loaded with snow, were bringing an early night, a good night, I hoped, with no Jerry upstairs, and twelve hours respite from the cold.

'Good night, Mick, I won't forget.'

'Good night, Lar.'

'The light was off as I let myself into number 22, and Mrs Barnes was sitting in front of a fire that would roast a Bush Baptist. The place was clean and shining. A starched white tablecloth covered the cheap table.

'Took us by surprise yestiday,' she said. I smiled. Around her shoulders was a beautiful lace shawl, and her silver hair and luminous eyes were lovely in the firelight.

'Where's Dog . . . Mr Barnes?' I asked.

'Wun two quid on 'orses,' she replied. 'Said as we'd sup ale tonight, 'e's taken a fancy to thee, lad.'

'You're looking very glamorous tonight, Mrs Barnes,' I

said, slipping her the old Blarney, 'and I'll go halves with the ale.'

'No, tha'll not go 'alves, 'is treat, 'e wuddn't like that.' She smiled, delighted.

''e wuddn't like that last remark either! eeeee, 'im catch me in't dark wi' 'andsome young fella like you . . . switch on light, lad.' I did so.

'Why,' I said joking. 'Is he a terror?'

''e is, lad, though never wi' me. Best 'usband in world. But you doan't know 'im, 'e never finished story of 'im an' Captain last night! 'e wun Victoria Cross!'

'Who, the captain?'

'No . . . Jim!'

'The Victoria Cross!'

'Aye, Jim carried Captain ower No Mans Land an' 'id in shell 'ole. Covered Captain all night wi' his greatcoat, 'e did. Snipers 'ad 'em pinned down. Then, at dawn, when Captain died, Jim came out of shell 'ole screamin', an' charged Jerries on 'is own . . . . Killed sixteen of 'em wi' 'and grenades an' bayonet, single'anded, an' ower lads 'eard 'im screamin' an' cum over to 'elp. Jim were cut to bits, an' gassed a bit, an' 'is feet were frost bit, an' that were end of War for 'im. 'e's never told me anythin'. It were Ted Earls told me, after.'

'And that was when you married him?'

'Aye, in t'hospital. 'e were 'ome first, an' I'd made promise.' I caught the glimpse of tears in her eyes and looked away.

'On'y man,' she said softly to herself, 'I ever loved, were Ted Earls.'

Dogberry came in then, with a glow on, the pockets of his overcoat bulging with bottles, a bag under his arm with more in that, and the sweet smell of Jamaican rum off his breath. 'eeee,' he said, 'I'm right glad t'see thee, lad,' and shook hands again. Mrs Barnes nodded significantly.

'Rum!' she said. 'Dinner's near ready.' While she was looking after it, Dogberry produced the evening paper and rustled it importantly, put on a pair of Woolworth's wire-rimmed spectacles with one glass cracked, and sat down at the table. Over his shoulder I could see that things were going badly for England. Everywhere they were in full retreat, the Japs pursuing them down the Malay Peninsula, Singapore itself under threat, though its fall unthinkable. Britain's Allies in adversity, the Russians, had taken a terrible mauling with 300,000 prisoners taken at Minsk in July, 650,000 more taken at Viazma in October, and the Germans stood before the gates of Moscow. The only tiny gleam of hope that day was that the siege of Tobruk had been lifted. The blackest news was the sinking of two of Britain's greatest warships off Malaya, the *Repulse* and the *Prince of Wales*. Some young reporter with stars in his eyes had written a mighty banner headline across this local paper. 'Japanese Octopus Spreads Tenticles Over Far East'. Mrs Barnes sat down, and I could see that this was part of a well-established ritual.

'Read news before dinner, lad,' she said. 'Jim's a scholar,' she added proudly, ''e can read.'

'Ah can that,' said Dogberry.

''ow's war, Jim?'

'Bad, lass, right bad. Lost two battleships, we 'ave, an' Japs are spreadin' testicles ower Far East! Our generals, lass,' he added seriously, 'are makin' right balls of war, but doan't worry, in't end we'll get 'em!'

'Well,' I said to comfort him, 'with America fighting the Japs now, and about to declare war on the Axis, you stand a chance.'

'We'll get 'em anyroad,' he said, and put the paper from him, locking the black news out of his mind. 'Doan't really need bluddy Yanks, but they'll cum in 'andy, ah suppose. Did in t' last war, at end!'

And here, I thought, lies the greatness of Britain. They were too bloody stupid to know when all was lost! They wouldn't know the truth if it jumped up and bit them on the leg! And they had the devil's own luck, for three days before the Japs had blown the US Navy to hell at Pearl

125

Harbour. It was only a matter of hours, I figured, before America declared war in Europe, and, in fact, they did the next day.

But now Mrs Barnes stood up to serve dinner and slipped off the lace shawl.

'That's Limerick lace,' I ventured.

'Aye,' she said. 'It were grandmother's, ah got it from muther. She 'ad t'run from famine in Ireland. Died when ah was on'y five, she were always right poorly.'

'Then you're Irish?' Dogberry chuckled. 'Aye lad,' he said proudly, 'married a Colleen I did. We're 'alf Irish in this 'ouse!'

After dinner we sat around the fire and supped ale, and I whipped around to the pub when I went out the back, for this house had a flush toilet. It was only in the old centre city that the Muck Cart operated. I came back with half a bottle of black market rum, lunatic soup, to liven things up a bit. It did. Soon I was singing, 'She walked through the Fair,' Mrs Barnes sang 'Danny Boy,' in a high quivering voice, and Dogberry, transported with delight, volunteered to give us 'his comic number'. On the second time around I knew the chorus and we bawled it together . . .

> *We packed up an' away we went,*
> *It's cheaper to move than pay the rent,*
> *All we left for the Grow–ser was 'alf a pound of starch,*
> *An' Sataday mornin' without warnin'*
> *We were on the march,*
> *Were on the march, were on the march,*
> *Were on the . . . .*

We were abruptly silenced as the guns opened up with a roar. There had been no warning from the sirens on this snowy night. Overhead, the German bombers flew a familiar course, engines labouring with another load for Liverpool. Dogberry heard it first, the misfired conk-conk-conk of a plane in trouble. He flung himself on the floor.

'Down,' he roared, ''e's in trouble, 'e'll drop bluddy lot!'

And then it came, the blood freezing sound of bombs whistling through the night, louder . . . louder, the explosions, close at hand, while the front door blew in, and the lights went out, and, in the tingling silence that followed, the desolate sound of falling glass and the wailing of children.

'Are th' all right, Jim?' came Mrs Barnes's voice from the dark.

'Ay, lass, are thee?'

'Ay, is Pad all right?'

'Okay, okay,' I said from under the table. Dogberry struck a match.

'We'll 'ave lights on again in no time,' he said. 'Take more than bluddy old 'itler t'put lights out in Warrington.'

Three minutes later the light was back on again. I emerged from under the table and surveyed the damage. All the front windows had blown in and, but for Dogberry's advice to hit the deck, we would all have been badly gashed, perhaps killed by flying glass. Several people in Uniform Terrace died that night from just that, and scores were badly scarred. The ambulances started to arrive then, checking for casualties, and taking the injured to hospital. Dogberry, swearing softly, scrutinised the print over the mantelpiece, and picked up a splinter of glass from the plastic beauty's bodice. He sighed his relief. There was no more damage. He found a hammer and tacks in the kitchen press, and grinned.

'Good job ah sole me own boots,' he said. All the bombs had landed in a waste lot, about four hundred yards from the terrace, and only superficial damage had been done to the houses. Together we jammed the front door back into position and I started to tack newspapers over the holes in the windows. Mrs Barnes swept up, Dogberry piled coal on the fire until the room started to grow warm again, and then it was time for him to go to work. With the bombs the snow had really settled in, great heavy feathers already covering the scars in the waste lot.

He sat down, grunting, easing off his slippers, and painfully forcing his feet into the boots with the knife slashes. Mrs Barnes was strangely quiet as she handed him his sandwiches.

Dogberry kissed her, and this time she did not shrug him off. 'See thee in t' mornin', lass,' he said fondly. 'Goodnight, lad, luke after Missus for me.' He left by the back door.

While tacking up the last of the paper I watched the old man come out from the side of the house, braving into the bitterness of a Lancashire winter, in the big boots with the slits for his ruined feet, his wheezy goodbye from his busted old World War One chest, and then I had another look at the gallant hero over the fire, with his gallant wound, and confident stride across the Axminster lawn, and Lord Jesus, I swore to myself, England . . . Home . . . and Beauty!

I watched Dogberry wave from the gate, shoulders already white, and march off into the night with hope in his heart and a great confidence in England. I envied him, for I was lost!

I envied his courage and the courage of his fallen friends in Flanders. I envied his tawdry icon over the fire. I envied the gallant hero and his plastic beauty, I envied their two little Harry Whartons, grown up now, probably chasing the Germans back over the Channel, right this minute.

I envied everything and everybody, for they had come to terms with life as it was, and little neutral me . . . I had not!

The following morning Uniform Terrace presented a doleful spectacle. Most of the glass had been painted black against the Luftwaffe, and now, houses such as the Barnes's had tacked up newspapers, nailed blankets over the gaping windows, stuffed cloths in minor holes, and many of the front doors lay half covered with snow on the small lawns. It was like a brand new slum.

On the job it was all go. The firm had turned over to First Aid Blitz Repairs, and were mad for glaziers, carpenters being in great supply. Mick Gilbey, my socialist mate on the job, volunteered at once for the glazing, I could do a bit of it too, and together we made our way back to Uniform

Terrace. Naturally, we started at number 22. Old Mrs Barnes was delighted and kept us supplied with tea all day. Mick cleared off the kitchen table, got a couple of blankets from Mrs Barnes, and, when the glass arrived in great crates, was ready to begin cutting it. It came with a glass cutter, putty knives and tacks, and I was flabbergasted at the precision of the operation, for our site was notorious for foul-ups. The explanation lay in the fact that the ARP was in control and had long prepared for such an eventuality. Air Raid Precautions in Britain were well organised.

All along the Terrace, men were climbing ladders, hacking out old putty, taking measurements, and calling them down to the glass cutters, who did their best on kitchen tables. Mick and I were good at cutting and did most of it for the others, so we had it cushy, working inside in front of a roaring fire.

Before eleven o'clock the Barnes's house had all its glass, held in with tacks. It was secure enough for the present, squeezed into place, the final puttying-up could be left until later. The thing was to get the glass back into the freezing homes. We worked with a will, for a bitter Lancashire winter was setting in to stay. Mick made it his business to make a big hit with old Mrs Barnes, and, before the dark came and stopped us working, he had coaxed her into taking him as a boarder. I was delighted.

'Ah suppose I'll 'ave to,' she said. 'You luke right poorly, lad. Do they feed you proper in't huts?'

Mick could eat like a cormorant, but well I knew what his trouble was and why he 'luked so poorly'. That morning, before we started on the glazing, I had remarked to him on how bad he looked.

'It's the wet dreams, Lar,' he said. 'Jaysus, if I don't marry Rose Mary soon I'll go into TB. Why? Don't you get them?'

'Yes.'

'How often?'

'Maybe once a week . . . if I'm lucky!' Well I knew what one of them could do to a man. They left him drained, tired before the day started, and still not satisfied. It was

129

outraged nature taking its revenge for a life of enforced celibacy, a completely unnatural state for a healthy male.

'Christ,' said poor Mick, 'I'd throw up me hands an' thank God if I only had one a week. I'm goin' out of it, dreamin' about Rose Mary every night an' comin' off in me sleep.' He showed me her photograph afterwards, and God knows I could not blame him for wanting her. She was a nurse in the Meath Hospital and in the photo, taken with Mick, she came through with all her charms. She had everything in the right places, she was a beauty, womanhood personified, and more than ripe at twenty-five for love. But, of course, in the Irish Free State she remained a virgin, and would until Mick married her. He would remain a virgin too, I found out. Both were indoctrinated by the Church, and communist though he considered himself, had too much respect for his sweetheart to offer her love without marriage. The eleventh commandment reigned supreme: 'Thou shalt not dip thy wick without a jockey's licence!'

'There's one way to stop the wet dreams, Mick, the only sure way. Get yourself a woman!'

'I couldn't do that. Could you?'

'Any chance I get Mick, though they're not many.'

'Then you've had a woman?'

'Three so far. None now . . . unfortunately . . . though I had the day before yesterday, I mean the night. In fact, I had three . . . .'

'Jesus,' said poor Mick, 'if only I had your pluck . . . .'

'Look, Mick, when are you getting married?'

'We won't have enough saved until next year. We're gettin' married at Easter.'

'Well, Mick, an' don't misunderstand me, I mean no disrespect, but why don't you take home a few French Letters at Christmas. That's only a couple of weeks away.' Mick stared at me blankly, as if he could not believe his ears.

'I'm going to pretend I didn't hear that, Lar,' he said quietly. 'Only I know you meant well, I'd hit you now.'

'Sorry Mick. Forget I spoke.'

'I will, Lar. We'll be none the worse friends for that.'

'Anyway, Mick, I think I can help you. There's an old trick I learned in the Irish Army. You get a spool for holding thread, double a piece of string through it, and tie it in the middle of your back. I do it sometimes when things get tough.'

Mick was intrigued. 'How does that stop it?'

'Well Mick, you always have a wet dream lying on your back. Now, with the spool in the middle of your spine you feel pain in your sleep, and turn on your side. It doesn't always work, but it cuts it down to hell.'

'Jaysus,' said Mick, 'I'll try that tonight. I have a spool of thread in the hut.'

Mick moved into number 22 that night, and old Mrs Barnes was again in the firelight with her lace shawl and silver hair shining, and her eyes, the eyes of a gentle tigress, reflecting the flames. She stopped Gilbey in his tracks, and almost purred with delight when he let loose a flood of Blarney. She was not too old, and quite vain enough to lap up the compliments. I had to warn Mick.

'Don't give her the Blarney when his nibs is around. He's made about her, Mick.'

'At her age?' said Mick.

'Well, won't you be mad about Rose Mary . . . at her age?'

Gilbey grinned. 'Probably,' he said, 'twice as mad.' It was 11 December, the day Germany and Italy declared war on the USA, who promptly took reciprocal action. England's bacon was saved again, their long and courageous stand alone brought to an end. Although the United States had been doing everything short of warfare to help them, nevertheless, nothing except total war by their bigger ally would save them.

'You're going home for Christmas, Mick?'

'Yes, thanks be to God. I'll see Dublin an' Rose Mary again. Why don't you come too?'

'I'm only on indefinite leave from the Army. I don't think I'm supposed to be over here. I might be picked up.'

131

'But you haven't been recalled, have you?'

'No, an' I don't think I ever will be. The threat to Eire was over before I got out on leave. I would have stayed if there had been any chance of a scrap, but my sweet Jesus, Mick, there's a big Culchie sergeant waiting there for me, and he'll do for me if ever I cross an Irish barracks' square again.'

'Chance it,' said Mick. 'You can always make a run for it across the Border, if the worst comes to the worst.'

'No, I wouldn't do that, I couldn't. That would mean joining the British Army, and, with my father a Shinner, I need never show my face at home again. I'll think about it, going home, I mean.'

I thought about it for four or five days, and, on 16 December, made up my mind to go home, for as long as the money lasted. That was the day the Japanese invaded Borneo, a day I was never to forget, for I wrote to Mam that night, told her I would see her soon, and forgot to post it. Several times I looked for it, but in the end decided I must have posted it, for I always carried postage stamps. In the rising excitement of going home, I forgot the whole matter. Everywhere the British and American forces were in full retreat, and Mick and I left for home on 23 December, the day that Wake Island fell to the all-conquering Japanese hordes.

The only gleam of hope left was in Russia, where at last the mighty Nazi war machine had ground to a halt before the gates of Moscow, and was giving ground before the Russian counter assault. Stalin was in the front lines, commanding every commander. His word was absolute, his grasp of every aspect of the war, masterly. Brute as he was, it took a brute to defeat a brute, and Hitler, who had taken complete command of the German forces four days before, would prove no match for the murderous Russian. It would take time and a few more million lives, but nobody could be certain then of the final outcome.

The Mail Boat had been attacked a couple of times, and old Mrs Barnes was worried for us, but go we would. Mick, I think, would have swum the Irish Sea, and our hearts rejoiced when we reached Holyhead to see the battered old tub that had taken us here, waiting to take us home.

It was a night-time sailing, but here in Wales there was little sign of the bitter winter we had left behind us in Lancashire. Naturally it was cold, being winter, but the terrible Siberian frost and snow were gone, and I knew it would be even milder on my side of the Irish sea. We could look forward to a soft, almost spring-like Christmas in Ireland. Already Gilbey was transformed. He stood six feet tall, but he seemed to — my mind searched for a word and came up with an old-fashioned one — he seemed to burgeon, to expand, the drawn face had disappeared, and he was a handsome figure of a Dubliner, taller than most.

We were quietly waiting in queue to board the ship when I spotted the little weasel the big 'Prod' had thrown through the window on my first day in England, and I looked away quickly as his eyes swept the queue. His face carried a barely healed scar under the right eye, probably put there by the iron fist of Trevor Baird. For the first time in weeks I wondered anew what had happened to him, after the coppers stopped kicking him. I kept my eyes meekly fixed on the ground. This little bastard was spoiling for trouble, I could almost smell it, and, when it came, my heart nearly stopped.

'You there,' snarled the Ferret. 'Yes you, Paddy . . . that's right, you beside the tall one . . . step aside.'

'Yes, sir,' I said, smartly stepping out of the queue and standing respectfully before him.

'Over to the office, Paddy.'

I gave Mick a despairing glance, and followed the vicious little fucker. I knew better than to revolt, or show any sign of resentment, but, on the other hand, I would never grovel. Inside the office I was made to open my suitcase, and the small rodent went through my possessions one by one. The case was empty, my clothes lay thrown on the floor, I felt like killing the little bastard. At the same time I was mortally afraid of him, for I felt here a viciousness that

133

even exceeded the hatred of the Black and Tan Bateman, a ferocity that would cheerfully skin me alive and use my hide for lampshades.

'Ah,' he said triumphantly, as he spotted Mam's letter at the bottom of the case, 'what have we here?'

He opened the letter, read it, and called a policeman.

'Take this,' he said, indicating me, 'outside to the shed, and bring back his clothes.'

And so, five minutes later I found myself standing stark naked in a small corrugated iron hut, bolted in, shivering with cold, trembling with anger. But there was a terrible dread behind the anger. One wrong move and I would see the inside of an English jail. I was left there for half an hour before the policeman brought back my clothes again. I was blue with cold and my teeth were chattering uncontrollably. It was certain the Ferret had kept me there longer than was necessary.

Right away he started to throw questions at me. What was the code of the letter? Why was it not posted in the ordinary way? Why was I carrying it at the bottom of my suitcase when it should have gone through His Majesty's censorship? Did I have contact with any Germans resident in Eire? What did I mean by trying to sneak the letter through to Dublin?

'I wrote at the last minute to tell Mam I would be home. I forgot to post it. That's all there is to it, sir . . . .' Holy suffering Jesus, fancy calling this little Sassenach bastard 'sir', but there were plenty of better men than me who had to know when discretion was the better part of valour. In the end he reluctantly released me, with a venomous warning not to make the same mistake again.

'No, sir . . . Thank you, sir, I won't.'

'Get out,' he snarled. 'The boat for Paddy Land is about to sail. We don't want your type hanging around Holyhead.'

'Thank you, sir.'

There was no way this swine was going to provke this Irishman, yet something about his speech, some small tiny thing had come to my notice. He spoke well, very clear

English, almost accentless, yet was it my imagination, or somewhere, however faint, did I catch a trace of Dublin? Surely not! Yet the most bigoted Orangeman ever to rule in the six lost counties had been a Dublin man, the grandson of an itinerant peddler, Signor Carsoni . . . drop the 'I' . . . and Spaghetti Junction took on a very British sound. Carson, who stood for King and Country, the Union Jack, the H'empire on which the sun never set, Carson, the man who destroyed another Dubliner far more gifted than he would ever be, one Oscar Wilde, Carson, who had presided over the division of Ireland, and who left his native land with a legacy of hatred and bigotry that might take a thousand years to assuage. Signor Carsoni had been a 'Dub' all right. Was this ferret faced little swine another?

He was! Mick told me all about him on the boat.

'He's a bastard,' Mick said conclusively, 'an' his mother handed him over to the Prods when he was a baby. It was well known he was a bastard, an' of course, the Irish in his times were not exactly noted for their Christian attitude to children born out of wedlock . . . in fact, we're still one of the most unchristian countries in the world as regards that . . . an' not alone was your man a bastard, but he was a Prod as well. Ireland gave him a rough time.'

'How do you come to know all about him?'

'From the Da, he went to school just down the road from your man. The Da told me that they used to jeer the Prods, with their little pill-box hats . . . the Boys Brigade, he said it was. They had Dublin rhymes to jeer them with.

'Proddy Waddy on the wall, a half a loaf would feed yiz all?' I suggested.

Mick grinned. 'I see you know a bit about it too.'

'Yes, it was tried a couple of times during my childhood, but that stuff went out with my generation. We wouldn't join it, so it died out. That day is finished, I hope.' That was long ago, God love me, and I knew only hope then.

Mick, gazing over the blackness that was the Irish Sea, sighed gustily. 'Jaysus,' he swore impatiently, 'will we never get going?'

'What was that little bastard's name?'

'Sweeney . . . Toddy Sweeney, the Da called him.' The old steamer gave a couple of mournful hoots, the ropes were cast off, and we began to move out. It was all done by flashlight, as little light as possible, and we were leaving the pier, stealing into the sea like a thief in the night. Then suddenly I spotted the little rat who had given me such a going over. It was the briefest of flashes, yet still I spotted him. There was no way he could see me, and, standing back from the rail, I roared, 'SWEENEY . . . TODDDEEEE . . . SWEEENNNEEEY. THE BASTARD FROM DUBLIN.'

'Well, Jesus Christ,' Gilbey got out. 'But you're a right little whore, too.'

'Fuck him, he asked for it. He got it.'

'Under the belt, all the same.'

'Yes, well under the belt. That's the only language that bastard will ever understand.'

'Even so,' said Mick. 'A bit dirty.'

'Okay, okay, I'm sorry I did that, but that little ferret nearly got one of our gang killed coming over here, and he's just roughed me up, and Christ knows how many in between. To hell with him, he asked for it, the Quisling bastard. Gilbey grinned, and, in the dark, his teeth flashed.

'To hell with him and you,' he said happily. 'It's Rose Mary and Dublin for me.'

'And it's mortal sins for me if I get the chance. I've three dozen "Frenchers" with me.'

'Christ,' said Mick, 'I don't know where you get the nerve from. I'd never be able to walk into a chemist's and ask a girl for those things.'

'Nothing to it,' I lied brazenly.

'Where have you got them?'

'In my shoes, straight from Boots, the chemists!'

I did not tell him that I had bought them from a soldier in a pub, after I had bought him a pint. We had got talking, and he was flabbergasted when I told him that French Letters were a crime where I came from! We had met by arrangement the following night. He had sold me three dozen, army issue. But I was not going to tell Gilbey that! I wanted to come across as a tough guy who had shaken off the shackles of the Catholic Church. The truth was that that would take many more years, if ever!

We had arsed out in the dark somehow, into the open sea, and now the old tub picked up a bit of speed and headed for Ireland. There was no flicker of light to tell that we were leaving a country of forty-five million people, no moon shone to betray the land, the sea was as smooth as silk, no more ruffled than an English duck pond. But I knew and the crew knew better, far better, the way this tempestuous prima donna could change her moods, how suddenly she could arise from her present sulking and become a raging fury, a savage bitch of a thing, a raddled old whore with a misspent past who wanted to destroy all around her!

Gilbey went below to try and find a place to rest, perhaps sleep, and I wandered to the stern, savouring the quiet night. Overhead the clouds had gone, a little sliver of a moon lay on its back and the sky was bright with a million stars. It was as mild as spring, out here at sea, and it was then that I saw we were towing a large balloon, which must have slowed the old tub nearly to stopping point in heavy seas. It's purpose was obvious, of course. The Mail boat had suffered one machine gun attack, and this was an attempt to reassure the passengers. It did not reassure me, for if I was a German pilot and wanted to attack the ship, what was to prevent me shooting this bloody big bag of gas full of holes, and then machinegunning the bejaysus out of the ship? Nothing!

I went down, found a small space under the stairs, and, sitting on top of my suitcase, nodded off to sleep. It had been a long day, and anyway I had learned the trick of sleeping at will in the Irish Army. I had often slept standing up, on night guard, so this present position was no trouble at all. Three hours later I woke up, fresh as a daisy, and went on deck again. It was still dark, though the stars were fading, and on the breeze came the acrid smell of turf.

Here, far out to sea, the peat fires of Dublin announced that I was nearly there. Presently Mick joined me, and a few lights along the Wicklow coast broke the darkness, with much more as Bray slid past, and then we were in Dublin Bay, and the whole sky was lit up with the lights of home. My heart danced for joy. I glanced up at Mick, and saw that he was quietly weeping, tears silently streaming down his good-looking face.

And then it was Dún Laoghaire, Customs, me of course with nothing to hide except a pound of tea for Mam and a pile of condoms for me, with great hopes of going through the lot while in Ireland. At twenty-two you can rave anywhere, you do not have to wait for a fever, it is quite natural. You can rave anywhere at twenty-two. I was home.

7   Dublin

At Westland Row Mick and I shook hands and parted. He could not get away fast enough to get to the Meath Hospital and Rose Mary, who would be coming off night duty.

'Happy Christmas, Lar,' he roared, above the noise of the crowd. 'See you in Warrington.' And then he had gone, running, leaving me grinning and wishful behind. I had no Rose Mary waiting for me, and no wish to get married, still though . . . .

'Carry your suitcase, Misther?' I glanced down to see a small under-sized Dublin kid, scantily dressed against the winter cold, elbows coming through the sleeves of the dirty old gansey he wore, scuffed boots, down at heel, a pale eager face looking up at me, and I was shocked. All my life kids like this had hung around railway stations, but only now had I noticed their poverty.

I had come from a country at war, where everything was rationed, including clothes, but in all the places I had been had never seen anything like this. For the first time I was shocked into the reality of an arse-out-of-the-trousers Irish Free State. This kid needed a feed, not work, but he was prepared to work for a feed. And there was not enough of him to life the suitcase. I was reaching into my pocket for a couple of shillings to get rid of him, when half a dozen others descended on me.

'Carry yer case Misther . . . aw, Misther, looka me . . . .'
'Misther, Misther, I'll do it for a bob . . . .' Hastily I

handed the case to the first kid, and waved the others away.

'You can give me a hand with it,' I told him, to save his pride, and together we left the station, with both of us holding the handle. Outside I paid him off, gave him five bob, and told him to go and get himself some breakfast.

'Tanks, Misther,' he grinned. 'But there'll be another train at ten. Me mother 'ill be waitin' for the few bob . . . .'

'Have you no father?'

'No . . . he went t'England and never cem' back.' He shot off then, pale-faced, wiry, under-sized, the very spirit of the city that had spawned him. 'Poor little bastard,' I said to myself and made tracks for D'Olier Street. At College Green I went to the lavatory beneath the island in the centre of the road, put a penny in the slot, and, in the privacy of the toilet, took the condoms from my shoes and carefully placed them in my inside jacket pocket. Then it was on to the first number 50 bus for Crumlin. To hell with the 77, I had no time to wait for that, this bus would leave me at Crumlin crossroads, where the road split in two, one going to Crumlin village, the other to the Halfway House and Walkinstown. It was only half a mile, I was travelling light, I was twenty-two, it was nothing.

Half an hour later I stood on Walkinstown Road. The sun broke through the morning mist and there was our splendid house, silhouetted against the back drop of my beloved Dublin mountains. Nothing had changed. All about me were the green fields I had often dreamed about. I should have been full of joy, charged the last hundred yards to our house, invaded it like a burst of sunshine, yet I stood there, hesitant. The hurly burly of war-torn England was behind me, I felt strangely out of place, like a survivor of a storm, thrown up on a deserted beach, grateful to be there, yet bewildered by the sudden calm about me. Nothing here had altered, the tempo of life was slow, the noise of the outside world muted, and I knew my stay at home would be a short one. I had been shooting the rapids of life, too much had happened too quickly, and now I discovered that the placid lake I found myself upon would no longer do. I wanted to go back and shoot the rapids again.

I stood there until one of my sisters spotted me from an upstairs window, and then the whole family were surging through the front door, and I was running forward to meet them. The prodigal son had come home!

Mam wept a little and told me off in no uncertain fashion for running away without even saying goodbye. But a couple of kisses and hugs, plus a whole pound of tea, soon had her smiling. Breakfast was a noisy affair, I dined on sausages and eggs, the like of which I had not tasted for months. After breakfast, Mam and I had a long talk, which she cut short by making me go to bed. 'Now,' she said. My protestations fell on deaf ears . . . .

'I know you, young man,' she told me. 'You'll be off around Dublin all day — Christmas Eve, meeting your gang in the Oval lounge, and not coming back here until the small hours . . . . You're lookin' a bit peaky . . . bed for you.'

Indeed, I slept for hours, but was out of the house and in Abbey Street before four o'clock, on a lovely dusky mild day. Dublin, my heart's blood, was all around me, and old Nelson looked down on the sparkling city, blazing with light, crowded, noisy, lousy with English money as never before. Even when the Brits had ruled it there had never been so much of their money in Irish hands, and if Nelson wanted to preserve his integrity he would have to turn a blind eye on many things that were happening below.

Black market tea was selling at a pound for a pound, not quality brands by any means, but tea anyway, and the dealers in Moore Street were flogging it goodo from under their stalls. Little sold that did not contain some additive, like dried tea that had been brewed before, or dried hawthorn leaves, fragmented and mixed in with the rest. You could tell the hawthorn's presence in tea by the faintly aromatic flavour, but, in a nation of tea addicts, nobody cared. The average wage in Ireland for a tradesman was five pounds for a forty-four hour week, a pound note was one-fifth of their total income, and yet the Dublin women would

141

save up, neglect other things, in order to buy tea. The black market flourished as never before.

Bicycle tubes, car tyres and tubes, petrol, all smuggled from the Northern six counties were openly on sale in the little alleys off Moore Street, where a vigilante system operated better than any before or since. No copper came into Moore Street unnoticed. And, in the laughing crowds of Christmas shoppers, the disciples of Fagin, the pick-pockets, had a field day, unless caught in the act. It was difficult to believe here, right in the heart of Dublin, among the free spending crowds, that, only a few hundred yards away, desperate poverty reigned over all. Little boys, like the one who had gamely tried to carry my suitcase grew up, under-nourished, under-sized. Yet those who survived would be among the toughest of the tough. Here, nature's immutable law operated as it had done since the beginning of time. Only the fittest survived.

I had more than an hour to spend before I would meet the gang in the Oval Lounge, that is, if any of the gang remained. The War had scattered us to the four winds, and it was in rather a pensive mood that I entered the Gresham. It was packed, well-heeled business men and black marketeers were spending money like drunken sailors. The Mary Magdalenes of Dublin had put on their war paint early today, I recognised several of them who hung around Dublin pubs and hotels, and Americans and Canadians, no doubt on leave, in their civilian clothes, were vying for the attention of the prostitutes.

I passed one I knew to speak to casually, she was a rip-roaring Communist, and revered Stalin above all others, but well I knew that, in the dawn of Christmas Day, she would, drunk or not, be on her knees in some chapel, lighting a candle after Mass to God's son, He who had said, 'Let him who is without sin amongst you, cast the first stone'.

'Up Stalin' I whispered, as she went by, and she gave me a brief flash of a smile before turning to her prey. Later, on her way back to the 'ladies' she paused briefly to speak.

'You used to drink in McDaids,' she said. 'You're starting to look like a man, at last.'

'Thank God for that! Will you have a drink?'

'No . . . can't you see I have a prospect? An American colonel, no less, or so he says.'

'Happy Christmas to you, Stalin,' I said as she moved away. 'Make it a happy one. Take him for all you can get.'

'No better woman,' she smiled. 'Happy Christmas to you too.' And then she had gone to her American goldmine, with her cultivated speech and delightful brogue. She was a good-looker too, and the Yank would think he had just been lucky enough to meet an Irish lady, no doubt he would have to overcome her shy Colleen ways this night, with loads of dollars, and the Yankee key to all female hearts, 'Gee, I'll take you back to the States, Honey'. Boys Oh Boys, was he due for a surprise!

I finished my bottle of stout, and wandered out into O'Connell Street, speculating, not for the first time, on how Lady Stalin had come to this pass. Her speech bespoke an education in one of Ireland's more exclusive convents. Probably the daughter of a strong farmer, gone astray, a few drinks, a young man, a night of bliss, perhaps only an hour of bliss, and finding herself pregnant. Then the run for the Big Smoke, Dublin, to escape the wrath of parents, the Church, and a scandalised parish! There were thousands like her in London. Someone had told me that she kept her illegitimate daughter in an exclusive convent for young ladies, that she never went to see her, that some imaginary uncle in England paid her fees, and that the girl thought herself an orphan.

And I breathed a little sacrilegious prayer for Lady Stalin, that her purse might be heavy before dawn, and her American colonel's that much lighter. There was plenty more money where he came from and he had never gone to the Front in a better cause!

Dublin was a tight city then, a manageable city, with its compressed core of theatres, picture houses and dance halls. In a daze of happiness I wandered around, under the blaze of signs and lights and coloured bulbs that stretched across Henry Street and Moore Street, under which Dublin's dealers sold their wares. Their strident voices were all around me. 'Tuppence a poun' th'onions . . . thruppence each the cauliflowers.' A whole generation of Irish kids were growing up without ever seeing an orange or banana or even a grape. But there was little else missing.

The shops bulged with all those items that were rationed in England, the pork shops sold miles of sausages, tons of black and white pudding, whole herds of pigs arses, called ham, under the blazing light of this Christmas Eve in Dublin. I was happy. I, who had so lately been groping my way in the eternal dark days and pitch black nights, in a country with its back to the wall. It had been a bit too much for me. It was the light, the blessed sparkling light that brought this laughing crowd shopping! I was like a night owl that had suddenly been pitched into tropical sunlight, and, blinking happily, I sauntered along the street.

And then I stopped dead in my tracks, frozen to the pavement by the terrible sight before me, for, hanging outside a butcher's shop by their feet, was a row of turkeys, their blood-congested heads almost at eye level, blue black, the colour Ken's face had been when I had come upon him. I stifled a scream, and suddenly started running, out of my beloved Moore Street, dodging swiftly everything that stood in my path. across Henry Street and down the Arcade. When I stopped I was panting, shaking, trembling so badly that I thought I would collapse.

Facing me was the Capitol theatre, and, almost at its front steps, the lights of the Princess Bar beckoned. There was already a queue outside the theatre, and you always had to cross this from where I stood, which was no bother.

'Excuse me, would you mind . . .?'

'Not at all, not at all, son, come through'. And then I was in the Princess Bar and somehow was holding a double Irish whiskey in shaking hands, sipping it, and making my way to the back, where I could lean against the wall.

The Princess, one of the city's most famous bars, much

patronised by journalists, writers and poets, and, being beside the theatre, quite naturally the performers, stage hands and stars alike. They all drank here. The place was packed as always, for ordinary Dubliners came here to see the famous, or infamous, as the case might be.

It was a long, narrow room, and the bar occupied most of the space. There was little room left to the customers. This night the 'Holly and Ivy drinkers' had crowded the place to bursting point. Slowly, the whiskey warmed and calmed me. I hated the stuff, but was glad of it now. I ordered another, and the Dutch courage it gave me took over, I put Ken and Moore Street firmly out of my mind, the trembling ceased, and once more I was one of the happy throng. Youth had bounced back.

It was at this point that a tall man stumbled in through the swing-doors, carrying, of all things, a six-foot Christmas tree, and wearing the indestructable grin of the happy drunk. The maledictions from the queue, rudely broken outside, came through with him.

'Yeh bloody lookin' eejit . . . .'

'Bloody drunken thick . . . .' The bar had quite suddenly become silent, to enjoy the 'bit a' Gas' . . . .

'Yeh bloody long dip stick,' said an angry woman who was holding the door open. 'Bargin' yer way through people!'

'I assure you, Madam,' said the drunk, in a cultivated voice, 'that I did not notice the queue.'

'No, yer too bloody drunk, that's why. Don't tell me,' she screeched at the bar tenders, 'that yer goin' teh serve any more to that fella.'

'Madam,' said he, holding the tree aloft. 'You go too far. Flattery will get you nowhere with me.'

'Out you,' shouted the manager. The tall intruder completely ignored him, and, holding the pine tree aloft, made his way politely through the packed shop. The shelf that ran along the wall opposite the bar suddenly lost two pints, customers lucky enough to have stools at the counter lost their hats. And forward came the tall one, grinning fatuously, excusing himself, wishing everybody a 'Happy

Christmas, you merry throng', the shelf drinkers hurriedly grabbed their pints, more Trilby hats were swept away, and glorious mayhem reigned in the Princess Bar. This was exactly what I needed, this was what I had come home for, a bit of Celtic madness. My spirits soared. He came to a halt beside me and placed the base of the pine tree on the floor.

'Out,' roared the barmen. The manager was blue in the face with rage. 'Out . . . Yeh won't be served here.'

'What about me bloody pint he's spilt on me?'

'Landlord,' said the tall one grandly. 'Fill the flowing bowl . . . replace the pints that fell to my progress, and give them a 'small one', a Jameson, Powers, whatever they wish. It's on me . . . Happy Christmas, lads,' he roared, and the good-humoured crowd gave him a laughing cheer.

'And a double Jameson for me,' he shouted.

'No drink for you,' said the manager, 'you've had enough.'

'Aw, go on,' said the crowd. 'He's all right . . . Jaysus, it's Christmas, he's harmless.' In the face of this, the manager capitulated, but warned that it would be only 'the one'.

'And a Happy New Year,' roared the tall one beside me, knocking back the double at speed, and swaying slightly with the tree he held in his left hand.

'That fella beside yeh is a famous surgeon,' whispered a man on my other side. 'That fella can get thousands to do an operation.'

'I find that hard to believe.'

'It's true all right. He's a terrible man for the gargle, when he breaks out.' Pushing his way through the crowded bar, a man was determinedly fighting his way to the surgeon, and then he stood before us.

'God bless yeh, Doctor,' he said. 'An' may yeh have many another Happy Christmas. Yeh saved me wife last year. Veronica Murphy was her name. Do you remember her? Do you know her?'

'My dear fellow,' said the medical man jovially, 'I know your wife inside out,' and he gave a great shout of laughter, convulsed by his own wit.

146

'God bless yeh anyway,' said the other, laughing fit to burst.

'Well, gentlemen,' roared the inebriated surgeon. 'I must away . . . I must arise and go now . . . . Gangway,' he roared, and made for the door. Several men held the swing doors wide open to assist his going, the four deep queue slowly moving into the Capitol, as he shouted another Happy Christmas to all and sundry. Then he turned, moved forward, tripped over the butt of the pine tree, and fell like a log into the moving queue. As he was going down I heard him roar ' . . . Timbeeeeeeeer', the swing-doors slammed shut, and he had gone. From outside came a confused babble, but inside we were laughing so much that we could barely hear it. It had been an uproarious few minutes, and now, ready for the gang in the Oval, I made tracks for the door myself.

Outside, I watched the drunken surgeon being helped into a taxi by the man whose wife he had saved. I went over to help. Together we stuffed him in, pine tree and all, for he clung tenaciously to it to the last. By now it looked like something that had been run over by a double-decker bus.

'I'll tell the wife I met yeh,' said my companion.

'Do that,' said the surgeon happily. 'Biggest bloody ulcer I ever saw. Tell Vernoica she has great guts.'

'Are yeh ready?' said the grinning taxi driver.

'Home James,' was the reply. 'And don't spare the black-market petrol.' Together we watched the taxi roar off.

'Will yeh come back an' have a gargle wit' me?' said the man.

'Sorry, I'd like to, but I have an appointment. I'm late now,' I said.

'Okay, son. But that man yeh helped can get thousands for an operation, and he saved Veronica for nuttin' . . . God bless him.' I set off then for the Oval, just around the corner in Abbey Street, went upstairs and looked around. There was no one there. With a sinking heart, I ordered a bottle of stout. The lounge was crowded, but of our gang there was no sign. I sat down at a table and morosely sipped

147

the stout. I had missed being here last year, confined to Barracks, all leave suspended after the bombing of Dún Laoghaire. The bomb had landed in the middle of the road, had torn up the tram tracks, but little more damage had been done. This had been a reprisal for Irish troops shooting up some drunken Allied soldiers who had driven across the Border, armed to the teeth, hoping to meet the 'toy soldiers' of the Irish Free State. They had been challenged twice at checkpoints, and were roaring through the third one, when a burst of machine-gun fire brought them to an abrupt and bloody halt. Some had been taken to hospital, rumour said some had been killed, whatever, the rest ended up in the Curragh Internment Camp, and things had been tense.

Our company, 'Dirty C' were at the ready, transported, lined up, each wearing a bandoleer of fifty 303 bullets, sleeping in our clothes for three nights, ready to go at a moment's notice. I had spent St Stephen's night on guard beside the obelisk on Killiney Hill in a blinding snowstorm. Killiney Castle, where we were stationed, lay below, and I quietly did a perish for Ireland, gazing futilely down on the sea, which was below somewhere. I was supposed to be on the look out for lights at sea, enemy invasion. The German, Japanese or total Allied Forces could have landed below for all that I could see or care. It was this kind of stupidity, endemic in all armies, that I hated most, posting a lone soldier on top of a hill, in a blizzard. And the old 303 Rifle, older than myself, barrel pitted from the sodden trenches of Flanders, was wildly inaccurate. Even I, a dead shot, was lucky to hit the board on the rifle range, much less the bulls-eye.

But where the hell had the gang gone? Surely I would not be left here alone? I wandered over to the window overlooking Abbey Street. From where I was, I could see across O'Connell Street to where the Grand Central picture house blazed with coloured lights, strung around the glass roofed entrance, that totally covered the pavement and threw back a million sparkling diamonds of light. Directly opposite was the place where President Keely had set up his orange box a few years before and held meetings in opposition to the reigning Fianna Fáil party, who were banging their drums, and waving the Tricolour in front of the General Post Office, for nationalism, as the good Dr Johnson remarked, is the last refuge of a scoundrel, and very much in vogue in countries like Mexico and Ireland, where the chief export is people. The population of the infant Irish Free State had dropped to two and three quarter million souls, for, with emigration virtually ended to the United States, the Irish were fleeing to England as never before.

Keely would fix all that. He was quite mad, of course, but then, derisive Dublin had always had a soft spot in its heart for people a 'ha'penny short of a shillin',' and claimed that he was no madder than the people who represented us. He contested every election, and, alongside the posters of Fianna Fáil, and the opposition, Cumann na nGaedheal, came the information that Keely was running for President again. These notices appeared all over the city, scrawled in chalk or paint, and, when prominent politicians were holding a party rally, we young fellows would make sure to be there, for the 'bit of gas'.

Keely, mounted on his orange box, would set up close by, and most times would attract a larger audience. The Civil War that had racked Ireland only a few short years ago was still bitterly remembered, and election meetings could be violent affairs. Keely came along as a welcome relief!

He was a short stocky man with a mane of snow-white hair that reached his shoulders. He was endowed with the roar of a lion. The last time I had seen him in action he had, in ten minutes flat, removed half the crowd standing at the General Post Office, listening to a 'national hero'! The would-be President had a positive genius for what are known in England as 'Irish Bulls'. He had the colourful speech and accent of the native Dub, and there was no avenue of fractured English that he had not explored and made his own.

149

Looking out of this window I could still see him, in my mind's eye, standing on his orange box, proclaiming his programme for the improvement of the Free State. One item, a matter of some urgency, it seemed, was that, once in charge of the nation's affairs, the statue of Nelson, on top of his lofty Pillar, would be made to face north instead of south! 'That bloody womaniser has no right teh be lookin' down on Daniel O'Connell, the hero of Catholic "imagin-ation".' The laughing crowd roared their approval and applauded madly.

It was still the Dublin that James Joyce knew so well, squeezed between the two canals, where poverty reigned supreme. Twenty-five per cent of the city lived in 5,000 tenement houses, living, on average, four to a room, a seething down-at-heel Irish kasbah on the Liffey! Thousands of children, summer and winter, roamed the streets and went to school barefoot. Keely's proposal, 'Boots for footless children', was naturally greeted with uproarious approval. Not, mind you, that he ignored the problems of delinquent youngsters. 'The yout' a' today,' he would roar, 'have no respect for th' elders, but I'll soon fix that when in office, be openin' a few more reformatories, I don't blame the mothers and fathers so much as the parents! If them boys were in Russia, they'd be thrun inteh the Liffey. An yeh won't believe this, but when I cem' outa the pub last night, there was me bike . . . gone.'

President Keely's reign was short, though sweet, and he gave Dubliners many a happy hour. He disappeared off the scene quite quickly, and I often wondered what had become of him. Unless he changed his name, he never made it to Leinster House. He used to proclaim passionately to the crowds, 'I'm a Dublin man. born an' bred in this towen, and if God spares me I'll be buried in Glasnevin.' Perhaps God intervened quicker than he expected.

And, below me, I spotted Jerry and Hughie, making for the Oval. 'Thanks be to Jesus,' I sighed, and ran down the stairs in case I missed them. They both looked 'half cut', they were both wild, and capable of any indiscretion when jarred. I loved them, birds of a feather, and I was as mad as either of them or both. At last it was turning out to be a great Christmas Eve.

'Redmond,' they roared in unison.

'Dr Livingstone, I presume?' I said, and embraced them.

'That,' said Jerry, the mad red-head pointing to Hughie, 'is Livingstone. I, Sir, am Captain Langsdorf. I scuttled the *Graf Spee*, in Montevideo Harbour.'

'Jerry,' I said, 'you're twisted.'

'Naturally. It's Christmas Eve, isn't it?' Together we returned to the Oval Lounge, hopefully waiting for some more of our gang to turn up, but none of them did. The War had scattered us, and denied us, like millions of our generation, the privilege of being young. One who had been a class mate of ours did appear, unexpectedly, with the sleeve of his coat turned up where his left forearm used to be. He had never been one of the select Christmas Eve gang, and meeting him like that, upset us. He had been among the British who had escaped from the shell-torn beach at Dunkirk. He started to tell us of the retreat in France. It was the last thing we wanted to hear about. The bloody war was with us every day, and now, to have to suffer this 'shoneen' with his fake English accent, and put-on phlegmatic air, dogged as does it . . . .

'We'll get 'em, mate,' he told me. 'An' this bleedin' country should be in there with us.

'You better get yourself back with "us" then,' I told him. 'We are not one of you. Go back where you belong.'

There would have been a fight there and then only he had one flipper missing, but even at that, Jerry and Hughie had to get between us. Reckoned he could beat me with one arm, and I spat at him that he could never do that when we were at school, even with two arms, and, if God gave him a spare and made it three, I'd still beat the shite out of him. Eventually, he departed, obviously a ha'penny short of a shilling, and we returned to our drinking, going on shorts to forget Murphy with the one arm.

'You're worse,' said Hughie to me. 'Taking notice of an

151

eejit like that. Couldn't you see that he was shell-shocked or something?'

'We'll get 'em, mate,' I imitated. 'Cor . . . we'll get 'em.'

Hughie grinned. 'Really got to you, didn't he?'

'Yes, I meet bastards like him every day in England. I won't suffer them here.'

'I'd love to have seen his arse running up the gang plank,' said Jerry. 'With the bullets kicking up sparks,' and suddenly, without warning, he burst into song, in a thick Culchie accent.

> *And whin wit' foemen wreshlin'*
> *Where the balls like hail are whishlin'*
> *An' the bloody bay-nets bristhlin', Molly Bán*
> *An the lasht words I'll be spakin', Molly Bán*
> *When me sowel its lave is takin', Molly Bán*

'No singin',' roared the barman, 'no bloody singin' . . . .'

Ara Grá mo Chroí mo Stóirín, your sweetheart, Brian O'Riain
For you his blood is pourin', Molly Bán . . . .

'Out,' shouted the barman. 'No more drink for you lot.'

'One for the road, then,' said Jerry. 'Give us a kiss an' we'll make it up.'

'I'll road yeh,' said the barman, red-faced from the laughing crowd, 'If yeh don't make tracks out a' here.'

'Okay, boys,' Jerry roared, 'let's go somewhere respectable, like Dolly Fawcett's.' The same Dolly Fawcett's was a notorious brothel. The crowd in the lounge were enjoying the antics of Jerry, laughing and egging him on. 'Give us another song, Redser, will yeh?'

'No . . . he won't,' shouted the furious barman. 'He'll do his singin' somewhere else.' Jerry had a good voice, when he wasn't skylarking, and now he sang to the barman.

> *Ooooohhhh, stay as sweet as you are,*
> *Don't let a thing ever change you,*
> *Stay as nice as you are,*
> *Don't ever let a soul rearrange you.*

'Jaysus,' roared the infuriated barman, and came with a rush from behind the counter, but he had no hope of getting his hands on Jerry, who was lightning fast at strategic withdrawal. I left at a more sedate pace, and went down the stairs to find a grinning Jerry waiting for me. We had been in babies' class together, gone on to Primary School, and shared the same desk. All our lives we had never been too far from each other, until the accursed war split us up. I loved him, especially when he had a few on board, when the quiet companion who would discuss literature in depth, who loved poetry and Autumn woods, would disappear, and this hilarious character take over.

We waited for Hughie, who now joined us with a doleful countenance.

'Jaysus,' he said viciously. 'Every bugger in the whole world has Christmas Eve off . . . except me.'

Hughie worked as a van helper for one of Dublin's biggest emporiums, Todd Burns, in Mary Street.

'But I thought you were off,' I said.

'No . . . I paid a fella a quid to stand in for me from four till seven.'

'It's ten to seven now,' I told him. 'You'd better go.'

'I suppose so . . . Happy Christmas, Lar an' Jer.' We watched him slouch off in foul mood, then Jerry grinned at me.

'Hughie,' he informed me, 'fiddles while Todd Burns.' There was no way he was going to let anything spoil Dublin for him this night. He too had worked and groped his way about Peckham Rye in the blackout, and had had his share of English cold shoulder.

'Gentlemen songsters out on a spree,' he sang as we went from pub to pub. McDaids saw us merry, the Scotch House saw us boisterous, the Pearl Bar saw us tipsy, and O'Mara's saw us fluthered.

'Time,' said Jerry, 'to go for a feed.'

'Yes,' I hiccupped, 'jusht about.' My head was beginning to spin, but a good plate of rashers and eggs would put that right. We found a small restaurant in Talbot Street, found a table inside with some difficulty, and gave our order. Jerry had been here before and knew the form.

'And a bottle of Chateau La Filth, the best, mind you,' he told the grinning waiter. The place was packed with Christmas revellers, and from a table opposite three pretty girls flashed us an occasional smile. They were in the company of two middle-aged men, but when the men went to the toilet Jerry was away like a flash.

'Are those two your fathers?' he asked them. Giggling, the girls told him that they were their bosses and that they were standing them a meal.

'Big deal,' said Jerry, glancing around the shabby place. 'Which of you are they after?'

'Both of us,' said the brunette. 'But they won't get anywhere.'

'You should be at our table,' said Jerry.

'I wish we were,' said the blonde. 'I'm bored sick with these two oul' fellas.' However, Jerry had his eye on the toilet door, and beat a hasty retreat when the men opened it.

'Now, sir,' said the waiter, 'your bottle of Chateau La Filth.' Jerry filled his glass, tasted it, took a good gulp, and, with watering eyes, looked at the waiter.

'Excellent,' he pronounced, 'my compliments to the Bootlegger.' I tasted the stuff and it was vile, some kind of cheap sherry topped up with poteen. It was dynamite!

'That's some bottle of steam.'

'Mother's milk,' said Jerry, pouring another glass, and trying to focus on the pretty girls.

'You're going to be good and twisted,' I told him. 'That stuff is lunatic soup.'

'Oh, to be demented,' said Jerry sonorously and without any warning jumped up on the table.

'I'm Captain Langsdorf,' he announced. 'And I scuttled the *Graf Spee* in Montevideo harbour. I have sought sanctuary in this lovely neutral country.'

'Good on yeh, Captain,' said someone. 'Have another drop of depth charger, an' you'll scuttle yourself.' The place was in an uproar, people falling over laughing at this gangling red-headed son of Dublin, who now descended and, bottle in hand, gravely made his way towards the pretty girls, and their middle-aged escorts.

'Gentlemen,' he said, 'with your permission?' and drew up a chair.

'Permission be damned,' roared the bigger of the two men. 'Get yourself to hell out of here.'

'Certainly,' said Jerry, standing up. 'I can take a hint . . . Madam,' he said to the laughing brunette, 'will you walk?'

'Jesus Christ,' said one of the men. 'Will I hit him or will you?'

'Come on, Jerry,' I said quietly, 'or you're going to be in trouble.'

'But,' Jerry protested, pointing to the brunette, 'she's too young for him.'

'But I'm not too old for her,' snarled the big one. 'Now . . . beat it.' Jerry shook his head sorrowfully as we made for the door, but once at the exit he turned and faced the two middle-aged men.

'De yeh know what?' he called over. 'You're like an oul' dog chasing a bike . . . if you caught it you couldn't ride it!'

He shot out into the street then, and, fast and all as I was I lost him in the crowds. Fuelled on rocket juice he tore through everything, hitting nothing, and I came panting into O'Connell Street with a heavy heart. Jerry gone! The only one of the old gang left to me, and now I faced for home disconsolately. However, passing the monument to the great Catholic Emancipator, my spirits picked up, for dancing 'ring-a-rosie' around its base were some two hundred young people, in festive mood, singing. Among them the red head of Jerry came in view, and I ran across the road, broke the circle, and joined hands with him. All the misery of blacked-out, war-torn England was forgotten, the lights of Dublin seemed brighter than ever before, as we, the generation whose youth was being stolen, grabbed the little bit that was available, and made merry in the brief time that was left to us.

155

Ring-a-Ring o' Rosies
A pocket full o' Posies
AAAAAASSSSSHHAAH . . . AAAAAASSSSSHHAAH
We all fall down.

During the cheering that followed Jerry broke free, and was clinging to one of the bronze angels that protected Daniel O'Connell. He now took the bottle of *Steam* out of his pocket, took a slug, and roared . . . .

'I'm Captain Langsdorf . . . .'

'You scuttled the *Graf Spee* in Montevideo harbour,' screamed a teenage girl beside me, laughing.

'That I did, Madam,' Jerry roared. 'Have you ever suffered the effects of being torpedoed?' Finally he fell off, and I caught him as he fell. He was very drunk now, almost unconscious, and I knew I had to find a taxi, and fast. But taxis were few and far between in this neutral city. Half dragging him, I made for Foster Place and the traditional taxi rank.

'We're all out a' petterell,' a driver told me. 'I'm goin' home. I've about enough in the tank teh get me there, that's all. I can give yiz a lift as far as Christchurch, if that's any good.'

'Thanks,' I told him, and together we loaded Jerry into the back. It was only a few hundred yards nearer home, but it helped. On top of Christchurch Hill I looked down into Patrick Street and the Coombe, the place where I had served a hard apprenticeship in life, sighed, and took up my burden. Jerry could barely walk, he lived on the South Circular Road at the Rialto end. It was going to be a long trek. In the shadow of the old Dean's Cathedral, I let Jerry slump on to the footpath and took a breather. It was a beautifully calm Christmas morning, with a sky full of stars shining like diamonds, the city had suddenly grown quiet, and, here in the slums, each window held a large red candle showing the way to the three Wise Men, to where the Nazerene was being born all over again. Here, in the houses around me, old falling-down Huguenot tenements, with ten families to a house, poverty reigned over all, and little Dublin infants came into a world of swaddling rags, akin to the baby who had been born in Bethlehem, nearly two thousand years before.

And suddenly I had a bad taste in my mouth, my stomach turned over, and I got sick through the railings of Patrick's Park, 'The Lousy Acre'. The spasm over, I leaned weakly against the iron bars, and regarded Jerry sleeping peacefully on the pavement. I felt dirty, the only dirty thing in the whole world was me. Only a few years ago I had come this way, every Christmas morning, an innocent boy with a voice of gold, to sing the praises of the child who was born this day.

The city slept, turbulent Dublin was still for a while, and drunken gurriers only, like Jerry and myself, were abroad upon the face of the Universe. I lit a cigarette, physically much better, but my spirits were at rock bottom. I decided to let Jerry sleep it off as long as possible, then kick him awake, and make him walk it as best he could. It was then I saw the police squad car round the corner from Bride Street. Jerry got kicked before his time. He staggered up, me propping him, trying to look as if we were walking naturally, but the police car drew alongside anyway.

'You there,' came a country brogue. 'Lar Redmond . . . over here.' I left Jerry propped against the railings and went over.

'Well, Lar,' said Garda Kinsella, who lived not far from us, 'yiv had a fine oul' time on it tonight. Get your friend inteh the back, before I change me mind.'

'Are you going to arrest us, Mr Kinsella?'

'What for? Sure there's nothin' wrong with you, an' yer friend only has a few jars too many. I'm goin' off duty. Garda Nolan here beside is drivin' me home, an' you're in luck tonight. Where does your friend live?'

'Near the Dolphins Barn Bank, Mr Kinsella, and thanks very much. You won't tell Dad or Mam, will you?'

'Not at all,' said this decent man. 'sure it's Christmas, God bless it, an' young fellas go mad like, sure I did it meself, many a time.'

157

I got Jerry into the back of the car without difficulty, for he was sobering up rapidly, though still capable of anything. Blearily he surveyed the two policeman.

'Do your duty then, if you must,' he told them. 'Take your mechanical tumbril to the Bastille, and confine me to a dungeon. Madame Guillotine awaits . . . . It is a far far better thing I do now than I have ever done, a far far better rest I go to . . . .'

'It's Grangegorman you'll go to, with the rest of the nuts, if yeh keep that up,' said Garda Kinsella, but he was laughing fit to bust.

At Dolphins Barn Jerry was put out, to make his way home the short distance as best he could. He was okay for walking anyway, and we made a date to meet on Stephen's Day in the Red Bank at three o'clock.

Jerry gravely thanked the policemen, said he would recommend them both for promotion. 'Look out for stripes early in the new year?' He had influence and so on . . . .

'Look,' said the laughing driver. 'Under the influence is what you mean. Now get to hell home before we really run you in, and a happy Christmas to you, and a big fat head in the morning. Goodnight.'

As we drove up the Crumlin Road, Kinsella remarked that my friend must be a bit light upstairs.

'Not really,' I told him. 'But he's great gas when he has a few, and he never causes trouble.' I conveniently forgot his remarks to the two men in the restaurant.

'Nor uses bad language, either,' said Kinsella, 'A touch of quality there.' I was let out at the Halfway House, and slowly made my way home under a bright starry night. All around me the quiet fields of Walkinstown lay like a great carpet, that spread to the hills, covered them, and went on unspoilt across Ireland, stopped only by the sea. This was my land, my heart would always be here. Yet the sense of being unclean persisted, although I drew the cold air from the mountains deep into my lungs. It cleared my head anyway, but the memory of this Christmas Eve and morning would last me for a lifetime. I had been sick through the railings of

Patrick's Park earlier, and, recovering, had seen in my mind's eye the ghosts of two little boys, my young brother and I, walk softly past on the far side of the road, bound for Clarendon Street Chapel to receive Holy Communion, and afterwards sing through the Mass. And then the breakfast, followed by biscuits and lemonade and sweets galore, with something stronger for the men. And home to a happy family and a new pair of roller skates, tearing along the concrete 'right of way' that was called 'The Back of the Pipes.' And coming home ravenous, to a little house that was full of the smells of Christmas, roast turkey, with stuffing, mince pies, jelly and tinned pears, sisters and dollies and prams, little brothers who played with humming tops and Mechano sets, paper hats and crackers that went off with a bang, a jolly father, and a tired but well contented mother. This was her brood, this day the result of all her thriftiness.

'I heard you sang beautifully in Clarendon Street this morning' — a proud mother. But what of her son, now? Where had the guileless child gone? Who was the drunken gurrier who had vomited last night? Where had he come from? There had been no sign in my childhood of the lecher that would emerge in youth, whose only thought was to get the knickers off some woman as soon as he could. Who was becoming expert at the art of seduction, or thought this Christmas morning that he was.

At the end of the hedges our three-storey house was ablaze with light, and the pine tree, now ten feet high, that grew near the gate, was multi-coloured with 'Fairy Lamps'. Mam and Dad were at the front door, wishing a few neighbours goodnight, as I came through the gate.

'Happy Christmas, Lar,' they said.

'And many of them to you. Goodnight.' In the hall, Mam gave me her squinting hard stare that could see through me.

'Would you like a cup of tea, Lar?' she said softly. 'Just you and me, in the kitchen? And I'll make it like I did in the old days . . . I haven't touched the pound you brought home.'

'Yes, oh yes, I would like that, and a couple of sandwiches.' I knew what she was up to, apart from talking to her favourite son. She knew all was not well with me. And I knew she knew.

'You're looking a bit peaky, Lar,' she said as she poured. 'How do you feel?'

'Okay, Mam, okay, just a bit tired, that's all.'

'So you're not goin' to tell me?'

'Tell you what?'

'Don't fence with your mother, Lar. She knows you too well. Something terrible happened to you over there. What was it?'

'Ah, sure it's over now. I don't want to talk about it.'

'Take my advice, Lar, and start talking about it or you'll have a nervous breakdown. You nearly had one at fourteen years old . . . when you were going to James's Street School . . . only I let you leave it . . . .'

She sighed, a long sad sigh, and looked at me through misty eyes.

'Don't, Mam,' I said quickly. 'Don't cry.'

'No . . . not this night of our Lord, anyway.' She wiped her eyes on the corner of her apron. 'Drink up your tea, Mam.'

'I'm always afraid for you, Lar, above all the others. You're too sensitive, too easily hurt, and, in your own quiet way, wilder than any of them. And you lash out with that tongue of yours when you're hurt, or frightened. I know you do it to hide yourself from the world . . . the same as me . . . you're the one I fear for, Lar, the one I worry about.' I stared at her wide-eyed. That she could see through me I knew, but she had never since I had grown up confided in me as she had when I was a boy. Until now.

'But, Mam, you're supposed to have stopped worrying about me a long time ago. I'm an ex-Irish soldier . . . I'm a fully fledged carpenter . . . I can hold my own with the best. Never lose any sleep over me.'

'I wish I could stop worrying about you, but I know when all is not right with you.'

160

'How?'

'You get a funny tight look about the eyes . . . the same as you used to get when you were a child . . . when the bloody Tans were knocking in the panels of the door in Gardiner Street . . . .'

'Mam, please, for God's sake, don't cry.'

'I can't help it,' she wept softly. 'I know what's wrong with you. I was frightened out of me mind all the time I was carryin' you . . . your poor father "on the run" an' the terrible times that were in it . . . oh, Lar, you're too highly strung, an' that's the reason. You were terrified even before yeh saw the light a' day . . . I used teh feel yeh kickin' inside me, an' the heart jumpin' out a' me breast.'

Her speech, which had gradually improved over the years, now reverted to the old Liberties' style, and she put her head down on the table and silently cried. I stroked her hair until she ceased, poured her a fresh cup of tea, and she silently drank it. As for me, I was too shocked and frightened to say much. That she and I were fey, I knew, that we both occasionally possessed second sight, and it was whatever premonition of disaster had come upon her concerning me that frightened me most. I knew she would close her mind against me, as was her wont, that she would never tell me, but pass it off as a woman's foolishness.

'Mam,' I said at length. 'You are right. Something terrible did happen to me in England.'

She raised her head. 'I knew it,' she said quietly. Then I told her of the way Ken had lived a life of agony, of his compassion for his young wife who had fled a loveless marriage, 'Poor little sod, married to a cripple like me'. The way I had come home to the house where this man with blood-blackened face hung over the stair-well. I told her about the turkeys in Moore Street that had nearly unhinged my mind. I did not tell her about Lucy Bottle, though!

'So,' she said at length. 'That's why you had the tight look about the eyes . . . I knew it.'

The clock chimed three then, and we both stood up. It was long gone past time for bed.

'We'll talk again, Lar,' she said, 'but I don't want you to go back to that country.'

'Okay, Mam,' I said, and kissed her goodnight. 'We'll talk again.'

'Knock off the radio, Lar,' she called from the stairs. 'It's still on.' As I went into the dining room the music which had been blaring away abruptly ceased and an upper class British accent intervened.

'News has just come in,' he said tonelessly, and I could almost see the stiff lip of the invincible Brit firmly in place, 'that Hong Kong has fallen to the Japanese Army. Malaya has been completely over-run and is under Japanese rule for the present. This is a special news bulletin.' I switched off the set, and went upstairs to bed. Yes, the Brits were taking a hammering everywhere, but what the hell was that to me? I had no reason to love them, I wouldn't miss Hong Kong. The Japs had never menaced me, the Brits had, and anyway it was all a long, long way from Walkinstown and the quiet fields where dawn would soon break. So to bed and the end of my first twenty-four hours back in Dublin.

I woke up to a spring-like Christmas morning, with bird song and sunshine. I had no hangover. Thanking the good Lord, I made my way down to the kitchen, where I luxuriated in the first cup of tea of the day, smoked a cigarette and, hearing a distant cough from Mam's bedroom, took the hint, and brought up a pot of tea.

'Happy Christmas, Mam.' I kissed her. 'Happy Christmas Dad.' I spent a smiling time with them, and then went out into the garden. It was almost as warm as summer, difficult to imagine the misery of winter in Warrington, even thinking about it made me shiver, but that was where I was returning to, and why? Why leave this lovely house and the coming spring for the hazards of a hostile country? Why could I no longer be content with a trout rod and a river? Bloody well I knew why, but I asked myself the question anyway, just to get things straight in my mind.

The reasons were many and varied. The most important was that in Walkinstown I felt life to be passing me by, there

162

was no chance of getting a woman, and no way I could grow in experience if I ever wanted to be a writer. Yes, except for the 'nooky', that was the most important.

At breakfast I glanced around the family as they came in one by one. My sisters were young women now, girls I hardly knew anymore, what with the age difference, my absence in the Army, and now my exile in England. They were warm and friendly, all ready to go to Mass, and grudgingly I went with them, where I met many neighbours briefly. When the Mass ended I sloped off to a nearby quarry and I longed for my fishing rod, for it was full of large perch, gliding through the reeds. It was the season for coarse fishing. I arrived home about two o'clock and sat in the kitchen with Mam for a while. In the dining and sitting room, now transformed into one, with the sliding doors pulled back, there was a goodly sprinkling of family friends, taking a Christmas drink. I mingled with them, but refused all drink, and stuck to tea. The memory of last night was too recent. Outside, the sun had suddenly gone away, dark clouds had moved in, though it was still unseasonably warm, a 'Pet' day, according to my mother.

The doorbell rang and she rose and went to it. She came back to me, ushering in Mick Gilbey, who stood among the crowd of strangers, slightly confused. Where he had come from there had been no crowd, of that I was sure.

'It's your friend Mick,' she said. 'He wants to see you about something. Take him into the other room, Lar.' Together we went into the large kitchen, with its built-in cupboards, its washing machine and fridge, its lovely fire-place built of Courttown rustic red brick.

'Jesus,' said Mick softly. 'This is a lovely house. How in God's name do you ever stay in a place like oul' Dogberry's, in Warrington?'

'I didn't always live in such style, Mick, and anyway, whatever about the house, I'm still only a carpenter . . . .'

'But you don't have to be over the water, do yeh?'

'No, but if I want to be a writer, I've got to see the world a bit. I'm not one of the fellas who'll never be three miles

163

from a cow shite. What 'ill you have to drink?'

'Nothing, Lar, thanks just the same?'

'All right then, Mick, out with it. You didn't come all this way out from Dublin just to see how I lived. What did you come for?'

Gilbey grinned. 'You don't change, do you, Lar. Direct an' to the point, as always.'

'Yes. What is it, Mick?'

'As if you don't know!'

'I know, but I'm not going to say it. You'll have to do that yourself!'

'Well, it's Rose Mary . . . Lar, I've been a bloody fool. I should have listened to you, instead of turning on you.'

'Say no more, Mick, I understand.'

'Have you any left?'

'Unfortunately, plenty. I'll go upstairs and get you some. I can spare twelve.' I left him then, to get over his reddening face, and ran upstairs to my den, Berchtesgaden, on the third floor. From this high vantage point I could see Drimnagh Castle and all the green fields for miles, all the way to Clondalkin village. I had the French Letters hidden behind my books on the shelf under the gable window. Glancing out as I found them, I saw the form of a woman lurking behind the hedge at the gate of Norton's Farm. She was no more than two hundred yards away and I recognised her at once. It was Mick's woman, the fair Rose Mary herself. One of my hobbies, before I joined the Army, was birdwatching, and now I focussed my field glasses on the woman below, and, 'Jesus,' I whispered to myself, this one was all woman. Even though she was well muffled up against the winter, nothing could conceal the beauty of her face and form, a woman in her prime, ripe for love, ready for love, eager for love. She kept looking expectantly towards our house.

'Well dear,' I said aloud. 'Never let it be said I kept you waiting.' With that I ran down the stairs to Mick. I handed him the pack in silence, he stood up, and we shook hands again.

'God bless you, Lar,' he said. 'I'll see you back in Warrington.'

'Have a lovely Christmas, Mick.' Mam came back in to the kitchen and looked in some surprise at my friend.

'Off then, without even takin' a drink, is it?'

'Yes, Mrs Redmond. It was just something I wanted Lar to do for me. He'll be going back before me, I think. I'm sorry I can't stay for a drink, but I have someone waiting for me. A Happy Christmas to you and yours.'

'And the same to you,' said Mam. 'See Michael out, Lar.'

At the gate, Mick turned to me and shook my hand.

'Thanks, Lar, thanks for everything. I'll see you in Dogberry's.'

'Yes, but in the meantime don't delay. It's starting to turn cold and your woman will be freezing. I grinned at him. 'Nothing as bad as a cold woman, Mick.'

'And you're the right little artful get,' said Mick. 'How did you know she was down the road?'

'Saw her from the attic, when I went up for the Frenchers. She's a right armful for any man, you're a lucky fellow.'

Mick grinned and strode off, and I shot back to the attic to watch his departure from on high. I saw him reach the gate of Norton's farm, Rose Mary came from behind the bush and, right there, on the gravel path of this country road, she put her arms around him and kissed him long and hard. I watched through the field glasses enviously, wishing I was in his shoes, for the night, anyway. I had no idea of marrying, and Gilbey had nothing else.

But tonight, Gilbey, another virgin boy from Ireland, would go out among the stars where I had been only too briefly and would know the glory of fulfilment with the one he loved. I envied him so much. The woman clung to him, promising everything with her body. In the end, ashamed, I lowered the field glasses and went downstairs. Gilbey, the Phantom Rider, would ride this night, aided and abetted by his deputy, one Lar Redmond, a hard ridin' cowboy from west of the Liberties, end of story. Gilbey, tall in the saddle

165

rode off into the gathering twilight, Redmond put away his
six-shooter and went into the dining room. I was for ever
doing a Walter Mitty. In 1941, maybe it was not a bad thing
to do.

All the visitors had gone, the table was set for dinner, the
turkey lay streaming in its own juices, I was home, for one
more Christmas.

8   The 11th Commandment

St Stephen's Day came mild and sunny to Dublin that year. I
had a date to meet Jerry, and great hopes of picking up
some pretty little 'mot' and making love to her. With Jerry,
the mad one, all things were possible. Girls seemed to be
drawn to him like wasps to jam, and the lounge in the Red
Bank was a likely place for what I had in mind. I was there
on the dot of four o'clock, and ten minutes later Jerry came
in, grinning.

'You've had a few already,' I accused him.

'Why? You only starting now?'

'Yes.'

'Well, you'd better get yourself a couple of doubles then,
and catch up on the form.' Half an hour later, I had caught
up, and, in the rosy glow of anticipation, watched two lovely
girls come in the door.

'Cop that,' I said to Jerry. 'There's a couple of smashers.'

'They'll keep,' said Jerry, winking at them, and ordering
two more drinks. The pretty ones, we found out afterwards,
were named Carol and Noelle, two most appropriate names
for the time of year. They smiled demurely at us and sipped
lemonade. At least, that is what we thought it was, and Jerry
gave it as his opinion that they could be softened up by
introducing them to the demon alcohol. I thought so too
but stiffened in my chair as a man at the counter turned to
meet a friend. He was an officer in the 7th Dublin Infantry,
an arrogant bastard who had once put me on a charge

because I did not freeze, trembling under his gaze, as he inspected the company for that day.

'What's wrong?' said Jerry. 'You've gone a bit white about the gills.'

'That get with the chestnut moustache is an officer in the Army,' I whispered.

'Jaysus, what about it? He doesn't know you're working in England, does he?' And that was perfectly correct, too, but I had a sudden premonition of danger. I was only on indefinite leave, I had no right to be out of the country. I could be lagged back into the accursed army at any time. The sooner I made myself scarce and got back to England the better. Once again, I bitterly regretted the way I had bull-baited the sergeant at the gates of Santry Court. That old savage would have my guts for garters if ever he got near me again.

Well I knew the brutality of an army jail, any army, called the 'Glass House' on both sides of the Irish sea. A young soldier had been killed in Aldershot jail the week I left England, broken on the wheel for some trivial mis-demeanour. There had been a hue and cry in the news-papers. Someone had leaked the circumstances of his death to the press, there was an uproar, but it would be stifled quickly and the 'Glass House' would continue unaffected and unaltered. No civilian prison could match the brutality of the army ones, and the Irish prison on the Curragh was no exception. Terrible things were done there to young soldiers in the name of 'discipline', especially to those who had deserted and were unlucky enough to be caught.

Two in our company had been sent to the Curragh, poor Rock and Cushy O'Brien, both hard chaws from the inner city. They were charged with desertion and were sentenced to six months. O'Brien came back to us broken in spirit, Rock as defiant as ever, but his health let him down. He was quietly discharged, having contracted tuberculosis from hardship, and I had heard a rumour that he was dying in Crooksling Sanitorium. The brutality of the British had passed on to the Irish, via ex-officers and non/Comms, when our army was founded. Not that we needed any lessons. It seemed we had our own plentiful supply of brutes who enjoyed their work. We had no need to ask for foreign volunteers, or be taught anything by the likes of the German SS And if that Culchie bastard ever got me back . . . Jesus!

'Jer, . . . I'm going to make a run for it the day after tomorrow. I think my luck is running out!'

'But there's no reason why they should call you up again, is there? After all, no matter how long it takes, Germany is going to lose, the North is stuffed with Yanks, and the English threat of invasion is over. Too many Irish Americans,' said Jerry reasonably.

'I know that. With America in the War, the Jerries are finished. But the Brits are still on the run. They lost Hong Kong two days ago, and the *Barham*, one of their biggest warships was sunk in the Med' . . . .'

'No matter,' said Jerry, finished with the subject. 'The English always lose every battle except the last one. Now for the girls.'

He rose, made his way across to their table, and came back with them in tow a couple of minutes later. Mistake number one, they were not drinking lemonade, but Pims Number One, and these demure Dublin Colleens proceeded to drink us under the table without coming within an ass's roar of losing their virginity. Even though Jerry and I were only drinking stout at a shilling a bottle, we were well on before the girls even started to sparkle, and what they were on was two and six a go, and had a kick like a mule.

Even dinner did not soften them up and all the time their hands were very firmly on their ha'pennies. I arrived home, broke, at two o'clock in the morning, sobered up from the long walk, with my mind made up. Mam would be very upset at this second desertion, but go I must. My intuition, when I took note of it, was rarely wrong. It was only when I brought common sense to bear on a situation that I fell down. And all the alarm bells were ringing.

The next day the feeling of imminent danger hung over

me like a pall. I stayed quietly at home. In the evening, Mam and Dad went out to visit some neighbours and I volunteered to mind the house. Our family was rapidly growing up, I had two younger brothers in the Irish Army, and teenage sisters who were flirting or courting. I sat alone, listening to the radio, when a sharp knock on the French doors that led to the garden made me jump. I pulled back the heavy curtain and looked into the smiling face of Mary Evans. Jesus, this was it! More than once, in passionate love sessions, I had nearly made it with her, but with her knickers half off she had always jibbed at the last moment. Now . . . if I had had condoms, things would have been very different. Knowing I was home, she had watched our house from her own, not far away, and had struck when the coast was clear.

'Well, God bless you,' I said to myself, as I opened the door, 'but I'll make all your dreams come true tonight, and never a danger of giving you a baby.'

She was a lovely red-head, with blooming breasts, and a curvaceous body that I had explored many times, and maybe tonight was the night.

'Hello, Larry,' she said softly.

'Hello, Mary,' I said. Drawing the curtains over the closed door and putting my arms around her, I kissed her willing lips. I found out at once that she was still mad about me, for the kiss went on and on until she lay back slowly, pulling me down onto the big settee, and, from that position, my hand roved over her body at will. Eventually, gasping, she pushed me away.

'Larry . . . Larry . . . stop, I only came over to have a chat with you.'

'Like hell you did,' I thought, but was glad of the respite, for the condoms were up in my room, and I had to get them. This neighbour's daughter had been in love with me for years, too close for me to regard her as an adventure, but I had learned a lot since the last time I had felt her and I knew better now. Every woman was a strange and dangerous adventure!

'All right, Mary, love,' I said with mock piety. 'I'm sorry. I'll get you a glass of lemonade, or would you like a glass of sherry or port?'

Unleash the demon alcohol, it might work.

'No, thank you,' she said, rising and smoothing down her frock. 'What would your mother or father say if they came home and found me here?' Her face was flushed, her flaming red hair was lovely under the light from the chandelier, and her breasts were rising and falling with the tumult in her young heart. This girl loved me, but I was aroused and angry.

'Why did you come then?'

'I just wanted to see you, Lar.' Yes, she just wanted to see me, to see if I had changed towards her, to see if she stood any chance with me at all, or would she make up her mind, woman-like, to settle for some other young man who had more honest intent on his mind.

'I'll be leaving soon again, Mary.'

'When?'

'Maybe next week,' I lied.

'Well, I'll be home alone tomorrow night. Dad is going out to meet "that one" of his, and I'll stay at home.' Her father was a widower, a very young widower at forty-seven, but to Mary he was an old man, and 'that one' of his was a lovely woman of thirty-five, a nurse, who could easily give birth, and provide Mary with a couple of sisters or brothers she did not want.

'I'll come over then.'

'About half eight, Lar. The coast will be clear by then.' I let her out by the same way she had come in, and kissed her passionately at the gate. She clung to me, promising me, with all her woman's guile and body, how it would be between us the following night, and, with that implied promise, my plans for leaving Ireland the next day fell through. I would postpone for a day, but the sense of peril persisted, though I confided in no one.

Mam was serenely content the following morning, taking my quiet ways as my intent to remain at home, but it was the

171

quiet of a sleeping volcano. It was all right with mother if I was called up again, she had no comprehension of the hatred I held for the Army, especially a neutral one, pretending danger when all danger was over. 'Soldiering', as far as I could make out in the Irish Army of that time, was a way of getting off the dole, a roof over your head, a feed, and a few bob a week. The backbone of the original Free State Army was still there when I had joined, 'Oul Swallies' they were called, most of them barely able to write, speaking fractured English, nearly all of them elevated in rank to cope with the onrush of patriortic young fools like me, or boys who fled from the slums and cramped quarters, for what to most of them was a better life. It was not a better life for me!

By the time eight o'clock came the following night I was in a state of excitement. Mam thought I was going to the pictures. I went for a walk to kill time, having to leave the house at seven if I was going where I said. I crossed the field behind Mary's house at eight thirty, sliding in the back way. And now at last I was here, Mary was embracing me, and without a word she led me into the dimly-lit sitting room and straight onto the couch. There would be no messing around tonight. I had a packet of Durex, opened in my pocket, Mary loved me, was wild for me, and we could make love without risk. I had tricked myself into this way of thinking, but at the back of it all, I knew I was behaving like a bastard. But all that was firmly put aside now, as my hand caressed her silk knickers and satin thighs, and she moaned with pleasure as I found her again and kissed her with open mouth, tongue to tongue, kissed her as she had never been kissed before, with her heart pounding so hard I could hear it. Slowly she went limp and was mine for the taking.

'Mary . . . Mary . . . love me tonight . . . really love me . . . now!'

'Lar . . . Lar . . . you know I want to, but I'm afraid.'

'Afraid of the priest, is that it, Mary?'

'No . . . afraid of you, afraid of having a baby. You wouldn't marry me.'

'I would.'

'But you wouldn't want to, and that's what I'm afraid of.' I found her mouth again and kissed her and kissed her until we were both half out of our minds, and then I asked her again.

'Don't be afraid, Mary, I have some of those things with me. There's no fear of you having a baby.' I felt her stiffen under me and then suddenly I found myself on the floor, having been pushed, and pushed hard, by an enraged Irish female. Stupidly, I came to my feet, and Mary stood like a fury over me, for she was three inches taller.

'So that's what you had in mind, you dirty blackguard. You've learned a few tricks over the water, haven't you. How many of the English ones have you used them on?'

'But you said you didn't want a baby.'

'No, and I didn't want a whore-master who carries those things in his pocket, either!' So here it was again, I thought, as I stumbled out the back door only twenty minutes after I had come through it, the bloody brain washing of the Church, Mary was another victim, welded to it with bonds of steel, destined to open her legs to celebrate the sacrament of marriage only, and if that was a sacrament there must be something wrong with my mind. Irish women all over the country were yearly crucified with yet another baby, their husbands better at celebrating sacraments than any priest. Jesus . . . let me back to England! The people there did not think of a bit of 'crumpet' as celebrating a sacrament, and no wonder. The sexual act was beautiful, but the heat and the fire, the sheer animal-like pleasure of the act put it right out of the sacrament class. Sacrament my arse, I thought savagely. Born in guilt, the deck stacked from the start, lousy with original sin, inherited from Adam and Eve, who had only done what came naturally, and with the equipment given to them by their creator. What did He expect them to do? Was Adam supposed to stir his tea with it? Was Eve given a body irresistible to men only to spend her time resisting?

I looked at my watch. It was still only a quarter past nine, that was how fast things had happened at Mary's. My case was packed, I was ready to travel, why not now? I crossed the road and entered our house for the last time. It might be years before I entered it again. Everything was okay, Mam and Dad would be back in an hour. It was time I was off. Never had the sense of disaster been stronger. I was lucky enough to grab a bus, and got off at Dolphins Barn. Jerry was in his favourite pub, sipping a bottle of stout. Money was running low with him as with me. He regarded me with surprise.

'Jesus, Lar, you're not going back so soon, are you?'

'I am, Jer,' and I told him of my premonition of being called up again, and the bastard who was waiting for me.

'How are you fixed for money?'

'Nearly broke . . . those two little lynxes in the Red Bank just about did it.'

'Yeah,' said Jerry sighing, 'and the taxi . . . and the dinner. Jesus, Lar but we're a right pair of eejits when we get on the booze.'

He finished off the stout and put down his glass angrily. 'And not even a bloody feel for all the money we spent. Have you any money at all, Lar?'

'About thirty bob. It'll have to do.'

'Where will you spend the night?'

'In the railway station, if I have to.'

'Have you still got any French Letters left?'

'Yes.' I told him morosely. 'Two bloody dozen.'

'Ah,' said Jerry softly, 'sweet mystery of life. Give them to me. It won't take me long to convert them into cash.'

In the toilet I gave them to him, and stood alone at the bar drinking a pint, while Jerry was absent. He was back just before closing time and, with a grin, placed four pounds and sixteen shillings on the counter.

'The "Mickey" money,' he told me.

'Jesus . . . Jerry, you're a genius.' I divided the spoils equally and pushed Jerry's half across to him.

'No, Lar,' he said, 'I'll take a quid, and that's all. Buy us a drink before they close.' We embraced at the bus stop, and

I departed with a lump in my throat. Jerry I loved, he was part of my life since babies' class and we were as close as brothers, or as close as brothers are supposed to be, but rarely are.

I booked into a bed-and-breakfast joint beside the railway station, sharing a room with a quiet country man, who placed the legs of the bed inside his boots before going to sleep. So, I thought, he was an old hand, a 'Long Distance' man who was used to the Roughton House, the Sally Arms, and sleazy lodging houses. I had no worries about missing the train the following morning, for this place was geared to travellers. At five in the morning we dined off a solitary egg with plenty of bread and butter. Surprisingly, the cup of tea was strong and delicious, but one look at the landlady told me why. She was a fine buxom widow, who positively oozed sex, one that I knew could not do without a man for long, and, no doubt, she had a string of men who brought her back pounds of tea from England, and the miserable half ounce a week ration did not worry her.

In the railway station nothing had changed, a seething mass of Irish all headed for England. I was worried but not too much. My travel permit was in order, there was little chance among this horde of being spotted. Yet I heaved a sigh of relief as I walked up the gangway, and immediately disappeared below, until she sailed. Then, and only then, did I come up on deck, to watch Ireland fade and disappear. The War would be over before I saw it again, and only God knew when that would be.

At Holyhead I kept a low profile, too, praying that Toddy Sweeney, the ferret faced Dublin bastard turned Sassenach did not spot me, and my prayers were answered. And all over again, a crowded train, all change at Crewe, but this time I saw plenty of American uniforms scattered among the Brits. While waiting for my train, I stood close to a group of Yanks, listening to their talk, they seemed a little disappointed with England. They had been looking forward to a country in the front line, Britain in the trenches under shell fire, but they were a bit late for all that.

I had missed the Blitz, too, the Jerries had shot their bolt, and turned their back on a country too tough to be frightened into submission. Hitler's dreams of a panic-stricken population running around like headless chickens screaming for mercy, were gone. And besides, he was up to his hocks in Russia, where right now more of his troops were dying from cold than from Russian bullets. The Brits had expected this, and had quietly bought up everything woollen in Spain and Portugal last summer, at the cost of twenty-six million pounds. When the Nazis arrived, desperate for blankets, pullovers, anything off a sheep's back, and loaded with money, the cupboard was bare.

You had to admire the bastards, I decided, and love their women. Now these disappointed Americans in their uniforms of fine cloth, lousy with dollars and lust, would get more chances than I would! Had they been here earlier they would have seen a country that had lost 40,000 civilians, 86,000 seriously injured, 156,000 who would carry the marks of Der Führer's rage to their graves.

It was much colder here than in Ireland and, as the train sped inexorably north, it became bitter, snow flakes flew past the window, and the landscape turned white. Jesus . . . it was just the same as I had left it. Did it ever stop snowing in the north of England? At Warrington, I moodily made my way through packed snow to Uniform Terrace and the Barnes's shabby home. Gone were the bright lights of Dublin. I shuffled uncertainly through the blackout. It would take me a little time to get used to the dark again, but back at the Barnes's all was the same. The old lady sat at one side of the table, Jim, the scholar, was reading the news to his old wife, who turned her splendid eyes on me with affection and welcomed me 'home'.

'Ee, lad,' said the old man, rising to greet me, 'but it's naice to see thee again,' and gave me a vice-like handshake. Still as strong as a lion, I thought, nearly worn out, like his country, but still a lion, a British lion.

'Wud 'ave thought, lad,' said Mrs Barnes, 'as you'd 'ave stopped longer in Eire. 'Ave you no Irish Colleens waitin' for you? A good-lookin' lad like thee?'

'Plenty,' I told her. 'But I don't want to be tied down.'

'Want to sow wild oats first, eh?'

'That's right, Mrs Barnes,' I said. I could have gone on to tell her that sowing wild oats in Eire was a short walk up the aisle with a lady who had a figure like an inverted question mark, and that the reason for the walk was unquestionable. The alternative was to risk a dose of 'clap' from a 'Brasser', like Lady Stalin, and that was all the bloody wild oats you'd ever sow where I came from. But I kept my own counsel, just for once.

'Did you see Mick, then?'

'Yes, once. He'll be after me very soon, I think.'

'But 'asn't 'e got a lass? 'asn't 'e marriage on mind?'

'Yes, Mrs Barnes, but he's not earning any money over there. If he wants to get married this Easter he'll have to come back soon, and save like mad.'

'Poor lad,' said Mrs Barnes, 'leavin' lass be'ind. She shud cum over wi' 'im.' Poor lad be damned, I thought. He'd be back soon all right. He would have ploughed his way through the dirty dozen I had given him, twice over by now, the lucky bastard. But there had not been a 'Workman's Friend' among the condoms he got from me. You could not put patches on the ones I had given him.

So, the following morning it was back to work on a frozen building job. The days of the bonus scheme based on production were gone, for the present anyway. The plasterers and bricklayers had been stopped short by the weather. However, we were still paid to stand around, or at best make an hour's work last the day. Hard work would have suited me down to the ground, helped to keep my circulation going, but, day after day, a leaden sky unloaded another dollop of snow to keep our spirits at an all time low. And, to make things worse, no sign of Gilbey.

'Could 'appen as 'e's found a job in Dublin, luv,' said Mrs Barnes.

'Unless he has a separate kit of tools I don't think so. His tool box is upstairs in the bedroom.'

177

'But you've been back ten days now, Larry . . . .'

'Thank God for that. I've a full week's wages coming this week.' It was two weeks later before Mick arrived. He looked taller, bigger, better than I had ever seen him, a picture of glowing good health.

'An' fresh and well you're looking, Mrs Barnes,' said Mick, kissing her on the cheek, and shaking hands with old Dogberry who was too stunned to be jealous.

'So you got back at last,' I said shaking hands. 'Jesus, Mick, I missed you.'

'Well,' said the tall one, 'I thought of you now and again. But I was pretty busy.'

'I know,' I said grinning.

'And you're right, but the reason I stayed so long was that I got married.'

'Married . . . ! Thank God for that. Congratulations, Mick.' We shook hands again, Dogberry shook hands again, and old Mrs Barnes kissed him on the cheek. Her beautiful golden-flecked eyes sparkled, and she gave him a knowing smile.

'So,' she said softly, 'you've found out the wonder of your lass, 'aven't you, Mick?' Gilbey did not even blush, but gave her back look for look.

'Even more wonder than I expected, Mrs Barnes, the wonderful world of women.' With Mick back on the job everything seemed suddenly to come right again. I had already written to Mam and said how sorry I was, weeks ago, but she never answered. Now, on Mick's first day at work, we came home to find two letters, one from the fair Rose Mary, the other from my mother. My intuition had been only too right. The day I had sailed for Holyhead two Army officers had come to collect yours truly. I had had a narrow escape, but now all thought of Ireland must be left behind, home-sickness, however bad the attack, must never be allowed to drive me to risk going home again. I was here for the duration of the War, however long that took. With this thought came a kind of relief. Like Cortez, I had burnt my boats, and would have to tackle this country on my own.

I was back on the Correspondence Course again, and making progress. I wrote an essay on fishing for trout, which was accepted, and, in due course, I received two guineas. I was on my way. The whole field of literature opened up before me like a flower. I would take the world by storm! I had actually earned money from writing, I hated the building game, if I buckled down to work I could make it. Edgar Wallace and Dickens had done it with no more education than I. So would I!

Old Dogberry, following the War avidly, was up and down like a yo-yo. The Brits had knocked the bejaysus out of the Italians in the western desert, and flung them out of Egypt. Huge stores of war equipment had been seized, tens of thousands of prisoners captured, the war there seemed to be over.

'Bluddy spaghetti merchants,' growled old Dogberry, bristling. 'Time we put bluddy Saw-Dust Caesar, in place.'

However, in the Far East, the Japs had descended like a tiger on the Dutch and British Empires, and had taken on America as well. They conquered all before them, soldiers who travelled light, could live off a handful of rice, and who fought with unparalleled ferocity. They destroyed the myth of the white man's supremacy completely and absolutely in a matter of weeks. But old Dogberry and the British public hung on to their victories in Africa, while, as the spring came to Warrington, their generals again made a blunder that would cost them dear. Major General R.N. O'Connor, a man with a good Irish name, had bludgeoned the Italians into the ground with a small force of battle-hardened men. He was not allowed to clear the rest of Italian Tripolitania. Instead, his 19th Corps was broken up and sent to Greece and Crete, where they were destroyed. And with the arrival of General Rommel on 12 February, 1942, the Brits' easy conquests in Africa came to an end. They faced a man who could tactically run rings around any British general.

He fought clean and fair, and the Brits, albeit reluctantly — and who could blame them? — admired him and wished him to hell and Connemara. He fought with young

Germans who were used to winning, who thought themselves invincible, and damn near were. They left a lasting memory behind them, for their song, 'Lili Marlene', became the marching song of their British opponents and in time came to epitomise the Second World War. And right now, in this bitter begrudging Lancashire spring, Lili Marlenes waited under lamp posts with their lights out, all over Britain, waited for their free French lovers, or Norwegians or Poles who had managed to join forces with the Brits, they waited for Australians, New Zealanders, Canadians, but mostly they waited for the Yanks and the mighty dollar.

With hundreds of thousands of married men posted all over the world, young British women, left to wither on the vine, decided not to, and, with the help of the indispensible condom, issued free to soldiers, managed to avoid becoming frigid. The glamour boys of the forces, the RAF suddenly found themselves taking second place to the Yanks, fickle females having forgotten for the present their heroism in the Battle of Britain, when these young eagles of the air had faced the might of the Luftwaffe and won. the Irish too found favour with English women, their Blarney irresistible. Also, like the Yanks, they had plenty of money to spend. Unless, that is, they were married, like Mick.

'I thought you'd wait until Easter, Mick,' I said, during lunch hour. We were back on bonus again, and there was no time for talk during working hours.

'I couldn't, Lar. I was mad about her, and she about me.'

'Was?'

'Am! You know that. But I made my journey to you for nothing. When we went to bed that day, an hour after I saw you, she told me she would not suffer me to wear those things. So we did what Adam an' Eve did, just the same as the Garden of Eden.'

'I suppose she's in the family way now, Mick.'

'I suppose so, but it's only a few weeks to Easter, and what does it matter? We're married! That's why it took me so long to come back. We had to put up the banns for three

180

weeks in the local chapel. In the meantime we slept together.'

'Where?'

'In her flat, where else?'

'Mrs Barnes was saying that it was a pity you didn't bring her over to England.'

'She wouldn't even think of it. Anyway, she has a good steady job as a nurse, an' where would you expect us to get a place over here?'

So, Mick was taking the same sorry road as the poor Dublin glazier, O'Riordan, who had had to leave his beloved Alice, to glaze the windows of Buckingham Palace.

'It's going to be a hard road for you, Mick.'

'Maybe not that hard. I'm going home for keeps, at Easter.'

'Yes, but what to?'

'You'll hardly believe this,' said Mick, 'but there's that many tradesmen left Ireland that I could have got a job.'

'Then, in God's name, what did you come back for?'

'The bloody tools, what else?'

'Oh . . . I forgot that.'

'Mind you, the money is lousy, no overtime, but then it was never any different.'

'It wasn't as lousy as the money over here. We're paid more than the English — the Dublin rate is tuppence an hour more.'

'An' that's a big bloody deal,' said Mick, bitterly. 'But from what I hear on this job, there's going to be a real big change after the War. It wouldn't surprise me if they came up with a Socialist Republic, or even a Communist régime.'

This conversation took place in the canteen, during lunch hour, and the man sitting on the opposite side of the table burst out laughing, a derisive laugh.

'You might as well rave here as in bed,' he told Gilbey, in a heavy north of Ireland accent. 'Their class divisions here are nearly as bad as in India. An' what's more,' he added savagely, 'they like it that way!

Mick gazed at him blankly, stuck for an answer in the surprise attack from this man.

'Not from what I hear,' he said eventually.

'No? Well I think different . . . the workin' class, with their caps and jerseys, office workers apin' the city gent, bowler hats and rolled umbrellas, the lower middle class, a four-bedroomed house, an' a woman that "does for" twice a week . . . .'

'You seem to have made a good study of it all,' said Mick.

'Aye, I have. It's not much different in Belfast, but over here sickens me. The upper class, rollin' in money, the village squire next on the list, with his tenant farmers, touchin' their forelocks, or maybe it's their foreskins . . . .'

Mick laughed. 'By God,' he said, 'you've a talent for invective!'

'Well here's some more of it,' the other spat out. 'Their fuckin' establishment, Eton an' Oxford for them, an' an old school tie that will carry them through life nice an' cushy, an' at the top, their Royals, all teeth an' no chins, fuckin' parasites, no job! I know the job I'd give them, a pick an' shovel an' a cutting from here to Dover! Or maybe start them on a tunnel under the Channel.' He stood up abruptly. 'Socialist Republic,' he spat out. 'Wake up. Th' English like it the way it is!'

'Well,' I said with a sigh of relief as he went off, 'that's a red hot Commo' anyway.'

'Maybe I am too,' said Mick. 'For it's not much different where we come from. A Blackrock scarf or a university pin can get you anywhere.'

'It's not as bad as here, though.'

'It is, twice as bad. It's just that it's better concealed, we're a nation of hypocrites, a priest-ridden island, ruled by the bishops. Our workin' class are afraid to speak out! And priests that are never drafted more than fifty miles from home. That's why the Irish priesthood is so backward. They've never travelled.'

'What about the Missionaries? What about them?'

'Either dedicated priests or poor ones who have had to

182

be subsidised. Do you know what, Lar?'

'What?'

'If Jesus, the carpenter in the sky, came back to Ireland tomorrow he'd scatter the crowd he has workin' for him like snuff at a wake. He'd kick their arses from Ireland to Timbuktu. He'd destroy their cushy life style as surely as he kicked over the stalls of the money changers outside the temple in Jerusalem.'

The whistle blew then, and Mick came slowly to his feet. He was starting to look peaky again, from too much hard work and sexual starvation. I knew the signs. He was six years older than I was and his want was even worse than mine, and Jesus Christ, that was bad enough!

'Come,' he said grinning, 'blue collar worker, back to the Salt Mines an' earn your bonus. Be like the English . . . like being working class!'

That'll be the day, I thought. Jack London had written about work beasts, the never ending treadmill of the steaming laundry he worked in, and this bleached hell I was suffering, would go on for ever unless I broke the mould. Despite being tired, despite a sixty hour week, despite everything, Gilbey and I worked just as hard in our off time at home. Mick was doing an advanced course in higher mathematics. Trigonometry, he took the trouble to explain to me, was a branch of mathematics which deals with relations between the sides and angles of a triangle.

'Mick,' I said, 'don't go any further. Maths and me are strangers, I might as well be looking into a bush.'

'Don't tell me you're not able to strike out a stairs.'

'I am telling you . . . I can't. And I know nothing about striking out windows or doors, or joinery of any kind. I was never trained for that.'

'Name a' jaysus,' said Gilbey indignantly, 'what were you trained for?'

'To be a foreman. To be able to strike out foundations, know enough about all crafts to be able to supervise all tradesmen, to be a boss's son. I know I'm a good carpenter, fast and neat, but that's as far as it goes. I'd be lost in a joinery shop. And if what I'm working nights at shows results, maybe I'll never need to know any more about the bloody building line.'

That spring, very near the time for Mick to depart, my first real breakthrough came. I had been taught to aim at a market, and my love-starved life dictated the road. I chose a women's magazine and struck oil first time with a story about a crux in a marriage. It was real shit, but I got five guineas for it, and the lady editor requested more. I obliged with an avalanche of crap, real literary diarrhoea, that brought me a passing fame in this factory girls' magazine. I looked into a glorious future. But dreaming stopped in the face of the fact that I had paid an office girl half the money earned, to type the story. If I was to be a real writer then typing was a skill I had to learn. If I could play the piano by ear, I figured I could do it on the typewriter as well. I bought a second hand portable, and it did not take too long to turn out a creditable typescript.

But nothing could ever overtake the joy, the memory, of the acceptance of that first story. The morning it came I was facing into a bitter day on the job. A sleety wind sent dark *Wuthering Heights* clouds racing over the town, and I was shivering at the thought of the muck and slush that I was going to have to endure, when the postman pushed a letter for me through the letter box. Suddenly I was on Miami beach, the coconut palms waved in a balmy breeze, and the blue tide of my coming fame came in never to ebb. In a daze of happiness I gloated over my first cheque!

After that, I wrote like a fury at nights, and within a few weeks I received a letter from the editor. 'Dear L.C. Redmond, (Mr, Mrs or Miss). Since you are becoming well known to our readers, we enclose a form which we hope you will fill in, with a view to devoting an editorial to your career . . . .' How old was I? Male or female? How many children? When had I taken up writing? And many other things that I had no intention of answering truthfully. Remembering Lucy Bottle's husband, I said I had been taken out of the Army so that I could do more damage to

Der Führer in a factory. The next issue of the love rag contained a glowing tribute, which I treasured until Gilbey woke me up to the fact that I was writing rubbish.

'Mind you,' said Mick, 'it's a great achievement for a carpenter to get anything published, but you're capable of better things than that, far better.' A left-handed compliment that I could have done without. It stuck in my craw, spurred me on to do better, and 'better' had no place in this factory girls' Never-Never Land.

I sat down and wrote a real story, which came back like a rocket. 'Rather "red" meat for our readers,' said the editor. 'Our ladies do not want to be distressed, only entertained! We would welcome another warm-hearted love story from you. We are sorry to have to return this, but we are sure you can revert to your old style at will.' It was signed by the editor. I put the rejected story away and immediately plunged into another suburban pot boiler. This was also rejected. I had lost my touch, I could not revert as the editor had hoped, and a nice profitable sideline was lost forever.

I did not know then that it would be many years before another story of mine was published. In the meantime, I was only twenty-three. 'Writing,' as R.L. Stevenson had so truly remarked, 'is a mighty bloodless substitute for living', and I must dance down the Yellow Brick Road that lead to where?

'To a woman, that's where,' said my mind, 'and get her into bed as quickly as possible, if not sooner.' I had had little luck in this grimy town, I was sick of it, I must engineer a transfer at all costs, as far away from here as possible.

I lay in wait for Lucy one Saturday evening, but she resolutely refused to 'take up' with me again. 'Nay, lad,' said practical Lucy, 'we've 'ad ower little moment, an' it's finished. You're a good-lukin' lad, what's wrong wi' you?'

What indeed? Nothing, except that the girls in this town seemed to prefer anything to an Irish civilian. Although, I knew I was wrong about that. Most of the men on the job had a woman on the side. Well then, this town was just unlucky for me, and anyway I hated the seventeen smoking chimney stacks I could see from my bedroom. I hated the grimy, cobblestoned backstreets with their doorsteps gleaming white against the sooty brickwork, and even the river I had come across outside the town was polluted, a splendid stream until industry ruined it, for it had a waterfall that crashed down into a deep, foamy pool, from which multi-coloured bubbles ascended forever. Like me, I thought, forever blowing bubbles.

As the day for Mick's departure approached, my spirits, at an all time low since my second rejection by the Rag-Mag, dropped even lower, while his soared. I could never endure this town when he went. So, on a Monday morning, when timber supplies had failed to arrive and the Devil made work for idle hands, I was ripe for trouble.

'What's goin' on?' Mick called out to the crowd of men walking past our particular house.

'We're jackin' up,' came the answer. 'It's over the huts.'

'C'mon, Lar,' said Gilbey, who was quitting in two days time anyway and didn't give a damn. 'Let's help them out.' Rose Mary and Dublin beckoned, to hell with the rest, including me!

Gladly, we lined up alongside the others, about a hundred in all. It was none of our business, we did not live in the huts, but anything to break the boredom of life in Warrington. 'Jackin' up' was the favourite recipe for this, and tormenting the English office staff was good for the morale. The martyrs from the huts took up the cry, and we with them.

'WE'RE HERE ABOUT THE HUTS . . . WE'RE HERE ABOUT THE HUTS.'

The man elected as spokesman walked importantly onto the board walk outside the office and knocked on the door. A terrified typist opened it a tiny crack, snatched the written petition, and banged it shut at once. The chanting grew in volume and edginess as the minutes went by and nothing happened. The truth was that the entire office staff were afraid of us. Reared on a diet of the 'fighting, drunken Irishmen', we were judged to be barely human, and they reacted accordingly. If they could not avoid dealing with us they treated us with contemptuous frigidity, neutrals who watched their Merchant Navy and Royal Marines go to the bottom, week after week, and denied them the shelter they needed so desperately. All in all, not a menu geared to win over rebellious Irish hearts. Soon, the first stone struck the office. The windows had long since been covered with a heavy, stone-proof steel grid, prudence learned from former 'Jack-ups', but the galvanised roof was still there, and we rained stones on it, a satisfying sound.

I was having a ball, it was all a 'bit of gas', and Mick was grinning like a Cheshire cat. It was a piece of mock ferocity, but the staff obviously believed their lives to be in danger, and kept the door locked. If one of the pretty typists had emerged, and like Dorothy, in the Land of Oz, had given our spokesman a good slap in the puss, his reaction would have been immediate. Like the cowardly lion, he would have slunk away, tail between legs, and all of us mock lions exposed for what we really were. Irishmen playing 'stage Irish', which the English expected.

'What about the huts?' the crowd roared.

'Aye,' shouted a tiny painter beside me who had the voice of a baying wolfhound, 'an' whar' about the earwigs?'

A couple of labourers came up then, each wheeling a barrow of stones, and the staccato clangs on the galvanised roof turned into an avalance of noise. Suddenly, the office door opened, and out on the board walk appeared the impeccable form of our new Public Relations man, the old one, it was rumoured, having been removed to hospital suffering from a persecution complex. He was hearing Irish brogues all the time and his Lancashire staff had begun to be accused of being Paddies and Biddies. His replacement would go the same road if we had anything to do with it.

He stood there, quite coolly appraising us, until the hail of stones stopped. Once more I had to give grudging credit to the English, for guts.

'Good morning, men,' he shouted in a public school accent. 'I'm here to listen to your complaints and, if possible, to rectify them. Now, who is your spokesman?'

'I am,' shouted our man, Cooney, from the front of the crowd, 'an' we're here about the dirty bloody leakin' huts.'

'That, my friend, is already receiving attention. As you all know there's a war on . . . .'

'We know there's a bloody war on, we're not here to discuss that!'

'Yes, my dear fellow,' said the other patronisingly, 'but unfortunately it takes precedence over everything else. I have to go through all the fiddle-faddle of bureaucratic boards who allocate materials as they see fit. However,' he continued, raising a hand to silence the gathering rumble, 'I have good news. The materials we need will arrive this week and I will undertake to have the roofs repaired at once. Now, you people, is that not fair?'

In the slight pause that followed the small painter gave tongue.

'But nobody has said an'thin' about the bloody earwigs!' He was pointedly ignored.

'While yer restin' yerself, what about appointin' someone teh keep the huts clean? Like washin' the floors now an' then,' Cooney shouted. 'Or de yiz think the Irish live like pigs?'

'Come . . . come . . . I'm sure nobody in this firm thinks that. But I'll consider your request and see what can be done.'

'Y'ill do no considerin', y'ill do it this day or we don't go back teh work!' A little ruffled by now, the superior one's complexion was rising.

'That is not a proper attitude,' he said, his voice trembling slightly. 'Striking is against the law, and carries a prison sentence or deporation with it.'

'Why don't yeh deport some a' the shaggin' earwigs?' said the long-suffering Dublin painter, amid an explosion of laughter.

Cooney was not laughing. 'There's no need for threats,' he bawled. 'We've been complainin' for mont's now, an' nuttin's been done.'

'I can assure you this time it will be done.'

'When will yeh do somethin' about the poxy earwigs?'

'If I may speak without interruption, I'll concede a point. I'll have it done today.'

'Yis, but yeh keep glossin' over the earwigs!' The small painter was hanging on like a bulldog, but again he was ignored.

'Today. I promise. Now men, back to work.'

'Back teh work, ses his Lordship,' roared the painter. But how would yew like teh come home teh twenty t'ousand fuckin' earwigs?'

In the roar of laughter that followed we were watching the Public Relations man with interest. It was plain he was under pressure. Under the cool exterior he was shaking, his hands were trembling, the rosy cheeks had vanished to be replaced by an ashen face, and eyes that were jumping out of his head. He focussed the Dublin painter with a baleful glare, and spoke. And like snow in rain our sham ferocity disappeared.

'Jaysus Christ,' he ground out, his voice curdled with rage. 'I've had enough of yer fuckin' earwigs, yeh bloody little get . . . the whole lot a' yiz 'id get down on yer bended knees if yiz had the pay at home yer gettin' here. An' there'll be no strike! Get that in yer head,' he snarled at Cooney, 'or you'll be on the next boat home. Now, Fuck Off . . . the whole fuckin' lot a' yiz, back teh work or off the fuckin' job!'

So this was my courageous Sassenach, a Dublin gurrier in disguise, a smart bastard who knew on which side his bread was buttered, who could see through us, and was quite capable of dealing with us. A diamond to cut a diamond!

In the shock of revelation, we slunk off, beaten. Gilbey was openly laughing.

'Jaysus,' he said repeatedly, 'can you beat that? A bowsey from the slums, apin' the English upper class and gettin' away with it.'

'He has us sized up anyway,' said Cooney with a grin, '"Jackin' up" is about teh go out a' fashion.' And it did!

189

The following day would be Mick's last in England, and we decided to go to the local music hall, to cheer me up. Accordingly, we groped through the freezing blackout, a little late, and managed to get the two worst seats in the house. Like all music halls this one was semi-circular, best seats on the ground floor, the Stalls, next best Upper Circle, on top of that the Gallery, or 'The Gods'. Our seats were at one end of the half circle of 'The Gods', where we had to lean over and see the stage sideways. A couple of hours of this left one 'gunnereyed'. It was not a promising start to what turned out to be a memorable night of sorts.

The Chorus, a dozen shapely girls scantily dressed, made our sex-starved hearts miss a couple of beats. Sequined bras covered softly ample bosoms, lush bottoms beckoned, and the lovely slopes of their bellies made ours turn over. After the girls retired, to lack-lustre applause, from an audience composed of factory workers, their wives and sweethearts, all sated with sex it seemed, a couple of comedians came on, with the usual smutty jokes that had the crowd in knots, while scarcely raising a smile in Mick or me. This stuff would be booed off the stage in Dublin, a ribald city where outrageous stories were swopped in pubs, but frowned on in public.

The stage was regarded as public, the pubs were not. We had only contempt for comedians who could not make a crowd laugh with good clean fun. For Mick and I had, despite our resolutely anti-clerical pose, been well brainwashed in childhood, and suffered from the Irish disease, the double standard.

When the comedians mercifully departed, the orchestra played the nostalgic strains of 'Mother Machree' and on stage came a small Irishman, dressed in 'Paddy me arse' eighteenth-century attire, singing the song. He had a loud, raucous Dublin voice, and the English, who could not distinguish one Irish accent from another, listened to him with reverence. He sang with great feeling, a real 'Ham' who laid it on with a trowel. He would have been belted off 'the boards' in Dublin, if ever he got past the stage door, which was unlikely. The applause was rapturous!

'Jaysus,' Mick exclaimed. 'Did you ever hear anything like it?' I had, many times, in theatre queues, where dead beats sang for beer money.

There was worse to follow. As the applause died down, the singer went into a monologue, his voice choking with emotion, about his old Irish mother who waited in a thatched cottage in the glen, silver-haired, rosary beads in hand, praying and waiting for her lost son to return. The blue mountains lay bare against a winter sky, banshees and leprechauns haunted the night, and the wind that blows across the sea from Ireland, blew moistly over this hard-headed, north of England audience, and the Blarney, dipped in bullshit, had them gulping. Many of the mill girls, who could mix it with the best, were unashamedly weeping.

'The nearest that fella ever got to a thatched cottage,' Mick said in a grinding whisper, 'was the pisshouse on O'Connell Bridge.'

'Maybe he was on a couple of excursions down the country,' I whispered back.

'He might have got across a country softie!'

'Or her mother!'

'Shush,' came the indignant voices of people close by and we had to shut up and endure the torrent of verbal diarrhoea that poured off stage. They brought him back three times to sing 'Mother Machree', and, in the deafening applause, we were able to voice our feelings.

'De yeh know what?' Mick moaned, 'That fella'd be et', bet, an' thrun up again where I come from.'

I agreed, but privately thought it a very revealing inter-lude. It had shown me once again that, for all the stiff-upper-lip façade of these people, they were, at heart, kindly, like the two Kens and the mother, like Lucy Bottle, like old Dogberry and his amber-eyed wife. I was learning slowly and reluctantly, but learning anyway. However, I was never going to like the grimy face of the north of England, and the War was never going to give me the time to explore the

Yorkshire Moors, or go to that place I venerated, the Vicarage at Haworth, where *Jane Eyre* and *Wuthering Heights* had been written by two gifted sisters, and had opened up Yorkshire to the world.

But the same books, especially *Wuthering Heights* with its animal-like younger Heathcliff, grunting mangled English in a 'wuthering wind', had formed my dislike for the North. I was used to a soft climate and a softer voice, and the strident, sometimes fractured English spoken all about me set my teeth on edge. Tomorrow night Mick would sleep with the fair Rose Mary and I would be alone again with my writing, and no pal to confide in, and the longings that never left me. I would have to get away from this place.

An elbow in the ribs brought me out of my rêverie, to face an excited Gilbey. 'Will you for Jaysus sake have a look . . . through the wings on the far side!' Mick hissed. 'Have a ging.'

From where we were sitting we could see into the space back stage, and my eyes popped. Dressing and undressing casually, the chorus were making ready for their next appearance on stage. Quite naked, as they changed costumes, a vision of twelve lovely women unfolded, flashes of snowy white breasts, Venus de Milo forms, shaped like the hour glass, rounded bottoms and soft thighs that lead men to paradise, or, if denied, to madness. It was all there, a better show than they would ever put on, on stage. The aged stage hands wandering in and out casually, bringing costumes, fetching things, without raising an eyebrow, but on us two God-forsaken refugees from the world of women it was worse than the thumb screw or the rack!

'Sweet Mother of Jesus!' I gulped. We watched for a minute, then Mick stood up abruptly.

'C'mon, Larry,' he said, and gladly I followed him. It was all too much for us, stupid Irish who had been reared on a diet of mortal sins, young men who could not even manage to seduce a woman. It might all have been different if we had worked in a factory alongside girls, but we were in a reserved occupation, vital to the war effort, and we toiled in a land of men.

In a pub on the way home we looked for the comfort of whiskey, but in vain. 'Doan't thee know there a waar on, whiskey's on ration. Sup ale, lads, in t' long run it's better.' We sat there in the crowded pub, gloomily 'suppin' English piss, a travesty of a wholesome pint of Guinness, sunk in the deepest depression, until Mick remembered that this time tomorrow night he would be in heaven with Rose Mary. 'All over her,' he told me, 'like a heat rash,' and then suddenly he shut up as he observed my stricken face.

In the bedroom, back at the Barnes's, I watched him tie a spool of thread firmly in the middle of his back! No erotic dream was going to spoil his reunion with his love mate! I found my own spool in my suitcase and followed his example. I had need of it that night!

9   Plymouth

Easter came and went, and with it, Mick Gilbey.

With Gilbey gone, Warrington became unbearable to me. I decided that pastures new were of paramount importance. I had taken up a new Correspondence Course, run by one man. He admitted only those who were published writers, and then only if he considered that they might make it as writers of note. He had a long waiting list, but even though I had been writing crap, I was accepted at once.

He had three tests. Describe the moon, or the sea or "The English countryside'. I chose the first, and to the present day I can remember it word for word. To qualify for this demanding man's course in writing was not easy, for the descriptions had to be no more than one paragraph. I submitted the following.

'Terence had always feared the moon. It reminded him of death. A dead world, lost in space, shedding its palid light upon the marsh; for the marsh too was dead and corrupting. It caught the moon's light and held it. When no moon shone it gave back an eerie phosphorescent glow that he feared even more, and glittered, like sequins thrown on mud.'

But there was no way I could take up the course in this accursed town. I became a nuisance on the job. I led every protest, however silly. I was threatened with being sent back to Ireland, but protested that all I wanted was to get out of this town. My past record was that of a skillful and fast carpenter, and the foreman, who liked me despite the trouble I gave him, was sympathetic, for he was a cockney and hated this place as much as I did.

When the break came, like most things, it took me by surprise. It was 29 May, the day the Japs took Lashio, the terminus of the Burma road. Reg, the foreman, came to me about nine o'clock and told me to go home and pack. I was due to travel to Plymouth, damn near the length of England. All I knew about Devon was that it was famous for Devonshire cream, and that they spoke very differently from this harsh voice of the north, a west country 'burr'. I had a vague notion that it was Long John Silver country, 'Ow be yer turnips a'growin' ter day, Garge' . . . and that it was the home of Dartmoor and its grim and terrible prison. That Sir Francis Drake had played boles on Plymouth Hoe and considered he 'had time to beat the Spaniards yet'. Outside those important pieces of information I knew nothing. But one thing I was sure about, and that was that I could never detest it as much as here.

We were into May, and yet the winter had only slightly loosened its grip. It was cold, wet and breezy, the 'wuthering wind' whistled through the houses we worked on, and even the watery sun brought little warmth. Far to the south where I was headed I knew was a more genial climate.

Old Mrs Barnes and Dogberry were upset by my going and gave me a tearful farewell. And truly I was sorry to leave them. My dislike of the north of England made me ashamed when I thought about it. For these two old people had treated me like the son they never had. Lucy Bottle had defended me and given me a night of joy. Poor Ken, until life became unbearable, had treated me well. The Sally Arms had sheltered me in my hour of need and Ken number two and his mother had treated me as one of their own. I had not got all that much to complain about, even if the savage treatment by the pig-like Mrs Beeby, and her Irish-hating husband had soured me against this place from the start.

Also, the climate, so much colder than Ireland, was not

to my taste, for even now, in early summer sunshine, one could get goose pimples in the thin wind.

Spring had just departed and had been a terrible one for England. Three German Pocket Battleships, the *Scharnhorst*, *Gneisenau* and *Prinz Eugen*, each capable of taking on the best the Royal Navy could offer, had broken out successfully and dashed up the English Channel. Lord Haw-Haw, alias William Joyce, in his broadcast from Berlin that night, thumbed his nose at the Brits, and haw-hawed with delight at their discomfiture. That had been on 11 February.

Four days later, Singapore, mighty bastion of Empire, symbol of British power in Asia, fell like a rotten fruit to the Japs, and its mighty garrison marched away to brutal captivity, and set to work like Coolies building the Burma Road. Many of them would never live to see Blighty again. Worse, the myth of the indestructible Brit had been extinguished forever and would never again command respect or fear in Asia. A Japanese Aircraft Carrier launched an attack on Darwin, capital of Australia's Northern Territory. No part of the Empire was safe anymore.

March had brought no cheer either. Seven days into the month the Japs landed in New Guinea, poised now to strike at Australia, whose fighting men were at war thousands of miles from home. Britain's Burma Army had to get to hell out of Rangoon, another 'strategic withdrawal'. Two days later, the invincible Japs conquered Java, completing the occupation of the East Indies.

Through all this old Jim Barnes never faltered. England would win through. 'Bluddy squint-eyed Japs 'ill get what they 'ave coming, an' Jerries 'ill really cop it this time, no bluddy mercy for this lot, an 'itler won't 'ole up in Holland like Kaiser Bill! We'll 'ang bluddy lot,' he told me, and by God he was proved right!

But at that time I would not have given the Brits much chance of continuing on alone. America was now in the War, England's proverbial luck still held. The Russians still bore the brunt of German might, but the Russian Bear, though horribly mauled, presented a ferocious front to the invader, and had ground him to a halt, with six million men under arms. The world was in flames, Devon beckoned, and I sat on the train tearing southwards with a happy heart. Maybe some Devonshire maid, or her mother, I was not too particular, would fancy me. Sure I might as well rave here as in bed.

London, where I had a wait of almost five hours, changed my mind about Britain's chances of winning the War. The station was seething with soldiers, many of them Yanks. It was obvious that, between the Russians, the USA and Britain, Germany could no longer hope to win, that in the end, even if it took years, Hitler would be brought to heel.

In mainland Europe resistance fighters were growing in a strength and boldness that no German atrocity could halt. Burning villages, shooting the population, only increased the hatred and recruited thousands more to the 'Underground'. Nightly the Brits dropped machine guns, rifles and explosives to fuel the fire, accompanied by soldiers of unimaginable courage to drill and train more Freedom Fighters. No doubt about it, this country was proving its mettle and was to be admired, even by people as biased as myself. My childhood memories of British rule and the terror of the Black and Tans had blinded me to the truth about the present war.

It was not hard for me to remember how that gentle Prime Minister, Neville Chamberlain, had debased himself, almost grovelled, to try and stay the hand of the mad Adolf, to no avail. A Prime Minister whose inoffensive hobby was 'bird watching', had no notion how to deal with an Anti-Christ. Churchill, after years in the wilderness, swept Chamberlain into oblivion and took a bulldog grip on the nation.

His determined face, cigar jutting out, was plastered all over the country, especially in railway stations, whose shattered glass roofs bore mute testimony to Der Führer's rage. Churchill's coalition took the best of all parties and welded the nation as one. In the long wait for the train to Plymouth I had plenty of time to think. I had been recruited in Dublin to work in Britain, but quite a few of the men I had to work alongside were openly hostile. That Britain needed its Irish labour force was obvious, but the fact that young men like me were sometimes the object of open contempt was hard to endure. And it was not possible to explain my situation to any English person. Terrible stories of the rounding up of Jews and gypsies all over Europe were leaking through, to trouble me. If these stories were true, it would be my duty to join up at once, despite the fact that I was a reserve soldier of the Irish Forces.

But were they true? Had not Britain circulated terrible stories about the barbarous Hun in the First World War, the happy pastime of making lamp shades out of the skin of British soldiers, especially those who had been tattooed. Thousands of my countrymen had swallowed the propaganda and joined up to fight for the freedom of small nations like Belgium. My father did not believe the Brits and decided to fight for his own country — in it.

My childhood had been warped by the Irish struggle and the Civil War that set brother against brother. Many of my father's friends, fighting alongside him, had been caught and hanged or shot out of hand by the Brits. In our house, as in most of Ireland, the British propaganda machine was treated with open scepticism, if not utter disbelief. If I ever joined the British Army I need never go home again, for I would be ostracised by my own. I would be a maverick, forever banned from the family circle. I would never be forgiven.

Anyway, I hated the Army, any bloody army, except the Salvation Army. I had been described by a discerning sergeant as 'the best bloody civilian in the 7th Battalion' and he had been correct. I was one of the finest shots in the company, could march as far as the best, was efficient and clean, but there was something lacking, and the sergeant had spotted it. I kept in step when marching, but I had an easy stride. In no way would I ever become a military goose-stepper. And I had an enduring contempt for peacetime soldering. I was, as usual, a square peg in a round hole!

The journey to Plymouth seemed endless. In fact it took eight hours. Frequent stops in sidings to allow trains which, bearing everything it took to make war, had precedence, and before darkness fell I watched tanks by the hundred trundle past, lorries by the thousand. It was clear the great build-up for the invasion of Europe was on. Before I fell asleep, weary of this long day and hungry — for my diet of weak tea and buns did little to sustain me — I wrote a letter to Mam. I woke up in the morning at eight o'clock, in Plymouth Station, starving, to a cheerless prospect. It was pouring rain, and I humped the tool box and suitcase along a platform that had puddles and streams of water, for there was not one pane of glass left in the roof.

Outside, and directly opposite the station, a huge pile of bricks and stones that had once been a prominent building sent up little puffs of smoke through the debris. All around had been blitzed, tall houses gutted by fire or ravaged by bombs. It looked like something from World War One in France. I felt myself to be in the front line at last. A truck pulled up then and a huge bear of a man clambered out, grinning, and made straight for me.

'You'll be the new arrival from Warrington,' he said, and shook my hand in a huge gentle paw.

I smiled back at him and said, 'Larry Redmond here.'

'Oi'm 'arry,' he replied in a soft Devonshire burr. 'Larry an' 'arry.' He swept my tool box up and into the back of the truck without effort, put the suitcase beside it, and covered both over with a canvas cover.

''op in,' he said.

Compared to Dublin Plymouth was a small city, but of far greater importance that my own birthplace. It was a major port of the English Navy, then one of the world's most formidable. Harry was about forty-five years of age, ruddy-faced and strong, a gentle giant, whose face saddened as we passed a terrace of blitzed houses.

'No one,' he said, 'got out of that lot alive. Ower Vera, that worked for us, got killed that night. That was 'er little 'ouse,' he informed me pointing to the last ruin. 'Our Vera?

She worked for Gran. 'ad a kind of understandin' with 'er, maybe get married some day. 'ad nothin' worked out, mind yew, but I'd probably 'av'. Sorry arrhur I didn't.'

He fell silent then as we wound through the traffic, mostly Army and Navy lorries. I was becoming a bit of an expert in assessing the damage to English cities and decided that this one was the worst hit. I was correct. Churchill stated later that Plymouth had had the most terrible experience of any English city, and now, driving slowly through it in the pouring rain, it was a sad sight.

London, though terribly scarred, was largely intact. Coventry had had its core neatly removed, with its suburbs still there. Here the Luftwaffe had torn the centre of Plymouth apart and then run amok in what was left. Devonport, another naval centre close by, was even worse, Harry told me, but this I could not imagine. I was wrong. I saw after the War what the Allies had done in Germany, in Düsseldorf, Cologne, Hanover, and along the industrial Ruhr, cities that had been pounded into pulp, and even then the bombing continued. It was something like kicking a corpse, the terrible whirlwind of hatred delivered with precision against those who had sown the wind.

But all that was years in the future as we drove into Oxford Street. It had once been a street of tall, Victorian houses, but now there was only one left and it stood quite alone among its fallen fellows, all of them reduced to safe levels. Harry pulled up before it and went inside. He came out after a couple of minutes and got back into the truck.

'Sorry,' he said, 'Ol' Gran got a notion ter visit ol' Violet, that's 'er sister. Were a sneak raid over that way last night. Oi 'ave ter pick 'er up.' And that was very much okay with me. I was having a ride around Plymouth. I could see all I wanted in the firm's time, and it would hardly be worth bringing me on site that day. Lovely!

'Oi were in Dublin durin' the Troubles,' Harry informed me as we wound our way through the shattered streets. 'Noice people they was, an' very kind tew. Know Ringsend, Larry?'

200

'Yes, but not much. Around the Docks, isn't it? We call it The Village.'

'Fancy yew not knowin' about Ringsend!'

'But Harry, Dublin is getting to be a big city now. I was miles away from Ringsend.'

'Well, that's where Oi used ter be on patrol, supposed tew be lookin' out for Shinners — bluddy stupid it was, 'ow was Oi suppose ter know the difference between Shinners an' other people? They was all dressed the same, an' looked the bluddy same. An' anyway, the people in Ringsend were very fond 'o me, arrher I tipped 'em off that the Tans were agoin' ter raid them that noight. An' Oi did it everytime, arrherwards. The Tans were scum. They robbed 'an killed 'an disgraced me . . . an' England.'

Open-mouthed, I gaped at the big man beside me, but he gazed steadily ahead, untroubled by his treason to Britain.

'Me an' Eric, we was the tew that were always on patrol in Ringsend, an' it didn't take us long tew click with a couple of the local maids . . . .'

He chuckled. 'Mots is what they call 'em in Dublin, ain't that roight?' I laughed.

'That's right, Harry, but were you not afraid to be seen with Irish women?' What I should have said was, 'Were they not afraid to be seen with you?' The Shinners had a swift way of handling women who went with British soldiers, and among their neighbours they were social outcasts, shunned by all. Some, I knew had had their hair hacked off and I had heard of at least one case of tarring and feathering, but she had been going with a Tan.

'No,' said Harry thoughtfully, 'nor were Eric. He'd 'ole up in Carmel's 'ouse, an' I'd 'ole up in Mary's . . . an' a sweet maid she were. An' mad about me an' me about 'er. She was lovely.'

The rain increased in force as we pulled up at a traffic light. All about were sodden ruins. Even as we waited, great lumps of bricks and mortar broke loose from one of them and joined the heap on the ground with a sodden thud.

'And you two never married?'

'No. She warn't game ter chance it in Devon, thought as my people wouldn't take to her, an' I couldn't leave ol' Gran, that's me mother, ter struggle on with the boardin' 'ouse alone. Tina, me sister, got married tew a no good bastard, 'ad tew, an' she only seventeen. 'ad twins for 'im, she did, before she found out he were already married. Got jailed for bigamy, 'e did. So there yew 'ave it. Ol' Gran 'ad 'ole bluddy lot of 'em ter keep, when I were in Dublin, an' I 'ad me duty ter do by 'er.'

'Where's your sister, Tina, now?'

'At 'ome, 'elpin Gran, wi' Audrey 'elpin tew. Audrey's sister, Gladys, is in the Air Force, you'll meet 'em all soon enough.' So here was a story that touched my heart. This gentle giant beside me had never married because of his Ringsend sweetheart.

'Did your Mary ever marry, Harry?'

'No. She wrote ter me once, from a convent. Last I 'eard of 'er she were goin' ter Calcutta in India. She was gentle, my Mary.' We had cleared the centre of the city by now, but the devastation did not lessen, if anything it got worse. Eventually we pulled up before a row of small cottages that miraculously were still intact. Two old ladies talking on the pavement kissed each other goodbye and one of them scuttled over to the truck.

'Move over, Larry, an' let Gran in. 'ow yer keepin', Vi?' he roared through the window at the other old lady. Hastily I opened the door, jumped out, and helped Old Gran into the truck. She was spritely, with a rosy withered apple face and startlingly blue eyes, and I liked her at once. Squeezing over to her son, to make room for me, she gave me a sidelong glance.

'Oi see,' she said to Harry, 'we 'ave a gentleman on ower 'ands. This the one we was expectin'?'

'It is, Gran. Name of Larry, from Dublin.'

'Ah,' said Gran knowingly, 'Dublin, eh! A good-lookin' lad, Harry. The maids 'ill be arrher 'im.'

''alf 'is luck,' said Harry, and, waving to Vi, roared off

through the wrecked city. I saw a beautiful granite church laid open to the sky, the pitiless rain pouring down on this medieval masterpiece, with the stone statues that had graced the entrance lying on the steps before it. I had seen it all before, especially in Coventry, but the desecration of a church never failed to sicken me, as though the hand of God had been spat upon, Mount Calvary all over again. A minute later we turned into Gran's in Oxford Street, where I would live for a time.

The street, as far as I could make out, had had about twenty tall Victorian houses each side, but now on one side none were left, and we pulled up at the only house still standing, opposite. It was heavily shored up, braced from the ruins of its former neighbours, its peeling white gables once the inside of the houses next door.

''ere we are,' said Harry, matter of factly. I jumped down and helped Old Gran to alight. The rain had suddenly ceased, the warm sun shot through the scudding clouds, and I had arrived in a different country. Gone was the reluctant, tardy summer of the north, for the trees around me were almost in full leaf. Old Gran smiled at me.

'Are you so 'elpful with the young maids, Larry?' she said. I could have told her I was twice as helpful, three times as much, especially if there was a chance of helping them into bed, but naturally I kept silent.

'My mother taught me to respect women, all women, Ma'am'.

'You'll call me Gran,' she said swiftly. 'The same as all the rest.'

'Right, Gran,' I said, and took my suitcase from the truck. The bloody tool box could stay where it was, it was bound for the building site anyway, but if anyone wanted to steal it they were bloody welcome to it. We entered Gran's boarding house by the basement door, the front door being boarded up. That day I found out that it was sandbagged behind. In the basement, which was the dining room, there were tables laid out for twenty people. Nine-inch rolled steel joists, or girders, were held firmly against half-inch

203

thick steel plates, about three feet square, which supported the ceiling against another Blitzkrieg from the sky and a possible collapse of the three storeys above. I stood there, gaping. I had never seen an air-raid shelter like this dining room.

Gran chuckled, for she was observing me closely.

'Take more than 'itler to get old Gran,' she said. 'Now, take a seat, lad, an' us'll get yew some breakfast. Yew look famished, lad. Yew're w'ite as a sheet.' Indeed I was exhausted from hunger and the long journey and sat gratefully down. Very soon breakfast was placed before me — and what a breakfast! I had never seen anything like it since I left Ireland. Two eggs, real eggs, with sausages and rashers, a plate full of white bread, and a pot of lovely strong tea. Gran sat nearby as I wired into the lot.

'We don't 'ave this all the time, Larry,' she said. 'But, lad, yew'er real dawny lookin' an' ole Gran be very friendly with ower local farmers.'

'Keep up the good work, Gran, and may you be half an hour in Heaven before the divil finds out.'

Gran burst out laughing, slapping her knees with her hands.

'That's Oirish, an' all, that be! Did yew 'ear that, Audrey?' I glanced over my shoulder and looked into the simpering face of Audrey, who looked about eighteen, bursting at the seams with feminine charm, broad hips, lovely fulsome breasts, and strong over-large legs. She would never win a beauty contest but no man would complain if he had her in bed. All cats are black at night.

I stood up and said good morning to her, smiling innocently, but I think she read my mind, knowing that young men lusted for her.

'This be Larry from Dublin,' Gran told her and Audrey, giggling, left the room.

'That be me grand-daughter,' Gran told me. 'Eat up, lad. Yew're gettin' a bit of colour in yer face.'

Replete at last, I sat back exhausted. What I needed was a good sleep, but there was a 'waar' on and I supposed that I would be required on site that day. Harry came back then with another older woman, his sister.

'This be Tina,' he told her and I gazed at Audrey's mother. She was a fine woman, about forty, I guessed, and lacked none of her daughter's charms, though she was much better looking and quite obviously more intelligent.

'I'm pleased to meet you,' I said, standing up.

'Proper Oirish gentleman we 'ave 'ere,' said Gran. 'What do yew think . . . ?'

'I think,' said Tina, and I noticed at once that her speech was much better than the others. 'That it won't take him long to capture some maid, if he's willing.' Willing! Jesus Christ if only she knew how willing the young man who stood before her was, even desperate. That his intrusions into the world of women had been too brief, just enough for him to know that his world was a desert without them, that soon he might br frustrated enough to look for solace in the arms of a prostitute, and risk a dose. The docks around Plymouth, I had been told, were a fruitful hunting ground for men like me, even though I still looked like a boy. It was the bloody long eyelashes that gave me the appearance of a boy and concealed the fact that I had a fine well-developed body from hard work, that I was all man.

'Well,' said Harry, 'Oi'd better show yew where yew sleep, an' then it's change yer clothes an' out ter work.'

'I'll show him,' said Tina.

'An 'e'll not be goin ter work this day,' said Gran firmly.

'But Gran . . . ,' Harry protested.

'But nothin',' said Gran, 'Oi know yewer supposed tew take 'im out to the job, but yew can easy cover up.'

'Ow? What'll Oi say?'

'Say he didn't get 'ere till the afternoon. That train was 'eld up.'

'All right, then, Gran.' And so it was Tina who led me upstairs, into a room at the top of the house that held four beds.

'That one,' she said pointing, 'is yours.' My heart sank. This was not for me if I wanted to continue my Writing

Course. On the way up I had noticed a tiny room, little more than a cubby-hole, with one small bed in it, the door being open.

'Any chance of the little room across the landing, Tina?'

'Why, don't you like company?'

'Not this much.' And then I told her about my ambition to become a writer and that I needed solitude for my Writing Course. I went into the tiny room, Tina followed.

'You're lucky,' said Tina. 'The man that was in here only left this morning. We were glad to get rid of him, a grouchy old bachelor.'

'Then I can have it?'

'Yes, but you'll have to wait until I change the sheets. Come back in about an hour I'm rushed off my feet preparing dinner for twenty men. Sorry, Larry.'

'That's all right, Tina, I'll sit in the kitchen and talk to Gran. But I'll unpack now, all right?'

'All right,' she said, and squeezed past me, her breast brushing my chest, for the room was that small, and my heart skipped a couple of beats. There was a window set in the sloping ceiling, with its glass painted black against the Luftwaffe, but it opened when I tried it and I had an unparalleled view over Plymouth, this bomb-blasted and fire-gutted city. In the distance the dark expanse of Dartmoor, with its grim prison wall, down on the horizon, and all around the fair countryside of Devon. Already it was moving in on the shattered city and the piles of debris and stones were rearing a healthy crop of wild flowers. Yellow ragwort waved in the sunshine, thistles springing up all over, and a hundred other plants that had not grown here for centuries were reclaiming their own. A couple of hundred yards away a circular water tank, sited against another incendiary attack, gleamed like chromium plate and, serenely floating on its surface, a wild duck and her seven chicks. I was excited about my tiny room with a view.

Clothes being rationed, my unpacking was soon done, and I reverently laid my tiny portable Corona on the bed. If I got myself a piece of board and placed it under my typewriter the bed would be okay for work. This, I told myself with all the confidence of youth, is where my masterpiece would be produced.

Back down in the air-raid shelter-cum-dining room, Gran was placidly knitting a jumper for one of her grandchildren in the Forces. She seemed happy to see me. No doubt I had struck it lucky to find this household, warm as any home in Dublin's Liberties, and infinitely more prosperous.

Gran, like the rest of Britain, although surrounded by ruins, had no doubt that 'Old 'itler' would be hanged. It would take a bit of time but England had plenty of that. It was 30 May and that night there was jubilation in Oxford Street, for Britain had struck back, and hard, with the first thousand bomber raid on Cologne. The flattening of German cities had begun.

'Ole Drake 'ad time for a game o' boles, before 'e 'ad 'is set-to wi' the Spaniards an' Oi recken we 'ave time on ower side.'

She glanced up from her knitting and gave me a shrewd eyeful.

''itler 'as 'ad it. 'e made 'is big mistake takin' on the Russians. You'll see. Loike a cuppa, Larry, seein' as we're 'avin' a natter?'

'Not half, Gran.'

'But why are you not in bed, Larry?'

'I'm moving into the little room. Tina wants to change the sheets. I'll go up when she does.'

'All roight then.' We settled down to enjoy a 'natter' and Gran surprised me by accepting a cigarette. She was a hardened smoker, had only started a little over a year ago when the fury of the Luftwaffe had shaken even her iron spirit.

'Tell me, Gran, why is the front door boarded up and sandbagged behind?' She shook her head slowly, sighing.

'That was a bad noight for me,' she said sorrowfully. 'That were the noight Devonshire lass were killed . . . bluddy Germans!' I got the whole story from her. Devonshire Lass was a greyhound, an Irish import that

207

Gran had bought from a Dubliner, that had won all before her. In fact Gran had, by one means or another — all of them crooked — won a pile of money on the bitch. The whole boarding house had been in on the act, the bookies' losses were considerable, and growing, before they began to make her an odds on favourite.

'Oi soon put a stop tew that,' said Gran. 'Oi gave her a good feed before the next tew races, an' when 'er odds went back tew four tew one the 'ole bluddy 'ouse were on her, an' we took the bookies for 'undreds. Lovely,' she said laughing, 'tew see them crooked buggers 'aving tew fork out.' The upshot was that she was banned from every track in Devonshire.

'And what did you do then, Gran?'

''ad 'er dyed by an expert, an' ran her under a different name. Only once, mind. Oi 'ad tew dress up as a man tew get into the track and place a bet. But Oi did it, an' got away with it, an' the bluddy bookies were 'it in the pocket again, an' they don't like that.' As far as I could make out bookies were the lowest form of animal life that Gran had ever seen, and existed solely to be taken as often as possible. Over the years Gran had owned greyhounds who had won little and cost much. All that had changed with the advent of Devonshire Lass, the Irish speed merchant, and she was of the unshakable opinion that all she had to do was to get another Irish greyhound and all would be as before.

I told her the truth, that all Irish dogs were not winners, but made no impression at all.

'You'll buy me a dog when you go over on 'olidays, won't you?'

'But Gran, I don't know one end of a greyhound from the other.'

'No matter,' she said firmly, 'Oi'll be lucky again with an Irish dog.'

'Well, anyway, what happened to Devonshire Lass?'

'Arr,' said Gran sorrowfully, 'that were a terrible thing. It were the noight o' the first big raid by the bluddy Germans, the night this 'ole street were wiped out, all except us. The

208

good Lord didn't want us lot yet, 'ad other plans for us, Oi suppose. We was all 'idin' down 'ere, an' terryfyin' it was, with the bombs burstin' all around, an' 'ouses close by going up . . . an' the bluddy whistlin' noise them bombs made before they 'it . . . Arr . . . ,' she said, her voice dying slowly away as the terrible memory, etched on her mind for ever, took hold.

'Don't worry, Gran,' I said softly. 'It's all over now. They'll never do that again.'

'They moight.'

'They won't, not as long as I'm here. Hitler isn't able to make the bomb that will kill me!'

'They was over Plymouth last noight.'

'Only a couple of planes, a sneak raid. Harry told me about it. As long as I'm in this house there won't be another bombing near here.'

'Why,' said Gran, wide-eyed, ''ave yew some special charm, or somethin'?'

'Maybe. I just know that there is no bomb with my name on it, Gran, I'm certain of that!'

'What makes yew so certain, Larry?'

'I just know, Gran. You'll see.' I could not tell this woman that I had ESP, extra sensory perception to a high degree. She might not understand. Many people, better educated by far than Gran, treated ESP with derision. If you did not have it, how could you understand it? And if you did, how could you explain it, when you did not understand it yourself?

'That's all roight, then,' said Gran, believing me, and looking very relieved. 'You're our lucky mascot, the one who 'as the four-leafed shamrock.'

'Anyway,' she said pouring another cup of tea, 'Devonshire Lass were out in 'er kennel an' Oi wanted tew go an' bring 'er in, but the others wouldn't let me. If Oi 'ad she'd be 'ere today.'

'Well, it were 'ell all around, and in the middle of it, a stone from that old church you saw on the way 'ere, were blown up, and it landed square on Devonshire Lass's

209

kennel. But first it came through the front door, straight through the stairs, an' out through the back wall, an' killed 'er. Come on, I'll show you.'

She dabbed her eyes with a handkerchief, and led me upstairs and out the back. 'There,' she said, pointing, 'is where the Lass is lyin'. That be 'er tombstone. Oi'll not 'ave it removed.' Sure enough, a four feet long bevelled parapet stone from the church had flattened the dog, flat as a tram ticket, I said to myself, and no harm done. I was deadly afraid of greyhounds, and sensing my fear they always came at me.

'Maybe,' I said with mock sorrow, 'she's better off where she is. It's a cruel world, Gran,' I added hypocritically, for at twenty-two I didn't know that.

'The Lord giveth, and the Lord taketh away', said Gran resignedly, and then she added, 'That's what Oi used tew tell the bookies when I took 'em.' Laughing, we went back to our pot of tea, and Gran produced the family album. I have always detested family albums of people I hardly know. I was thinking up some excuse to go when she opened it, and opened my eyes as well. For this was no ordinary family album. This was a photographic record of two wars. Big, young and handsome there was 'Ower 'arry' in Flanders in the last months of that old and frightful war, the one that poor Dogberry had got trench feet in and a busted chest from 'whiff from Kaiser Bill'. Then there was Tina, first with twins, standing beside the no-good bastard who had bigamously married her, and then standing alone, holding the babies he had left her with. Tina was still a handsome woman and she had been a winsome Devonshire 'maid'. Privately I thought her better looking now than then.

'That's ower Audrey she's 'oldin,' said Gran. Audrey, by coincidence, came in then, but left after being asked sharply what she wanted.

'Just lookin' for something,' said Audrey.

'Well you won't find it 'ere. Try the kitchen,' said Gran. 'An' give yewer mother a bit of a hand.'

She subjected me to a penetrating stare and, after a few

seconds, decided to speak her mind. 'Yewer a good-lookin' lad, Larry,' she said slowly. 'Maybe too good-lookin' with noice manners an plenty of Blarney, Oi've no doubt, but ower Audrey is spoken for, gettin' engaged week arrher next. Yew won't get any ideas, lad, will yew?'

I felt my face going red. No doubt old Gran had seen one of my sly glances in the face of Audrey's obvious charms, but I hastened to reassure her.

'No, Gran,' I said quite truthfully, 'I won't get any ideas.' That was easy, for I already had them.

'That's all roight, then,' said the old lady. 'Now 'ere we 'ave ower 'arry in Dublin during the Troubles, as 'e calls it. And sure enough there was Harry, standing at the bullet scarred General Post Office in Sackville Street, as it was then, a fine figure of a man against the stone columns. So this was the man Ringsend Mary could not resist, and who could blame her?

'Arr,' said Gran sorrowfully, gazing at her son, ''e were always a lovely lad, bluddy big softie, as left 'is 'eart in yewer place, Dublin. Mary, I think, that's roight, Mary it was, "My Mary of the curling hair," he calls 'er when 'e gets drunk, an' sentimental.'

'"My Mary of the curling hair, The laughing eyes and scornful air",' I told Gran. '"Our bridal morn dawns bright and fair, With blushes in the sky . . . ." It's a lovely song, Gran.'

'No doubt, an' no doubt either that yewer Dublin Mary stole my son's 'eart, an' 'e never got over it proper. We was tryin' tew make a match for 'im a while ago, but 'arry just kept on duckin' marriage. A nice widow, she were, an' very fond of ower 'arry — 'oo isn't? — an' I think she would have got 'im in the end, but poor lass, she was killed last year in the air-raids. Don't suppose as he'll ever marry now.'

I remained silent as Gran turned over a page.

''ere's some of bluddy Adolf's work,' said Gran. 'Take a good look, Larry. That were taken on the footpath outside this house the mornin' arr'er the big raid.' I scrutinised the picture carefully, missing nothing, something to be always remembered, and with loathing for war. There were twenty-four bodies laid out before Gran's house. Some soldiers appeared to be covering them with sheets. However, they had not finished yet, and the beautiful form of a young woman lay rigid on the pavement; she seemed uninjured, unmarked, and the wind had blown her long blonde hair across her face.

'I knew 'er,' said Gran, pointing to the girl. 'I knew 'er well, saw 'er grow up, an' a bonny maid she were. Killed by the blast they tells me, blew her lungs in or somethin'. Oi don't roightly know.'

But I did. I had heard of and seen some of the freak effects of blast. I had seen a four-storey block of flats, not far from Big Ben, with the front wall blown off and the entire contents exposed to the public view intact. Even the pictures on the walls were still hanging on unblemished wallpaper. I had met a man who was the only survivor of a bomb which exploded close to the pub where he was drinking. Everybody in the bar had been killed by the bomb blast, the titanic rush of air that follows the explosion, all except himself, and he had stumbled out of the pub, naked except for his shoes. All his clothing had been ripped off. He could not account for it, or how he had lived through it, nor could anybody else.

There were several more photos of Oxford Street, before and after Nemesis, before the war a quiet place of genteel boarding houses, shrubs in tubs, and hall doors that were covered with gaily striped canvas coverings against summer sunshine.

Tina came in then and said that my bed was ready, and Old Gran firmly closed the Album. 'Off to bed wi' you,' she said firmly. 'Sleep till dinner.'

'Yes Ma'm, an' no Ma'm, an' Ma'm if you please,' and I saluted.

'If yew look up the Duck's arse you'll see the green peas,' said Gran and left me open-mouthed. That was an Irish saying!

Gran grinned wickedly at my discomfiture. 'Didn't think

as I'd know, did yew? Ower 'arry brought a few things back wi' him from Dublin, an' yew're a naughty boy.'

I fled up the stairs, into my cubby hole, and hit the sack. I slept like a dead man and was awakened by the boarders returning from work. The loud clatter of heavy boots, noise from the room next door, the whole house suddenly buzzing with life, after a long quiet summer day, with the sun setting on the ravaged city, and the RAF assembling from all over England, their thousand bomber raid headed for Cologne. There would be plenty of Oxford streets in that city tomorrow, and blonde young girls with shining tresses laid out on the pavements. Death, destruction and fire would rain down from the skies, laying waste all before it, this no 'gentle rain from heaven' but the vengeance of hell let loose, done by men who had lived through a similar inferno, and here to exact the price of that act!

The searchlights would be blazing, I knew, the ack-ack fire would find a few targets, and an English Eagle, with flaming plumage, would plummet to earth, but the main force would live to return again and again until they had reduced German cities to rubble. This was the first big British hit at a German city, the first small sign that England would survive and exact bloody tribute for a bloody German past.

Somebody downstairs was ringing a bell, and down we trouped to dinner. I threaded my way through the steel poles, found a vacant place, bequeathed to me by the old bachelor who had gone. Here I would sit until I left the house.

And surely this was the best dinner I had ever received in England. Roast beef! Real Gravy! Fresh vegetables . . . floury potatoes! Impossible! I got stuck in before this feast vanished from in front of my eyes. Old Gran, smiling, presided over the meal, served by Audrey and Rosie.

''ows the dinner, lads?'

'Lovely, Gran,' came the chorus.

'No bluddy Woolton Pie for my lads,' said Gran. 'Nor Carrot Pie neither.' The British Ministry of Food, headed by

Lord Woolton, provided well meaning nutritious menus, especially in British Restaurants, run by the State, while exhorting the public to make them at home. Spam came on the market, to a derisory reception, and whale meat proved a total failure. The British public could not stomach it, and Lord Woolton, in the Music Halls, was the butt of every second joke.

> *There was a young lady of fashion,*
> *Who was very addicted to passion,*
> *Well, one thing she said,*
> *As she jumped into bed,*
> *I've got something Lord Woolton can't ration.*

All in all, though, the rationing of food worked. Britain's children had never been as well fed as now. The hungry thirties had gone forever it seemed, and Britain's Coalition Government could, when things were at their worst, when the U Boats hunted in packs and sank thousands of tons of shipping a week, provide a better meal for their workers than the Tory Government could in the days of plenty — plenty for the upper class, that is. The four million unemployed, many of them soldiers who had been through the hell of Flanders, stood listlessly on street corners, existing on bread and tea, but as long as they had a Lucifer to light their fag — as the old war song they had marched to told them — they got a 'drag' from a Woodbine against the daily hunger.

The diet of war-time Britain was monotonous, but sufficient. Eggs were rationed to one a fortnight, either because too many chickens had been eaten, or because they could not feed them. The dried egg powder which made its appearance on the market in June, never crossed Gran's door while I was there. This delicious dinner that I was wolfing presented a few questions that I was not interested in, but I found out all about it in due time.

The 'roast beef of old England' was Dartmoor pony, the eggs supplied blackmarket by Gran's many farmer friends, who also supplied the dozen hens in the back yard that were fed on scraps. Old Gran's attitude was the same as Lucy Bottle's, that the 'Landed Gentry' knew little rationing and her boys were doing a better job for England. In Oxford Street we were fed on the best, and I never wanted to leave it. I had even more reason not to leave it a couple of weeks later, but that lay in the future.

I made a few friends that night. They came from all over the British Isles, from Scotland, Wales, England, and one, a Jew from Germany called Charlie, was to alter finally my bigoted attitude to the Brits and their war. His real name was Helmut and the stories he told me of Germany under the Nazis tormented me for the next two years. There was no disputing this man's evidence, for he still bore the marks of the SS interrogation he had undergone. He had escaped from Germany just in time to avoid Hitler's final solution to 'the Jewish problem'.

The British Ministry of Propaganda was not lying. Terrible things were happening to Jews and gypsies, anybody who believed in justice and humanity would fight this evil that was Hitler, the Devil himself walking abroad over all Europe, Lucifer unleashed at last, and triumphant. Had he not poisoned the minds of a whole generation of young Germans, taught them that they were superior to other races, that they were unconquerable? And they damn near were!

And I, what was I going to do about it? I need never go home if I donned an English uniform, my family memories of the Brits were too bitter. I loved Ireland, that green and pleasant land, the greenest spot on the whole earth, the incredible green that flashed against the blue mountains, and always the white scudding clouds that threw shadows across the landscape, to light it up a minute later brighter and greener than ever. The beauty of my country was unequalled, even here in merry England, also a beautiful land, where it had not been despoiled by greed, even here could not match the beauty of my Róisín Dubh, my Dark Rosaleen.

There was plenty of time, I told myself, and in the

meantime Britain needed army camps, and for that reason I was in Devon. I was a war worker, badly needed. But Helmut's lacerated back and crooked maimed hands remained to haunt me. He told me they had been broken with a hammer, after he had been lashed. In the end they had decided that they had the wrong man. They threw him out into the street, a broken man. He was an industrial chemist and useful to Britain, a pale, sad man who worked long hours with furious energy that could only be sustained by hatred. He would never see his family again. They had disappeared into a concentration camp. He held out no hope for them.

And the terrible thing about my own situation was that had I been able to join the American Army, or the French Army in exile, or the rag-bag of European Armies that had escaped with the Brits at Dunkirk, I would have returned home to a hero's welcome!

'Yew're very quiet, Larry,' said Gran, and jerked me back to the present.

'Just listening, Gran. Still a bit tired.' All about me the armchair strategists were running the war, debating fiercely on the merits of the Commander of the 8th Army. Most of them seemed to think that he was a bloody fool, at best, a coward at worst, and I held my tongue. My private opinion was that General Rommel could run rings around anything Britain could put up against him. Two days before, he had launched an attack, and desperate battles were raging right now. Gibbo, my old army mate, and John Duffy were probably in the thick of it. A chill ran down my spine. I was glad I was not there. My confidence that no bomb could kill me did not extend to shells, mortars and machine-gun fire. I was still the best bloody civilian in the Irish Army!

I went to bed early, slept the sleep of the guiltless, and woke to a lovely summer's dawn, an early breakrfast, and I was ready for work thirty miles away by eight o'clock. A ten hour day, a tough life — but what was that? I was young.

10 Little Audrey

That morning the firm's truck collected me at the end of Oxford Street. It had a removable canvas canopy and long wooden seats that tipped over easily. It was draughty, dangerous, uncomfortable and I was grateful that summer was here. Winter on this thing would be rough. It was already crowded when I got on, barely room for one cheek of my arse on the end of the seat. I nearly went overboard a couple of times. On the way we passed three buses conveying men to our site, a project to house WRENS, the women's branch of the Royal Navy, if and when the work was completed, for at the rate we progressed for the first two weeks that day would never come.

My workmate was an amiable, stupid lad from some nearby village, colour-blind and not acceptable in any branch of the Forces. He stood placidly around while I quietly went bananas. For the fact was that this was Warrington all over again, we had no timber to work with and got paid for a sixty-hour week while doing nothing. Red tape in Whitehall was largely responsible, but not wholly, for the civil service had no control over the U Boat packs, that hunted and killed in the wild Atlantic. Some of the huts were near completion but most, and there were scores, were only in their initial stage. And to make matters worse we had to appear to be doing something whenever a Naval Inspector showed up.

Being a builder's son, I knew the game this firm was

playing. Contracts were on 'time and material', fifteen per cent on labour, ten per cent on materials, and builders were becoming millionaires by looting the coffers of England, accumulated through bloody conquest over the centuries, and now disappearing fast. The First World War had reduced an obese and bloated England to a plump John Bull, but this war would leave him on the bones of his arse and speed up the decline of a great power.

Idling around all day in the sunshine, with nothing to absorb my energies, became purgatory to me, for with it came the longing for a woman that haunted my dreams at night. And always at dinner time there was Audrey, straining at the seams, to remind me of what I was missing, her coy come-hither glances driving me round the bend. We rarely spoke to each other, for Gran and Tina missed nothing.

In my little room I slogged away at the writing that would make me famous, but always the words of Stevenson were there to jibe. Writing, 'a mighty bloodless substitute for living'. I heartily agreed. This sorry state of affairs went on for a couple of weeks, and then one night, when the window was open, when a golden moon shone through to disturb my restless sleep, I suddenly awoke to catch sight, of Audrey standing silently in the moonlight, arms over her head as she removed her nightdress, naked as the day she was born before she turned and stole in beside me.

'Audrey!'

'Hello, lover,' she whispered softly, 'you've been longing for this.'

'Yes . . . I have,' and I kissed her breasts and her willing lips, and my hands roved over her young body until she moaned softly and then I was inside her, and all heaven was mine. We made love three times that night, before Audrey stole away, silent as she had come, and I slept the sleep of the just at last. But before my eyes closed I thought about what had occurred, with me wearing no condom, nor had Audrey seemed to care. I hoped for the best. She had not been a very active partner, she knew nothing about kissing with open mouth, but placidly absorbed my passion, absolutely content. She was, I decided, the eternal woman, she needed a man, did not question her need and knew none of the guilt that always tormented me. That she was no virgin had been obvious, that she had a lover I knew. She would make a good wife for some Devonshire lad as uncomplicated as herself. She had never been exposed to the fire and brimstone of the Catholic Church which, despite my rejection and supposed liberation, still clung to me.

I was late for breakfast the following morning and would have missed it altogether but for Helmut. Another lazy day on the job and I would be ready for Audrey again, should she come. And oh joy, oh bliss, I was certain she would! On the truck the lovely countryside rolled past, the sun blazed from a cloudless sky, my mood as serene as summer. I was jolted back to reality when we hit the job. Sometime during the night the firm's trucks had rolled in, bringing the much needed materials, the leading hands and foreman vibrant, we were suddenly on a production bonus and a long sweaty day's work ahead.

The curse a' jaysus on it, I thought viciously. It was either a feast or a bloody famine with me. Thankfully Audrey did not come that night, but on Saturday night she snuggled in beside me and everything was okay except that we were now working Sundays. Sod Sunday, I gave myself utterly into her keeping, for these delights came not often and Audrey, if not the most passionate woman I had ever known, was quietly insatiable. I wobbled onto the site and went to work with all the enthusiasm of a stranded jellyfish. I had dark circles under my eyes, I was banjaxed before I began. I prayed that Audrey would not come again for a while. But she did, that night, and powerless to resist her charms I gave the last of my flagging strength in satisfying her. She just lay there, almost purring like a cat, a beautiful plenteous young woman, made for love and little else.

'You're a randy young bugger,' she whispered softly as she stole away, and I collapsed into sleep.

The next morning I seeped into work. By ten o'clock I

was used up. I was on finishing work, known as second fixing, and now with no one around I opened the wardrobe which lay horizontally on the floor, climbed inside, closed the door and went to sleep in my temporary coffin. The leading hand came in once and I heard him ask where 'that bloody wreck' was for he had noticed the dark circles under my eyes and had voiced his opinion on the subject.

'Yer'er agettin' too much "crackling", Larry,' he had said with a laugh. 'Oi suppose yew'er thinkin' yew can eat it, but by the toime yew'er my age yew'll think it'll eat yew . . . bloody hot-arsed Irish yew are.'

'No bloody fear,' I had replied, but I was beginning to agree with him now. He seated himself on the wardrobe but I lay doggo until he went, and then I went back to sleep. The lunch hour whistle woke me up, much refreshed, and I opened the door and stood up. A small feminine gasp followed and I was staring into the eyes of my new labourer, Lucy. Twenty-nine women had been drafted onto the site to assist in the general mayhem.

'Jesus,' she gasped. 'So that's where you were. Larry, isn't it?'

'Yes, but who are you?'

'Lucy,' she replied. 'An' this is me sister, Rita.' Lucy was not a bad looking young woman, Rita was, as the Yanks had it, 'homely', but in their blue tradesman overalls, which bulged in all the wrong places, they had little chance to impress. The group of women labourers caused uproar on the site and a jubilant male work force went to work with a heart and a half that day. It could hardly have been otherwise. All these women were in their late twenties or early thirties, half a dozen were widows of Merchant Navy men that the U Boat wolf packs were sending to the bottom in unprecedented numbers, the rest had been deprived of their soldier husbands. The men on camp came from all over, conscripted into the workers' army, going wherever they were sent.

Women without men, men without women, married couples separated and used to a sexual ration. The basic needs of the two sexes had never been more forcibly illustrated. Within a week all of them had paired off, some openly, others on the sly, but paired off anyway. Lucy had no eyes for me, thank God. She fell at once for the leading hand in charge of my section, pursued him relentlessly and without much trouble got him into bed. And I took malicious delight in reminding him about the dangers of too much 'crackling', noting his haggard appearance from time to time.

These women were, to say the least, 'earthy'. They had foul tongues and to my romantic young heart were a disgrace to their sex. But they were not interested in me. They were looking for men, not boys, and my sexual needs were more than catered for. Little Audrey saw to that. But, as always in war, an inexorable law of nature took control. The Old Reaper's scythe, dripping red with blood, was sweeping men off this earth. A series of ferocious battles was raging in the Western Desert. Rommel had broken through the British lines before being held in a pocket, aptly named by the few who survived as 'the Cauldron'. On 11 June Rommel's panzers broke out of the cauldron and by the following evening some two hundred and sixty British tanks lay smoking in the desert.

The 8th Army had to retreat, and a little over a week later Tobruk, that desperate last bastion that had held through everything, fell in a single day. Vast supplies and 33,000 Brits taken prisoner. In all it had cost Britain 75,000 men, and the Army dug in for a last desperate stand between El Alamein and the sea. I saw the result of the terrible tank battle on the Movietone news. The British had, as far as I could make out, been intercepted in a sandy depression, outwitted by the Desert Fox, and decimated by the killing power of Germany's dual purpose 88mm anti-aircraft, anti-tank gun, and the veteran panzers. Ripped apart, still smouldering, the tanks littered the desert floor, a mangled testimony to the brilliance of Rommel, who was promoted to Field Marshal on the day Tobruk fell, 21 June 1942.

The number of young widows on our job went up

significantly, there was a careless wild wind of 'tomorrow we die' sweeping the land, and men and women fell into each others arms and made love, or satisfied lust, nature did not care as long as the fallen numbers were replaced. It was against this background that my love life proceeded, though it did not need any encouragement from the Old Reaper. I was young, I loved women, it was as simple as that. And although my Catholic conscience told me I was a blackguard, a womaniser, a disgrace to my family and my chastity belt country, I carried on cheerfully enough under this burden. My mind had broadened considerably since my arrival in England. Even to the point where I was prepared to forgive a priest if he had a bit of 'nooky', even if he was not prepared to forgive me. The eleventh commandment had no more control over me! 'Thou shalt not dip thy wick . . . .' This was a summer of blazing heat, blazing passions, and blazing guns. All over the earth, from Pole to Pole, men were busily engaged in exterminating each other as fast as they could.

The Western Desert that affected England and our job so much was a mere sideshow compared to what was going on in Russia, where titanic forces were unleashed and casualties were counted in millions. In May the Soviet forces had gone to the offensive in the Kharkov area, but in sixteen days of bloody fighting were once again defeated. Badly mauled, the Russian Bear limped away, growling, to fight another day. History would yet reveal that the mighty tank of the German panzers would not travel as far as Napoleon's horses, that Hitler would never stand in Moscow's Red Square, but that was all in the future.

Now, right now, the forces of evil it seemed were everywhere in the ascendancy. On 9 June the Japs had completed their conquest of the Phillipines, and even the mighty USA seemed unable to stop them. But the great build-up behind the lines was on, British factories were churning out tanks and planes, all destined for the Western Desert and the coming decisive battle with Rommel. Weekly I watched the Movietone news and the growing confidence of the Brits. They had noting to compare with Field Marshal Rommel, they knew it and prepared an old fashioned World War One plan to conquer him. They would place their field guns wheel to wheel, a mighty barrage would open their offensive, with the infantry moving steadily forward. Sheer weight of armour was to defeat Rommel, though, with twice as many troops opposed to him and twice his armoured strength, he gave them a run for their money, came close to winning, and even in retreat made Montgomery's clumsy efforts to trap him look foolish.

The first battles of El Alamein raged through July, followed with breathless interest by the British public, but neither side was strong enough to win. By the end of August the attacks on Rommel's supply lines were taking their toll, while all the while the British were growing stronger. On 31 August Rommel struck viciously and scored another success but the Brits dug in on the fortified ridge of El Hamman, and finally brought his spectacular run of mobile offensive actions to an end.

With Rommel held, Montgomery stolidly built up unassailable odds. Now it was his turn. He had been lucky enough to get the command of the 8th Army when British factories were turning the tide, and now, on the night of 23-24 October he opened a tremendous barrage on a six mile front, and the British infantry began to move forward.

This attack was widely shown on Movietone, watched in awe by the public, including me. Never had I seen anything like it, for the field guns were wheel to wheel and under a silver desert moon all hell was unleashed on the Axis forces, the Commonwealth soldiers moving slowly forward under this umbrella of shrapnel. Nothing could survive the assault, nothing that is but Rommel and his battle-hardened troops and tanks. He launched a counter offensive and ground Montgomery's 8th Army to a halt. Battles raged all along the front, but Rommel's tanks were being slowly decimated with no replacements and no petrol, while the British reinforcements inexorably spelled out his doom. By 4 November it was all over, the Desert Fox was beaten at last by sheer weight of numbers. The British regarded him with reluctant admiration. He had fought fair and clean, no atrocities were ever marked up against him, he was all that a professional soldier should be. And his contempt for Naziism and Hitler were to cost him his life eventually.

During this summer and autumn, while the whole world was in flames, the WREN camp in Devonshire lurched towards completion. Long periods of idleness, due to shortage of materials, followed by frenetic bursts of activity as the stuff arrived, was the order of the day. The order of my nights was just as unsatisfactory, either a feast or a famine. Sometimes Audrey would not come for a week or even more, but when she did she made up for it, tireless, placidly absorbing my strength while showing no signs of a sexual climax, wearing me out with a satisfied smile. She just loved making love, she was built for it and liked arousing men to a frenzy of desire. She played a cat and mouse game, she had a puppet on a string.

The long Indian Summer of 1942 was coming to an end, the early mornings were cold and sometimes lightly frosted, scarves and top coats had to be worn now in the back of the truck. From my high up window the view was changing, the yellow ragwort waved no more. All the wild flowers that had cloaked the ruined city with a passing beauty were gone, and the ugly mounds of rubble could be seen once more. With the autumn came another wild surge in my spasmodic writing and I settled down to finish the book. So intense was my effort that I literally fell into bed each night and never noticed that with the passing days Audrey came no more.

She was missing a whole week from the dining room before I even noticed. When I did, I asked Helmut where she was. He told me he thought she had gone for a holiday near her 'intended's' Army base and I went back to my writing. But I damned well noticed when she came back, for it had been over two weeks since we had been together and I was yearning for the comfort of her ample body. And still she did not come near me. Her boyfriend must have satisfied her for a while, I thought savagely, and was

224

probably near the truth. I slogged it out on the book for another week, despite a growing conviction that it would never be published. My intuition was correct as it proved. And here was the winter of my discontent upon me, I reflected morosely, as night followed night, and Audrey kept to her room.

I took to going to the local pub, The Oxford, where a dazzling redhead, the daughter of the owner, served behind the counter. Like most of the customers I was bewitched by her smile, which produced one dimple on the right cheek. She had a flawless complexion, the peaches and cream of a redhead, and large green eyes like a beautiful cat. Jessica! Half the pub was in love with her and she smiled kindly on me. But I knew I stood no chance with this Devonshire Maid, whose future was assured. She was part of Plymouth, well above working class lads, and I was part of the flotsam and jetsam of war. Now, if this had been Walkinstown! But it was not.

Sometimes, for variety, I went down Union Street. There the nations of the Commonwealth congregated. Aussies, Canucks, New Zealanders, Scots, Welsh, and inevitably, Irish from north and south. In or out of the Commonweath the Irish were bound to be there. Also the Free French, Poles, Dutch, all sailors serving under the umbrella of the Royal Navy. When the Americans came to port things livened up considerably, for they were hated by the other nations who were paid a pittance compared to these Yanks who threw dollars around like confetti and monpolised the women. The Merchant Navy was here in force too.

Union Street, as I vaguely remember it, for I only saw it once by day, was a pot-pourri of sleazy pubs, jammed with servicemen and whores, who fought for service at the bars and jostled each other in the blacked out street. Under the cloak of night Plymouth's Mary Magdalenes did a roaring business and the police, unless called in to suppress some bar-room brawl, kept discreetly away. For what I was observing, like a pale civilian ghost, were men who had little predictable future. The U Boat campaign of hunting in packs, took toll on every precious convoy that kept England alive, sending merchant shipping and their escorts to the bottom in dozens. Thousands of seamen died every month in the icy waters of the Atlantic, these survivors on Union Street had run the gauntlet many times, lost many comrades.

They got drunk in the face of death, made love to the harlots with desperation, no thought given to tomorrow, when they might live to contract a dose of the pox or worse. As always, when the Old Reaper was on the loose, when the sea ran red to his scythe, the sexes came together defiantly, mating in the long shadow of eternity. I was just a straw in the wind that swept the world. The wild flowers and trees that had encroached on the ruins of Plymouth so swiftly, were there to fill a vacuum. Nature abhorred a vacuum. Young bucks like me, and these sailors, had no choice in the matter. Procreate, said nature silently, or die. And all over the world men and women fell into each others' arms, and the whores of Union Street had plenty of competition from their more respectable sisters. For there were 'blue birds over the white cliffs of Dover', Judy Garland and the Strawman danced down the Yellow Brick Road, the wonderful 'Land of Oz' had come to England, and there was no rationing under the bedclothes, where, in this new urgent climate, lay Fairyland!

Union Street fascinated me, for it was always night for me there. I came to know its bars and haunts and the frenetic activity that it engendered. There was one place, shaped exactly like a key-hole, a long narrow shank, where the stalls side by side — gambling games, a shooting gallery, a coconut 'shy' and suchlike — and, at the end, the 'hole', a circular carousel where a mad collection of crazy-looking wooden animals not only swirled around but up and down, blaring music that was yet barely heard above the racket of the engine that made it work. It was a storm of noise, and drunken sailors rocketed around, sometimes with their ladies screaming on their laps. Quite often they failed to hang on, and landed in the deep sawdust put there for just that purpose. Everything here was a dirty, drunken, mad escape from the blackout, the perils at sea, and the ever present danger of another blitz on Plymouth itself. Even now, in the early mornings going to work, there were still people to be seen who preferred to sleep in the fields rather than risk the indoors. Trudging wearily along towards Plymouth these were mostly old folk who had been unnerved by the fury of the aerial assault. Coventry had been ripped apart in two raids, in which an estimated 800 tons of high explosive had rained down, two nights of hell, but it finished at that. Plymouth and her smaller sister city, Devonport had been pulverised in night raids by an estimated 1200 tons. The evidence of those awful nights was all around.

But, in the place I called the key-hole, all that was forgotten, left behind in a drunken haze. The Rifle Range was my favourite, for it was attended by a glorious blonde, about seventeen, ripe for love at an early age, with a flawless complexion and a voluptuous figure squeezed into a red dress which emphasised what it concealed, and soft round arms that were dimpled at the elbow. I never won a prize at her stall, I made sure of that, but it got me nowhere. Never once did she acknowledge my presence, my frequent visits. She was, I learned, the owner's daughter, her family's background was the Circus, there was little she did not know about boys and girls, though I refused to think of her as anything except the essence of femininity. She had captivated my foolish young heart. I got over my infatuation in a hurry the night 'Mickey Rooney' came in. He was a 'look alike' of the famous star, the shortest American sailor I had ever seen, maggoty drunk, and supported by a long dip stick from Kansas, named Hank.

They staggered along, 'Rooney' trying to extricate himself rom his gangling companion.

'Okay . . . okay . . . lay off me, Kansas. I'm okay.'

'You sure?'

'Sure I'm sure. Get the hands off the body, Hank.'

As they lurched towards the rifle range where I was

foolishly spending my money, 'Rooney' passed a filthy remark to my lovely blonde. I saw her face light up with affront, then without hesitation she came from behind to confront the two sailors.

'Right, Shorty,' she hissed, and, standing like a man, threw a straight left followed by a beautiful right cross that stretched him flat on his back. The six-feet-four 'pull through' that was Hank, helped him to his feet.

'Lemme at 'er,' he roared and pushed Kansas away.

'C'mon, Shorty!' Shorty came on, this time her left found his nose and her right finished the job on the same battered organ, which spurted blood. She had, as the sporting Brit put it, tapped the Claret, and Shorty was down and out. In fact, nobody seemed to notice the lonely young civilian, not even the whores, which, in retrospect, was a good job. I was missing Audrey so badly that I would not have taken much persuading. And I was drinking too much. I was Mr Nobody from Nowhere, I did not even have an Army number . . . the key-hole held no voluptuous temptress who wanted me. Life was at an all time low. Then Audrey came again.

I got back from the key-hole a little later than usual, for the incident with Shorty had developed into a terrific fight between a passing British sailor and the gangling Hank, who could fight like a thrashing machine. Others joined in and it was a glorious free-for-all while it lasted. That was until the British and American Military Police arrived. When I got home some of the boarders were still chatting in the steel-propped dining room, for I could hear their voices as I mounted the stairs, but I kept going. Back in my little room I opened the window and let in the silver moon that rode high in a clear sky, a good night for Jerry to strike, but those days, I figured, were long gone. As far as I could make out, Jerry was up to his balls in trouble in Russia. The massive German offensive that had carried them into Stalingrad in September had been halted at last. Graphic pictures of the savage fighting, in which the German Army had to take the city house by house, were shown on the

Movietone News. It was impossible to keep up with the happenings of this global conflict, but it seemed that the Japs and the Germans were now on the defensive, that the high tide of their victories was on the ebb, the Americans were poised to land at Guadalcanal, the long march on Germany and Japan had begun.

I was a November child, a Scorpio, and a November moon had always held a peculiar enchantment for me. I gazed long over the shattered city, the ruins softened by the moonlight, and, sighing, went to bed as a dark mass of clouds moved across, plunging the earth into darkness. I fumbled my way into bed and fell asleep at once.

Sometime during the night, I awoke to a familiar scent and the soft presence I had been longing for. Evidently Audrey had kept away until she could no longer control her desire, for she went to work silently, passionately kissing me with open mouth, French kissing, that drove me wild. Little Audrey, it seemed had progressed a lot since we had last been together, her breasts had grown larger, her charms even more voluptuous. We made love slowly, gently, experienced love, prolonged as far as possible until nature would not allow more time, and together we rode the storm of ecstasy, the only heaven that ordinary men would ever know on earth.

After it was over I lay beside her panting, peaceful at last, and still no word spoken. I was reaching for a cigarette when her voice broke the silence.

'You've been having a high old time with our Audrey, haven't you, Larry?' Jesus Christ, I nearly had a stroke. It was Audrey's mother!

'Tina!'

'Aye, lover, Tina!' I lit two cigarettes and passed one to her.

'What do you intend to do?'

'Come here more often, lover. You have a beautiful body.'

'So have you, Tina, so have you,' and the love-making started all over again.

Coming towards dawn she slipped away, and I, to my all too brief sleep, but not before we had had a long conversation. Audrey was pregnant, she had told me, and shocked me into silence.

'Worrying if you're the father, Larry, eh?'

'Yes . . . it's possible . . . I never used a condom. How long have you known about Audrey and me?'

'More or less since it started.'

'But you're her mother! Why didn't you stop it?' In the darkness she had laughed softly. 'Stop Audrey? You must be joking.'

'But she's pregnant now!'

'An' about time, lover. Our Audrey has been playing up since she were a girl. Started at thirteen, or I'm not her mother. She's had a good run for her money, an' likely it's the soldier she's going to marry that's the father. She was with him for a whole week a while ago. I saw to that!'

So, this was the guile of women!

'It's a wise child knows its own father, isn't it, Tina?'

'That it is. Audrey's being married next week. Jack's more than willing, he's delighted she's pregnant. He's mad after her, been havin' her on an' off for years. Now he reckons as he has her.'

'And has he?'

'Aye, as long as he keeps her well supplied. She'll make a good wife, I reckon, when the baby comes.'

'And that's why she's kept away from me?'

'I told her to keep away . . . I didn't want her bumping into me,' and she smothered her laughter under the bed clothes.

'I don't mind you bumping into me . . . you're a lovely woman . . . and far better in bed than Audrey.'

'Rubbish! All cats are black at night. Anyway, you Irish are full of Blarney.'

'But you are better in bed, Tina. You really know how to make love?'

'Doesn't Audrey?'

'No, not in the race with you.'

'You're having me on, I know, but I like it. Not bad for an old one, eh?'

'You're not old, not with a body like yours. Never!'

'I'm too old for you!'

'By God, you're not. Come here, me ould dote, and love me once again before you go.' Very soon I discovered that Tina was in love with me, though she was too wise to expect me to be in love with her. But I came to love her, and told her so.

'You love me, but you're not in love, is that it?'

'Yes, and I'll always love you, Tina, long after we've parted. I'll remember you with love.'

'And I'll remember you with love, always.' And she reached out for me and found me and I found her all over again.

But six o'clock, when I had to rise after my orgy of love, that first time, was a disaster. I toyed with the idea of stopping out of work. But Tina, fresh and wholesome looking, shook me awake and I faced the day like a sodden bootlace.

When I got to work Lucy took one look at me, at my peaky face, and, laughing, took a flying leap that wrapped her legs around my body and sent me staggering back.

'Yew've been on the bloody nest again, 'avent yew? Look,' she screamed at a group of fellow women labourers, ''e's been on the bloody nest.'

'Us don't believe it,' said her sister. 'Let Oi 'ave a look, an' see if 'e's got 'un!' They made a run for me then, and violently I broke loose and took to my heels, chased by the screaming crowd of women, the men roaring them on to catch me. I took refuge in the men's lavatory and stopped there until they dispersed back to work. I had seen what these beauties were capable of doing to a man once they got his trousers down, though I do not think they would have done the same to me.

A week before, Lucy had come into the hut I was working in, disgusted, and in turn had disgusted me, for I was, despite my nocturnal activities, still a prude at heart. I

231

expected women to behave with decorum, and this tribe of Amazons that had erupted on to the building site were not my cup of tea, to say the least. Lucy had cocked up her arse and deliberately farted, and shrieked with laughter at my scarlet face. That she took delight in shocking me I knew, but this behaviour, even from Lucy, was over the top. The cause of her disgust was even more revolting.

There was a swarthy Ganger on the site, who looked like a tall Arab, and he had when Lucy was passing, pulled his penis out through a hole in his pocket and waggled it at her! Her affront was not based on his behaviour, but on the colour of his penis, a 'dirty brown thing' she called it, and went on to say that her husband's was at least 'white'.

'Dirty filthy bastard,' she had said, 'Oi'll fix 'im.' She did too, she and the other harridans. The whole gang of them attacked him at once, and despite his lusty resistance overcame him and held him down. Off came his pants his legs pulled apart and a liberal dose of red lead paint plastered all over his 'crown jewels'.

'An,' Lucy told me, 'When we 'ad 'is balls well covered, we rolled 'im over an' painted his arse as well. 'e'll keep that thing well covered from now on.' The Ganger was transferred in a hurry, and was seen no more.

Alongside this bawdy life ran the inevitable tide of tragedy, and one never to be forgotten morning I came in to see Lucy, face bloated from crying, sitting quietly in the corner of the hut. She stared unseeingly before her and fretful sobs racked her body from time to time. Silently, I gave her a cup of tea from my flask and coaxed her to drink it. Her young husband had gone down with his ship, she still held the telegram in her hand.

She had been unfaithful to him for months, but in her book that was no harm. ''e won't be goin' short when 'e's in port,' she had once told me. 'An' what's sauce for the goose is sauce for the gander. There's plenty left for 'im.' Thus she had justified her adultery with the leading hand, and this bloody war was ripping the last of my Irish guilt-complex to bits. Just like an unfrocked priest, I'd end up worse than the rest, I thought. Venial sins had gone out the window a long time ago and my newly acquired thinking was that a 'good mortaller' was worth a bucket of them.

The raw facts of life had been presented to me since my arrival in England, not least in my own behaviour, and here before me was the woman taken in adultery. She had spent the night before with the leading hand, Harry, and now, just out of her bed of sin, she wept bitterly for her lost love.

'Oi really loved 'im, Paddy,' she sobbed, ''e were my childhood sweetheart . . . 'arry were just a stop gap . . . lonely like me, separated from 'is wife . . . no bloody 'arm done. No tears, no fuss, hooray for us, and thanks for the memory.'

I saw down beside Lucy on the stool and put my arms around her, rocking her gently. 'There, love, there . . . . There love, there . . . . until the worst of the storm had passed for the present, anyway. Then we both sighed and went back to work.

There was no bloody sense to this life. What was it all about? Where was I going? Where was Lucy going? That was easy if I believed my church. Straight to Hell, for being a whore. But was she not in Hell now? Was she not receiving the wages of sin, on the double? And would she not have received the same even had she remained faithful and pure? What kind of a God was it that I had been taught to love? I had no idea.

'And what would you do,' said the priest in my mind, 'if God took you now? Filthy as you are, a lecher, steeped in mortal sin, you leave God no choice. He has to consign you to the eternal flames of Hell if you die this day.'

Why? Because he made women irresistable to men? Am I to be damned for all time because I can't go without a bit of 'the other'? Who made me as I am? Who made Tina the way she is? Who made the whole lousy set up? God! And I'm to be damned for his handiwork! If that's the case I might as well be hung for a sheep as a lamb . . . Lamb of God who takes away the sins of the world! What happened to that gentle creature? Who thought up Limbo . . .

Heaven and Hell? My church, the Catholic Church, and all the breakaway churches that came after it, had the same idea.

'Fuck it,' I said aloud.

'What!' Lucy had never heard me swear before and was shocked. 'Oi'm surprised at yew. It sounds terrible, comin' from yew! It don't suit yew!'

'Doesn't it? I can swear better than any of you, in men's company.'

'Well, don't do it in front of me. Oi'm a woman, too.'

'Sorry, Lucy. I stand corrected.' As if I needed to be reminded that she was a woman! Lucy was all woman, and she could not help it either. I leaned moodily on the bench and went back to my brooding. What would I do if God took me now? Ascend into Heaven in foamy white clouds as Jesus was depicted in stained glass and oil paintings? Hardly that way for mortal sinners! Then what way? Shot from earth, Heavenwards, to stand before the Gates of Paradise, that would be always closed to me. No just God, I speculated, would ever consign an infant to Limbo because it had not been baptised, or gloat in the temporary sufferings of me in Purgatory, if there was such a place.

Maybe there was a Hell, but surely I was not bad enough to go there, just because I loved women? After all, if there were no people like me, where would the saints come from? Perhaps reincarnation was the answer, or something like it. Maybe there was a separate department for slightly worn sinners like me, and I would be returned to earth for a re-thread, perhaps in the form of a dog. But if this did happen the first thing I would do would be to sink the fangs into the arse of the first 'sky pilot', or bank manager or millionaire I met, and of course, having outraged the law, I would be put down at once. And back to the Gates of Heaven I would rocket again, to stand before St Peter, stern custodian of Paradise. But this time my reception would be very different, if Peter was the man I believed him to be.

'Welcome, my son, welcome,' he would say, 'welcome forever to Paradise. As a man you were no better than a dog, as a dog you displayed the finest qualities of a man. Welcome St Laurence!'

Sure I might as well rave here as in bed, no one could hear my thoughts, no danger of being locked up. Not now, anyway.

This day had started badly, and there was worse to come. When I got back to Gran's there was a letter for me, and as I opened it a newspaper-cutting fell out. It was the Death Notice column and the names jumped off the page. Gibbons (James), Duffy (John), both dead from wounds received in the Western Desert. Jesus, Mary and Joseph,' I whispered aloud, and burst out crying. Unfortunately, the letter was given to me in the dining room, where all mail for the boarders was handed out, and there was a stunned silence before I fled upstairs to my room. Nobody followed, in this kindly house I was to be left respectfully to get over my grief. Through blurred eyes I read my mother's note, for she was not very hot at writing letters.

Dear Lar,

This is bad news I am sending you, but you might as well know it now. I came across this in the Evening Mail, and may God comfort your friends' mothers this day. Write more often, Lar, I worry about you, you know that. Put pen to paper now and tell me how you are. Your father and all the family send their love.

Mam

I sat down on the bed. It was dark and cold, but I did not switch on the light, nor did I feel the chill. My stunned mind refused to accept the fact that my pals were gone forever. In my mind's eye we were marching through the green lanes, the valleys and mountains of Wicklow on a summer night. We were leaving the International Hotel in Bray on a long march that would take us close to the Border and the six severed counties of the Province of Ulster. Marching out from the town at nine o'clock, the sun setting behind the mountains, the darkening lanes, the heavy sleepy smell of the Irish countryside, the overpowering scent of lilac and wall-flowers announcing an unseen cottage, the bark of a dog or the hoot of an owl, night sounds, our marching footsteps the only alien sound in this beautiful scene.

Sharing a cigarette, when we 'fell out' for a rest, with John Duffy and 'Gibbo', pals who shared all, it could not be that they were dead, sharing the same desert, and I left alone . . . I refused to accept that. In my mind they would always live, eternally young, young as the age-old mountains around us. And then, at last the dawn, the sun, giver of life, bursting over the mountain tops, lighting up the green valleys, and the gentle majesty of county Wicklow, the Garden of Ireland. We were not alien now, our uniforms merging with the green of hedgerow and field, in this, the loveliest of all places on earth.

'Ye greene and pleasant land,' said one of my invading Norman ancestors, 'and well worth fighting for.'

And nearly nine hundred years later, I thought so too. In a kaleidoscopic cavalcade the events and pictures of two years as a soldier flashed on the screen of my mind, and always with Gibbo and John.

Lying in a ditch outside Drogheda town, when the manoeuvres were under way, waiting to trap a company of 'the enemy' at dawn, and the dull roll-like thunder that came from Dublin, thirty miles away, as the brightly lit city's North Strand was devastated by a blitz from the sky.

Finding the traps of a rabbit catcher in the fat fields of Co Meath and stealing every succulent victim, for we were hungry. We were always hungry, we marched too hard and ate too little, we were still growing. Taking a bucket from a farm house and, safely hidden in a wood, boiling the rabbits and devouring them without salt when they were half cooked. There was no end to the pictures that flashed through my mind.

The derisive comments of my friends when I returned from my one man invasion of the Six Counties and told

236

them about it. I had been made a Company Runner. Armed with a compass, a bicycle, fifty live rounds of .303 ammunition I was sent out to locate B Company. Very soon I was hopelessly lost but recklessly cheerful as the green hedges flashed past. B Company was supposed to be somewhere in the region of Ballyjamesduff, I would soon come across some farmer who would show me the way to Paddy Riley's village. God was in His heaven, not to worry, the world was all right. My world, that is. After about an hour I arrived on the outskirts of a small village, pulled up beside the first man I saw, and asked him was this Ballyjamesduff.

'Begod,' he said in a heavy northern accent, 'it's not! Yid betther high tail it back to the Free State Army before a "Peeler" sights you.'

'Are you joking? I'm not really over the Border, am I?'

'I'm tellin' yeh, yeh are! An' it's a guid job ye're talkin' to a Catholic or yid be in throuble!'

'But I never saw any Border . . . .'

'Just get teh hell out young fella. You're a target here.' For answer I unclipped the Lee Enfield .303 from the frame of the bike, slapped five rounds into the magazine and one up the spout, slung the rifle over my shoulder, hanging by the hard canvas strap, grinned and set off.

'Thanks,' I shouted over my shoulder, and set about creating a new world record for a soldier on an old 'upstairs bike'. I had never been near the Border before, did not know that only the main roads had Customs Posts, that the maze of small country roads and lanes that led north and south could never be sealed off. The rivers that ran south could not be made to run north, or vice versa, the natural boundary of this island was the sea, only hatred and bigotry on both sides could sustain this impossible monster that divided farms and villages.

However, discretion being the better part of valour, I tore back the same way I had come, and fervently hoped I was not going in a circle in these featureless lanes. Eventually I came to a crossroads that I recognised, asked a farmer, and found B Company. So much for the compass. But, when safe, I wondered what would have happened if an RUC man had tried to arrest me? That they were armed I knew, and I did a Walter Mitty about the events that might have happened. Me in a ditch, picking off British Soldiers, a Spartan defending a pass, and eventually fighting my way back to the Free State and sanctuary. In no way did it occur to me even in my dreams to die for Ireland, not on thirteen and twopence a week, anyway!

'I'm bloody sick of this mickey mouse money,' I told my pals that night. 'My father has a bit of influence and I'm getting out of this Cowboy and Indian outfit. Anyway, we're not going to be invaded, and, as sure as Christ, we're not going to invade the North. So I'm out.'

'Not before me,' said Gibbo.

'Nor me either, Gibbo,' said John. 'We'll beat him to it when the time comes.' And they did, gone over the wall two hours before I walked out through the gate, and left word for me that I had lost the bet. And now they were dead, Gibbo at nineteen, though he looked far older with his heavy black stubble, Duffy dead at twenty. They had gone the way of thousands of Free State soldiers, bored with the dull routine of a neutral army, over the border and into battle before most, for they were trained soldiers when they joined the British Army.

Gibbo, the comedian who kept us laughing, Gibbo, the songster who raised our spirits singing until we joined in, Gibbo, the bawdy composer of pardodies, the famous afternoon marching down the main street in Bray after a punishing trek through the mountains, Gibbo, defiantly raising his voice in song, and one hundred and fifty young men bringing the traffic to a halt with their singing.

Gibbo . . . Gibbo . . . Gibbo, unforgettable Gibbo.

'God rest you both,' I whispered in the dark, and felt a timid hand on my shoulder. It was Tina. She had silently entered the room, and now gently led me, like a sleep walker, down the stairs into the steel-posted dining room. It was warm, lovely and warm, compared to the cold place I had been, somewhere between Heaven and Hell. Old Gran was there, looking worried.

''e's like a ghost,' she said, and put her arms around me. They had kept my dinner hot, all this time, for it was after ten. Tina made no pretence in front of her mother, loving me and kissing me back to sanity, and making sure I ate the dinner. Old Gran made no comment, gave no look of disapproval, but, smiling, made her way upstairs to bed.

'Good night, Larry,' she said quietly. 'Oi'll leave you in good 'ands.' And did. I drank a couple of cups of tea, and felt a lot better, but far from well.

'Sleep with me tonight, Tina, and don't go 'way. I need you.'

'I won't go away,' said Tina. 'But no funny business, you need sleep. Come to bed now, lover, I'll fill the hot water bottle.'

Together we went upstairs but not to my little room and single bed. Tina's room was large, the bed had a soft feather mattress, and I needed no hot water bottle as I snuggled into her love and warmth, and came back from the cold of the grave where my two pals lay.

I fell asleep almost at once, Tina stroking my hair, kissing me now and then, holding me until I felt safe. Sometime during the night we made love, gentle love that she could not resist, sleepy love that went back to Dreamland when it was done, with our arms still around each other and my cheek on her breast. I was safe from the world here, I could never repay this woman who had protected me through the night, who gave herself to me completely, who loved me, a mother and passionate mistress at once. I was never to know another love like Tina.

11   Plymouth with Tina

As the year 1942 came to a close the fortunes of the Allies, in particular the Brits, improved dramatically. Everywhere the forces of aggression had been brought to a halt, the greatest of these events being the encircling of the German 6th Army at Stalingrad, the Russian Bear, maddened by suppurating wounds, tightening his ferocious grip on the doomed men of the Third Reich.

Despite the terrific efforts of one of Germany's ablest commanders, Field Marshal von Mannerheim, to break the stranglehold, the Bear held on, at his last gasp, and the world held its breath. Finally, in the early part of 1943, the Germany Army, starved, frozen, half dead, surrendered and were marched away. Few would ever live to see Germany again. The great Russian march on Berlin had started, tremendous battles lay ahead, more millions would die, but the Red Army would end up in Berlin.

In Africa the Brits retook Tobruk, and the 8th Army opened the drive on Tripoli. Hitler's day in Africa was coming to a close, as it was in Russia.

The Americans were hitting back too and Japan's days of easy conquest were over. From now on their fate was sealed. Here in Plymouth, the days of the blitz were over, but they were just beginning in a big way for the Germans. There was to be no mercy, they were to experience at first hand what they had been dishing out for so long.

The British were gathering strength with every week,

their air-raids of Germany were pressed home with a vengeance. The Americans too, thick on the ground, joined in, and between them they incinerated the mighty city of Hamburg in a man-made fireball. Throughout this year I followed the fortunes of war and I knew more about it than any soldier fighting in it. I knew this from my experience of manoeuvres in the Irish Army, when orders came that made no sense to the soldier on the ground, when we were rushed from one place to another like headless chickens. The men fighting in this war knew only the immediate enemy that confronted them. That was all they had to know if they expected to see Blighty ever again.

Our job came to a close in March 1943, the last of the WRENS installed. A new site opened beside it, this one to house sailors, and I was lucky enough to be transferred to it. I did not want to leave Plymouth, I had it too good here, with Gran's blackmarket grub, and Tina to love me now and then, and my firm conviction, which turned out to be wrong, that Plymouth's days of agony were done. And then there was the Oxford Arms, with the delightful Jessica of the one dimpled cheek. The few locals left in this devastated area pointedly ignored me but as the pub was filled with displaced persons from all over this did not distress me in the least. I had made plenty of new friends, spent money freely and lived for the day. With the whole world on fire, I sat on a hill and, like Nero, fiddled while it burned.

One night about ten, while sipping a pint, the air-raid sirens wailed their warning, followed at once by a terrific barrage that rocked the pub and stunned us. It was a sneak raid, a few German bombers that, by flying low, had managed to evade the radar so that they were over the city before the alert.

Now, fascinated, I watched the searchlights probe the sky, catch and hold a glittering squirming plane. I covered my ears against the storm of noise and shrapnel that rent the sky. Suddenly, a tiny, bright spark erupted from the plane and in seconds a fiery cross twisted slowly earthwards, followed by a distant explosion.

The customers went mad, cheering, shouting, making V for victory signs, and one of the clannish locals, overjoyed, deigned to speak to me. He said, 'That were the o'ly fuckin' Jerry Oi've seen ever shot down over Plymouth.'

The following morning a young German pilot was found on a local beach, crying from the pain of a broken ankle. He was only eighteen! Hitler must be getting short, I thought. The raid was over almost as soon as it had started. Little damage had been done and my companions in the pub were quietly satisfied, like myself, that Plymouth would never be blitzed again. Sneak raids, maybe, but no more than that. The Germans were fighting for their very lives in Russia. The country that had been expected to fold up in six weeks had taken everything that Germany could throw at it, and confounded the world by pushing the German Army back, with all England applauding. And the Brits were doing more, they were sending convoy after convoy of tanks, guns and shells, supplies that were vital to Russia in her hour on the cross, in her agony. But Russia's pleas for the opening of a second front fell on deaf ears.

The communist elements on our job were vociferous in their clamour for the Allies to invade Europe. They were saying openly what I had thought privately for a long time, that America and England would fight to the last Russian, as long as he was still killing Nazis. They were delaying the invasion of Europe to allow the combatants in Russia sufficient time to bleed each other white, thus killing two birds with the one stone. When their invasion did come it would only have to face a Russia and a Germany on their last legs.

'Good old Joe,' said the Brits, knowing well that Stalin had saved their bacon. An unprecedented wave of communism swept Britain, if my job was anything to go by, and the wealthy upper classes were compelled to remain silent and suffer. The talk among the other lodgers in the dining room was as red as Russia, and red Russia was red with blood. Old Gran was among the most rabid, holding bitter memories of the First World War when the expected land fit for heroes turned into a nightmare for the working class, when hungry millions had stood on the street corners and produced a breed between the Wars that Hitler had called a C3 nation. Over a third of them would be found unfit for Army service, and the men I worked among were a living proof of this. Mostly, they were badly underweight, never really looked fit, and lacked drive. They worked well enough, but never seemed to get enough to eat. Their conversation was, when not cursing Britain's upper class, solely devoted to ways and means of augmenting their food through the black market. Their comments on the War, as Stalin started to roll back Hitler's hordes, were bitter, though true.

'Watch the bastards open a second front now,' they predicted. 'They don't want old Joe in Europe!'

'And do you?'

'Too fuckin' right, Paddy,' I was told. 'Old fuckin' Winston 'ill do for now, but when the War's over, out 'e goes.' They had not forgotten the bitter hardship of their youths, the insult of the 'Means Test', and those among them who were eventually called up to serve on 'The Home Front' left with a cynical rancour in their hearts.

I had been shocked from time to time since I had come to England, at the attitude of Britain's working class towards the War, from Lucy Bottle to old Gran, from the men on the job to the women in the factories. If one were to go by what one read in the papers, Britain was 'Going To It', a nation welded together in shared hardship against the forces of evil. But if one had one's ear to the ground, as mine surely was, then a very different pictured emerged. Factories still went on strike for more pay. 'Sod the War, you'll pay us more or we stop work, bastards, you've 'ad your day. You need us now to save your bloody property, but wait, just wait till after the War . . . .'

'They're feedin' the workers better now,' said old Gran, carving up a blackmarket roast without a twinge of conscience, 'than ever before. They needs 'em now, for factories an' fightin'. That's all us were ever wanted for, workin' an' fightin' — an' fightin' for what? For bloody rich people to 'old on to what they 'ave.'

'And they won't let go easy,' said Tina. 'You'll see! Wait till they don't need workers any more and you'll see the unemployment lines growing — that is, if we let them get away with it. But we will not, not this time.'

Once more the difference between Tina's speech and the rest of the family struck me, and I made a resolution to ask her about it, next time we slept together, which would be tonight if I had my way.

'So,' I said to old Gran, for devilment, 'you're not worried about eating blackmarket beef?'

Gran turned to me smiling. 'If Oi didn't know yew were jokin', Larry, Oi'd give yew the door. No,' she said thoughtfully, 'not livin' beside that bloody funk 'ole, Torquay. The 'otels out there are packed wi' war-dodgers — bacon an' eggs every mornin', roast beef every day for dinner, pheasant an' venison too, if yew're able to pay for it!'

'Are you pulling my leg?'

'No,' said big Harry, 'Gran's not. Tell yew what, next time we 'ave a Sunday off Oi'll take us out an' yew can see for yewerself.'

That night I sneaked silently into Tina's room. We had made no date, but the bedroom door was unlocked and a nod was as good as a wink to a blind horse.

Tina heard me, her bedroom window was open and through it poured the light of a full golden moon. She sat up when she heard me lock the bedroom door, her full breasts showing pale in the bright room. She turned back the bedclothes and engulfed me with love when I got in. She said no word, just loving and kissing, passionate kissing with open mouth, adoring me with her body until I felt, somewhere far off, buried beneath the loving, a sense of shame that a woman like Tina could lose her head over a young man she could never hope to have.

'Take what the Good Lord sends', she had once told me, and meant it. She resisted my urgency for a time, prolonging the loving, and when eventually she let me take her I was ready for the long trip among the stars, where suns and galaxies counted for nought in the face of these two meteors who blazed a trail of passion, exploded in fiery joy, and returned to earth, spent.

Presently I lit two cigarettes and we lay there, lazily smoking. The cigarette afterwards is the best, I had once been told, and that was another bloody lie. Looking back it seemed that everything I had been taught up to lately had been a bloody lie, especially about the English. My baptism of fire at Holyhead had warped me for a time, but here in Plymouth, as in Warrington, I had been made to face the facts.

And the facts were that the English were no better and no worse than the rest of the human race. The Germans claimed that they were the master race, the English thought that they themselves were, and their belief lay in their victorious past. England lost every battle except the last, a country with the Devil's own luck. From the Spanish Armada, scattered by a storm, up to the present, luck had saved them every time. Hitler had had them on their last legs when he turned on Russia. Another blitz or two on London would have done the trick, panicked the population, as had been done here in Plymouth. I had been listening to enough tales to know the score. After the hammering of 20-21 March 1941, this small city of 200,000 was in a state of shock, 18,000 homes destroyed, their two largest hospitals badly damaged, the city centre wiped out.

With its morale badly shaken, Plymouth had tried to cope with this frightful event groping its way back towards some kind of normality, but the five nights of blitz that April brought had finished the job. This city was broken, 30,000 homeless, 50,000 sleeping rough in the surrounding countryside, in barns, in sheds, in mine tunnels, in ditches and on Dartmoor itself. The facts were hushed up, glossed over in the press. 'Britain can take it. None better than the sons and daughters of glorious Devon, of Drake!'

All bullshit, I reflected. They were, after all, only human. When they were cut, they bled, when their loved ones died, they cried, when their homes were destroyed they panicked. There was no master race on the ground when all hell was unleashed from the sky, as the Germans were now finding out.

'Tina,' I said softly. 'Why is it that you speak so much better than Harry or Audrey? Or Gran, come to that?'

'You're observant, aren't you?'

'Just curious, Tina. It's sticking out a mile.' Tina sighed.

'It's a long story, Larry. I don't want to go into it.' There was silence for a while.

'I was sent away as a child. I was reared in an orphanage, Larry, and had a better education than the rest.'

I digested this for a while, but could not see old Gran sending her daughter to an orphanage.

'You mean that your mother, old Gran, sent you away? I can't believe it. Not her.'

'No, not her. Old Gran is not my mother. She could never do a think like that.' Another long silence, this time broken by me.

'I'm sorry, Tina. It's none of my business. Forget I asked.' I slid down beside her, cradled her in my arms and kissed her neck and cheeks. My lips came away wet with her tears. She was crying silently, and now holding her close, I could feel her whole body convulse as she was racked with pain.

'Jesus . . . Tina . . . forgive me. I never meant . . . .'

'It's all right, Larry, it's all right. It's me. I'm wrong, I always have been, ever since the day I was born!'

'Hush, Tina, don't cry any more. I'm sorry, Jesus I'm sorry. No more questions, ever.' Tina dried her eyes on the sheet and lit a cigarette with hands that trembled in the flare of the match.

'You might as well know the rest, Larry. I want to speak about it, I've wanted to tell you for a long time. If you don't

246

understand, then I'm lost. But you have to know.'

'Okay, peg ahead, if you feel that way about it, if it helps.'

'Right, Larry. Now ask me . . . If Gran is not my mother what is she to me?'

'What is she?'

'I don't rightly know. Maybe she's my half sister. Maybe you can figure that one out. I'm the incestuous child of Gran's brother and sister, got that? Gran's brother and sister made a baby, and that baby was me.'

'Jesus!'

'Yes, Jesus! That's why I could not grow up in Plymouth. The family were too ashamed, so I had to be hidden away. When I left the orphanage I was sent as a servant to a lord's house in London. It was there I met my husband and that was when I found out the whole rotten story, for I had to produce my birth certificate, hadn't I?'

'Did you ever meet your mother?'

'No, she died.'

'Your father?'

'Yes. He's probably still alive, somewhere in Harrow. That's where I caught up on him. He's a Church warden with his own cottage in the grounds. Funny.'

'Go on, Tina.'

'Well, I don't quite know what I expected, but whatever it was it was not him, as he turned out . . . he was quite tall, good-looking, very quiet . . . shy. He didn't know what to do or say when I told him who I was. He went as white as a sheet, I thought he was going to faint.'

'And then?'

'I grabbed him and helped him inside, and sat him down on a chair. There was a little open cupboard over the gas stove, with tea, sugar . . . the lot. So I made him a cuppa and had one myself.'

'And still no words between you?'

'Oh, we got going eventually. I remember him asking me if I had come to accuse him, and I didn't know how to answer him. I didn't know what I had come for, actually, except to see what my father looked like. So I told him that.'

'"And what do you see?" he said.

'"A man, like any other. You don't look like a . . . ."

'"Queer?" says he, "Neither do you. You look the same as any other pretty girl."

'"But I'm not any other pretty girl, am I . . . Father?"

'"No. You're very like your mother, not as beautiful, but like her."

'"Where is she now? Do you know, or did you desert her when you ran away?"

'And then the whole story came out and I knew the lot, at last. He told me about this house, and his sister, old Gran, and it was her I turned to a few years later when I was in trouble. But that day I shall never forget.'

The room was growing darker now, as the moon climbed higher in the sky, the floor shadow lengthened, the moonlit patch withdrew, and from somewhere in the ruins around came the hoot of a barn owl. Yes, the countryside was moving in, and rapidly. A long silence prevailed. Soon it would be time to return to my own room.

'Well, Tina, finish it.'

'All right, love. Well, he took me a short distance away into a graveyard and showed me her tombstone. It said, "To my dear wife, Alice. Every hour I spent with you was precious to me."'

'Jesus, Tina . . . had they married?'

'Yes. They managed it somehow, in a Registry office. It wouldn't be very difficult if you think about it. And then he had got this job and they had lived together until she died.'

'And it never troubled either of them that they were brother and sister?'

'That's exactly what I asked him, and he said, beyond making sure that they had no more children, it did not trouble either of them. "Don't you understand, Tina," he said, "we loved each other!"

'"But it was wrong," I told him.

'"The world said it was wrong, but we didn't think so. She loved me just as much as I loved her. It wasn't possible for us to spend our lives apart."

'"But she was your sister!"

'"She was the fairest of the fair . . . like no other woman ever was, the one that God made·for me. There will never be another."'

'And that's what your father told you?'

'Yes. And I knew there never would be another! Larry?'

'Yes, Tina.'

'Larry, I've always been confused about the whole thing. The way he saw it, they had only broken the rules. They had done no harm to anybody, except me, and he was sorry for that. But nothing else. If he had to live his life over again he would live it with her, and her only. He spoke about reincarnation, about a past life he was sure he had spent with her, and that they would meet and love again. He was an educated man, Larry. I left him, confused . . . I've been confused ever since. Can you make any sense of what I've told you?'

'No, it's too deep for me. Ask me when I'm eighty, I might know then. But one thing, they did no harm on anybody, much. You have always been a lovely-looking woman, it's hardly their fault you married the wrong man. They gave you life, Tina.'

'But still I worry, Larry. For instance, is it bad blood that makes me sleep with you, am I a whore because I need a man, and you I can't resist? Answer me.'

'I can't answer you. How could I when I can't resist you either? I'm a man, you're a woman, and we're both lonely. I love making love to you. I love your thighs, your lovely swelling breasts, the softness of you, I love every bit of you because you are a woman and I was meant to love you, if only for that reason alone. Tiny, it's getting late, I'll have to go.'

'Will what I've told you make any difference to us?' Her voice trembled as she asked the question, and then it came to me that she was lying as far away from me as she could get, that she had braced herself for rejection. For answer I reached over and drew her gently close to me and reassured her in the only way possible, the only way she wanted to be reassured.

249

I was learning fast, growing up in a hurry since I had come to England. The sheltered celibate monastic life of Ireland was far away, here in the full hurly-burly of life was all that I sought to know, good and bad, black and white, all mixed up together, the rigid line drawn by my religion melted and blurred by the pitiful humanity, the weak frailty of men and women, the loving, the living and the suffering.

'Tina,' I said as I kissed her goodnight, 'you're God's blessing to one lonely Irishman, you are the only thing in this whole godamned crazy world that makes a bit of sense right now. Tina . . . what would I do without you?'

'Look for another woman,' said Tina cheerfully.

'Looking is one thing, finding is another.'

'You need a maid, Larry. You're made for marriage. You need a good maid to love you and look after you. You wouldn't have to look far if I was twenty years younger. Now, off you go, lover. See you tomorrow.'

She would see me sooner than that, but neither of us knew than then. My little cubby hole was on the opposite side of the house, the window was open and the same moon that was leaving Tina in darkness, was creeping like molten silver across the floor. A glorious August night. I looked out over the ruined city. Saplings of chestnut, beech and oak waved gently in the warm breeze, lording it over the weeds and wild flowers that were hiding the piles of rubble that had once been Plymouth. The roads between the ruins gleamed like chromium plate, the roads that led to work. Jesus, but I was ready for sleep — and no wonder! I tumbled into bed and was instantly unconscious, dreaming once again that I was home, on the banks of an Irish trout stream, fishing a pool below a waterfall crashing down, filling my mind with its glorious roar, and . . . .

'Larry . . . Larry . . . .'

The scream penetrated my mind like a red hot iron, and, confused, I shot bolt upright in the bed. Tina, a frantic looking Tina, clutching her clothes to her breast with one hand and shaking me with the other.

'Come on,' she screamed. 'Jerry is back!'

The roar of my dream waterfall had been the roar of approaching aircraft and Tina, survivor of the last blitz, knew only too well the sound of German aircraft. Stupidly I tumbled out onto the floor, grabbed my clothes, and in the wake of Tina ran for the stairs. Together we raced down as the first explosion rocked the house. All hell broke loose when the anti-aircraft battery close to us opened fire and the sirens belatedly added their wail to the mayhem outside. Most of the other boarders were already in the dining room. Tina had risked her life trying to wake me up.

An ashen-faced old Gran huddled shivering in the corner, clasping and unclasping her fingers. She was white as a sheet and trembled visibly. They had not expected this, nobody had. We had all grown complacent in the face of Russia's victories, the Nazis had no planes to spare for England. We were all wrong. People were right now being blown sky high outside, the floor under our feet jumped to the thud of bombs as battered Plymouth was mutilated all over again. Dwellings that already gaped at the sky, roofless and burnt out, were now completely demolished, heaps of rubble that had once been the city centre were once again blasted onto the roads, the only living casualties here the wild flowers and saplings.

But houses that had been patched up and were occupied were also going the way of the countryside intruders and the next day would reveal that over a hundred people had died that night. It would also reveal how the German Luftwaffe managed to arrive undetected. Their own cities were now daily subjected to air-raids, and they had flown over Plymouth by following closely in the wake of returning British aircraft, a cunning move that they would repeat in the coming November. It was foolproof. No radar ever invented could tell one aircraft from another when practically mingled, but Tina and a good many others could. They needed no radar to tell them that German aircraft were overhead. Tina had known before the first bomb fell. They could tell by the different beat of the engines, they could tell a loaded bomber from one that had already done its deadly work, they had their own built-in radar!

So had I, the one that told me that I would never be a casualty. Now, on a crazy impulse, I who had never known a really heavy attack from the skies, had to see for myself. Unnoticed, I crept through the door and back up to my room, to gape at Plymouth under fire. A great blanket of cloud had obscured the moon and the search-light beams, looking thick enough to walk on, were probing the night like solid columns of chalk. The old house seemed to sway in the storm of sound and all around the deadly gunfire mingled with the roar of planes and bombs. Explosions blossomed like red flowers in the mangled remains of this city. And cowering like rats in their holes, in the Anderson Shelters, in the ineffective brick ones that studded the streets, and in basements reinforced like our own, men, women and children had to endure a hell they were never designed to endure, ordinary people, some of whom would be mentally scarred for life. People whose gardens had become 'The Front'.

And just below me, in the ghastly light of incendiary bombs, an old man and woman bent beneath their burden of bedclothes were heading for Dartmoor and safety. Beside them, cowering close, was a whippet-like dog, tail between legs, scared witless, sometimes making little runs, only to return at once to its owners.

Somehow, that picture was to stay in my mind forever, always to be remembered, an old couple, trudging slowly through the mayhem, while young men in the flower of their youth slammed shells into guns, aimed at the sky, where other young men showered terror and death on the city below, neither of them doing much hurt to the other!

And an ambulance swerved aside, barely missing the dog, racing towards the skyline that was glowing red.

My hatred of violence and war, which was rooted in the terror of the Black and Tans and the Civil War of my childhood in Dublin, now rose from deep within me and curdled my guts. I could have vomited with rage. I had no sense of fear, just a wild lunatic rage, not only against the Luftwaffe above, but against the whole bloody concept of war itself, the tit for tat that left mothers weeping. But this war was like no other that had ever been. Here, in Britain, for the moment anyway, the soldiers were safe enough, in barracks buried deep in woods that bristled with ack-ack guns: it was their mothers and sisters that were taking the brunt of battle, they who would be mutilated or killed outright, if they were lucky. And only too many were not.

Now, around and all about, the incendiaries rained down, turning night into day, though few bombs followed in their wake. Evidently, the Germans could clearly see what was worth bombing and what was not, and turned their attention to what was left of Plymouth. There was nothing around here except our house, and so it survived once more. However, the planes left a calling card that could have spelt disaster to all.

A loud bang on the roof, and the plaster on the ceiling spattered onto the floor followed by a fire bomb, blazing whitely. It landed in the corner against the wall, and in seconds I had emptied three buckets of sand onto it, for the buckets were in every passage and room in the house.

God bless old Gran. She was a survivor, all right. The raid lasted about half an hour, maybe more, maybe less. It is hard to be certain when one is under attack, time ceases, only life counts. Half a mile away the glowing red skyline spurted from time to time as the bombs struck home, but here all was over. The roof by some miracle had not caught fire, and through the gaping hole came an acrid wind, the hot wind of war.

Now racing footsteps on the stairs came to my ears and I heard one of the boarders shouting. He was a cockney, who fancied Tina, and I also knew that he suspected me of sleeping with her. We avoided each other as much as possible.

'Down't risk, it, Tina,' he was shouting. 'I'll see w'ere the stupid young sod is.'

'The stupid young sod is here,' I told him as he burst into

my room, and there would have been a row but Tina was on his heels.

One glance at the room told the story and I grinned happily at the Cockney's obvious discomfort.

'Good job the young sod was here,' said Tina, glaring at the Cockney, who fled.

'You all right, Larry?'

'Course I am, Tina. I told you . . . Hitler hasn't made the bomb that can reach me.' The raid was over. The ack-ack guns close by still made the old house tremble, but they were wasting ammo', trying to fluke a retreating German plane. Suddenly they stopped, and, in the blessed silence that settled like dust, the clouds cleared and the full moon shone, straight through the roof and onto my floor.

'I can reach you,' said Tina softly.

'Come on, then,' and in seconds we were in bed, naked as the day we were born. We made love as the dawn broke over Plymouth, slow tender love, snuggling into each other, Tina clutching me close to her, desperate for the comfort of another human being after this terrible night. And before we slept I wondered if this love in life, this love of life, was a natural reaction to death and destruction, if the women in Berlin threw themselves at their men, like Tina, before the guns had stopped firing, helpless pawns in a never ending game between the Old Reaper and Mother Nature.

It was eleven o'clock before we appeared in the kitchen and started to make breakfast. Nobody had gone to work that day, all asleep from the exhaustion of the blitz. I went around waking them, some came to breakfast, some did not. Old Gran kept to her bed and I brought her up her breakfast. She looked her age this morning, this grand old lady who had been through too much, but grinned defiantly at me as she turned into her food. The radio beside her bed stopped its blaring music and on came the twelve o'clock news.

Gran nodded significantly. 'That'll teach 'em,' she said. 'Four thousand of ower planes knockin' bloody 'ell out a' bloody Berlin. Good for us! Tell Tina Oi'll be down soon.'

Just as I was leaving the room she called me back.

'Did Torquay cop it last night, Larry?'

'I don't think so, Gran.'

'Bloody war-dodgers,' Gran spat out. 'Livin' in luxury in that bloody funk 'ole. Oi'd love tew see them bastards cop it. Moight convince them there's a war on.'

Downstairs again I turned to Tina. I had wanted to see the much maligned Torquay for a long time, and now I questioned her closely.

'You'd really like to see it then?' said Tina. 'Well, we'll both go next Sunday if you're not working.'

'I won't be. I'm beginning to do a bit of war-dodging myself, I think. How will we get there?'

'I've a little car stashed away just down the road. Harry keeps it topped up with petrol from the truck. We'll make a day of it.'

And so it was all arranged at last, I was going to see Torquay and it had all been so simple. I had never suspected that Tina had a car. I gave her a hand with the kitchen until old Gran came on duty, and then made myself scarce. The sun was blazing, there was a brisk wind that blew the scent of wild Dartmoor into Plymouth and I set off to see the damage that the raid had done last night.

It was no different from anything that I had seen before except that these ruins were hot and the ARP people were busy digging among the bricks. I passed several groups before my conscience got to me, and then I peeled off my coat, grabbed a shovel, and set to with a will. The men were friendly, offered me tea during a brief respite, and called me Paddy. There was one frantic looking woman helping, who never stopped. Her fingernails were broken, she looked exhausted and dirty, she had been at it since the bomb struck, I was told. It was her sister and baby that the bricks covered, they could still be alive. Stranger things had happened, but not that day.

At half past five an arm appeared among the bricks, and a couple of minutes later the battered body of a young woman clutching a baby was taken out. Both were dead.

Dead and dirty, said my mind, which had suddenly become clouded, and I started to tremble. From the moment the arm had appeared I had frozen on the job, unable to lift a finger to help. The same terrible paralysis of fear that had come over me when Ken hanged himself, the same, all over again, as I had experienced in Moore Street, when confronted with the blood congested heads of the turkeys. Only this time it was worse. The trembling increased until I was shaking from head to foot.

'Steady on, lad,' said one of the grave-faced wardens. 'We've 'ad to deal with worse than this.'

Worse than this? There could not possibly be worse than this. Maybe there could have been more bodies, but worse than this? Never! A young woman aged twenty, the baby under a year, both sleeping forever, dirty and dusty in death, she in a flimsy nightdress, her lovely breasts uncovered, the child still with its napkin on.

'Got to 'ang on,' said the warden. 'Keep a stiff upper lip, lad.' But I had not been born with a stiff upper lip, I could never acquire the phlegm of the British. My race were more emotional, endowed with more of everything, we sang too much, drank too much, cried easier, fought harder and with more fury, we had too much of everything. And always with the built-in knowledge that our time on earth was short. The Brits, it seemed, never thought about death, and carried on as if they would live forever.

A wave of homesickness engulfed me as I wandered home, for Oxford Street had become home now, but I would never put down roots in this country. The stream and mountains, the lakes and rivers of Ireland would always call me, the incredible green of my island home would never set me free.

I had left Ireland because I wanted to be in the real world of the present, because I wanted to be free of the shackles of a priest-ridden country, because I wanted to experience life at first hand in the front lines. I had left with the cocky idea that I was as tough as they come. In the Army I had marched with the best. Sometimes, on the gruelling

256

mountain passes I had carried a weaker comrade's rifle, in the building game I knew no fear of heights, sure-footed on a single plank. I had fought young men, two, three stones heavier than myself, and come out on top. I had come to England fancying that I was among the toughest of the tough, that I could take anything, but now I was realising that I had been born flawed, that when the chips were really down I went to pieces.

Was this the reason my mother feared for me? And, word for word, I remembered the last time we had spoken and what she had said.

'I know what's wrong with you,' she had wept. 'I was frightened out of me mind when I was carrying you . . . your poor father "on the run" and the terrible times that were in it. Oh, Lar, you're too highly strung, and that's the reason. You were terrified even before you saw the light of day . . . I used to feel yeh kickin' inside me, an' the heart jumpin' out a' me breast.'

So, that was it, was it? The last exploration left to mankind would be the exploration of his own mind, I had read. Well that would be never in my case. Or any other man's mind either.

The long walk to Oxford Street brought me back to myself, though Tina's face dropped when she saw me. I had gone out in a decent suit, which was not dusty and spoiled. I was filthy from dust and smoke, suddenly much older, pinch-faced and careworn.

'Oh, my God,' she gasped, 'what happened to you, Larry?'

'Tell you later, Tina,' I said, and headed for the bathroom. The house was almost back to normal, all the boarders turned up for dinner except the German, Helmut. He had been given a terrible reminder of what was happening every night now — of the pulverising Nazi Germany was taking — and somewhere over there, if they still lived, his mother and two sisters were being bombed to hell and Connemara every night. He arrived late, blind drunk, but a gentleman to the last.

By Sunday I had fully recovered from the harrowing experience of the air-raid, quite back to my normal self, confident and capable: it was my armour against the world. I could put it back at will, I had to to survive. It effectively covered the flaws, though I did not deceive Tina. She had come to know me too well.

I lay on as the others went to work, and had a late breakfast with my buxom love served by an efficient looking woman about Tina's age, her 'stand-in' for the day. And then it was off to Torquay in glorious sunshine, in a Vauxhall motor car that had a sliding roof, and, with the wind in our hair, we left Plymouth and its desolate aspect behind, far behind, out of sight, it no longer existed as we sped along the road. Tina looked ten years younger, driving carefully, smiling, loving every minute of being with me and the day that was in it.

The fragrant countryside rolled past. Fat farms, manor houses for squires, were thick on the ground, and estates where great titles dwelled, thatched cottages, beautifully kept, that produced sturdy yeomen for England. The class divisions were clearly to be seen, if one had an eye open, though here was not to be compared with the conditions that had existed in northern towns like Warrington, between the Wars. The country labourer could always augment his income by tilling his garden, sometimes quite large, or the odd rabbit or pheasant poached from His Lordship. Though his income might be disgracefully low, compared with the denizens of the northern coal towns or the unfortunate miners in Wales, he lived on the fat of the land. Every cottage had its quota of hens, these people would never come to know dehydrated egg-powder, fresh vegetables were always to hand.

They were a sturdy breed, compared with the hollow-chested, sallow-faced products of industrial towns, whose staple diet consisted of jam 'butties' and fish and chips, when they had the money to buy them.

Torquay knocked my eye out when we eventually came to it. Tall palm trees waved from parks that blazed with flowers, the small harbour was filled with expensive yachts, a sedate Fun Fair was in full swing and the beaches around the town were colourful with umbrellas erected against the sun. Hundreds of people swam in the blue sea, children built sand-castles, hundreds lazed in the sun, shining with oil, naked brown bodies that had been exposed a long time.

'So,' I said to Tina, 'this is old Gran's funk hole!'

'Aye,' said Tina. 'Look at 'em, Larry, that's as close to the war as they're likely to get.'

We strolled around the small town before going to Kent's Cavern, that prehistoric cave, deep in the bowels of the earth where time stops. The cafés and restaurants were doing a roaring business, thousands of men and women lingering over coffee and cakes, or just lounging around the town, in light expensive summer frocks and blazers that carried a college or university crest. Upper class accents everywhere, arrogance on parade. So these were the children of privilege, Britain's élite, top of the heap, who took wealth and status for granted.

'They'll get a bloody big shock when the War is over,' I said.

'Maybe,' Tina replied, and then she made the remark of the century. 'They'll lie low for a while,' she predicted, 'and plot and plan behind the scenes until they can strike again. They won't lose their power easily. They'll fight for that if nothing else.'

Close to the harbour we discovered a house where Elizabeth Barrett and Robert Browning had spent the night, and I told Tina of the wonderful romance that had been between the two poets, about Elizabeth's fragile health and domineering father who had failed to prevent the couple running away. This house, I told her, must have been their last stop in England before they sailed for Europe.

Europe? Where was that? What was it like, now that the sign of the Crooked Cross waved from Estonia to Greece? According to the British press, which I treated with inbuilt suspicion, thousands of Jews and gypsies were daily herded into concentration camps, but what went on there was pure speculation. In no way would I believe what the papers hinted at, that they were being destroyed in thousands. And once again, of course, I was wrong. But one thing this glorious day in Devon did for me — it finally removed any guilt I felt for not joining the Army and fighting the forces of evil on the continent.

For one thing, I hated the wooden discipline that turned living men into zombies, who marched to order, slept to order, and finally stopped thinking and thought to order. For another, the Airforce, if it accepted me, would find a good job for Paddy as a rear gunner, and they, I had been told, survived on average about five raids. After that they hozed them them out of the rear of the planes. And, although I knew that Hitler had no bomb with my name on it, I was not so certain when it came to bullets or shells. Hitler had enough bullets for the whole world and, in the face of this crowd of war-dodgers, lazing about on a sunny beach, content to let the lower orders fight for them, my decision hardened, crystallised forever.

These bastards who would not fight were not worth fighting for: this was not my country, nor ever would be. I was a war worker, recruited to build Army camps and Airfields. I was doing that, I was worth a dozen of these privileged gets who used their paters' influence to avoid going to war. And it was inevitable that soon Europe would be invaded. Sicily had been invaded by the Allies in July and the fighting there was almost at an end. In the face of imminent invasion of mainland Italy, Mussolini had resigned, and now the 'saw-dust Caesar' was on the run.

'You've gone very quiet, Larry.'

'Yes, love. I've been tormenting myself for a long time, wondering if I should join up. But not after today, Tina, not after Torquay. I never really understood old Gran's hatred for this place, but I do now.'

'Don't let it spoil our day,' said Tina smiling. 'Anyway, I don't want a crippled hero on my hands. A live coward is much better for a woman.'

'Am I a coward?'

'I don't know and I don't care. I don't want you hurt, blinded or mangled like the lads I looked after in France in 1918. Bloody slaughter it was, an' they came back home to nothing. Don't mention war to me. I've had enough of it in my lifetime.'

'Jesus, you were in the last war! I never knew that.'

'There's a lot about me you don't know. I joined up to get out of service. "Yes Ma'am, an' No ma'am, and when would His Lordship be wanting his breakfast?" Nothing has changed, Larry, or ever will, though I must say there was not as many war-dodgers then as now. Two of His Lordship's sons were killed in Flanders, another crippled for life. I don't want that to happen to you.'

'It won't, not after today, not until that bloody lot go first.'

'And that will be never. They've all got important jobs, doing nothing, somewhere in Whitehall, organising man power or something . . . . Sod it, Larry, let's enjoy the day. We could be dead tomorrow.'

And so we went on the swings, rode the hobby horses, ate fudge off a stick, lost money in slot machines, rode the ghost train where howling noises and gangling skeletons made Tina scream and hold me fast, and gave me a chance to feel her thighs. It was a great day altogether, livened up with a sneak raid by a single German plane, who scooted over the waves, dropped a couple of bombs near the beach, sending the loungers running, and took off for France with two Spitfires hot on his tail. One could almost feel the heightened mood of the war-dodgers after this little charade, entering the water with a shout, feeling joyously happy to have had a little taste of war, a very little taste I reflected, after what I had seen in Plymouth. And I had not seen the worst of it yet.

It had all seemed like some trivial episode in a movie, sunny sands, carefree crowds, balloons on sticks, straw hats, and a couple of bombs that had sent up two great clouds of water, hurting no one. But suppose the bombs had landed

261

on the beach? How many arms would have been dug out of the sand? How many babies would have died?

'Cheeky blighter,' said this old Etonian. 'Turned tail fast enough, when our chaps got on to him . . . .'

'Won't be long now, old chap,' was the response. 'We'll be chasing them over the Siegfried Line soon.'

'Hang out our washing, eh?'

'Let's drink, my dear fellow, to that.' Already the indestructable British complacency had reasserted itself. I could feel it at work, among my fellow workers. With America and Russia pitted against Germany, the end result was never in doubt. But the titanic effort that would be needed was being badly underestimated in England. The feeling in the air was that it was almost over, Musso' gone, Hitler next, German cities being pulverised every night. The Jerries could not hold on much longer. There was lots of loose talk abroad about Italy, the soft underbelly of Europe, and about being in Rome and Paris by Christmas. In the end I was also convinced and started to dream of home again, of trout streams and blue mountains, of reed-fringed lakes that were home to enormous pike. But on this day, in Torquay, with my buxom mistress, I threw all care to the wind, to hell with tomorrow, today was all. And today flew by all too soon.

As the sun sank lower in the sky Tina headed for the car. Driving at night was a hazardous experience in blacked-out England, where one had to go along with the aid of two tiny slivers of light, all that was permitted to escape from the headlamps. We wanted none of that. As it was it was growing dark by the time the familiar smell of wet ashes announced that we were back in Plymouth, and Tina docked the car. We headed then for a pub she knew, where there was a band of sorts and a 'Mike', an old fashioned pub almost unknown to the Forces, a local pub where locals sang. On this night there was a bottle of Scotch whisky for the best singer and the place, quite large, was crowded. To my surprise, Tina entered the competition and was the seventh to sing among eleven volunteers. Never had I seen her look so well, a fine and lovely woman, who radiated joy. Looking at me and singing for me she brought down the house. She had a magnificent mezzo-soprano that needed no 'Mike'. Standing back from it she nearly rose the roof off.

'When You Come to the End of a Perfect Day,' she sang, and the storm of applause as she rose gloriously to the last note left no doubt that she was the winner. I was stunned. I had never suspected that she could sing at all, but then, as she had said earlier, there was a lot I did not know about her. And if I lived with her for a lifetime there would still be a lot about her that I would never know, her, or any other woman either. For I was learning and learning fast, that these strange creatures without whom no normal man could live, were as unfathomable as the deepest ocean, as mysterious as the most impenetrable jungle, each one was a Mona Lisa unto herself, waiting, watching, smiling not on men but at them. They reigned supreme.

Anyway, I was young and ardent, and Tina reigned supreme this night and well into the following morning. I had no way of knowing it, but this 'Perfect Day' marked the end of my happy days in Plymouth.

That night before we slept I questioned Tina as to why she had never had her voice trained, a stupid question. For it was rarely that girls from the orphanage ever made it from kitchen to drawing room. His Lordship had heard her sing one day and had offered to sponsor her, if she became his mistress. Tina, young and stupid, had declined the offer from a man old enough to be her father, and instead had gone on to marriage with a dark-haired charmer, who gave her two kids before his ex-wife caught up with him and he went to jail for bigamy.

'Thanks for a lovely day,' I whispered, before returning to my little room. But Tina had gone, far away, into the land of dreams.

12 Goodbye, Tina

The following morning I looked around the bus. The days of travelling on the back of a truck had long since gone, as had the women labourers. Things were better organised now, materials more easily available to building contractors, the frenetic madness of 1941 had gone and, except for the recent raid on Plymouth, it might have been peacetime. Suddenly I realised that my days in Plymouth were almost over. The bus was only half full, the job on hand almost finished. I knew I would be facing the unknown very soon.

That evening the unknown suddenly presented itself in the form of an identity card. it was not my yellow Aliens Identity Card, but a blue one, which meant that I was now regarded as a British citizen. That in turn meant that I was liable to be called up to serve in the Army, Navy or Air Force. I had no intention of serving his Majesty in any of these capacities. Strangely, the card had come via the Food Office, and there I presented myself on Tuesday moning. A toothy young lady of the upper class languidly presented herself smiling, but the smile went off her face very quickly when she realised the purpose of my visit. Bluntly, I told her I did not want to become a British citizen and wanted my yellow identity card back. She was speechless for a few seconds.

'Am I to understand that you are refusing British Citizenship?'

'Yes, you are. I'm Irish, I'll stay that way.'

'Don't you know,' she scorned, 'that thousands of your countrymen would give anything for what you are rejecting?'

'That may well be so, Miss, but I'm not one of them.'

'Then what are you doing in this country, may I ask?'

'Doing what I'm paid to do. Building Army and Navy Camps, anywhere I'm sent. That's all I contracted to do when I came over here. That Blue Card is the thin edge of the wedge. Next thing I'll be called up . . . .'

'And you're afraid of that?'

'Very much so. I'm going in no bloody army. I'm a War Worker, nothing else.'

'Well,' she said witheringly, 'you'd sooner let other lads do the fighting for you?'

'That's right,' I grinned. 'We are two of a kind. You've got yourself a nice little cushy number here. Daddy's little girl is not going overseas with the Red Cross, is she?'

'How dare you!'

'Look, Miss, just replace my identity card. That's all I came for.'

'Well, you'll not get it here. The police will want to see you about this matter.'

'Why, is it a crime not to want to be English?' Anyway, that afternoon a large and hostile copper arrived at the Digs, and told me to report to the station at seven o'clock. I had often been there before, being made to report to the police once a month, but this time it was a bit rougher. I reported on the dot and entered the station to be confronted by a sergeant, a superintendant and the big copper I had seen before. They ignored me as I stood before the desk, a slightly built young man in the presence of three large and hostile Brits.

'What's this matter all about, Sergeant?'

'This Irishman wants his yellow identity card back. Says he don't want to be British, sir.'

'I never said that,' I said, 'I want to remain Irish.'

'Hold your tongue,' the Super snapped. 'You'll speak when you are spoken to.'

265

'I'll speak when I like. I'm not in your army, not yet. I'm a civilian and I intend to remain one.'

'Ah,' said the Super thoughtfully. 'So that's the crux of the matter. Afraid you'll be called up, is that it?'

'Yes, that's it. I was in one bloody army, the Irish one, and I didn't like that. I'd like yours even less.'

'Beggin' yer pardon, Superintendant, sir,' said the big English culchie from Hampshire, 'but it seems to I that we 'ave an IRA man on ower 'ands 'ere . . . sir.'

'Have we?' said the Super turning to me.

'No . . . sir,' I said grudgingly, 'I was a soldier in the 7th Dublin Infantry, Leinster Command. I'm still on indefinite leave, still an Irish soldier.'

'Don't look much, do 'e sir?' said turnip-head from Hampshire, grinning.

'Probably a dangerous little bastard with a gun, just the same. Are you?'

'I'm a dead shot with a rifle. I was the company sniper. The company sergeant said I was the best . . . the best bloody civilian in the Irish army.'

'That's some recommendation,' said the Super, smiling. The sergeant and the Hampshire culchie were not amused, and I could see that they would have liked to rough me up a bit. I was suddenly glad that this superintendant, who represented a higher social order, was here. But not that glad, not when I remembered that the higher one went in the British caste system the more ruthless they became.

There was a long silence in the room and I stood there, fidgeting, scared but trying not to show it.

'Where do you work?' said the Super taking out a nail file and inspecting his hands.

'Bickley . . . building a camp for sailors . . . it's nearly finished.' Another long silence in which the Super filed his nails. He was toying with me, playing cat and mouse with an inferior. He was ten years younger than the other two, about thirty-eight, over six feet with a slim, perfectly formed body. His dark hair was receding slightly, perfectly arched eyebrows over a handsome face, a clipped 'Ronnie' under a straight nose. All he lacked was a pith helmet and a rattan cane. He should have been in India or Burma or Hong Kong, anywhere in Britain's far flung Empire he would have represented the King in style. He was the perfect Brit, cool, hiding behind his face, a gentleman by world standards, but a bastard that was capable of anything from pitch and toss to murder, in the name of King and country. And I was the small representative of the small country that had spat in the King's eye, taken them on when they were up to their balls in trouble in Flanders, and kept on taking them on until they cleared out.

The Empire that had fought for the freedom of small nations had written their darkest pages of history in my green and pleasant land and had been matched by a ferocity that they would never forgive. We had shown the world how to get rid of a conqueror, we had invented guerilla warfare, shown other nations how to fight in cities, fight from within. And that sort of talk was all right in Ireland, on St Patrick's Day, but by Jesus, it was a different proposition in an English Police Station, in 1943. The other two yobbos, quite prepared to give me a going over, were to be feared, but this cool Super put the fear of Jesus into me. I stood there, trembling.

'Give him back his yellow identity card,' said the Super suddenly, 'we can win the War without him.' He glanced up and smiled at me and suddenly my skin crawled.

'You're a good-looking lad,' he said. 'The ladies must envy you those long eyelashes. Do they?'

'Yes, sir, sometimes. I wish I could give them away, though.'

'Why?'

'They get me in trouble, with other men.' I was going to add that they took me to be effeminate, that now and then I had to throw off the coat and persuade them otherwise, but he interrupted, thinking I had finished.

'Ah, yes, no doubt,' he said thoughtfully, still smiling. 'No doubt.' The culchie from Hampshire tapped the counter.

''ere be yer yellow card,' he said. His tone had become

267

civil all of a sudden, and the sergeant was equally subdued. The Super, still smiling, was courteous to a degree.

'Redmond . . . Laurence,' he said. 'We'll be seeing more of you in the future. Report the first of every month at seven p.m., Okay? Unless I send for you. Got that, Paddy?' And he smiled.

'Yes, sir,' I said, trying to smile back, but the sweat was running off me. This bloody Super was a homosexual and he fancied me. That was why the other two cops had suddenly backed off. They knew what I knew, that he fancied me, and they were keeping their distance. The next day I fronted up the foreman on the job.

'So,' he said, 'transferring you shouldn't be too difficult. The job's nearly finished. But I'm surprised. I thought you loved it here in Plymouth.'

'I did,' and I went on to tell him about the blue identity card. That this man had just been released from the Army I knew, also that he was a rabid communist. I was sure I could trust him, that he was a kindred spirit.

'The next move will be to put me under surveillence, make it awkward for me in the Digs. I need to get away, George. I've been too long around here. I'm regarded as a local now.'

'What about your bit of crackling?'

'How do you know about that?'

'Saw you with her in the pub that night, the night she sang. Lovely voice, lovely woman. Wouldn't mind a slice of that meself.'

'Join the queue, George,' I told him. 'Eat your heart out.'

'She really fancy you? I mean, really!'

'Unfortunately . . . yes. It'd be different if she was twenty years younger, I'd never look further. I'm not looking forward to telling her that I'm going.'

'Well, you're not gone yet. We've plenty of sites to send you to, airfields, housing sites, first-aid blitz repairs. Where would you like to go?'

'The airfields, preferably where there is accommodation

268

on the job. I want to get back among the Paddies again. I'll feel safer.'

'What about Alconbury, Huntingdonshire?'

'All the same to me. I've nothing against the place, I know nothing about it.'

'Well, I'll see if I can arrange it. I expect I can. We're nearly finished here.' That night I told Tina it was on the cards that I would soon be leaving Plymouth, that the job was coming to an end. She took the news calmly, quietly, just one long sigh and then a smile that trembled on the edge of tears.

'I've been expecting that for a while now. Harry told me the job is almost finished. I'll miss you, Larry . . . but I always knew this day would come.'

'I'll miss you too, Tina.' This conversation took place in the passage leading to the dining room, and just before we entered she gave me a fleeting glance.

'See you tonight, lover,' she whispered.

'Of course.' We were old lovers now, used to each other, Tina fitted me like a well-loved coat. She had taught me everything I knew about love-making, serious long drawn out love-making. She had made me a man. My previous encounters with women, all too brief, had left me still a boy, but that day had gone with her. I was now a young man who was used to his ration of sex and I vaguely wondered what I would do when she was far away. I would never again be lucky enough to have a woman like her to love me and protect me from myself.

'Maybe I'm too old for you, Larry,' she had once said. 'But I've no conscience, about sleeping with you. What would you do if I was not here? Go down to the 'key-hole' and maybe get yourself a dose? You need a woman — every man does, but you more than most. Thank God I'm here to look after you.'

'What makes you say that I need a woman more than most?'

'Because you're a randy little bugger,' she whispered, pulling me into her, 'and thank the good Lord for that.'

I slept with Tina every night after that until the time came to leave, and that was 3 September, 1943, the day the Allies landed on the Italian mainland and Italy threw in the towel. We had many conversations lying side by side or snuggled up, the poignancy of our imminent parting drawing us closer together. The night before I finally left was a memorable one, and sex, although it played its usual important role, had little to do with the memory.

'Tina,' I said to her sleepily. 'Will you and I meet somewhere for a weekend when I'm settled? Will you?'

'No, lover,' said Tina gently. 'After tonight we're finished, completely. I've had my little run, now it's over.'

'Tina!'

'I know, Larry, it sounds hard but then life is hard. And anyway, you'll soon find another love, young and fair this time, not an old bag like me.'

'Don't say that, love. I never think of you like that.'

'No, you don't Larry, you've made me very happy in the time we've had together. I will never forget you, but life goes on, and it has to be lived. I'll be married before Christmas, I've just made up my mind.'

'Married!'

'Yes, Married.' I lay there, boggled, hardly able to comprehend what this woman was telling me. My Tina was going to marry another man, chop our relationship out in one swift stroke, guillotine it!

'Who is he? Have I ever met him?'

'To the first question, love, he's a small farmer, a widower, a fine man about fifty. To the second question, no, you've never met him, or ever will. He's been after me for years, and now, after tomorrow, I'll marry. And I'll be a good wife to him. So no more hanky-panky with you. Sorry lover.'

'I don't know what to say.'

'Then let me say it. I'm forty-three years of age and it's time I had a steady man, a husband, while I can still get one.'

'Do you love him?'

'Yes, but in a different way from the crazy way I love you. I'll be happy enough, Larry, never fear. I hope you'll work the future out as good as me. But I fear for you, I'll always remember you and worry how you are getting on. You're not half as tough as people think you are.'

'What's wrong with me, Tina? You're not the first woman who loved me that has told me that.'

'What other women?'

'Woman, singular — my mother. Answer the question, please.'

'Well, for one thing you're too easily hurt, too sensitive. For another, you don't fit in with the other men you work with, I never heard of a carpenter before who wanted to be a writer. I think,' she said, slowly, 'that's the real trouble . . . you are a writer, you see too much, feel too much . . . .'

'I do all right,' I said squeezing her breast.

'Not that way, you dirty little bugger,' said Tina, smothering a laugh. 'You feel too much about life. It gets to you too easily . . . you're a dreamer, Larry, in a world of cruelty, half the time your feet are not on the ground at all.'

And then she said something that I was to remember.

'Do you know what, Larry?'

'What?'

'That movie you're so crazy about . . . "The Wizard of Oz".'

'What about it?'

'That's where you belong, dancing down the Yellow Brick Road with Dorothy and the cowardly Lion. You and that Lion would have got on well together?'

'How so?' I was nettled.

'I'll tell you how so. Because you're both full of huffs and puffs and roars and wishes, and acting tough, but underneath it all you're as soft as jelly. Any woman can see that.'

'As long as only women can see it it's not too bad.'

'And of course you're a wild romantic in a world of reality. That's why you'll always be in trouble with women. Women don't like reality. They suffer it but they don't like it and they'll gladly follow a good-looking young fool like

271

you down the Yellow Brick Road . . . .'

'Okay, my love, okay. That's enough, too close to home by far.'

'But true,' said Tina gently. Yes, what she had said was true all right, only too true, it was always 'Somewhere, over the Rainbow' with me.

'Anything good to say about me, Tina, me oul "segosha"?'

'Segosha,' said Tina dreamily, snuggling close, 'I'll never know what that word means but it's a lovely word. I'll always be your "oul segosha". And take credit for this, you have made a woman of me, at last. I've had a rough life, I've had plenty of loneliness, no man aroused me for years until you came along.'

'Why did I arouse you? Do you know?'

'Yes, I know, and don't be offended. I pitied you, so young, so easily reached, so innocent in your wickedness, so lost, whistling in the dark, looking for a love. So I decided I'd be your love while I could, and now it's nearly over.'

'And you're going to settle down and get married.'

'Yes. I've had my little run.'

'And I have to find someone else to walk down the Yellow Brick Road with?'

''Fraid so, lover.'

'You've spent your Indian Summer with me and now it's a warm fire and a safe room gainst the coming winter, is that it?'

'More or less, Larry, more or less. Jesus, love me one more time, forget tomorrow, it'll be here soon enough.'

Big Harry had seen me off at the station and now, tearing across England headed for Huntingdonshire, I felt the usual rising excitement of travelling towards the unknown. The train was full of soldiers and sailors, with a sprinkling of airmen, packed to capacity, the corridors jammed. I had managed to get a seat and, despite the fact that I could see plenty of young women standing, I clung grimly to my seat. The only train I could get on had been an evening one, I would travel all night, arriving in London the following morning, and I needed sleep. Tina had seen to that, made sure that for a while I would be content with my own company.

Ten of us were jammed into one small carriage, four WAAFs, two sailors, three airmen and me, the only civilian. The sailors were drinking Navy rum, ninety proof I was told, from two lemonade bottles. The oldest was a tough-looking old salt about forty-five, weather-beaten from facing into Atlantic gales, a hard man. Beside him the youngster, about twenty, looked frail and rather pathetic. From his accent he was a product of a northern industrial town, the Navy surely had lowered its standards to accept him. Reared on 'jam butties' between the Wars, he must have been, as Jane Eyre's housekeeper had remarked, 'tenacious of life.'

What they were doing was totally illegal and would have got them six months apiece in 'the Brig' had they been seen by an officer. It was a grave offence in the Royal Navy to hoard the daily ration of rum and that is what these two had been at for some time. Both bottles were three-quarters full when we pulled out of Plymouth, and now, a couple of hours along the road, the young sailor was beginning to have a sickly pallor that boded ill for him and us.

'Come on, lad,' said the tough one in a soft Hampshire burr, 'knock it back like a man.'

To show him what a man was he took a hefty swig. Jam Butty followed his example, started coughing, turned green and suddenly, in one convulsive jerk, emptied his stomach onto the luggage rack.

The poor bastard had jumped to his feet and aimed at the ceiling in an effort to avoid us, but the force of his convulsion sprayed the carriage and a vile reek filled the air as he collapsed onto the floor.

Screaming with rage, the 'ladies' of the Airforce gave vent to their feelings. 'You dirty filthy pig . . . ! You filthy fucking bastard . . . ! You Lancashire fuck-pig!', as they fled from the carriage. We all followed as the 'old salt' picked up his companion and laid him gently on the vomit spattered seat. Then he made himself scarce, for I never saw him again. The hours slowly went by. Once we pulled up and lay doggo on the track with all the lights out, as a squadron of Luftwaffe pasted some town. Although there had not been one night in 1943 when there had not been a raid on some English town or city, yet the feeling of complacency that the War was almost over persisted, until it became clear that the Allies would have to take Italy a foot at a time.

But right now men and women began to lie down of the floor, weary of standing, and some with the bright idea of making love at sixty miles an hour, hoping for a collision I stood in the corridor until I was falling down tired, and then I opened the door of the carriage that was shunned by all. There was one small corner that had escaped the deluge and there, despite the smell, I collapsed and fell instantly asleep.

I woke up to a small noise. It was the door of the train being opened by two ambulance men, carrying a stretcher. The platform was quite deserted, how long the train had been in the station I would never know.

'You know this man?'

'No.'

'What happened to him?'

'He got drunk, that's all I know. I was too tired to stand up any more so I came back as you see. That's all I know.'

They lifted the still form of the youth onto the stretcher. His childish blue eyes were wide open, gazing into eternity. He was quite dead. As they made off I stumbled to my feet, grabbed my suitcase off the rack, cleaned it with a handkerchief and slowly made my way along the platform. I was supposed to make my way from here to Huntingdon station, but I threw my luggage into the luggage room and went out into the streets of London.

A lot had happened since I had seen it last, the Big Smoke that I had first seen in 1941. To hell with the war and the firm. A bit of war-dodging wouldn't do me any harm. So I spent the day and night in London, seeing the Wizard of Oz all over again and getting a little drunk before heading for the firm's hostel at Shepherds Bush. I felt sure the friendly manager would put me up for the night, and I was right. But on the way I had a glimpse into the underground life that went on in the city almost to the end of the War.

I rode on the Inner Circle for a couple of hours, geting out at some of the stations to have a closer look. London's Tube dwellers were settling down for the night. Some I spoke to had been coming down since 1939 and were now part of an extended family. One old man I spoke to grinned happily as he told me the War had saved his life.

'Sittin' in a bleedin' bed-sit night after night . . . talkin' to me bloody self, this war suits me fine.'

He waved across to a crowd of people who waved cheerfully back.

'Made more friends since the War started than ever I had before. Lovely comin' dawn 'ere night ar'er night, safe an' warm, among friends till mornin'. An' no charge for light an' 'eat.'

'It's an ill wind that brings no comfort,' I told him.

All along the platforms of the Underground people were casually undressing beside the double-tiered bunk beds set back against the wall, while London's teeming hordes came and went, used to the spectacle.

'Thought it was all over fer a while, Paddy,' said the old man cheerfully. 'Crowds fell off . . . but old 'itler woke 'em up last February and they've been comin' back ever since.' And that was true. The Luftwaffe, supposedly too deeply engaged in Russia had found time to give London another dollop in the spring of '43. And to this old man Der Führer had come as a blessing from heaven, to fill his lonely, bedsitting years with happiness. He and thousands like him would never think of it like that, but for the rest of their lonely lives they would look back on this brutal war with a sigh 'for the good old days.' It surely was an ill wind that brought no good.

And the Londoners, tough though they had had it, had fared better by far than those in small cities like Plymouth and Coventry. They had had no Underground to flee to, no haven left when the bombs rained down, and no city centre left when they had stopped. London was too vast a target to be wiped out completely by any one raid, people would still be able to see familiar landmarks that had survived the holocaust, but smaller cities had their ancient cores ripped out in a single night of terror, all the sights of a lifetime removed at a stroke. The citizens, dazed and shocked stumbled about the ruins hardly able to tell one street from another.

Quite often, although it was never mentioned in the press, the people's morale was broken. The bravado displayed in the press, the dashing daredevil 'Britain can take it' attitude found no echo in the small cities that had been 'Coventrated', where there was little heart to continue a war that missed the soldiers but did not miss their families.

At Bethnal Green, just as the train was pulling out I saw something that left a question mark with me for a lifetime. A small man with a large roll of brown paper in his hands was walking around a very substantial female, quite slowly wrapping her, in mummy fashion, against the hot wind the trains brought. She, towering over him, stood still while the little fellow completed the job. Craning my neck I kept them in view until the train entered the tunnel and they were gone, and so was I. What the hell happened when he completed the mummy job? How did he get her into the bunk bed? How did he get her out of it? How did she manage if she wanted to visit the toilet during the night?

These questions would plague me and remain unanswered. And the cosy scenes I witnessed in the Underground, the almost 'party' atmosphere that prevailed, the family fireside scenes of little children being made ready for sleep while thousands left and boarded the trains, this had become the norm in the London of 1943.

The following morning I left for Huntingdonshire. I was lucky, for one of the firm's trucks was leaving for there and I knew the driver, a Mayo man, who remembered me from my days in Coventry. He picked up my suitcase and the tool box from the station and as we drove northwards and deeper into the midlands he told me about Alconbury airfield and the place I was destined to work.

''Tis a kip, Larry,' he said. 'Way out in the fields on the edge of the RAF Station. Fuckin' planes roarin' over yer head all day an' all night, an' that's all yeh ever see. No Irishman is welcome on the airfield, unless a' course yer in uniform. Then yer all right for hozin' out a' the back of a Lancaster, and it's "Good Old Paddy".' He was a big redheaded son of the West, and now he burst out laughing.

'Good old Paddy,' he said, 'Good old Paddy had guts . . . great guts, an' there's nothin' bether to an Englishman's eyes than an Irishman's guts . . . splathered all over the place.'

'You seem to have no love for them, anyway, to say the least.'

'Ah, some a' them is okay, I'll have to admit that, an' bether employers than the Irish, bether be a long shot, but sometimes th'old bitherness comes over me an' I say things I suppose I shouldn't. But I'll never join their fuckin' Forces, that's for sure. Me father'd turn in his grave, an' I need never show me head back in ower house again if I ever put on a British uniform.'

He was in the same boat as me and there were plenty more like that, whose fathers had fought the Brits to a standstill, and only too many who had been hanged or shot for fighting for freedom.

'Is your father still alive, Paddy?'

'No . . . I never knew him except as a very small child. The Tans cem' to ower house wan day an' his body was found on the dump outside the town afther, with a bucket over his head, shot full a' holes. They used him as a cockshot.'

'That was done in Dublin, too.'

'It was done all over Ireland, Larry, be them murderous bastards. An' then they expect teh turn us into British soldiers if yer over here for a few years.' But the truth was that there were thousands and thousands of British soldiers from the Irish Free State, who had taken the King's shilling because they could not get a job in their own country, many of them deserters from the Irish Army who had fled over the Border into the Six Counties, trained soldiers who were just plain bored with life in a neutral army, as I had been myself. The danger to the Free State had passed long since, many of these men were the sons of soldiers who had fought in the First World War, and had been reared somewhat differently from myself and the Mayo man who drove the truck Our families had had too much hardship and grief during the Troubles, suffered too much, cried too much, starved too much for his and mine ever to forget, much less forgive.

'Have they ever tried teh get you teh join, Paddy?'

'No, not yet anyway, Larry.'

'They will, Paddy, they will, mark my words. Your job and mine are getting less sure by the day. The big rush is over, all they'll need now is to maintain what has already been built. The day of the big money is over, Paddy. Have you noticed how scarce Sunday work is getting?'

'Aye, bejaysus, now that yeh mention it, I have been startin' teh notice.'

'Well, watch out for the day they give you a blue identity card. That's the beginning of you ending up as an English soldier . . . . ' I went on to tell him about my experience in Plymouth and how I had defied the coppers.

'Bejaysus,' said Paddy in admiration, 'but you're a right little terrier at the back of it all.'

I said nothing. Just grinned, letting him think well of me. I did not tell him how I had nearly shit my pants with fright in the Plymouth police station, how the smile of the tall Super had sent shivers up and down my spine, how I had panicked and run for it as fast as I could. Or how I had left Tina and a bit 'of the other' behind, the loving, the sex, the exquisite experience of Tina, who loved me as no woman had before, or how I was facing the future lost and lonely, and never knowing when, if ever, there would be another woman in my life.

For I was in no way likely to have sex casually — a one

night stand. It had become too dangerous, I was never going to repeat my experience with Doreen in London. I had been very lucky not to have ended up with a dose of the 'Johnny Rocks' and since then the situation had become much worse. In every public toilet there were warnings of the rise in syphilis and gonorrhoea, where to go if you had contracted the 'social disease'.

The War had torn England apart, scattered husbands in industry or conscripted them into the forces, wives had been left lonely and had gone into the factories, where their sisters had already taken up with a Yank or a Pole or an Irishman or just any man, origin unknown, to comfort them in the long, blacked out nights. Down came the moral standards, down the knickers and up went 'Fagan' and the incidence of sexual disease.

The further north we went the smaller the towns and villages became, quaint names like Biggleswade and St Neots were left behind. Paddy told me the names, for all the signposts had been removed long since, against a German invasion that never came and never would. It was flat, lush country and now, within an ass's roar of 1944, winter was closing in. The hedgerows were bare, the odd copse of trees, stripped of their summer plumage, slept quietly, and I envied them their lot. They knew no winter, only spring and summer, days of thrusting life, bursting into leaf when all the bitter weather had gone, standing in all their green glory through balmy summer days.

'Wouldn't it be great, Paddy, if we could go to sleep all winter, like the trees?'

'Begob it would, an' y'ill wish that harder before this one is over. The camp at Alconbury is the worst kipp I was ever in. I spent last winter there and bejasus I'll never spend another. I'd go home first.'

'That bad?'

'Yes, that bad. Galvanised huts. Bare tin, unlined. When yeh wake up in the mornin' yer breath is iced just over yer head. No wardrobes for yer clothes. Wan pot-bellied stove teh keep the kipp warm. An' a nice wall teh wall concrete floor the

279

help yeh wake up quick like, of a winter's mornin'.'

So, that's what I was facing. It sounded like some Soviet concentration camp in Siberia.

'Jaysus, Paddy, surely it can't be all that bad!'

'Y'ill see for yerself soon now. We're nearly there. This is Huntingdon town.' We rolled slowly through the narrow main street, flanked by tall stone houses and shops, a beautiful well kept old medieval town, little better than a village by English standards, but the centuries had rolled down its streets and left it untouched. Now a new invasion, that would also come and go and leave it unscarred, rolled along in front of us, a large convoy of US Airforce trucks, each with its white star painted on its doors.

Cigar smoking Yanks sat behind the wheels and a couple of big shots raced past in a jeep. Behind us came the tanks, massive lumbering monsters, each with its black snout of a gun thrust aggressively forward. Any one of them could have reduced this town to rubble in a matter of hours, destroyed the work of centuries in minutes, as was happening all over Europe. And the pavements were crowded with American servicemen, all dressed like officers, beautiful expensive cloth, so that one could not tell the difference between a private and colonel. I was impressed. More than anything else this emphasised the enormous wealth of the United States. And again, every second American was holding hands with a woman. The few British Airforce uniforms I detected walked alone, the Yanks had taken over the women. And the full meaning of the derisive British saying 'Over fed, over sexed and over here' hit me with force. And there were wonders to come, though that still lay in the future.

I had been reared on a diet of American movies, the Broadway musicals of the thirties, the glamour of Hollywood, the close up kiss at the end, where an American Dagwood went home to Blondie, where 'Whippoorwill calls and evening is nigh' and, Sweet Jesus help me, I believed he hurried to 'my blue heaven'.

If I had not been such a bloody young 'eejit' I would have

observed, from the life around me, that young and beautiful brides turned into married women, with swollen bellies and varicose veins, that they were constipated, that they farted and belched and that sometimes sex was the last thing they wanted. But that is not the way Hollywood projected it. And I had swallowed it all. I, the bloody young fool who sat in this truck and watched and envied every American who passed by.

I had also been exposed to the movies that depicted the other side. For instance, the 'Dead End Kids' movies, which showed the other side of America, the terrible side of a society in which, if you had not made it by the age of forty, you were a gone duck. A failure, an also ran. No, for me it was always down the Yellow Brick Road, the Never Never Land that was just beyond. I would always be like that. But I did not know that then.

Eventually we came out of the town into deep countryside, just a few miles and then we were there. Alconbury! It was just as Paddy had described it. A half dozen blister corrugated huts on the edge of the road, and behind, somewhere, there was an airfield, and that was all.

It was only two o'clock in the afternoon, everybody was at work somewhere else, and I was shown my bed by a surly Yorkshireman who was in charge. And so I went to bed, worn out. I slept until five o'clock. When I woke up I was starving, but there was no way I could get even a cup of tea. Just another Paddy, who would go to work the following morning. I wandered disconsolately around until it started to grow dark and then the trucks rolled in, full of hungry men. All Irish, thanks be to God! I was, in a way, home at last. And the canteen opened in a hurry. I paid for two dinners and ate them both.

13   Alconbury

Alconbury was all that the Irish lorry driver had predicted and even worse than the impression I had of it at first sight. There were six corrugated huts, a dining hall and a run down recreation room with sagging table-tennis nets, scarred tables, worn linoleum on the floor that was not often swept, much less washed. The whole scene had a faded look to it that told its own story of a camp once crowded with workers who had built the airfield and then moved on. The Irish here, too, belonged to another generation, mostly middle-aged, quiet, thrifty men who knew that their working life was coming to an end and who hung on in this backwater, where the forty-four hour week had come back, where there was no overtime.

This one fact impressed on me even more surely that the War was already lost and won; that England as usual would come out on top. But here, in this miserable kip, it was hard to believe that there was a war, except that the constant roar of planes skimming our quarters kept us reminded. Even then, after a week or so one failed to notice the planes. It was like standing at the bottom of a waterfall, fishing for trout: for the first ten minutes all was sound and fury but after twenty minutes you were used to it. Alconbury was like that.

The first night I spent there was a nightmare. Every few minutes planes roared over the hut. The first time it happened I nearly jumped through the roof, much to the amusement of my companions, who chuckled quietly and assured me I would soon get used to it. They were right. But by then a worse evil had taken over, pure utter boredom. The only relief was the recreation room and its piano, which was, surprisingly, in fair condition, and I filled in many a lonely hour playing to myself. Once, a buxom wench of about thirty came in and sat beside me, asking me to play different popular tunes of the time. It was not difficult because I played by ear. Once — and once, only — she came, for after about an hour a long gangling red-faced Irishman presented himself in the doorway and glaring at me asked her when she intended to iron his shirt.

'So,' she said jumping up, 'we're going out after all are we?'

'Yis,' he snapped, 'we are, to Bedford. I'm fed up with the pubs around here.'

'Where did you get the petrol, Paddy?'

'Mind yer own business, an' come on.'

'Okay. Thanks, Paddy,' she said to me, and left.

I soon found out that she was the cook, that she was sleeping with the boozy-faced Paddy, who was about twenty-eight and years younger than the camp average. I was probably the youngest man on this site, but I was painfully aware after he left that I had made an enemy. I made a decision to keep clear of him, for he was big enough to take me apart with one arm. Thankfully the cook never again came near the piano, and, as he was living with her in her quarters, our paths did not cross.

I started to write again. With my little portable I typed away many an hour, and the two occupations of writing and playing the piano set me apart from the rest. But I made many friends in a hurry. There were half a dozen men from the West who could not write, and to me fell the task of doing it for them. They would sit quietly on my bed and whisper their letters home. There was even a little Dublin man who was illiterate — and this I found hard to understand because he was as smart as a tack. I had not yet heard the word 'dyslexic', or found out that this was a

283

medical condition, a malfunction of some of the brightest minds, and that the condition was irreversible. My offer to teach him to write he gently rejected. The men from the west told me that they were too long in the tooth to learn new ways. Of course this meant that when a letter arrived for one of my friends I had to read it to him. So, gradually, I was respected, especially because I never spoke to anyone about the letters, or discussed their contents.

The work on Alconbury airfield was as boring as the workless weekends. It was merely routine maintenance, fixing a lock here, a door there, a window somewhere else, working apart from the rest of the Irish, alone as I had never been before. And all around lay the lush fields of this very comfortable part of Merrie England. The farms about the airfield were enormous by Irish standards, three hundred acres being ten a penny, with their big houses of stone or brick, set well back from the road. My companions, some of whom had been here for years, told me how much they looked forward to the summertime when they went picking peas on weekends and got paid by the bag. And so the dreary winter passed into spring, with Christmas just a vague memory of something that did not happen. I sent Mam a few pounds for a Christmas box and wrote a long letter for once. While I was at it I wrote to Tina, a short impersonal note in case her man was around when it arrived. A week later I received a photograph from Plymouth. Tina, fine and good-looking as ever stood beside a huge Hampshire farmer, a kindly looking man who grinned happily at his newly acquired treasure, as well he might. I looked long and hard at the wedding photo before tearing it up. On the back she had written 'Goodbye, lover' and had stepped irrevocably into my past.

'God bless you, me oul' "segosha",' I whispered.

'What was that, Larry?' said Johnny from Mayo, who I had forgotten was beside me.

'Nothing much, Johnny,' I said, 'just day dreaming.'

'You ought to get out of the camp now and again, Larry,' said this kindly man who was old enough to be my father.

'It's not natural for a young fella like you not to go to Bedford an' chase the women like the other young fellas around here.' And that was the strangest thing of all. Since Tina, I had never felt the slightest desire for sex, and had no intention of going anywhere to pick up 'a bit of stray'. The risk of 'getting a dose' was only too real, but that was not what prevented me. I seemed to have reached some kind of an oasis in my life since my arrival in Alconbury, and, after a fashion, I was grateful for it. But while I was vegetating quietly in this corner of England, the tumultuous year of 1944 went inexorably forward.

By January the Allies had driven the Germans back in Italy to Rome, and the Red Army re-took Kirovagrad. In the same month the allied airforces began an operation they called 'Pointblank', directed against the German aircraft industry and the hated Luftwaffe. This was swiftly followed by the liberation of Leningrad as the Russians swept forward in a drive that would eventually take them to Berlin. General Eisenhower assumed supreme command of the Expeditionary Force, to a snarl of envious rage from the ordinary Brit on the ground. But the press remained silent. America and Russia were now the superpowers, Brittania no longer ruled the waves and her far flung Empire had been overrun by the Japs. Never again would a British officer quell an Indian mob with a flick of his rattan cane. The myth of the invincible Brit, the myth of the all powerful white man had been trampled into the dust by the Japs. Had not Singapore fallen in 1942, symbol of Imperial might, all its great guns pointed the wrong way and its mighty garrison kicked up the arse all the way to the Burma road?

Here, in Alconbury, spring was bursting out all over, and although the nights were still cold, gone was the accursed winter in that cheerless iron hut, where the Irish lorry driver's prediction had been proved correct. The half circular construction of the galvanised huts with the beds close to the walls ensured that the ceiling was only, at most, two feet over one's head and usually in the morning a thin film of ice from frozen breath glittered above, a nice start to another day on the job.

'You're very far away, Larry,' said Johnny. 'Dreamin', as usual.' So, Johnny had me spotted, too. I grinned at him.

'Sometimes, Johnny, it's better to dream about Fairyland, or the other side of the rainbow, better to leave this world altogether for a while and leave behind the sickening things that are happening all over.'

'Yeh could be right,' said Johnny non-committally, 'but there's a poor divil in the hut next door that wants a letter written.'

'Well . . . that's no trouble.'

'He's too backward to ask yeh, Larry. I was wonderin' if you'd get talkin' to him sometime, an' maybe he'd ask yeh.'

'Who is this man? What's his name?'

'Yeh know him well enough, everybody does. He's the man wit' the crippled leg and the head full a' wire, yeh know, the wan we call Wire Head . . ., Clancy from The Glenties.'

'You don't call him that to his face, surely?'

'By Jaysus, we don't. Nobody does.'

Well I knew this man and I avoided him like the plague. He was a terrifying figure with a battered face, white and fierce, a man who had been born deformed but, like Quasimodo in Notre Dame, tremendously strong. He moved, after his crooked fashion, with unexpected speed. Above the waist he was built like a tank with great muscular arms hanging almost to his knees. A man to avoid.

'Jaysus, Johnny,' I blurted, 'I'd be afraid to go near him.'

'An' y'd be wrong, Larry. That's one a' the nicest fellas God ever made. He's over here supportin' a mother an' father an' two imbecile sisters at home. Y'd never think that, would yeh, teh look at him?'

'No, you never would.'

'He was a blacksmith, wit' his own forge, before the horses became too scarce. Will yeh meet him if I bring yeh?'

'Yes, of course.'

Of course I would. Who the hell wanted to get into the

black books of a man like that? Not me, anyway. I liked being alive, even in this doleful kip called Alconbury, where my life seemed to have come to a dead stop.

'Will yeh come wit' me now?'

'Sure, Johnny, if he's stuck for a letter, I'm his man.' Five minutes later I met the man. He was dozing on his bed as we came in, his short grey hair standing up like a hedgehog's spikes.

'Well, Clancy, me son of Erin, here's the little Jackeen yeh wanted teh meet. Yeh know his name, I'll lave yeh wit' him.' I spent an hour or more talking to Clancy and discovered, as Johnny had predicted, a generous decent man. I would never meet better. So much for judging the book by the cover. When I told him I would be delighted to write home for him, he opened up like a flower, and I had made an invaluable friend. A couple of months later this man saved me from being battered senseless by the drunken brute who slept with the cook. However, that night I knew nothing of the future, or any other night since, and that surely is one of God's blessings. For to be able to see one's own future would surely be the road to madness.

The following night I took my little portable up to the recreation hall, for Clancy was too shy to whisper his letter in his hut, and I wrote to Glenties for him. His family's misfortune was only too common in the depopulated areas of Ireland, as generation by generation the native stock dwindled — famine and emigration stripping the hills and valleys — and blood ties came too close.

Clancy's father had married a first cousin, and two imbecile sisters and himself were the result of this disastrous liaison. The father, I gathered was 'not the full shillin', either.

On 13 June, ill-fated for England as the date suggested, I was transferred to work on the American airfield, twenty miles away. June was a hell of a month for the Allies in Europe. Rome fell to the US 5th Army on the fourth of the month, Normandy was successfully invaded on the sixth, and the first VI flying bomb fell on London on the unlucky thirteenth. These bombs were swiftly christened 'Doodle

Bugs', a reference to the peculiar whining stutter made by their engines, and once again London was the chief target for Der Führer's wrath. They caused horrific devastation on impact, for it seemed they did not penetrate the earth to any great depth but exploded at ground level, and, for a quarter of a mile around the impact point, the casualty rate was high, mostly from flying glass splinters.

With certain defeat staring him in the face, Adolf was still mad enough to think that he could turn the tide with this last horror and bring Britain to her knees. And it was on the unlucky thirteenth that I gleefully went to work for the American Air Force. Anything for a change. Most of the men in our hut were transferred with me, labourers whose job it was to keep the runways in perfect order. Me? Back to the same old routine, maintenance of living quarters. But it was like being in a different country, and in a way it was, for here America reigned, GI territory.

On that first morning the lot of us had to present ourselves before an American colonel, in order to get an airfield pass, and it was here that the fundamental difference between the Americans and the British surfaced. On my first day at the British airfield I had had to apply for a similar pass, with amusing results.

Ramrod-straight, a British sergeant had marched into the CO's office, where a tall, languid officer lounged behind his desk. I was told to wait outside the open door as the sergeant's boots crashed deafeningly on bare boards, the 'bang-bang' as he came to attention and saluted.

'Sah,' he roared. 'Permission requested to bring in civilian worker.' The bloody officer must be stone deaf I thought, but he was not. This was an exhibition of the iron discipline of the British Army.

'Permission grawnted,' the officer replied, with a bored salute in return.

'Sah,' roared the non-com, and banged his way back to me.

'You may report to the colonel now,' he bawled at me, still ramrod-straight. I bloody near burst out laughing in his face. I went quietly into the officer and presented my pass to the colonel. He looked at it indifferently, and murmured something I could not catch. I think it was 'another Paddy'. However, he signed the pass and flicked it across the desk to me.

'Thank you . . . sir,' I said hastily, and his eyebrows rose a little.

'Sergeant,' the colonel drawled. Bang-bang-bang-bang. Lead boots with the leather lungs was back.

'Sah,' he roared and nearly burst my bloody ear drums.

'His pass is in order now, sergeant. Put this man to work,' drawled His Lordship and resumed filing his nails.

Thus Alconbury, but this application was a very different kettle of fish. The sergeant who had escorted us from the gate rambled casually into the Pass Office. Behind the desk a long Texan lounged, with his shoes on it. He was also a colonel.

'Gotta bunch of Irish here, Al, who need their passes signed,' said the sergeant.

'Okay, Mickey. Send 'em in one at a time. Lost my goddamn lighter somewhere. Got a light?'

'Sure, Al,' said the sergeant and took the proferred cigar and lit both. He strolled over to the doorway where we all stood.

'You guys can come in now, one at a time.' And so our passes were signed. We now had the right to work in GI territory. The foreman of the gang already working there collected us then and we went to work, me alone as usual. I had plenty of time to look around and was enormously impressed. It seemed at first to me that I was not really on an airfield at all, for the gaudy signs, beautifully done, reminded me of Disneyland. Outside the hut where I was fixing a window, a kind of Indian Totem Pole stood, with a grinning demon on top, pointed teeth bared, spiky fingers aimed earthwards, the malevolent personification of aerial bombardment. At its feet the sign said . . . 5th Bomber Command.

Out on the runway a couple of Flying Fortresses were being checked over prior to another assault on Germany. One had fourteen miniature bombs painted on the fusilage. on the other, one of the crew standing on a ladder was adding the twentieth bomb. Each bomb stood for one mission over Germany.

Beautifully painted right along one of the plane's length, a fulsome blonde reclined, smiling at all, the spitting image of Betty Grable. Other fortresses I was to see later were painted as well, displaying Mickey Mouse, Goofy, Donald Duck . . . but at this point frivolity ended. These massive planes, the like of which I had never seen before, brought daily and nightly terror to German cities, unloading their deadly cargo with impersonal precision. Betty Grable, Goofy, Donald Duck and company grinned and smiled over carnage on an unimaginable scale. The easy-going American existed only on the surface. Underneath, scratch the paint, and you had a pilot and crew that faced a shrapnel-filled sky, inches from death every day. Betty Grable came back one morning with both her diddies shot away, Goofy had lost his head, and I never saw Mickey mouse or Donald Duck again.

The Yanks had machines for every type of work. A cigar-smoking groundsman, sitting behind a front-end loader, could shift a mountain of ammunition boxes in an afternoon without rising a sweat. It was the same all over. Casual endeavour concealed deadly precision. I was overawed, stunned by the wealth of the US. From their expensive uniforms to the handmade shoes of the officers, everything here was too much to take in that first day. After years of rationing the dining hall, where we were allowed to dine with the air-crews, was another revelation. You could help yourself to as much as you wanted, you could eat like a pig if you were that way disposed, but a notice behind the counter said, 'Eat What You Take'.

Confronted by mountains of beef, chicken legs, vegetables galore, and a lake of steaming gravy, we attacked our meal with a vigour displayed by few of the Yanks. We had not tasted such food for years, even the best of old Gran's blackmarket meals hardly matched the food these Americans ate so casually.

It was the same story when it came to dessert, simply no limit to the supply of ice-cream and tinned fruit. A big cook, wielding an axe like a tomahawk, expertly hacked the top off a tin of fruit damn near as big as a dust bin, and emptied its contents into an aluminium tank on the counter. A long ladle hung on its side and we could, and did, gorge ourselves on mixed fruit, pears, peaches, apricots, pineapple, and other exotic fruits unknown to a whole generation of young Brits, and certainly never tasted before by many of our gang. To a man we gorged and that afternoon little work was done.

Stomachs began to churn and, green of face, men stumbled towrds the lavatory. Some failed to make it there and were compelled to squat beside the runway much to the amusement of the Yanks. Rich food, after the Spartan diet of years proved too much, there was little dinner eaten in the dining hall that night. On the American base we were fed like turkey cocks, but even then the pampered Americans were heard to complain.

They were outraged at being served 'Shit On Shingle' twice in one week and, overhearing the conversation, I grew curious as to what they were referring to.

'God damn it, Hank, shit on shingle again for breakfast this morning!'

'Jesus H. Christ,' snarled Hank, 'I'll blow if I get that shit on shingle one more time.'

'Ain't fit food for a hawg,' a Southerner drawled bitterly, 'Fust thang a' do when a' gets home is go out in the woods an' shoot maself a mess a' squirrels.'

'Squirrels?' said a Brooklyn voice, 'Jesus, we got 'em in Central Park. Don't tell me yah eat the things.'

'Sure do,' said the Southerner, quite unperturbed. 'Beat's chicken t' hell, turkey too, man,' he drawled. 'Yah ain't lived till you've tasted Maw's squirrel pie!'

'Yuk,' said Brooklyn, 'I'll stick to my side a' the Mason Dixon . . . Squirrels an' woods is out, concrete and burgers is in.'

They were both, however, in heartfelt agreement about

'shit on shingle', which I found out was their derisive name for minced meat on toast, a luxury that British civilians had not enjoyed for years.

As a wet June turned into a wetter July the 'Doodle Bug' barrage on London intensified and another evacuation took place. Anyone who could got to hell out of the city, an estimated one million fled, as the battered old giant that was the heart of an empire came under bloody assault, for the third and last time.

Among these refugees from Adolf's wrath came a fair maid from Kent, who was to love me with the passionate intensity of the very young, and in her turn brand herself on my heart forever. Mina, who walked in beauty, Mina, my beloved one, a dazzling blonde with the figure of a goddess.

On the first evening that I saw her standing behind the counter in our dining hall, I was struck dumb, love at first sight, head over heels, and suddenly I became afraid I would be transferred to some other place. All that day, and for many days before, I had used every means in my power to get a transfer. It was just too boring here. I had come to England to see some action in the first place, not to spend lonely evenings in this rural backwater, and with my inbuilt confidence that Mr Hitler had never made a bomb with my name on it I had no fear of bombs, 'Doodle Bugs' or other missiles, whatever they liked to call them — they would never hurt me. I just hated Alconbury.

The few locals I encountered were surly and ignorant, bucolic louts who resented strangers. I thought it was just the Irish they hated until one night I decided to walk to the Barley Mow, an ancient tavern with a roof of thatched reeds. It blended in beautifully with the bountiful fields around, where partridge and pheasant abounded, with little now to fear except the fox. The local gentry had larger game to kill these days. It was hot, I was thirsty and looking forward to a pint when I reached it.

The place was crowded with locals. I had not thought there were so many of them and not a few were young and strong, men who had had their 'call up' deferred because they were needed on the land. Burly healthy types who in no way resembled the 'Jam Butty and Fish 'n Chip' lads of northern English cities. Like most men who are safely tucked away behind the lines, they were twice as ferocious as the soldiers at the Front, mad to get at the enemy.

There was a queue at the small serving hatch in the pub and I took my place in it, behind two splendidly tall American flyers. When it came their turn to be served two locals walked in front of them and were immediately dished up two pints. This happened again and I heard the smaller of the two — he was only about six feet — say 'Jesus God, Jer, is the bloody man blind, or are we goddamned invisibile?' When the locals were served he stepped straight in front and faced the proprietor. 'Two pints of beer,' he said civilly.

The red-faced landlord, another ignorant looking lout, faced him squarely. 'No Yanks served in this 'ere pub,' he said stubbornly.

For a second the American stood there, stunned. Then he exploded. 'Jesus H. Christ,' he roared to his companion. 'Did you hear what that bastard just said?'

'Yeah . . . I heard. You meet pigs all over. C'mon, Jer, don't disgrace your uniform. He's not worth it.'

'Disgrace my uniform,' shouted Jer. 'We've saved these fuckin' Limeys in two wars, an' this fucker won't serve Americans. Jesus, Gawd, I'll fuckin' . . . .' There came a low growl from the collected yokels, a savage sound in a place gone suddenly quiet.

'You'll fuckin' what?' snarled one of them.

'Come on Jer,' said the tall Texan. 'They're not worth it.' He put his arm around the incensed Jer's shoulders and gave the crowd a scathing glance. 'I'll be droppin' bombs on Krauts tomorrow,' he drawled, 'but I'd sooner be dropppin' 'em on fuckers like you!'

They left, I with them. There was no point in waiting to be insulted, and anyway these yokels were in a dangerous mood. It was no place for a neutral Irish civilian! From that moment onwards my desire to leave Alconbury reached fever pitch. I felt trapped and became insolent and careless in my work in the vague hope of being sacked, but that too was unlikely. The Labour Exchange decided when you left and where you went. The foreman in charge was another local who had, from the first, made no attempt to conceal his contempt for me. He rarely deigned to speak, just handing me a written order for the day's work, 'Fix lock on door, Hut 28 . . . .'

He received on the double what he dished out, silent contempt, but not anymore. The next time he criticised a job I had done, and done badly, I effed him with a venom that stopped him in his tracks. At all costs I had to be transferred. However, that provocation ceased from the moment I laid eyes on Mina. Suddenly Alconbury was a heavenly place to wake up to. The winter of my discontent had lasted too long. Spring had passed me by unnoticed, the fresh growth that powders the trees and hedges had only evoked a scowl, the call of the cuckoo had only served to remind me of the green meadows of my home that I had not seen since 1941. Nothing had been happening. Every day I saw Flying Forts limp back on a wing and a prayer, riddled with shrapnel, some with their landing gear immobilised, or the wheels shot off, skidding along the runway in a cloud of smoke and sparks, before exploding. The ground staff were never allowed near when this happened, but from a distance we could plainly see the results of war and the terrible fate of the loser. The lucky ones died.

In the meantime I was the diminutive representative of a neutral country that in those days hated England, an exile not to be spoken 'down to' by any Englishman, an unhappy young man who remembered the past too clearly. Wilhelmina — Mina — changed all that. Suddenly I loved Alconbury, I could tolerate anybody, and the rustic gobshite who was my foreman was so astounded that he started to call me Larry. The 'Paddy me arse' days had gone, that much my small mutiny had accomplished. Right now the hares that lived on the vast airfield danced in the sunsight, the sweet call of the cuckoo rang an echo in my heart, the hedgerows exploded with blossom, woodbine, wild roses, mayflower, and at their feet the ditches were a riot of colour. The breeze that fanned the fields was perfumed as never before and all this had come about because Der Führer had sent one English Rose my way.

Her father was in charge of the dining halls that served camps such as ours and he had ordered his daughter out of London, despite her protests. She too had to go where she was sent, and fate and a 'Doodle Bug' had sent her my way.

Among the few young men in the camp she created a storm and seemed casually unaware of it. Standing behind the counter, coolly serving dinner with the detachment of a duchess, the half dozen who chanced their Blarney got nowhere, and christened her 'Stone Wall Jackson'. Some of them were six feet tall, good-looking, and had a way with 'the women'. If they could get nowhere, what chance had I? Anyway, I was too dazzled to try.

Although I had loved a few women, all older than myself, I had never been 'in love' and could not handle a situation in which the woman was obviously younger than me, and by far the most beautiful I had ever seen. Because of her the dirty old workers' camp was suddenly lovely, because of her I was among the first up in the mornings, and lingered long over breakfast. Because of her I returned to camp every night, glad to be back in glorious Alconbury, to see my angel again. All the bullshit I had seen on the movies was true, after all! I was in love, too shy to speak to her, content to adore her from afar. She appraised me as coolly as the others and never smiled, always quite unapproachable.

Then one evening, paying for my dinner, I handed over a ten shilling note, and she pushed the same amount back to me in half crowns. I made to correct her mistake but met an icy glance. 'Next,' she said curtly.

At breakfast the following morning it was the same. I handed over half a crown and received the exact amount back two shillings and six pence. Meals for nothing! What was happening? I was sorely puzzled and one day spoke to my friend Billy Power about it. It had been going on for about a week, and Billy, who had tried his luck with her and failed, burst out laughing.

'Jaysus,' he stuttered, 'you must be the most innocent Jackeen that ever cem' out a' Dublin! She wants yeh teh take her out, y' eejit.'

'Never!'

'Don't bet me, you'll lose! I'm ten years in England an' I know the English wans inside out. She wants to make a date.'

'But Billy, she never smiles at me, or even gives me a second glance.'

'She doesn't want the whole camp to know, for Jaysus sake use your head. This is England, not Ireland. The Irish wans are all flashin' eyes an' coaxin' smiles, but yeh have to have a jockey's licence from the priest before they'll take their hands off their ha'pennies.'

I made sure to be last in to dinner that night and approached her with wildly beating heart. She placed my meal before me, took the ten shilling note I gave her, and swiftly banged four half crowns on the counter. She did not look up, but commenced stacking plates. She was waiting. Billy Power was right!

'I'd love to take you out,' I whispered.

'When?'

'Last night!'

A tiny flicker of a smile for answer. 'Play the piano again tonight,' she said softly. Half past seven saw me in my best sports coat, open-neck cream shirt and brown gaberdine trousers, shoes shining almost as much as myself. My dream girl was coming.

She did not, but at eight o'clock a girl I had never seen before approached me at the piano.

'Hello,' she said smiling. 'Are you Larry?'

'Yes.'

'I'm Barbara, Mina's friend. I only just arrived this afternoon. She told me to tell you she is waiting down the road.'

'Thanks very much, Barbara, thank you,' and I shot out of the recreation room like a bullet. She was waiting where the road turned as I left the camp, but quickly disappeared when she saw me coming. I sauntered along casually, just in case anyone was looking, but past the bend I ran like hell and soon caught her up. She stood there waiting, smiling, and without thinking I put my arms around her and kissed her. There on a quiet road in Huntingdonshire, while RAF Bombers and American Fortresses headed across the sky, bound for Germany and mayhem. In Russia four million communists had fallen upon three million Nazis, the battle of the 'Hedgerows' was raging in Normandy, the US Marines were locked in battle with the Japs at Sahibganj — but these minor events were ripples compared to the earthquake that rocked my world as she kissed me back. For this girl was as madly in love with me as I was with her!

She had been stationed here before, knew her way around, and brought me to a little old pub down a leafy road, where we sat in a bay window with coloured leaded panes, while the sun set slowly and the long twilight began. She sipped a gin and tonic and there being no whiskey on offer I drank foul English mild beer, which now tasted lovely, and on the slow walk home we stopped often to hold each other close, passionately kissing, mad for each other as the very young can be.

And here was the Yellow Brick Road I had been searching for all my life, here was love and the wild joy of being loved in return, here was desire, above all — desire, for love demands consummation. It is the way the good Lord made the world!

When Adam first knew Eve a hundred earthquakes could have rocked the earth, a thousand storms could have raged across the oceans, but in the Garden of Eden there was only love and the planet could have been knocked out of orbit and flung headlong into space for all those two cared.

> *Oh, the Garden of Eden has vanished, they say.*
> *But I know the lay of it still.*
> *Just turn to the left at the bridge of Finay*
> *And stop when half way to Cootehill.*

Percy French was wrong. The Garden of Eden was right here, in Alconbury!

14   The Enchanted Wood

In the four weeks we were together I played the piano often, especially on rainy nights when we could not walk to our special seat in our special pub. Mina and Barbara would be there in the recreation hall, with a few of the younger Irish as well. The place had suddenly become popular again, with some of the lads hoping to 'get off the mark with Barbara' — for it was accepted that Mina was my girl, and she was. To complete my happiness I found out very soon that she loved music, that it was her joy to sing. I should have guessed from her slightly husky voice that she was a singer, but her soaring notes the first time I heard her sing, left me breathless. She left me breathless too and rainy nights always ended in the old disused air-raid shelter, where we kissed and cuddled. Other nights on our way back from the pub we ended up in the long grass, under a mid-summer moon, and came close to the final act of love.

Many times I could have taken her, but something always held me back. Perhaps it was the knowledge that she was younger than me, that I was an expereinced lecher, that she was only eighteen, and I twenty-four. Whatever it was, for all our 'heavy petting' we never consummated our love. But I taught her the ways of love. She had just escaped from the menace of the 'Doodle Bugs', the frenetic climate of war that always brought the sexes together. Where there was the threat of death there was lust, if not love, and to hell with tomorrow was the order of the day. Mina knew, better than

I, what it was to live in the front line, and the recklessness of the war years had left its mark on her forever. She was ready for love, wanted it, it was there for the taking.

One night, after a particularly heavy session in the grass, we sat up, panting, and I saw she was close to tears.

'Why?' she said. 'Why?'

'I don't know . . . I'm not good enough for you . . . though God knows I love you and want you. I'd marry you in the morning if I had the chance. Will you marry me?'

'No, next year maybe, but not this year.' She dabbed her eyes, combed her hair, and in womanly fashion removed all signs of the hectic hour we had spent.

'Why waste a year?' I said.

'I'm not wasting it, really. We wouldn't waste anything if you were willing. You couldn't love me if you won't make love to me.'

And that was 1944. I was lusty and ardent, and would make love to anything in skirts, so why could I not make love to the girl of my dreams? Perhaps I was afraid to spoil the dream or somehow to tarnish so lovely a creature who had captivated my heart for all time. Or maybe it was some remnant of my Catholic upbringing that said you did not sleep with the girl before she was your wife. I was torn apart.

The next night in the camp fixed everything. When I went in for dinner a middle-aged woman stood behind the counter and Mina was gone. Gone for keeps I was told. Her father had come in a car and taken her away. Barbara had gone too. I was stunned, too stupid with grief to sleep that night. She had gone without a word of warning, without leaving a farewell note. Desperate, I faced the cook, and asked her about Mina. The woman seemed tearful and upset, her eyes red from crying, but she had nothing to tell me. 'Perhaps,' she said, 'her father found out about you.'

The following morning the drunken-faced Irishman was aboard our truck, but I did not connect this event with the cook's tears. Billy Power whispered to me that this man had lost his cushy kitchen job and had been sent back to the hard labour of a pneumatic drill on the concrete runways. I was not interested, I had my own troubles.

I worked in misery all that morning under a blue summer sky that suddenly seemed black. The storm that raged within me raged all around as well, the centre of my world had gone and I was lost. So this was love, this was what blind fools wrote poetry about, this torment the price one paid for losing one's heart. The ecstasy of the past few weeks forgotten, the light suddenly gone from life, the whole lousy creeping Jesus world suddenly revealed in all its brutality, torment and grief.

At lunchtime that day Billy Power sat beside me, as usual.

'So,' he said sombrely, 'the girls have gone.'

'Yes, Billy.'

'Did you know they were going?'

'No . . . Mina never even left a note. The cook told me that probably her father had found out about me, and took her away.'

'An that's a fuckin' lie,' Billy swore. 'How could the father know about you unless somebody down here told him?'

'Beats me, Billy,' I said miserably.

'Well, it doesn't beat me. That red-faced fucker over there,' he said nodding in the direction of the cook's lover, 'is the cause of it all. He was tryin' his luck with Barbara an' Mina this long time — fancied himself as the whore master of the women's quarters. When the cook copped on there was a big heave between the two a' them, and it was her rang Mina's 'oul fella, an' blew the gaff.'

'How the hell do you know all this?'

'I'm not saying', but I know. Larry, for Jaysus sake, steer clear a' that animal. Mina was the wan he wanted, an' he'll have it in for you. He'll tell himself he could a' made her only for you. Watch out!'

I covertly glanced over to where he was gulping his dinner and met a savage baleful glare.

'You're right, Billy, but I'll give him no chance to pick on me.'

'He'll find wan, Larry, an' he's big enough teh kill yeh.'

300

'Maybe he'll get a surprise,' I said, but in my heart of hearts I was desperately afraid.

I did not have long to wait. On the journey back to camp I had instructions to report to the Labour Exchange over some trivial matter long forgotten, but the truck was kept waiting outside for a full fifteen minutes.

'Sorry lads,' I said as I climbed aboard.

'By Jaysus,' snarled lover boy from the bog, 'but y'ill be sorrier when we reach the camp.' And I felt suddenly relieved that I had prudently hung a nail bar on my belt, under the overalls, and now made up my mind that I would use it if I had to. And it looked as if I would.

I sat there trembling, white-faced, as the truck tore camp-wards and skidded to a halt on the gravel beside the dining hall. Before it had fully stopped I was over the tailboard and fifteen paces away before my enemy cleared it. He stood there grinning, savouring this moment when he could unleash his fury on me.

'I'm goin' teh bate the bejasus out a' yeh, yeh Jackeen bastard.' He came with a rush, but suddenly pulled up when the nail bar came from under my overalls. A nail bar or jemmy is about three-quarters of an inch thick, with a crook like a shepherd's hook about two feet long, a fearsome tool if used as a weapon. And I intended to use for just that purpose.

'An that won't save yeh either,' he snarled, and then from nowhere came Clancy, his wiry hair bristling, moving with his crablike gait at incredible speed and loosing a long right hook that seemed to come from the ground. Not knowing what hit him, Lover Boy was stretched on his back.

'Bejaysus,' said Clancy, 'lay wan hand on the little Dublin lad an' I'll fuckin' kill yeh.'

''Tis not yer business, Clancy!'

'I'm makin' it me business,' Clancy snarled, pointing at me, 'that's a friend a' mine an' y'ill rue the day yeh ever put a hand on him. Remember that, Mickey Hegarty, or y'ill never see Sligo again!'

So, that was his name, and Clancy the only man in the

camp who knew. He climbed shakily to his feet, cowed. Already a big bump was forming under his left eye and he would sport a beautiful 'shiner' for a few days.

But he lurched off towards the women's quarters without another word. Apparently his demotion did not exclude him from sharing the cook's bed. But I was wrong. He was seen carrying his gear after dark towards hut number six, which was half empty. As men left this camp they were not being replaced, a sure sign that the War had peaked, and that it was only a matter of time before Adolf's fate was sealed.

All across Europe, as in Russia, the Germans were in retreat and it came to me in my misery that I would be free to return home in a matter of weeks. Again I was wrong, for the resilience of the Third Reich was simply incredible. Hitler had told his people they were the master race, they believed it, and damn near proved it, for they had taken on the world and, but for Der Führer's fatal mistake of underestimating the Soviet Union, it seemed they would have won.

After dinner I made my way over to Clancy's hut, where as usual he was sprawled on his bed. His game leg gave him some pain from time to time, but only I knew this.

'Thanks, me oul' son,' I said, and sat down on his bed.

''Twas nothing',' said Clancy, 'anyway, I've wanted a skelp at him for a long time. That bastard ruined a girrill from my parish, when she was workin' in a hotel in Sligo. She had a baby for him, but yer man skipped it over here.'

Well I knew the fate of Irish girls in 1944 who had a baby outside marriage, but I asked him anyway.

'What happened to her, afterwards?'

'Don't yeh know damn well what happened to her? The nuns took her in until the baby came and then soon afterwards she ran for it, an' left them wit' the baby. I hear she is 'on the town' in London, an' that she sends money to the nuns every so often.'

He remained silent for a little while, staring hard at the roof of the hut. 'I'll fuckin' kill him if ever he gives me

302

another chance. Tell me somethin' Larry,' he said, changing course, 'would yeh have used the nail bar on him?'

'I'm bloody sure I would.'

'But yeh could kill a man easy wit' one a' them things!'

'Clancy,' I told him, 'in the old Wild West they had what they called 'The Equaliser', the thing that makes up for the difference in a small man and a big one, and that was a Colt .45. He was too big for me. The nail bar was my equaliser.'

'Bejaysus,' said Clancy quietly, 'you're a quare hawk at the back of it. I should a' let yeh at him. Maybe yeh would a' done the job for me.'

'Not a hope, Clancy. I'd probably have broken one of his legs. He expected me to aim at his head and he was wrong. I wasn't in the Irish Army for nothing, me oul' son. They taught us a few dirty tricks in unarmed combat there.'

Clancy grinned. 'Get th'oul' typewriter, will yeh? It's a while since I wrote home.'

And it was, I reflected, as I started his letter, but, in my fool's paradise, I had never noticed, no more than I now noticed the roar of Lancaster Bombers overhead, but I could hear quite distinctly the sad rain on tin, the rain that never seemed to stop since Mina left. I was grateful for the respite Clancy's letter gave me from my own heavy thoughts and the never ending longing for yesterday.

Back in my hut, the letter finished, I lay on the bed and stared at the corrugated roof, the heavy summer rain drumming away, a fitting accompaniment to my sombre thoughts. 'So,' said my mind, 'you're the great fella who came over here, because you were told in Ireland that English girls were a "pushover", that they were all "wised-up", that they were easy meat for an Irish brogue and the Blarney that went with it. You were too bloody stupid to imagine that you could fall for a Sassenach, too in-experienced to realise that women were women the world over with the same charms and wiles, too bloody bigoted ever to imagine that you could love an English girl as you do. You knew too little about yourself to know that you could never take love lightly or take advantage of a girl who adored you and had offered love many times. Too Catholic, too brainwashed, even though you had resisted the Church all your life. All piss and wind. Like the barber's cat.'

The Don Juan from the bogs of Sligo was on the truck the following morning, but this time carrying two suitcases. He was dropped off at the railway station. He was being transferred from Alconbury to God knows where. As I was at war against the world and still carrying the nail bar, I went over the side and in a moment of lunacy faced him, but well apart.

'You were telling me last night that you were going to bate the bejaysus out of me,' I called over to him. 'Well, here's your chance.'

I hefted the nail bar and stood there white-faced, a bad sign had he known it. He halted irresolutely and dropped the cases, looking over his shoulder at the truck, where he knew Clancy waited.

'Don't worry about Clancy,' I sneered. 'He won't harm you, but I will.' I think the logic behind my action, if there was any logic behind my action, if there was any logic at all, was based on the fact that this drunken animal had been molesting Mina, but the more likely cause of my sudden possession of courage was that I was half mad with grief over losing her and wanted to take it out on something or someone. Mickey Hegarty from Sligo would do just as well as anyone else.

'Dhrop the bar,' he snarled, 'an fight like a man, yeh cowardly Dublin bastard.'

'No,' I said softly, 'but swallow that remark or you won't catch that train.'

'Fuck off, yeh fuckin' little maggot.'

I came at him swiftly then — he knew what I intended to do, and he back tracked in a hurry. For the first time I saw fear in his eyes, and it would be a long time before he tried to beat up a small man again, especially a Dublin one. And then I was grabbed from behind by the powerful arms of Clancy and held. I stood no chance of breaking free and as suddenly as the moment of lunacy had come upon me, it went.

'Pick up them cases,' warned Clancy, 'an' get yer fuckin' self on that train before wan av us gets "hung" over yeh.'

'Okay,' I said to Clancy, 'you can let me go now.' I was tired, suddenly tired, sick to death of life, at the end of my tether, and I was only twenty-four. Life without my love held no meaning. Never had anyone meant so much to me before, I had had no warning of the intensity that love could arouse in me, for with the others it had been a little love and a lot of lust. Now, for the first time, I was made to realise what real adult love was.

The work on the airfield was mechanically done that day and it was no different from any other day here. In the afternoon I clocked the Flying Fortresses taking off. Every twenty-nine seconds as they hit a small rise in the runway they took off, bellowing, for the Third Reich. All day and every day and night, the great planes left this quiet spot, deep in the fields, where the corncrakes and cuckoos, like myself, had grown accustomed to the sounds of war, their bellies heavy with another load of death and destruction. Some of them would never return, but the losses were becoming fewer by the day. The German Luftwaffe had been almost cleared from the sky, the British and the Yanks could bomb at will, the only real danger now the ack-ack guns.

Germany was being systematically flattened, most of Russia's cities lay in ruins, London was daily belted savagely by the 'Doodle Bugs', ancient cathedrals, castles, monasteries were disappearing for ever like snow in rain and I did not give two knobs of goat shit if the whole world blew up. For my world lay in ruins!

That evening Clancy came to my hut for a change, and sat on the bed. He regarded me with something akin to pity, for in a face like his it was hard to tell a smile from a grimace. Poor Clancy, destined like Quasimodo never to know any woman except a professional whore and, even then, I speculated, only in the dark.'

'Ye're takin' it hard, Larry,' he said quietly. 'The girril goin', I mane.' I nodded, too miserable to speak.

'I know how it is wit' yeh, I've been that way over a woman, too, meself. Y'd hardly belave that, would yeh?'

'Of course I'd believe it,' I said, and meant it. Had not poor Quasimodo coveted the beautiful gypsy girl, couldn't the cat look at the King? And then, in a moment of blinding insight I knew who Clancy loved.

'It was the girl who went from your parish to Sligo,' I told him. 'That was the one, wasn't it?'

For a second he stopped breathing, then stood up abruptly.

'Bejaysus,' he swore, 'but yeh can look inteh a man's mind, yeh little fucker!' But he was not angry, thank God.

'That's why I'd kill that bastard Hegarty,' he confided. 'Though I'd no hope of ever marryin' her myself.'

'She could have done worse,' I told him.

'Well, she did. But yeh couldn't blame her for not throwin' an eye my way. A game leg an' a battered face like mine don't win the heart of a Colleen.'

'One day,' I told him, 'you'll find a woman who'll look beyond those things, and love you for the man you are. Wait and see if I'm not right.'

He stumbled to his feet again and, embarrassed, bid me goodnight. I did not believe that what I had told Clancy would ever come true, but it did no harm to bring hope to his heart. A few minutes later the hut door opened and the cook came in, leaving a folded umbrella running with water beside the door. The rain drummed heavily, it was almost dark, long before its time. Outside this dismal kip the puddles were turned into small lakes, the dreary hedgerows hung heavy with rain, crops were being flattened, rivers were running bank high, and for nearly two hours I had not heard the sound of the heavy bombers taking off. It was the silence, the abnormal silence, that told me the crews were grounded. The cook, a fine-looking woman, made straight for me. She held out an envelope which I took with beating heart.

'It's from Mina,' she said. 'I hope it makes you happy. She's mad about you, you know that, don't you, Larry! I'll leave you to read it.' And she went away.

'Thanks . . . thanks very much,' I called after her but she was already closing the door. I opened the letter with trembling hands and started to read. It was a passionate love letter, a declaration of love . . . 'I miss you in every possible way that a woman can miss a man,' she wrote, 'I love you so much, so very very much. I will not miss you next Saturday, for I will be waiting for you under the clock in Victoria station at mid-day. Be there, my darling, be with me and be my love.'

The letter was written in an unformed hand, which surprised me a little, because she was so very sophisticated and well spoken, but the beating of my heart told its own story. She had arranged a place for me to sleep, implied that I would sleep with her. And I would be there. I paced up and down the hut for a few seconds, then went outside. The rain had suddenly stopped and a weak dying sun lit up the dripping hedges so that they sparkled like jewels. A soaring rainbow arched across the sky in all its splendour. Never before had I seen a rainbow like this, never before had green fields and hedges lined so beautiful a road, the road that led to the railway station and the train that would carry me back to my love. This was Thursday night, I had only one day to wait, and then we would meet again.

But already my heart was dancing down the road, under the rainbow, that led to a land where 'dreams really did come true,' as mine surely would. Ready to go to bed for the night, the last rays of the sun slanted along the tarmacadam road, turning it to gold and the puddles to silver. The great Lancasters revved up and from far away came the roar of the Flying Forts, headed for the Fatherland, all with one purpose, to incinerate the next German city on their list. That day, 20 July, 1944, a group of German officers, Field Marshal Rommel among them, had tried to assassinate the unspeakable demonic fury, Hitler, and failed. Rommel, respected and even admired by the

Brits, paid for this with his life, and the diabolic monster that ruled the Third Reich stepped up the pace of eliminating the Jews, the final solution to all the world's worries, and threw in as many gypsies as he could catch for good measure, and the War dragged on.

But here, in Alconbury, God was in His heaven and the world, the lovely, magical world was very much all right. And all because one beautiful Sassenach had given her heart to an Irish Celt, traditional enemies who would love each other forever.

At exactly half past eleven I alighted from the train in Victoria Station. My heart was pounding, I had half an hour to wait — would she be there? Of course she would, why would she write me such a lovely letter if she did not intend to turn up? But still, my anxious heart held the smallest doubt. It was quickly dispelled, for walking toward the clock, here she came running, her face alight with joy, to throw her arms around me and, taking no notice of the seething crowds, kiss me long and passionately, clinging to me desperately, as if I might suddenly blow away, caressing my face, my hair, giving herself completely into my keeping.

Suddenly she froze and held back from me, and I could plainly hear the reason. Somewhere up there, in the sky, she recognised the waspish sound of a 'Doodle Bug', and the whole station came to a halt. Everybody froze, from somewhere came a muffled scream, and Victoria station was as still as Madame Tussaud's, people with wax-like figures, all still. And then, from close by, the terrific explosion as the bomb struck home. We were lucky, for Victoria Station had long since had all its panes of glass blown out — except for that there would have been many casualties.

A quarter of a mile away the ambulances were picking up the mangled bodies of a few more Londoners, another great hole had been blown in the face of the Old Giant, but here, within five minutes all was as it had been before.

'Let's get out of here, my love, it's safer where we're going.' In a blur of happiness we boarded a Mrs Miniver Train, and headed into Kent.

All the trains I had ever been on were downbeat and shabby, showing the neglect of nearly five years, too busy carrying workers and soldiers to be properly maintained, but this little branch-line train was painted green and gold and seemed to have escaped the rigours of war. Or perhaps it was the rose-coloured spectacles that I was wearing that made it seem so. Soon we were into the green fields and orchards of this part of England. There were two old ladies in the carriage who alighted clucking their disapproval one station before we got off. They had good reason, for we kissed virtually all the way.

At a tiny station, somewhere over the rainbow, we alighted and made our way along a country road, and found a café in Fairyland, actually Sevenoaks village, and dined on sugar and spice and all things nice, the main course being fish and chips, made by a master chef, specially imported by the Italian Underground to keep up British morale. Or so it seemed to this lucky young fool, exactly as it had been since time began, and would be until the world ended, until no more young fools were left.

Oh the days are gone when beauty bright my heart once stole,
When my dream of life, from morn till night was love, still love,
New dreams may come, and hopes may turn, to brighter calmer beams,
But there's nothing half so bright in life, as love's young dreams,
No there's nothing half so bright in life as love's young dreams.

So wrote Thomas Moore, nearly a century before, the darling of the old famine queen, Victoria, who had loved dear vacant-eyed, mutton-chopped Albert all her life, and mourned his passing for the balance of her days. The Queen had been a stickler for morality, but if judged by the large brood she inflicted on the British tax payer, there were no holds barred under the blanket.

The day passed in a dream, we went to an afternoon

dance, had tea in the same celestial palace and ended up in a pub where budding Bing Crosbys and Vera Lynns tried their luck at the 'Mike', but Mina did not go up. She would have left the rest of them for dead, I told myself, but then of course she left every other woman in the place 'for dead' when it came to looks. Naturally! Of course! We came out in a velvety summer night and, holding hands at the bus stop, waited for the chariot that would carry us to paradise. Mina had informed me that we would be staying overnight in the workers' camp where she was employed, some place called Petts Wood, and in my mind I had a fleeting thought of the grim half dozen huts at Alconbury, silhouetted against the vast plain that was the RAF airfield.

At the end of the bus ride Mina steered me into the perfumed 'blackout', for the scent of flowers was heavy on the air — sweet williams and 'evening scented stock' — as we passed unseen bungalows, old fashioned English flowers, and, over all, the heavy heart scalding odour of roses mixed with the smell of hay.

'We're nearly there,' she said softly as we began to ascend a slight hill, and then in the dark came the wild smell of pine trees and we were walking through a wood. The workers' huts were scattered throughout a small area of pine forest, craftily camouflaged, for Kent, unlike Huntingdon, had been in the front line from the start. But the overall 'feel' once inside the staff quarters, with pine branches brushing the window panes of my love's room, was of being isolated from the world, deep in a green forest. I panicked a little as I heard voices in the passage, and turned startled eyes on Mina.

'What will you do if anyone finds I'm here?' I whispered.

'Nothing,' she replied matter of factly, 'and don't whisper. All the others have lovers, why not me?'

There was no question now of where I would sleep, no hesitation on her part. She loved me, wanted me, and I was wild about her. Somehow, I forget now, but somehow we were suddenly in bed and consummating our love. She was lovely, fresh and young, unlike anything I had encountered

310

before, but towards the end of our first coming together she gave a sharp little cry that told me I had made love to a virgin, that I had sinned more than I had thought possible, for in the Irish camps it was an established fact, taken for granted, that all English girls were fair game, that there were no virgins among them. And all the bloody Irish camps were wrong.

'So,' I said presently, 'you were a virgin?'

'Yes, lover, I was.'

'But you never told me. Why?'

'I thought you understood, Larry. I thought you knew I was.'

'I never thought about it much. I love you too much to care, but now you're my girl forever. Will you marry me?'

'Next year, maybe. But marry on what?'

'We can save, make sure there are no babies until we're ready for them, both of us work.'

'I hope you haven't given me a baby already?'

'No bloody fear. I was wearing protection.'

'That's all right, then. Love me again.'

There was no fear of her having a baby, the US Airforce had seen to that little item for me, for on the airfield where I worked there was a large wicker basket hooked to a wall and it was brimful of 'French Letters'. The airmen just grabbed a handful when going out. I had done the same before coming here, several times. Sometime in the small hours our loving came to an end and we had fallen asleep with arms entwined around each other. Gently breaking free, I sat up and looked at the one who held my heart. She looked so beautiful, and so young, so very very young, to have all the charms of a woman.

I gently ran my hand over her lovely breasts and immediately she was awake.

'Good morning, lover,' she whispered and passionately kissed me.

'Good morning my darling,' and kissed her again.

'What time is it?' she asked, wriggling free.

'Twenty-five minutes to ten.'

'What! Larry, you have just twenty-five minutes to get to the dining hall. Breakfast finishes at ten around here on Sundays.'

'I'd better hurry then, love. Will it be all right? After all I don't work here.'

'Of course it'll be all right. There's always men coming and going that we don't know. Anyway, Barbara is serving. She'll see you're looked after.'

And so, dressed and shaved in a hurry, I made my way through the fragrant smelling pines, where a smiling Barbara served me breakfast. Mina breakfasted with the staff and, when I had finished, I took a walk through the pine wood, until I came to the end and stood looking over the enchanting countryside. This wood, located on top of a hill, would be etched on my mind forever, the laden fruit trees of many orchards made a pattern in the green fields now turning yellow, ready to be cut for hay. Some had already been mown and the hay-cocks in the distance looked like the tepees of the North American Indian.

Far away, the village I took to be Sevenoaks was visible, in the rising heat of this glorious July morning. It was a scene of quiet prosperity, of a way of life that had grown with the centuries, unscarred by war. Happily buzzing around the buttercups, daisies and other wild flowers, the bees went about their eternal task of providing honey. And in the sky I heard a sound which swiftly drew near, and for the first time I set eyes on a 'Doodle Bug' going about its business of destruction. Against the vast blue dome of the sky it seemed to crawl, but it would reach London soon enough, God knows. And then from nowhere three Spitfires raced across its wake and the rattle of their machine guns came clearly to my ears. The 'Doodle Bug' exploded with a bang that was heard for miles. The RAF were on the job. One more load of hell had not reached its target. In seconds the planes had gone and the countryside around basked peacefully in the sun, and my girl would be wondering where her dreamer was, where her lover had gone. I knew very well where I had gone, where I had been since

312

yesterday, where I wanted to stay forever.

I had been in a magic wood which lies at the end of the Yellow Brick Road, where dreams really do come true, that's where. And to cap it all I had another day left to spend in Fairyland, hurry, hurry, go back to her, time is flying, the day will soon be gone. She was waiting for me, a vision in a white summer dress, that emphasised her charms more than it concealed, her blonde hair gleamed in the shifting shadows of the pines, and she looked on me with love.

'Well, dreamer,' she said, 'have you come back to me?'

'I have. I dreamt you were waiting for me. You look beautiful.'

'Do all the Irish have as much Blarney as you?'

'No, of course not, I'm special. But I'm saving it all for you. Where are we going? I'm lost around here.'

'But you told me last night you knew all about here for years, that you were in Fairyland!'

'Maybe, but that was last night. Perhaps I'll go there again tonight, my love.' She smiled enigmatically, the eternal woman, the inscrutable Mona Lisa that hides in the heart of every female, holding a secret place that no man will ever penetrate.

'Perhaps you will, lover,' she said softly. 'How would I ever know how to shut you out?'

We had reached the road that ran alongside the wood and suddenly she stopped, almost like a doe sniffing the wind.

'There,' she said pointing. 'Another one for London. I hope Mum and Dad will be all right. I'll have to phone when we reach the village. They live in Sidcup . . . .' Tearing across the sunny sky, far away from us, a 'Doodle Bug' sped towards its target. The RAF did not succeed in intercepting all of them, most of them got through. Mina could be left alone anytime, for Sidcup was a dangerous place now. In fact, anywhere in London was a very dangerous place indeed, though on this day of days, the one to be treasured for a lifetime, London and Sidcup faded away after she had telephoned. We would be married soon we decided, though

313

not this year. She was adamant about that and gave me no reason. Where would we live in this land where hundreds of thousands of homes had been destroyed? Somewhere there would be a place for us. Of course! What would we live on? That was easy, we were both working, but if the worst came to the worst, and of course it would not, we could easily manage on love and kisses. Nothing is impossible in Fairyland!

We dined again in the Italian café, the afternoon found the temperature rising, we were both tired and we found a pond across a field where we slept in the shade of a willow, lying close together under an incredible green umbrella that hid us from the world. Sweet Jesus, I said to myself, never let this day end! Let it go on forever, for well I knew even then that happiness such as mine must be paid for sometime, though I said nothing of this to Mina. She lay with her head on my shoulder, fast asleep, and I was lost in the beauty of this creature until I too fell asleep.

The sun was low in the sky when we woke, and it was time for tea. Mina knew a little place just up the road where two spinsters served homemade scones and jam, blackberry, raspberry, strawberry, a luxury indeed in food rationed England. The middle-aged spinsters, incurable romantics it seemed, fussed over us like a pair of old hens, recognising at once that they had lovers under their roof, and, marvel of marvels, placed a section of honey in the comb on our table and invited us to 'sample the best honey in England.' Mina, city-bred, had never sampled the delight of honey in the comb, but I had and soon showed her how.

'And, certainly,' I reassured the younger of the two old maids, it was 'the best honey in England', and I threw in Scotland and Wales for good measure. And since I was in such a beneficent mood, I told them that we had honey bees at home in Ireland, and that our honey was nearly as good as theirs. Straight-faced, earnestly, slipping them the old Blarney, and though the English have been aware of the native Irish product for seven centuries, when exposed to it their defences seem to melt away. The spinsters were overjoyed, saw us to the door and asked us to come again.

'You're a right Blarney monger all right,' said Mina as we went towards the village and the pub. 'Charming the knickers off those two poor old dears.'

'I'd much sooner charm the knickers off . . . .'

'Me,' she said swiftly and in full view of the customers going into the pub she put her arms around me and kissed me with passion.

'You,' she said, 'can have me anytime. I love you, I'm yours.' And then the day fled fast, too fast, all mixed up with laughter and song and being young in the velvety blackness of a summer night on the way home, with the stars overhead, and now and again the fiery tail of a 'Doodle Bug' scuttering across the sky. With death so close, tomorrow might never come, and going through our magic wood Mina sang softly.

> *It's a lovely day tomorrow,*
> *Tomorrow is a lovely day . . . .*

Tomorrow was not a lovely day, not after loving half the night, and the wrench of saying goodbye.

'It's not forever,' I comforted the sobbing girl in my arms the following morning, 'I'll be back up again in a couple of weeks. In the meantime I'll phone you here every night at eight o'clock.'

'But where will you phone from?'

'The Camp office. There's an Irishman in charge there. Kiss me now, for I must be off.'

And so the sad journey back to Alconbury, with its narrow potholed, tarmacadamed road, its thick hedges and its wind-swept huts, miserable beyond description. Two of the huts were now completely empty and, except for the roar of planes taking off for Germany, the War had passed this place by. I rang Mina that night, she was frantic without me, she was coming to Bedford the following Saturday, she could not endure being separated from me. I went back to my lonely bed, strangely humbled before the enormous love of this English girl. She who had appeared so self-assured, so poised, so icily beautiful at first sight, so remote, had given me love like I had never known. Was this the way it was with the English? Did they all wear a mask to hide an inner warmth, perhaps exceeding the Gael? What about Big Harry in Plymouth? What about old Gran? What about Tina? The question answered itself, at least as far as the women were concerned, and there was an odd Big Harry about, I had to concede that. They were not all Irish-hating bastards like Bateman of Coventry memory or the Plymouth cops, though the feeling between the infant Irish Free State and the British was one of open hatred, shut ports, and a savage delight on my side's part that we were paying back old scores. 'Lurry him up, he's no relation.' In the meantime I had to earn a living here, among many who were openly hostile because of our neutrality. My yellow identity card was proof of that.

So, Bedford, thirty miles away, on Saturday night. I went to sleep with my heart singing. The question of saving to be married was shelved for the moment, tomorrow was a lovely day. Life was so tenuous a thing at any time, but more especially now when men, women, and children were dying by the hundred in London every week, and by the tens of thousands in Europe, not to mention the Pacific where Japs and Yanks were slaughtering each other with a vengeance.

I left for Bedford town on Friday night, found a bed and breakfast place over a pub called the Nags Head, and waited at the railway station the following morning for my young love. As before, she ran towards me, smothering me with love and kisses. She was all dressed in blue, her hair gleamed in the August sunshine, and although embarrassed, I secretly gloated at the envious glances of the young soldiers on the platform. Mina was wearing a 'Brighton Ring' she called it, a cheap imitation. I vowed the next one she wore would be real, and gold. A ring for a lifetime.

We went to a movie that night, 'Madonna of the Seven Moons,' with Stewart Grainger and Phyllis Calvert, an impossibly romantic film about an eminent doctor's wife whose personality changed from time to time, when she would suddenly vanish from his luxurious house, to live with Grainger in the slums of Naples. It was based on an actual case, I had read of it some years before. But here it was thinly disguised romance on our own level, two men torn apart by one woman, or perhaps two women, for the sedate wife of the doctor bore no resemblance to the wild Carmen-like creature who flaunted herself before her gypsy lover, Grainger. We were carried away, Mina in tears.

On Sunday we explored Bedford, went a little distance outside the town and dozed off in a meadow, the weather being as hot as ever. On the way back Mina picked a small booklet up from the road: sixty clothing coupons, scarce as hens' teeth! We flogged them for three quid and went on a spree in the pub that sheltered us. To hell with the expense, our love had taken wing, there was only this day and the coming night!

No tears the following morning. I was going to see her in the Enchanted Wood next weekend and return to Fairyland all over again. We would phone every night, it would be no time at all until I held her in my arms. We would be married next year, at Easter, the War would be over by then, all the church bells in England would ring, the lights would go on again, tomorrow would be a lovely day.

The future lay before us like a magic carpet. We had it all planned down to the last detail. We would make sure we had no children for a few years. I would get a job as a ship's carpenter on a luxury diner, she as a hostess or waitress, and together we would see exotic places like Fiji, and Hawaii, watch the flying fish sparkle briefly in the sunlight, see sharks and whales and lost atolls, go to a fiesta in Mexico or Brazil or both, stand in awe before the great redwoods in the Valley of the Giants in California, see Niagara and the Grand Canyon, go perhaps three times around the world and then, with plenty of money put aside, settle down in Ireland.

It did not work out quite that way. I never even got to see the Enchanted Wood in Kent again.

15   Hospital

I arrived back in Alconbury standing on cloud lucky seven. I slept the afternoon away with no worries about losing a day's pay. The new foreman on the airfield was an Irishman and he would cover up for me. And at nine o'clock Mina would be standing outside a phonebox near the wood and we would talk again. She was as besotted with me as I was with her. Dear God, we loved as only the young can love!

At ten minutes to nine I rang. Again at five minutes to the hour. Again at nine. This time the phone box was engaged. I rang again at ten past nine with mounting panic. No answer. At ten o'clock I quit and made my way slowly back to the hut, with a heart like lead. All my instincts said that something dreadful had happened to her, to keep her from me.

The Flying Forts came and went unnoticed by me the following day. I worked mechanically, counting the hours until it was time to ring again. It was one of the longest days of my life, but a million hours later it was time to ring, and I made my way to the camp office and dialled the number of the phone box with trembling hands. It was almost exactly the same as the night before, except that it was engaged at different times. But no Mina! What had gone wrong? Why was she not waiting for my call? I was like a zombie all day Wednesday, sick with foreboding, but I would ring again that night. I never did, for when I got back to the camp there was a letter waiting for me, postmarked Sidcup, Kent. Mina! At last!

In the privacy of the toilet I opened it with beating heart, and was glad I had chosen the toilet to read it, for in seconds I was vomiting uncontrollably, a violent retching that tore me apart and left me shaking and limp, my mind too stunned really to comprehend the unimaginable. But the unimaginable was there to read again and again, the words branded on my mind forever. It was from 24 Acacia Crescent, Sidcup, and had been written by Mina's father.

Irish Bastard,

I have read of worms like you, but always hoped my daughter would meet a decent man when she was old enough, instead of a rat like you, who took advantage of a girl who is still under sixteen. I could have you on trial for this, and the sentence would be severe, but I do not want the world to know about my daughter's problem. Christ help you if she is pregnant! My advice to you is to get to hell back to Ireland before I change my mind and put you in Dartmoor, where you belong, you bastard, you rotten sod!

Yours Faithfully

G. Davis.

P.S. Get moving!

How long I remained there, staring blankly at the page, between bouts of vomiting I will never know, but the whole camp was fast asleep before I crawled, shaking, into my bed, worn out. The following morning the letter was still there to read, but somewhere during my exhausted sleep, a resolve had formed in my mind. Come Saturday Mr Davis would meet me, and perhaps I could explain to him how I had been mistaken about Mina's age, and about my intention of marriage. Jesus, I told myself, wouldn't anyone think that Mina was eighteen or nineteen or even twenty, instead of being what was known as 'jail bait'? The

319

sophisticated way she held a gin and tonic, the lacquered finger nails, the stylish hair-do, her perfect figure, beautiful breasts and Grecian form, the whole image was of a woman in the early summer of her beauty. Who could blame me for thinking she was a grown woman? Nobody, except little Catholic me, that's who.

The strict moral precepts of my religion, which I had flouted several times, were still embedded in my mind, and I could not break free. I crucified myself, a scourging at the pillar far worse than anybody else could have given me, and the bitter hatred expressed by Mina's father, the just lash of his tongue, bit into me deeper as the days went slowly by. For this was a virgin I had sullied, this was a child woman I had bedded, this was the worst sin I had ever committed in my whole life. You seduced her, said my pitiless conscience, you are what her father called you, a rotten sod if ever there was one. And the sharp little cry she gave the first time we coupled kept echoing through my mind.

Through all this the radio reports on the progress of the War filtered through my misery. August had been one hell of a month for the Allies. In France they had to hold on grimly in the face of an incredible counter-attack by the Nazis, one that nearly succeeded. But the overall picture was coming clear. Hitler was beaten. By 12 August the German offensive ground to a halt, thousands of them were trapped and surrendered, and, in the Pacific, America's second war went well. The island-hopping towards the Japanese mainland was forging ahead, at terrible cost to both sides. In this month the last Jap resistance on Guam was crushed. In Russia the juggernaut that started at Stalingrad rolled inexorably on towards Berlin — it was only a matter of time.

It was only a matter of time too before Mina would be old enough to marry, and with this one comforting thought I boarded the train for London as planned. I was a seasoned traveller by now. Within three hours I was on the train for Sidcup, a short journey to outer London, enlivened by the snarling sound of a 'Doodle Bug' streaking across the sky and minutes later plunging earthwards. And then the deadly explosion and the rising column of smoke.

At Sidcup station I got general directions from a genial cockney as to where Acacia Crescent was, and I started out. It was about half a mile away. I was kept on course by the simple process of asking passers-by. The last man I asked looked at me quizzically.

'I 'ope there's no one belonging to you there, mate,' he said, 'Acacia Crescent 'as just copped it!' He pointed towards the billowing column of smoke high above the tall houses.

'That's Acacia Crescent,' he said grimly. 'Or wots left of it.' I started running. Sweet Jesus, how I ran — a sickening premonition of disaster driving me forward until I ran into the mayhem, the shambles that had been Acacia Crescent. Fire engines, amublances, wardens, the Red Cross here in force, carrying the dead and wounded from the ruins. A long line of covered bodies lay along the pavement which had been cleared of rubble, the road piled high with it, some of the houses still blazing, a gas main shooting a fiery fountain at the sky. It was a scene of appalling desolation. I stumbled over the rubble that blocked the road, and questioned a weeping woman. It was 25 August, the day that saw the French go wild, Paris liberated. 'Pardon me, Ma'm,' I panted. 'Could you tell me where number twenty-four is?' She looked at me with swollen eyes.

'There,' she said, pointing to a shallow crater. 'That's where it was. I lived there. I was out shopping when the 'ouse went up'.

'Did you have a family by the name of Davis in the house?' I asked hoarsely.

'Yes. They're all dead.'

'Mina Davis?'

'Yes, little Mina. Knew her all her life, yes, gone.' She started to weep uncontrollably again as I stood there frozen as if by some terrible swift paralysis, trembling, almost mindless. I was there so long that someone approached me. A warden.

'You all right, lad? You look bad.'

'Do you have the names of those killed?' I whispered.

'Yes, all here.' He opened a red ledger and started to reel off the long list.

'Davis . . . a Davis family,' I interrupted. 'Have you a Davis family in the book?'

'Yes,' he said heavily. 'Family of three, George Davis, Helen Davis, his wife, and Wilhelmina, the daughter. All dead, son. Did you know them?' I nodded and then my mind went blank. I dimly remember walking away, headed towards where? I have no idea, no memory. While I had been standing in the ruins of the Crescent I had become conscious of a dark cloud moving in over my mind, and I sought shelter under it; shelter from the War, from the world, and the anguish of this hour, sorrow too deep for tears. My mind was suspended in a vacuum, I had left all behind. 'Here,' I thought, 'you are safe, stay in the dark.' Time passed as I walked slowly along, although occasionally a brief flash of light penetrated the darkness, but I retreated under the cloud at once. It was much more comfortable there.

I was shaken out of my retreat suddenly by a heavy hand on my shoulder, to see a large London policeman before me. I looked stupidly around and realised I was close to St Paul's Cathedral, walking through the piled up rubble, weeds and bushes that had sprung up around it in the years since the blitz.

'Oi, Oi, and wot 'ave we 'ere?'

'Leave me alone,' I said.

'Another drunken Irishman,' said the copper. 'Come along with me.' I retreated back under the cloud, into the painless darkness, to be rudely awakened by the same man. This time I was in a room, sitting on a bed, and a glance at the iron bars before me told me I was in jail. The policeman was talking to another man, this one not in uniform.

'Found 'im staggering around the ruins at St Paul's, sir, and arrested 'im.'

'What for, may I ask?' said an educated Irish voice.

'Drunkenness, sir, 'e was falling all over the place. 'e's Irish,' he added.

'Indeed,' said the other icily, 'and that makes him a drunk, is that what you are saying?'

'No, doctor, no, sir,' the policeman stammered, 'No offence meant, sir.' The doctor glared at him and then came over to me. He briefly examined me for broken bones, took a swab from his bag, poured something from a bottle over it, and gently wiped the blood from a cut on my forehead, another on my cheek. Vaguely I wondered how I had come by them, but could not remember falling.

'Any identification?' said the doctor.

'No, sir, we've searched him thoroughly, no money, not even an identity card.'

'Probably robbed,' said the doctor. 'Did you observe the condition of his feet when you arrested him?'

'Yes, sir, of couwse.'

'Surely to Christ,' said this very angry Irish dcctor, 'you've had enough experience of air-raids to tell a person in shock from a drunk? Surely to Christ his feet should have told you that!'

I looked down. They were bloody and swollen, purpled in places, cut to ribbons. The ankles above them were no better, and I wondered vaguely how I could not have noticed.

'What day is it?' said the doctor, peering intently into my eyes.

'Saturday, sir.'

'Are you sure?'

'Yes, sir.' How could I ever forget Saturday?

'It's Tuesday. What is your name?'

'Paddy . . . .'

'It is not,' snapped the doctor, 'now tell me.'

'Paddy will do,' I mumbled. I had had enough of this horrible reality and started to pull the cloud over my head.

'Call an ambulance, Constable, and escort this young man to hospital,' he said, scribbling on a notebook and tearing out the page.

'Here,' he said handing the note to the constable, 'this will get him in.' Time to go, said my mind, and I went back into the velvety dark. Things came to me in occasional flashes after that, but after a few brief minutes was enough, and I always fled back to the shelter of my dark cloud.

It seemed I had been walking around for three days, days of which I would never have any recall, and was now in a London hospital, which one I neither knew nor cared. Twice a day I had to leave my cloud refuge, when the dressings on my feet and legs were being changed. My left foot had festered badly. I resisted every attempt to find out my identity, and was not pressed too hard, after I had 'blacked out' a couple of times.

The nurses, many of them Irish, soon had me identified as being from Dublin, but outside of that they knew nothing, and ended up calling me Mr Shamrock. And so, as the homeless Mr Shamrock I was sent from the general hospital to a psychiatric one, Winninger Hospital in the lush meadows of Kent, where all my troubles had started. But it was far from Petts Wood, there was nothing to remind me of what had gone before. And I needed nothing, it was all branded indelibly on my mind forever.

In Winninger, with its long cool corridors and large windows overlooking the well-kept grounds, I slipped away for a long time. In the darkness that had enveloped my mind I could be peaceful and quiet. I slept a lot, nearly twenty hours a day, but then I was under heavy sedation. I ate what was put before me sometimes, and at other times it hardly seemed worth it: I just went back to sleep.

But over a period of three months I started to improve, to surface from my depression for longer periods, to begin to display some little interest in the world around me, however slight. The hospital was full of men and women broken by air-raids or action in Europe, but of course a large portion of its residents were harmless incurables, destined to remain in care for life. My progress towards mental stability was erratic, a case of three steps forward and two steps back, but in the overall picture a very gradual improvement. I was now permitted to walk the grounds, which were kept in order by recovering patients, gardening being the best form of therapy for those who could do it.

It was late November now, and a mellow 'season of mists' was upon us, almost an Indian Summer, that was soon shattered by a sudden onrush of old man Winter who now sprang upon the countryside like a tiger, held back too long. The brown and golden-leafed trees that hung heavy in the still, autumn sunshine, glorious in dying, the beauty of decay, were set upon by a howling and bitter north wind and, in one stormy night, were stripped to the bone. The following afternoon, walking across the parkland under the shriven trees, my feet rustled through the thick carpet of leaves, glorious in death, and then my eye caught the only tree left with its leaves still intact. It was a young copper beech, about thirty feet high, and under it walked a trainee nurse, one of my favourites, a freckled-faced, cheerful Irish girl, who charged around the hospital, bringing sunshine and a glimpse of better things to this place of sorrow. She was crowned with a head of wild red curls, and now she waved to me from under the beech. It was Margaret Sutton from Limerick, and I called her 'The Local Express'.

I stood there, entranced by the picture before me, and 'click' went my mind and took a photograph of her and a copper beech that would stay forever with me. At the time I was unaware that I had been taking similar photographs for years, that I would be able to flash them on at will, that I was building a memory bank, that would serve me well as a writer some day, a blessing and a curse! That was the evening the headache began, a blinding migraine that lasted for three days, so bad that I was isolated in a small room with a high ceiling, drawn blackout curtains, barely illuminated by a tiny red electric bulb. There was no relief. I could not eat, I could not think, I could not even sleep. And nothing could ease the torment.

'And you were coming on so well,' said Terry, the male nurse, 'starting to write again, walking the grounds, making a good wise crack now and then.'

'I've no wise cracks to make now, Terry,' I said, 'I'll lose my mind if this keeps up.'

I must have been reaching some kind of a crisis, for the pain reached a crescendo in the small hours of the third day and I staggered out of the bed and into the corridor. The place was unnaturally quiet, or perhaps my headache was so bad that I could hear no sound, for psychiatric hospitals are rarely free at night from the moans of some soul in torment, but I managed to reach the office and find the head nurse.

'What is it, Irish?' he said.

'Jesus, Mr Gibson,' I said, 'can't you give me something to stop this headache.' He looked at me with pity, then made up his mind.

'Come with me,' he said, 'and by God I'll give you a cocktail that will cure anything.' He held on to me, for I was staggering, until we reached the dispensing room. He unlocked the door and went inside, returning quickly with five large capsules of different colours in the palm of his hand, and gave them to me accompanied by a glass of water.

'If that doesn't fix you nothing will.'

'If it does you should take up residence in Lourdes.'

'Still a little wit left, Irish. Don't worry, you'll be all right.' He escorted me back to my room, saw me safely into bed, and left. Within ten minutes the blessed relief of sleep came, though only for a short time, perhaps an hour. I woke up, still half-blinded by the migraine, and suddenly the picture of the Irish nurse flashed on the screen of my mind, the carpet of autumn leaves, everything in its smallest detail.

There was a note book on top of my bedside locker. I reached for the pencil that lay beside it and started to write, more by instinct than anything else, for it was almost dark.

> Red hair, under red autumn leaves,
> And a woman near her prime,
> Striding confidently through the dead leaves, of another
>   time.
> Fresh youth, wearing a nurse's cape,
> Striding the grounds of the hospital,
> Fresh as the fresh air itself,
> Escaped for a while from the mad ones,
> Who stare with mouths agape!
>
> Blue eyes that see no future, only now
> Caring for the living who have died,
> Dreaming of a husband in the sometime,
> While tending the battered flotsam of the tide.
>
> Walk, my Colleen, while your time is ripe,
> Tread the leaves not gently, they are the past,
> Stamp them under foot, they make little sound,
> There are leaves to come some day that
> Will cloak you under ground,
> Tread, stamp, break them, nearing Yule,
> As you walk the haven of the mad . . . and fool.

I finished, fell asleep again, and woke five hours later with no headache, thank God. White-faced and shaky, I stumbled into the corridor, blinded by the bright day. Lorna, and Liam, two alcoholic cases, were sitting on chairs outside my room, keeping a vigil, for I had come to know them well and they were anxious about me. I sat down beside them, blinking, trying to focus, and told them I was okay again. We shared a couple of fags, and only then did I remember the poem I had written in the small hours.

'I wrote a poem, last night,' I said, 'I'll go and get it and see if I can read it.' Incredibly, it was written in a clear

327

elegant hand, unlike my usual unreadable scribble, and I decided it must have been the slow pace, forced on me by the dim light that was responsible. I read it aloud, they were enormously impressed. I had barely finished when a pretty nurse, coming to check on me arrived, and I was made to read it again.

'Oh, Mr Shamrock,' she said excitedly, 'I'd give anything for you to write a poem about me. Here . . . Gladis,' she called out, 'Mr Shamrock has written a lovely poem to Margaret Sutton.' So it was read again and again, as more young nurses gathered around, and finally, the blushing Margaret herself, the envy of all the others.

From that day forward my full recovery was guaranteed, although it would be slow. I was to find out that a fractured mind took a lot more time to heal than a fractured leg or arm, that a broken mind would never heal, that fractured limbs would grow stronger but a mind that had broken down would never be quite the same again. In the meantime, my little rhyme had made me famous, I was besieged to write individual jingles, I was even loaned a typewriter, and excused all manual therapy. The psychiatrist who saw me from time to time surprised me on my next visit to him, for he was in possession of the poem. After that nothing surprised me, for every activitiy is noted in a psychiatric hospital, and the smiling nurses who inspected the wards were really doing a 'head count', making sure that none of the patients had escaped. For there were no locked doors or barred windows in Winninger.

All the patients here were non-violent and, as I slowly came back to normal, I found much fun around me, especially the alcoholics, who were usually in great form after a week's 'drying out'. They had outrageous stories to tell, and, in me, a good listener.

'So,' said my psychiatrist, 'it seems we have a man of some talent on our hands. When did you start to write?'

'About ten years ago, when I left school, sir.'

'And at what age did you leave school?'

'At fourteen, but I've been telling stories all my life.'

'Ever try to get anything published? I'm told you can type.'

'After a fashion, but I've been published quite a few times.'

'Where, in what paper?'

'No paper,' I said proudly, 'I wrote for a woman's magazine, *Feminine Era.*'

'So . . . not much formal education, right?'

'I'm afraid so.'

'It doesn't seem to matter with you Irish. It seems genius blossoms in every corner of your island.'

He scribbled busily in his notebook for a while, and then said, 'The young man who was admitted here was a manual worker. We know that by the calluses on your hands. You're not going to reveal your identity, I take it?'

'Sorry, sir, no.'

'Well, it won't take me long to find out now.'

'I don't follow you, Doctor.'

'You're not supposed to,' he said, smiling, and dismissed me, until the next time. Going out the door I paused, to ask a question that had been in my mind for some time.

'Pardon me, Doctor, but when do you plan to discharge me?'

'I have no plans for your immediate discharge.'

'May I ask why?'

'You may. For as long as you continue to have night-mares! Of course, if you are foolish enough to discharge yourself I will have to let you go, but you are far from well, even now.'

'Thank you, Doctor.' I walked slowly down the long corridor, thinking hard. For sometimes in my dreams I would suddenly be jerked into the past, and in rising terror an arm would appear from a mound of bricks, in a street, in Plymouth, and the battered body of a young woman clutching her baby would be dug out, and I would start running, running, running, to wake up sobbing into the bedclothes, so that no one would hear. Or the black, con-gested face of Ken would be beside me, asking me for a

329

light. Or I would be back in Acacia Street, where my sweetheart had been blown to kingdom come, and always I would run, to wake up half out of my mind, and the coming day would be a dark one, for now, with every ploy I could muster, I had to fight the black cloud that came over my mind. Under it was the way to madness. It no longer offered a safe refuge, I had come to understand that.

The night staff, vigilant as ever, had heard me trying to muffle my heartbreak and of course their notes had been read by the psychiatrists. They knew everything about me, and I had been told I was not as well as I thought I was. It was March now. I had been hospitalised for almost seven months. I would have to fight like hell if I ever wanted to leave this place. Most times I was quite happy to be here, for the sights and sounds around no longer distressed me, the abnormal had become the norm, and I was becoming institutionalised, and the news that sometimes came over the air was not reassuring. Out there was a terrible world of carnage and death, a pitiless place. Europe and Russia were slaughter houses, and London still produced its daily crop of maimed and mangled.

Here, in this quiet place, in March of 1945, with daffodils nodding in the breeze and swelling buds on trees promsing another summer, one could believe that the world would go on, despite mankind's ferocious desire to kill it. Or so it seemed to me. But one thing was clear. I would have to fight hard, very hard, to regain the confidence needed to face the great outside. At ever longer intervals, the black cloud would try to take over, and I fought it like a tiger. I came to know, on waking, that another day of battle lay head, for they all started the same way.

A sickening sense of loss, the result of dreaming of Mina. She would be beside me and I would see her lovely young face and reach out for her. I would grasp nothing, and then sit up, with eyes staring into the past. And for the past I could not forgive myself, ever.

I had seduced an under-age girl, nothing could alter that. The fact that she had been more than willing rarely

330

occurred to me. I was the guilty one, I was what her father had called me, an Irish bastard.

The next time I saw my psychiatrist, he was blunt to the point of rudeness.

'You are not making the progress I expected. You are keeping something back from me, something that is making you sick. What is it? Why, in the confidence of this office, will you not trust me?'

'I do trust you, Doctor. It's just that it's all in the past and nothing will alter it.'

'It's not all in the past,' he said angrily. 'It's very much in the present and you are allowing this secret to destroy your mind.'

He put his feet up on the desk, tilted the chair back, and regarded me intently while tapping a pencil off his teeth. He was a handsome man with a shock of black hair, in his prime at thirty-three, very Irish-looking I thought. But then I remembered his name and there was nothing odd in that: Vincent O'Callaghan. Although his speech was that of Oxford, there had to be, somewhere in his past, an Irish connection.

'My grandfather once told me an Irish fable,' he said slowly, 'all about an Irish king who had a horse's ear. Do you know it?'

I nodded, taken aback. Well I knew it, I had been taught it at school. Labhras Loinsigh, Laurence Lynch, the King who had kept his secret all his life, hidden under his long hair, until the need to confess it had nearly driven him insane. So he had gone deep into the woods and whispered his secret to a tree. In due time the tree had been felled and timber from it made into a harp. One day a passing minstrel had come into the king's court, and, after a royal meal, had been invited to play for the guests. The minstrel ran his fingers over the strings of the harp, and it sang 'Labhras Loinsigh has a horse's ear.'

At the time I read it as a boy, I had had a vague perception that it carried some kind of message. As I grew up I recognised it for what it was, the need to confide in someone, not something, and that the truth would out, some day.

I sat on my bed in the ward, knowing at last that I was in real danger of losing my mind, that Laurence Lynch had recognised this well over a thousand years before. Should I tell Dr O'Callaghan? I decided not to.

It was then he came into the ward, something he had never done. He stood before me.

'I know now what you need, I should have known a long time ago. You need a priest,' he said. I glared angrily at him and shook my head vehemently. The brain washing I had received from the Catholic Church in my childhood I had rejected, or thought I had. I was the one who had got away, little liberated me had cocked a snoot at all religions, I needed a sky pilot like a hole in the head, and told him so. He was not at all put out but regarded me with smiling tolerance.

'The confessional box in a Catholic church is the greatest solace any church has ever offered to mankind, the need to be cleansed of sin is universal. That, my dear Laurence Redmond, is what puts your Church before others. That is what you need.'

'Maybe . . . . So you found out my name!'

'I found out all about you, a week ago.'

'How?'

'Easy . . . through the magazine you mentioned. Then once I had your name, the police did the rest.'

'Have you contacted my family in Ireland?'

'No, not yet, but if you continue to be ill, I will have to, and soon.'

'How soon, Doctor?'

'That will depend on your progress here and as far as I am concerned that is being impeded by your reluctance to confide in me. So I have suggested a priest, the priest who is closely identified with this hospital. Believe me, Larry, he is an understanding man. I doubt if your terrible secret will shock him very much.'

'Are you a Catholic, Doctor. Please forgive me for asking.'

'I am, an English Catholic, but there's a big difference between you and me. Ireland breeds a special kind of Catholic, obviously you're not one of them, but you are more Irish Catholic than you think you are. Take my advice, and see Father Jerry. He may save you from yourself.'

'Is he Irish?'

'As a matter of fact, no. But as far as I know he is, as the Yanks say "legit". You don't have to be Irish to be a priest, Larry.'

And then, smiling, he left me alone with my thoughts. It was 1 April, All Fools' Day, a good day to decide to see the sky pilot, I thought, and then I felt a little ashamed as I looked through the window at God's goodness. It was not His fault that Russian shells were raining down on German cities, that Berlin itself was being reduced to rubble, that His beautiful world was being destroyed by men. Hitler was licked. I was taking an intelligent interest in the War again and knew that soon I could go home.

Here, in this hospital, where the Sassenachs had been so good to me, the perfume from a huge bed of wall flowers wafted into the ward, carried on the warm breeze, the sun blazed from a cloudless sky and the chestnut trees, fore-runners of summer, were bursting into leaf. It was a scene of the most serene beauty, such as Constable loved to paint, and, with a little help from man, this was God's handiwork which was everywhere.

And yet I was homesick, I longed for my Dublin and Wicklow mountains, my small fields, my trout filled rivers; I longed for the music of an Irish brogue, for Dublin itself, I even longed for the smell of the Liffey. Give me what they would over here, nurse me back to sanity with tenderness and love as they had been doing, feed me, guard me, cherish me, pave their streets with gold, and still it would not be enough, for my roots were deep in Ireland. Away from my Dark Rosaleen, I walked in alien corn.

A week later I went to see the priest. My psychiatrist had not seen me again, he had said his piece and rested his case. He was probably hoping I would take his advice. This

O'Callaghan was far cleverer than I had given him credit for, with the additional advantage of being able to see into a Celtic mind, as he had into mine.

The priest's house was a little way down the road from the hospital, and I had to be accompanied by a male nurse.

'Nuffing wrong with you,' he reassured me, 'it's just a bleedin' rule of the 'ospital. I'll wait in the 'all.'

And so together we walked to Father Jerry's house, which was on the outskirts of a hamlet, which would have been a lusty village of note where I came from, if not a small town. War and famine over the centuries had decimated my land, while this one fought with tooth and fang to own the earth, and withal, its numbers increased, its upper classes grew richer, and its workers in its factories lived lives of squalor in mean little houses. It had not been invaded in almost a thousand years until this war, when its skies had been full of Germans, who took dreadful toll for the humiliating terms dictated in a railway carriage at the end of World War One, and spawned Hitler.

Father Jerry Secombe was a genial Liverpudlian, a man used to big cities and their problems. In the heel of the hunt he turned out to be one of the best friends I ever had, but that only after many meetings, for I distrusted all priests. The ones I had become accustomed to meeting in Ireland had usually been sons of wealthy farmers or country publicans, priests who had grown up in the tradition of beating courting couples out of ditches. Transferred to Dublin they were out of their depth. Here they came face to face with real squalor, seething tenements, prostitution and worse. They never ventured down the 'Back of the Pipes' with a blackthorn stick, or explored the dark canyons of Guinness's Brewery at night, for some bowsy would have told them to 'fuck off' fast and a punch in the face might well have followed.

But this priest was a refreshing change and I liked him at once. He met me at the hall door, hand extended in welcome.

'I have been hoping you would come, Larry. Welcome to this house.'

'I'll take a little walk, Father,' said the male nurse, 'if that's okay with you.'

'That's considerate of you, David,' said the priest, 'come back in an hour.' Father Jerry was a good-looking man in his early fifties, silver-haired, small in stature, big in mind. He was dressed in a battered old jacket and soiled gaberdine slacks, and looked as if he had just come in from a stint in the garden, as indeed he had.

He led me into a lounge with an open fire of logs smouldering away, a friendly room with its well-worn leather armchairs and gleaming mahogany table covered with scattered papers and Church magazines, an untidy room that brought joy to my heart. A well lived-in room, far removed from the shining sterile wards of the hospital.

'Excuse me,' he said, 'I'm going to make a cuppa.' Presently he came back with good strong tea, scones, cups and saucers, sugar bowl and milk jug all crowded onto a perilous tray. He made the mahogany table with a sigh of relief, and we settled down to afternoon tea.

'Pardon me for not changing my clothes, Larry,' he said, 'but I'll be back in the garden "growing for Britain" after you leave.'

'You won't be doing it much longer,' I offered. 'Hitler is on his knees.'

'Thank God for that! I believe that man to be the Devil incarnate, though I'll still be digging away. I love the garden and the peace of this place. It takes a city man really to appreciate the country.'

And I wholeheartedly agreed with that, for although I loved Dublin, loved to know it was close by, I had turned my back on it since I was a boy and headed for the fields and mountains, wild places where I was never lonely. In the Walkinstown of 1938, when our family had moved there, I had had all that. Saturday night in the Theatre Royal was great gas, but Sundays found me with rod in hand, by a stream or a pond, or wandering through a wood. Trees in their tall magic brought me nearer to God than any cathedral and, in my mind, were infinitely more beautiful. I told him all this and in doing so revealed more of myself than I knew. I talked up a storm that blessed afternoon, I burst out of my self-imposed cocoon of silence, and he listened patiently, drawing me on with a nod or a smile.

An hour that seemed like five minutes passed, to be interrupted by the door bell ringing.

'That'll be your escort, Larry,' he said. 'Do you want to go now?'

'No!'

'Right then, I'll fix that. I'll see you back to the hospital myself.'

And this good man forgot all about his garden, and no doubt his many other duties, to rescue a young Irishman from himself.

Eventually I found myself telling him about Mina, my breakdown over my relationship with a child woman, the whole tragic episode. It was not a formal confession, it came pouring out, a heartscalding tale that left me in tears.

He said nothing, just let me tumble headlong into the past, until I broke down, and cried my heart out. He waited until the storm had passed, went outside to the kitchen and brought back some more tea.

'Drink that,' he said kindly. 'It will do you good. Feel better now?'

'No, Father, I don't.'

'You should and I'm sure you will, later on. Your trouble is that you can't forgive yourself, you have no faith in an all merciful God, who forgives those who truly repent. You loved this young woman, didn't you?'

'Love her? I worshipped the ground she walked on. I'll never forget her, there will never be another.' Father Jerry permitted himself a little smile.

'You think that now, Larry, but you are very young. You're a good-looking lad and no doubt, in time, some other woman will captivate you.'

I shook my head, vehemently. 'Never!' I said.

'In the meantime,' said the priest, 'I have, through the power of God, the right to absolve you from sin. It is here for you to reject or accept. You can walk free from this house this day, if you want to. Think it over.'

'There were other women, Father.'

'No matter. I am treating this as a general confession. If you kneel down I will give you absolution, through the power of Jesus Christ.'

'Just like that, Father? You say a few words and I am free?'

'Yes, confession followed by Holy Communion. Certainly! Repentant you are, but you are serving no useful purpose by hugging your guilt close to your heart, this self-flagellation will do nothing except drive you insane. The Church offers you an alternative. Why will you not accept it, why do you not believe?'

'I suppose it's because you've made it all so easy, too easy, Father!"

'Would you have been more impressed if I had spouted fire and brimstone, if I had unleashed a virtuous fury on you, if I had called you a lecher, if I had upbraided you with words like immorality, unchastity, wantonness, iniquity, evil, wicked, vile, foul? Would that have impressed you more?'

'Maybe it would. There would have been plenty of that where I come from.'

'Well, Larry, you're not there now.'

I knelt down before him and he said the prayers of absolution. I would go to Communion the following morning. My psychiatrist had been right. There was more of the Irish Catholic in me than I was prepared to acknowledge. I had been lucky enough to meet a priest used to the ways of the world. I trembled to think of what our local canon, who had never been more than three miles from a cow shite, would have said had I made my confession with him. He would have found a few more words than Father Jerry.

He would have told me I was a disgrace to the Church, the Catholic Church — for in his book there were no others — that the devil had marked me out for his own, he would have had me reduced to glancing down to see if I had a cloven foot! Sodom, Babylon had never produced the

337

like of me. I would be forever in debt to this English priest. I was permitted to go every day to Jerry, and we spent many an hour in his vegetable garden, and tending his roses. My pale face was gone, I was brown to the waist from long hours in the sun, the light summer wind blew the shadows from my mind, I was the picture of health. And still, Dr O'Callaghan did not send for me, there was no sign of me being discharged. It was May now, the War was over except for the mopping up. Hitler was dead, by his own hand, and faithful to the past, his mistress Eva Braun had gone with him. To where? The world hoped for once that there was a hell, and even that was too good for the bastard. This occurred on the last day of April, 1945. Two days before, Mussolini, the strutting sawdust Caesar who had crucified Abyssinia and helped Franco to do the same to his own people, was butchered by the partisans, and hung upside down alongside his mistress, Clara Petacci. On 2 May the Russians overcame the last fanatical resistence in Berlin. May the eighth brought VE Day, and still no move from my doctor.

The victory bells rang out from churches all over England and the bells of the nearby village rolled over the sunny fields, but to me they had a hollow sound. England was broke, skint, the future uncertain. But, nonetheless, there was much rejoicing among the staff, especially among the females, much of it spurious. Many of them had husbands who had been in Europe for a long time, had married in haste, and now faced the prospect of meeting comparative strangers. Nearly all of them had lovers, the War had broken down family units, it was a time of sweeping change; there were no blue birds over the white cliffs of Dover.

The returning soldiers had made their minds up long since. They were not going to take the dole and stand on street corners as their fathers had done. Their children were not going to grow up on a diet of Jam Butties and fish and chips, they sang 'The Red Flag' with gusto, they would throw the Tories out at the first chance. The labour MPs had even sung The Reg Flag in the House of Commons. But today was Victory Day, a Pyrrhic one, but victory anyway, and the staff celebrated by getting tipsy.

There was a celebration party planned for that night, discipline slipped a couple of notches, the surveillance and 'Head Counting' ceased altogether. It was in this genial climate that three alcoholic ladies — patients — decided to hold their own party, and quietly slipped away to the village and the pub. They were not missed for hours, and then the search began. It should not have lasted long, for the village had only three pubs, but the alcoholics as always were two steps ahead of the game. They had had three drinks in each of the pubs, nobody knew them, the publicans too were celebrating, and Scotch that had been 'under the counter' suddenly reappeared.

The three ladies, Hanna, Bridie and Ethel, had somehow managed to buy two bottles of the whiskey, plus a couple of dozen bottles of beer, and repaired to the nearest wood. By the time they were found in the late afternoon, they were uproariously drunk, singing 'God Save the King', using most unladylike language about the Germans, and, in that condition, were brought back to the hospital by car. Screaming, singing and whooping, as the mood took them, there was nothing to do but put them to bed to sleep it off. Somewhere about ten o'clock that night they woke up, to hear the noise of the staff party going full swing, and, resentful that they could not join in the drinking, they decided to liven up events. Bridie thought up the idea, Ethel seconded it, and Hanna did the job.

In the foyer of the hospital, where there was a public phone, Hanna range 999 and reported that Winninger Psychiatric Hospital was on fire. Within ten minutes the first of the brigades arrived, to be followed by another and another and another. In all, seven fire brigades roared into the hospital grounds, the main doors were flung open and firemen raced along the corridors dragging hoses, cheered on by the drunks.

The staff, half tipsy themselves, and stunned by this

invasion, poured into the corridor aghast, while Hanna and Co. slipped into the party and partook of the drink, as much as possible in the brief time before the heavy hand of the law descended. Singing lustily, they were eventually hauled back to their respective wards, proud to the last that they had celebrated England's victory in true British style. It was an uproarious day and night in Winninger Nut-House.

The following day, all being back to normal abnormality, I was requested to go to O'Callaghan's office. I knocked on the door, entered, and stood rivetted to the spot. There, in the middle of the office floor, was my accursed tool box and beloved portable typewriter. The good doctor was grinning like a Cheshire cat, enjoying my astonishment.

'Where the hell did they come from, Doctor?' I gasped.

'From Bedford police station. A friend of yours called Clancy took care of your stuff and left it in the care of the police. We got it from there.'

God bless you, I thought, poor old battered Clancy, the Quasimodo with a heart of gold, but I said nothing, except that yes, Clancy was a friend.

'I suppose, Doctor, that we're to discuss my discharge? I hope you haven't notified my family.'

'No, I don't think there's any need now, but I suppose you'll be heading home at once . . . Father Jerry tells me you are always talking about it.'

'I'll have to get a few bob together, Doctor, invest in some clothes before I go. I'll have to get a job.'

'That's what worries me, Larry. You've been here quite some time. You may find the great big world a bit much for you at first. You might fall down, and be back here in a hurry. I've often had this happen to a patient who is discharged too soon.'

'I'll have to chance it, Doctor. I can't stay here forever.'

'Of course not, Larry, but I have an idea, one that will bridge the gap between you and Civvy Street.'

'What's that?'

'Work from here. Leave in the morning, take a cut lunch and come back at night. We've done it before, and it works.'

And it did! The familiar, hated work came easily to me, we were 'on bonus', I was young and fast and the money rolled in. I kept a very low profile while on the job, after all I did not want it known that I was a psychiatric patient. I was regarded as a bit of a mystery man. I kept to myself and, despite the coaxing glances of pretty young nurses, managed to avoid getting entangled in their embrace, although the want of a woman was beginning to plague me again. But hard labour kept it in check.

After a month I came back to normal, my usual cheeky cocky self, with a smart answer for all, life went on. All things come to an end, I told myself, and although I would never forget my English love, self-flagellation, as Father Jerry had told me, was not what the Lord wanted. On that point myself and the Lord were in total agreement, if there was a Lord.

But sometimes, in the small hours, the dreams would come upon me, not horrific dreams this time, but lovely dreams of Mina and sunshine and a magic wood, and I would go to work, sad at heart, until the hurly burly of the day dispelled dreams — there was no money to be made dreaming, and I wanted to go home so badly. But of course I was not going to arrive with my mouth open, two arms the same length, and broke. I was too proud for that. Towards the end of my long stay in England I wrote home to Mam and explained my long silence, saying that I had been in hospital with a breakdown, after I had escaped a 'Doodle Bug'. No mention of Mina, now or ever, I decided. That part of my life was a closed book, never to be confided to anyone again. My mother, fey like me, would look through me, and suspect everything, but would not really want to know, all she would want to know was what this letter told her, that I was coming home soon.

Two weeks later a male nurse accompanied me to Euston Station in London, and helped me with my luggage. We had fifteen minutes left before boarding the train for Holyhead and we stood there chatting, as the whirling crowd came and went, a human ant hill that never ceased.

London itself looked forlorn and shabby, the change from producing the weapons of war to those of peace going sluggishly forward, but the great fighting spirit of this city, the reckless 'don't give a damn days' were past, the uncertain present subdued and sombre. This station, this train, had all seen better days, carriages with flaking paint, battered rolling stock all about, the huge glass vault left open to the sky long since, and now a passing cloud sprinkled the platforms unchecked.

'I suppose,' said the cockney nurse, 'we'll get around to cleaning up all this, one day. Bleedin' ole London looks a bit the worse for wear.'

'One of the ruins that Hitler knocked about a bit,' I said.

'Not 'alf.'

Just then a long train with a full battalion of British Tommies rolled into the station, to deafening cheers. These were the victorious troops returning from Europe, where the American army and the Russian one had given them a bit of small help in defeating the Germans, but it was their victory and they were home at last in the ''eart of the Empire'. They had been the first to tackle Hitler. Britain could take it! They had!

They tumbled out onto the platform singing, for they had come into the station that way and the words I knew well, 'Bless 'em all, bless 'em all, the long and the short and the tall' and so on, until the outrageous finishing lines.

> *Nobody knows what a twirp you've been,*
> *So cheer up me lads, fuck 'em all!*

And then it was goodbye to London, and the long journey to Holyhead, and singing Welsh voices. It was a changed place, gone the long lines of Irish waiting to be checked, one could come and go freely, the lights were blazing, it was peace-time again. The last time I had come to Ireland through here, we had sneaked like thieves in the night into the sea, a dark ship, leaving a country whose future was even darker. Now, all that was history.

It was a calm night, most of which I spent on deck

watching for the first glimpse of the Wicklow mountains to appear on the dawn horizon, but long before they came in view the lovely tangy smell of peat burning in Dublin's grates came wafting across the waves. It was autumn. As it had been when first I left. As the ship quietly pushed the sea aside, a bright glow on the horizon said dawn, and in the rising sun the blue mountains came in view.

Dún Laoghaire had not changed at all, and Dublin even less. It was still a city of bikes and cobble stones, poverty, piss and piety. There were more cars on the streets though, and the horse's day of dominance, all during the War, was coming to a rapid end. The canal barges, too, had had their brief resurgence, due to shortages, but they too were doomed. I was having a last look at the old way of life of the city. From now on the stinking motor car would take over.

But this morning, just before the bikes poured in, Dublin was quiet and elegantly shabby. O'Connell Street with Old Nelson dominating everything, the wide street with its monuments up the centre, a number 8 tram bound for Dalkey, resting in the shadow of the Pillar. The trams, nearly all gone now, would be totally extinct soon. I dallied in Dublin until the cafés opened, had a good breakfast in one, and then went shopping. No clothes rationing here, no rationing of anything much now, except the rationing the Irish were used to, money. If you had it you could get anything, the same then as now. Some things do not change.

I bought a new suit and suitcase, a top coat, new shoes, underwear, everything I needed for my return. The effing tool box was left at the station. After lunch I boarded the 50B, bound for Walkinstown and home. At the Halfway House I got off the bus and headed up the quiet country road, until I reached the bend, and there, as always, the mountains. This was still a place of green fields and singing birds. Nothing had changed yet, all still the same. I was home! I was safe, the terrible times all behind me.

And I suppose, said my derisive conscience that never ceased to trouble me, I suppose now you're going to look for a bride, a virgin of course, an unsullied Irish Colleen, and you are going to walk her into the chastity belt of a good holy Catholic marriage, and no doubt you'll go to mass every Sunday, while the dirty English are still in bed, reading the *News of The World*, sin and sex, crime and cunt, all on a Sunday morning, and you'll be an example to all of what a good Godfearing Irishman should be . . . in the chapel so all the neighbours can see.

'Shut up, you,' I snarled and started to walk back to the Halfway House. But ringing in my ears still was the roar of the Tommies coming back from Europe, exultant, sardonic — cynically facing the future with the past safely behind. It was safely behind me. Nobody need ever know! And the song roared in my ear, and drowned out all else.

'Nobody knows what a twirp you've been so cheer up me lad, Fuck 'em all.'

Amen to that, I said, and stepped into the pub to get some dutch courage. I needed it!